Hunter Killer

Shel Talmy was born in Chicago and moved with his family to California when he was fifteen. His prodigious success in the nationally networked teenage quiz programme – 'The Quiz Kids' – persuaded him that his future lay in the entertainments business. He became an international record producer, ultimately responsible for a sale of 85 million records, and amongst other groups he produced The Kinks, The Who and Manfred Mann.

Shel Talmy lives in London and is now devoting his career exclusively to writing. His previous book '*Whadda we do now, Butch?*' is also available in Pan. He has travelled the world in search of authentic material for his future books.

Also by Shel Talmy
in Pan Books

'Whadda we do now, Butch?'

Shel Talmy

Hunter Killer

Pan Original
Pan Books London and Sydney

First published in Great Britain 1981 by
Pan Books Ltd, Cavaye Place, London SW10 9PG

ISBN 0 330 26311 0
Typeset, printed and bound in Great Britain by
Hazell Watson & Viney Ltd, Aylesbury, Bucks

To Steven and Jonna

Prologue

Berlin, 12 December, 1940.

By 8.30 p.m. on a frosty night in Berlin, the four SS officers, captains all, had consumed two full bottles of whisky between them. Two more bottles stood unopened on the bar, put there by an obsequious bartender with a Hitler moustache.

Scotch was in plentiful supply, looted from Poland and France, who certainly had no more use for such luxuries. They would have to learn the role of the vanquished. The Germans would be stern task-masters until the lessons were ingrained and resistance vanished.

But the best part . . . the best part was that all good Germans would soon be sipping their whisky in Britain itself. The Führer had said so.

The tiny island nation stood alone, their allies utterly defeated, decimated by the Nazi machine. They were isolated without hope of surviving. No one would come to their aid, and they would be forced to surrender in a matter of weeks. The Führer had said that also.

The noisy bar was crowded with the black and silver uniforms and polished boots of the Führer's élite. The cellar room reverberated from the chorus of voices raised in the 'Horstwessel Lid' and 'Deutschland über Alles'. A fresh-faced Untersturmführer banged out an off-key accompaniment on the upright piano in the corner, and the singers beat out the rhythm with beer steins and stamping feet. The songs were sung with more enthusiasm than artistry.

There was a contingent of girls who mingled with the officers, red mouths glistening in the light that filtered through the smoke-filled room. They hung on the arms of the men, draped like so many gaily coloured flags. They gave the young stalwarts coquettish looks, and parried their rejoinders with mischievous smiles, but flattery was the first order of the day. They had quickly learned that flattery was soothing balm to these 'Young Heroes of The Reich', and when artfully applied, made a significant contribution to their pocketbooks. And so, the mouths that looked like they were painted in blood, smiled a lot, but the eyes glinted with avarice.

The four young Hauptsturmführers clustered together in a small group. They were contemptuous of what was on offer. 'Whores,' they muttered. Berlin had yet to receive the choice morsels from conquered countries.

One of them, slightly dishevelled from at least one too many, slurred his way through the information that he, Captain Rascher, had a brilliant idea, a far more interesting way to pass the time than just drinking.

'Four weeks ago,' he told them, 'I noticed an extremely attractive woman with a small child walking near the Reich's Chancellery. On the spur of the moment, I decided to find out who she was and followed her to an apartment building near by.'

Inquiries of the landlady had produced the intelligence that she was an American and the wife of a second Secretary to the American Embassy. Further inquiries into her background through his contacts, he winked slyly at the other three, had revealed that she was a Jewess.

'It would be an amusing diversion,' he suggested, 'to go to her apartment and check her papers. You must see her.' He rolled his eyes.

'That,' another protested, 'Jewess or not, would be stupid. They are Americans and we are not at war with America.'

'Not yet.'

They all laughed at the joke.

'And anyhow, what about her husband?'

Captain Rascher smiled, he had already thought of that.

'Her husband will be at the Embassy until midnight as he has been for the last three weeks and as he will be indefinitely, so why not go and have some fun. We are the SS, there will be no repercussions.'

In unspoken agreement they clinked glasses, downed the whisky and left the noisy cellar behind them. Boots crunched on a new fall of snow as they set off on the excursion.

In the apartment on Heinrich Kreussen Strasse, Natalie Sebastian was combing her glossy black hair in preparation for her husband's arrival. He had promised her that he would be home early from the Embassy for this, their anniversary. She had prepared a sumptuous, candle-lit supper. The aroma of food cooking drifted in from the kitchen, and a bottle of champagne was already cooling in an ice bucket. Four-year-old Mark was in bed asleep, and the maid had been dismissed for the evening. Everything was in readiness for the fifth anniversary of life they had shared. She examined herself critically in the mirror. At twenty-seven, no line yet creased the smooth skin of her face, and her dark eyes were lustrous and clear. She stood and whirled about, watching her reflection. Robert, she knew, would be pleased. He would desire her, he would have her. She wore a full-length semi-transparent négligé which she had bought especially for the occasion, the garment moulded itself to her body and emphasized the rounded breasts, the gentle curve of hips, the long legs. She went to a phonograph and selected a '78' from a stack she'd brought from America; Bing Crosby's familiar croon entered the room.

The serenity was broken by the sound of booted feet coming up the stairs. It wouldn't be Robert, it was too early for him, and anyway, there was certainly more than one person.

A loud knock at the door startled her. Who would be calling at this time of night? A twinge of fear knotted the pit of her stomach and she quelled it with difficulty. The knock sounded again, louder this time.

'Who is it?' she called.

'Frau Sebastian,' a muffled voice answered. 'Open the door.'

'Who is it?' she repeated. Her hands had balled into fists and the nails dug into her palms.

'We are the SS; we wish to speak to you. Open this door.'

She stood frozen to the spot. The fear was back again, and it wrapped itself around her.

'What do you want?' she managed weakly. 'My husband is not here.' She knew that it was an absurd statement to make as soon as she said it, but couldn't think of anything else.

'We must check your papers, Frau Sebastian; it is a matter of routine. Open this door.'

She moved haltingly to the entrance, slid on the chain, and opened the door a crack, peeking around the jamb. The whisky breath from the four men hit her full in the face, and instinctively she wrinkled her nose. She tried to close the door, but a polished toe cap had already occupied the space.

'Frau Sebastian? Is it correct that you are a Jew?'

'*Ich bin eine Amerikanerin.* I am an American.'

'But a Jew also,' the man persisted.

'What I am is none of your business. I am an American and the wife of a diplomat, and I have a diplomatic passport. You have no right to be here and no right to question me.'

The four of them laughed raucously.

'We have every right. We are the SS.'

'Go away or I'll call the police.'

They laughed again and louder, digging each other in the ribs to emphasize the obvious absurdity.

'I'll also report you to my Embassy. Now get your foot out of my door, you pigs.'

The laughter ceased so abruptly, it was as if it had never occurred. Very little had been needed to change their mood from mild aggression to naked hate. It blazed like pure energy, poured through the door, enveloped her. Natalie's heart thumped violently and she put her hand to her mouth, as a meaningless gesture of defence, when she took in the expressions on their faces.

'You should not have said that, Frau Sebastian. You dirty kike.'

With a vicious thrust, the speaker struck the door with his shoulder and snapped the chain in two. The door swung back, knocking her off balance, flinging her into the centre of the room where she just managed to keep her feet. The four stormed drunkenly in and Natalie screamed.

Other occupants of the apartment building heard the commotion and pretended that they didn't, they crept on silent feet to their own doors, locked, double and triple-locked them, and retired to remote corners of their apartments. It was better not to know what was going on. They knew about these things; if it was the SS or the Gestapo, neither one would brook any interference from an outsider. Those who interfered seldom had the opportunity to do it a second time.

The four of them surrounded her and stared at her body stupidly, in slack-jawed amazement. One licked his lips. Natalie covered her almost naked breasts with her arms and stared around her, wild-eyed.

'I am first,' Captain Rascher announced. 'It was my idea, I

told you it was a good idea.' The others agreed with grudging nods.

'No, please.' Natalie moaned. 'Please don't. Please leave me alone.'

The officers on either side of her grabbed an arm each, and Natalie screamed again, a high, piercing wail. Captain Rascher, with a smirk, slapped her face hard.

'Shut up, you dirty Jew bitch. It is because of people like you that good Germans are dying.'

'No, please don't.'

Rascher reached out a hand, grabbed the material of the négligé at the point of the 'V' just below her bosom, pulled straight down and the flimsy material tore like tissue paper. The officer behind Natalie took his cue from Rascher and ripped the nightdress down the back. When he was finished, the gown fell apart in two halves. Natalie writhed, but to no avail. The officers held her too firmly; she sobbed in complete panic, unaware of the tears coursing down her cheeks.

They wrenched off the torn halves of the négligé so that she was naked but for a pair of pants. Rascher took out his SS dagger with the insignia of an eagle perched on a swastika and grinned at Natalie with pure malice. She stared back at him in stark horror, all reason going or gone. He chuckled to himself, and, pointing the knife at her belly, he made as if to plunge it in, stopped within a fraction of an inch and laughed uproariously. Natalie screamed again. Then he took the knife and slit the sides of the panties so that they fell away from her trembling body on to the floor. He nodded to the two holding her, who forced her down on to her back. She began kicking wildly, and they laughed again at her puny efforts.

'Get her feet,' Rascher commanded the remaining officer. 'I don't want the dirty bitch to get me where it hurts.'

The other complied, and Rascher dropped his trousers, crouched down, and forced an entry. Natalie's screaming was continuous now and Rascher slapped her two, three, four times to shut her up. She subsided into whimpers and moans.

He was finished in thirty seconds, slapped her again for good measure, stood up, buttoned his trousers and took over from his comrade holding her legs. It was his turn next.

Four-year-old Mark Sebastian stumbled out of bed, ran a hand through his tousled blond hair, and rubbed the sleep out of his eyes. He had been awakened by a loud noise. Mommy had told him that, once he was in bed, he was not to get out, but a little peek wouldn't hurt and she wouldn't know . . .

Robert Sebastian ran up the steps to his apartment whistling tunelessly. He was a half-hour earlier than he had promised, and he knew that Natalie would be pleased. He had to shift the roses from one arm to the other to get at his key. Roses for Natalie, she adored roses, and it had taken him the best part of an hour to find a shop that still sold them.

It wasn't until the key was half in the lock that he heard the moans and grunts that came from inside the apartment. His mind went blank as he shoved the door open hard so that it banged on the wall, and witnessed the scene inside. Four Nazis crowded around his wife, naked on the floor, one inside her. No time elapsed when he went for the surprised Germans. He charged the closest one, bowled him over with a bone-jarring shoulder block. The roses flew high in the air, scattering all over the room. Sebastian grabbed the German on top of her by the hair, wrenched him away from the woman, trousers still flapping around his ankles. He punched the man in the nose with all his considerable strength. The bone crunched under his fist. As the man fell back, Sebastian grabbed for the Nazi's SS dagger.

Robert Sebastian was the perfect machine. Everyone but him seemed to be moving in slow motion, every sound was acute, every colour vivid. He tore the dagger out of the scabbard, slashed out at another German's face, the knife cut the man's cheek as if cutting through Swiss cheese. The other two had time to regroup, and jumped on him. One went for his knife hand and the other landed on his back. He shook his two-hundred-pound body violently and shrugged them off like fleas. His foot found the testicles of one, and he was going after the other when Hauptsturmführer Naumann shot him in the side of the head with his Luger from ten feet away. Robert Sebastian's momentum carried him a few more steps, and when he finally came to rest, he lay sprawled across his wife's naked and unconscious body. Naumann walked over and deliberately shot him twice more in the back of the head, then he turned the gun on Natalie, and without hesitation, pulled the trigger three more times. The blood welled out as red as the roses that were strewn about them.

Naumann's cheek was bleeding profusely and he dabbed at it with a handkerchief, already sodden with his blood.

'For God's sake,' one of them said, 'let's get out of here. What a mess!'

Captain Schmidt, in obvious pain, re-buttoned his trousers and gingerly fingered his broken nose. Another held his crotch to ease the throbbing pain. The four of them trooped out and clattered down the stairs. Bing Crosby finished his song and the record continued to turn, the scratch of the needle very loud in the silent room.

Mark had seen everything from the entrance to the living room, but he would tell nothing . . . His eyes were wide, staring and unfocused, his little fist was firmly in his mouth, his body was rigid. That was the way he was found an hour later by a tremulous neighbour.

Part One

Chapter One

Rudolph Werner was not his real name, but he hadn't used his real name for so long that, at times, he would almost forget what it was.

Lapses of memory were more frequent now. Old age had advanced in a dizzying rush. Arthritis had reduced a tall man with an erect carriage to that of an individual who had to shamble along, bent almost double. He looked at least fifteen years older than his real age of fifty-three.

His face was grimy and covered by a stubble of grey beard. He breathed through his mouth. It was half open and exposed yellow teeth. His lips were twisted into a perpetual sneer. His nose had once been broken and still made a dog-leg to the left, where a ridge of bone diverted it. The eyes were dull, overhung by salt and pepper brows, and as shifty as an Arab trader.

He clutched at the lapels of his threadbare overcoat, which offered little protection from the icy wind that whistled off the River Weser on this late November evening. His body made an involuntary shiver.

He plodded along the Bremen pavements, away from the dock area where he worked as a sweeper and occasional storeman in one of the many warehouses that littered the waterfront.

He walked towards the third storey walk-up that he called home, breathing heavily. His breath formed clouds of condensation in the chill air, his worn boots pounded out a steady tattoo on the sidewalk and echoed off the walls.

On this night, like all other nights in recent memory, he'd made his mind go blank. It was comforting. His feet would carry him automatically towards his destination.

It was better not to think; he had made a conscious decision about that a long time ago. That had happened when he had come to the painful conclusion that he had nothing left to think about; it was combined with the assurance that there was no one in the whole world that would give him the slightest thought. He was a nothing. An erasure mark on the sheet of life.

He had contemplated suicide, but had realized, well before any particular method suggested itself, that he hadn't the guts to carry it out.

It hadn't always been that way. Once he had had plenty of guts and the will to use them. Once he had been strong, decisive, on the way up. That now seemed like an incarnation away.

In the days of the Third Reich that was going to last a thousand years, all things were possible. It was easy to exert authority over the inferior races that populated the earth like so much vermin. He had not foreseen the downfall of the Nazi cause. How could he have foreseen it? Even the Führer himself had not included this eventuality into his calculations. And when the cataclysm came, the Führer had taken the easy way out. He would never know the conflicting emotions of being on the run that ripped the heart out of a man. He wished fervently that he had the sang-froid to take his own life. But it was no use. As miserable an existence as he now had, he was still alive, a far too precious commodity to be squandered by the peremptory use of a chambered 9 mm bullet.

So the SS major had run. His last posting had been at Dachau concentration camp, his function – to expedite the elimination of unwanted persons.

That had made him a war criminal. One was always a criminal to the victor. Obedience to orders was not to be countenanced. Instead, the honest recipient of such orders was to be singled out and hunted like a rabid dog. He had run to the organization that had been set up in the latter days of the war for such emergencies. 'Die Spinne' by name, it translated into English as 'The Web'; its function was to act as a conduit by which SS officers were passed on to safe locations. The SS major was provided with identification papers that said he was one, Rudolph Werner.

He reached into a pocket and withdrew a dirty handkerchief, he blew his nose noisily, without breaking stride. He didn't notice the man across the street who followed him at a discreet distance, soundless on rubber-soled shoes. The November night had already drawn in on the shortening day, although, by the dusty clock that sat in the window of a disreputable-looking bar, it was only 5.30 in the afternoon. A haze had already begun to form that presaged a thickening fog, so that when Werner glanced ahead of him, he saw the street lights as if enveloped in a gauze wrap. He turned into the tavern, marched stolidly up to the bar and ordered schnapps. He blew on hands that were raw with the cold, more susceptible now that they were bunched and gnarled with arthritis. When his drink came, he downed it in a gulp and ordered another.

Outside, the man across the road had stopped about fifty yards from where he would come abreast of the tavern. He leaned his back against a convenient wall, folded his arms, and waited. He looked very patient.

The warm glow of the schnapps suffused his whole being. The other half-dozen customers paid no attention to him, nor he to them. He finished his fourth drink and stood up. Ten more would not get him drunk, he was past the luxury of that sort of oblivion. It was purely for economic reasons that he curtailed his drinking and started on his way again for home.

The man across the road saw him re-enter the street, pause long enough to put up his coat collar, jam the cloth cap down on the balding head, and start off again in the direction in which he had been going.

The man exerted the tiniest bit of pressure on his back muscles. It was enough to push him away from the wall and land him on the balls of his feet, a graceful motion, accomplished in one continuous movement. He started after him keeping the same distance between them.

The older man walked down three more blocks and turned right into a street of dilapidated houses. The buildings were packed tightly together and gave the impression of leaning into the road, as if to snatch at an unwary stranger. What street lamps there were, remained unlit, shattered bulbs still in their holders. The only light by which he made his way, spilled out into the road from an occasional uncurtained window.

The man following reached the corner of the street and paused. He narrowed his eyes to focus on the dim outlines of the bent man as he picked his way around garbage cans and over broken paving stones. He started off again with measured tread.

Werner stopped in front of a house that was in complete darkness and climbed the worn steps to the front door.

He fumbled with his key before it went into the lock, turned it, and grimaced as a twinge of pain shot up his arm. He stepped into the hallway and shut the door behind him, stopping to listen for any reaction to his entrance. Silence greeted him, deep and forbidding, and laced liberally with the musty odours of unwashed bodies, dry rot and stale cabbage. The slut who owned the house would be dead drunk again, and the only other tenant, that fairy from West Berlin, would be off somewhere with his tongue up someone's ass. He smiled with malicious delight, flushed with the joy of hating. One day, he had promised himself, he would go into the kitchen, take the rusty butcher knife from where it hung on the wall, and then – while the fairy pleaded and simpered – he would cut his balls off. Werner cackled. He'd never miss them. And so, fortified and warmed by his resolve, he pushed the time switch that illuminated the hallway with a weak light, and chuckled his way up the creaking stairs to his room.

The man stopped outside the building and moved his head in a slow arc. He saw only dismal houses on a forbidding street. The man's sleeve brushed the side of his dark wind-breaker; it made a light rustle, only a tiny noise that was lost in the whine of the wind as it gusted past the houses. The only other sound came from a television with a cracked speaker, half-way down the street.

The man went up the steps lightly. He paused in front of the door, took a strip of celluloid from his pocket, inserted the clear plastic into the crack of the door and slipped the lock. He stepped into the hallway, closed the door without a sound. He paused to listen and heard a dull thud from somewhere above, the noise of someone stamping, heavy-footed, on a loose board. The man moved unerringly in the darkness to the steps that led upwards. He felt for and found the banister that wobbled at his touch, and started up. He kept to the outside corners of the stairs where they were least likely to creak. With all his caution, they still emitted groans of protest, but, as the whole house groaned and sighed as it settled for the night, it would have taken a sharp ear – specifically attuned – to separate his contribution to the whole.

He passed the first landing without stopping, knowing that that room was uninhabited, just as he knew that the tenant on the second floor was out, most probably for the entire night.

He slowed his pace as he reached the third floor, stepped on to the landing and stopped. The almost imperceptible noises he had heard on the way up were now more pronounced. From the other side of the thin door, he could hear the shuffling of booted feet, the clank of a pot hitting something metallic, and the grunt that followed.

Werner had tossed his topcoat on to the iron cot that occupied one corner of the shabby room. It slid down into the hollow formed by the sagging mattress. Next to the bed, a wooden crate served as a night table on which stood a shadeless lamp with a cracked green glass base. A few coins shared a Hilton ashtray with a half-dozen cigarette butts. Against the bare wall facing the door stood a scarred dresser with most of the drawer knobs missing. The top held a couple of bottles of cheap cologne, a comb with several of its teeth missing, and his one remaining possession of value – a pair of silver-backed hairbrushes in immaculate condition. A circular table with a leg missing was propped against the one window to the street. It was surrounded by three kitchen chairs with the paint peeling off them in curling strips. To the left of the window, he had rigged up a clothes line that served as his wardrobe, on which hung a suit, three jackets and two pairs of trousers. A pair of mud-stained boots were kicked carelessly into the corner.

He grabbed one of the chairs and dragged it on its back legs over to where a board, serving as a shelf, had been hammered into the wall with rusty nails. He plugged in the hotplate that lay there, and clumsy-fingered manipulated the can-opener. He poured the contents into a battered pot and gave an angry grunt as it banged into the side of the hotplate, spattering red drops on to the wall.

He had his back to the door, and so didn't see it as it opened under steady pressure. But he heard the creak from a hinge as the door stopped moving. He turned his head, unconcerned, and his eyes widened when he saw the man standing in the doorway. For a moment of time, the incisive Sturmbaumführer was revisited. He assessed the situation, took in the intruder in a flash, noted all the little things.

He was a powerfully built man in his early thirties, who stood 6 ft 2 in, or a little more, had dark blond hair that covered his ears and curled around the back of his collar; clean-shaven, the skin stretched tight over the cheek bones, a straight nose, a hard mouth, square chin, and the eyes . . . they were deep blue – bordering on violet – and totally devoid of expression. They seemed almost flattened, so that no light reflected from them – opaque, merciless eyes; the eyes of a killer. His turtle-neck sweater, trousers, ski jacket and shoes were all black, as were his gloved hands, one of which held a black gun. Werner recognized it as a Walther PPK 9 mm, and it had a black silencer attached.

He opened his mouth to speak, but the man beat him to it.

'Turn your chair around, and not a sound,' he ordered in a voice just above a whisper. Werner shifted his chair, obedience to authority was automatic. The man paused and smiled weakly.

'On second thoughts,' he said in a normal voice, 'yell your fucking head off if you like, not that it'll do you any good. There is no one around, and even if there were, I doubt that they'd give a damn. So it'll be just you and me for our little chat . . . Herr Major Schmidt.'

Werner's mouth fell open in true astonishment. He began to sweat. He said, without thinking, 'What do you mean? I am Rudolph Werner, you have me mixed up with someone else.'

The man shook his head, his expression regretful. 'I guess that was to be expected. I made a bet with myself that you'd say that. Let's save ourselves a lot of time. We can cut through all the crap and get down to the reason why I'm here. All of a sudden, after years of being patient, I find I have no more time to waste.'

'Who are you?' Werner asked. His voice came out in a croak, and a remote part of his mind took notice of the fact that his hands trembled and he couldn't stop them.

The man reached for a chair and swung it around in front of him. He straddled it and sat down, the gun steadied on the chair back. 'Some people think I'm a mad bastard, others, a card-carrying son-of-a-bitch. Then there are still others who think I'm a psychopath. You know, I've thought about it. Maybe you can help me. I can't decide which one I really am. Maybe all of them, maybe none. I think we'll explore it. What do you think about it, Herr Major?'

'But I don't even know you,' Schmidt blurted. 'I've never seen you before in my life.'

The man thought it over. He tilted his head. His eyes bored into Schmidt. 'Hmm, no, I guess you didn't. You were too busy to notice me. I can't really say that I remember you in any kind of detail, but I do know you. I've spent a good part of my life getting to know you.'

'But why? I'm nobody, I've got nothing you want.'

The man laughed, a deep-in-the-throat chuckle, without any sign of mirth. 'You're partly right. You are nothing, but you do have something I want. You have the names and whereabouts of three men that, shall we say, I'm anxious to find. They're former colleagues of yours, and I'm sure you've kept in touch with them.'

Schmidt took on a look of genuine dismay. 'Am I going crazy? I don't even know what you are talking about. I don't understand one word. You invade my house and point a gun at me. You want me to tell you things, and I don't even know what to tell you. I don't even know you,' he wailed.

'Well, then,' the man said laconically. 'I'll give you a clue. December 12th, 1940.'

Schmidt's mind raced, 'December 12th, 1940.' He looked perplexed, and felt anger rising in him. 'What are these stupid games all about?'

'Rascher, Naumann and Spitzweg.' The man dropped the three names like pebbles into a still pool.

Schmidt flushed with the heat of memory. Now he knew what the date meant. It had to have been around that time that he and the other three . . . he remembered with a clarity that forced an 'ohh' from a suddenly constricted throat.

The man smiled. 'I see you finally have it.'

'But that was thirty years ago,' Schmidt protested. He felt the sweat dripping down his face and into the collar of his shirt.

'Thirty years ago. True,' the man mused. 'Just a mere speck of time, the way the scientists figure it. Did you know that they look at things in millions of years? But I'm no scientist. Thirty years is a very long time when you live it from minute to minute.' The gun shifted from where it had been aimed at a nostril, down to the middle of Schmidt's stomach. 'Did you know, the Chinese believe that when you save a man's life, you become responsible for him for the rest of his days? When I read that, I thought about it for a long time and I couldn't see any reason why the reverse shouldn't also be true. When you destroy a life, you should owe the survivor something. So, I've something to collect that you owe me. Positively biblical, isn't it?'

'You're crazy,' Schmidt said.

'Maybe. But you're not likely to get a medical opinion in your foreseeable future.'

'Then, you are . . .'

'Yes. The son of the two people you murdered. The Sebastians. But I don't suppose you even knew their names.'

'But it was a mistake, it wasn't supposed to happen that way.'

'Oh, I know that. That wasn't the ideal scenario for the exalted members of the Third Reich. You were just supposed to have your fun raping a defenceless woman. And it was even sweeter because she was Jewish. Then you would go off, and nobody would bother you, because nobody bothered the SS. My father came in in the middle and spoiled your fun. Broke your nose and slashed Naumann's cheek. He would have killed you all with his bare hands, if you hadn't shot him.'

Schmidt sat silent. He slumped in his chair. His face sagged, etched with lines of resignation. 'You're going to kill me?' It was more a statement than a question.

Sebastian shrugged. 'Nobody lives for ever. But you still have a choice. You can die with the minimum of discomfort, or . . . it could be very painful. I don't mind either way. I'm very good at what I do.'

Schmidt shuddered. His mind shifted rusty gears. 'I must keep him talking,' he thought. 'If I can delay him . . . the longer he talks, the harder it will be for him to . . .' Schmidt's mind blanked with the shock of realization. Here, at last, laid out on a plate for him, was the situation he'd prayed for – the way out of the existence he hated, the final escape from shame and degradation. And what he was shocked about – truly shocked – was . . . that he wanted to live, cling on to the last filtered dregs of life, scrabble for the final toe-hold that would stop him plunging into the abyss. He had to keep him talking. 'If I tell you where they are,' he said, the harsh gutturals ran together, rendering them almost unintelligible. 'Slow down,' he told himself, 'don't be so nervous.' He took a deep, rasping breath. 'I'll make a deal with you,' he continued. 'I don't know where they are. I haven't been in touch with anyone. But I know where one of them is.' Pregnant pause. 'If you let me live, I'll tell you.'

'Well,' Sebastian said, judiciously. 'I don't see that you are in any kind of position to bargain.' His lips curled into a thin smile. 'Look at it from my point of view. I think you have information that I want – really want . . . I could even say, am desperate to have. If you don't give it to me willingly, you'll force me to get it another way, and I promise you that it won't be pleasant. But, you should know all about these things, Herr Major. After all, you had good friends in the Gestapo, and all those experiences in Dachau to draw on. You should be some kind of expert on what the limit of human endurance is. What is your pain threshold, Herr Major? Shall we test it?'

Schmidt's jaw quivered, but not with fright, as the man looking on supposed, or with revulsion, as vivid pictures of emaciated, half-torn bodies flashed behind his eyes, but with sexual arousal. He felt an erection starting and knew that he couldn't control it.

'How did you find me?' Schmidt asked, in a voice of command. It seemed to take Sebastian by surprise, but he made a quick recovery.

'Oh, that was tricky. It was like a real detective story, following your trail. I think you'll agree that I was a regular Sherlock Holmes when I tell you how I did it. You know how meticulous you Germans are. You keep records of everything. So there was the record of the murder of my parents, made out by the regular Berlin police. Officially, it says, "murdered by person or persons unknown". Witnesses, of course, were scarce, but one brave soul came forward and informed the police that the attackers were four of Hitler's élite, and that at least two of them had been wounded.'

'But how do you know all this?' Schmidt broke in. 'You could only have been a child.'

'I don't ever remember being a child.'

The silence stretched to breaking point, as Mark Sebastian, the man who had been a child for only a brief instant of time, sat as still as weathered rock, eyes unfocused, expressionless. Sebastian shook himself.

'I checked and found out that SS personnel had all their needs attended to at the Military Hospital near the Reich Chancery, and that on December twelfth 1940, three SS officers were treated in the emergency room at the same time. One for a slashed cheek, you know it took twenty-two stitches to close it up. Another for a badly broken nose, and they didn't set it too well, did they, Herr Major? And the third for what is delicately called a "groin injury", where my father kicked your friend in the balls. And the fourth man I had, because he was listed as having brought in the other three. Simple, huh, God bless bureaucracy. Then, I went to the American Document Center in Zehlendorf, and got the files on the four of you. It was all there, you know. Nazi party numbers, SS numbers, photographs, promotions and transfers. Then things started getting difficult. All of you managed to disappear after the war ended. Either you got out, or were helped out, or died. Do you know what I did? I prayed that you were alive. Understandably, I've never been much on religion. I couldn't see the point of praying to someone with a sick sense of humour. But I decided not to tempt the fates, just in case. I figured that I could use all the help I could get. So, I sent up prayers for all of you. I bet no one else ever did that.' Sebastian's smile was boyish and genuine. It took years off him. 'Don't know for sure, but I guess it couldn't have hurt, because here you are, and here I am, and I feel lucky. I think they are all still with us.'

'He wants to talk,' Schmidt thought. 'He wants to tell me everything, and I don't know why.' He remembered the dozens of interrogations in which he had participated as inquisitor. Apply a little pressure here, mental to begin with, although handling with kid gloves was unnecessary. He enjoyed playing with the wretches. Then something physical. Nothing drastic at first, a slap perhaps, then alternate between the two, from soft-with-compassion to hard-with-viciousness. Build it up, bit by bit, widen the contrast between the two extremes. And, in the end, all reserves vanished, and the words poured out of the mouth, tumbled over each other for pre-eminence.

But here was the classic role-reversal. He was the interrogated, and Sebastian, the inquisitor, but Sebastian was doing all the talking, pushing enough shit out of his mouth to fill a cesspool to overflowing. And then Schmidt understood. Sebastian was trying to expiate his guilt. He was apologizing for being there, for having to be there. Schmidt almost laughed. He felt no guilt at all.

He struggled for composure, began to relax, stopped twitching; a plan formed.

Sebastian stood up and started pacing the room, but never

took his eyes from Schmidt, or shifted the gun away from him. Schmidt sat, unmoving, in his chair, hands clasped together in his lap, his eyes following Sebastian's progress.

'The other three,' Schmidt thought with a vehemence that didn't reflect in his face. If only Sebastian knew what he really thought about them. He hated them with a fury and passion that seemed boundless. It was because of the other three that he had been forced into this rat-infested existence, reduced to being somewhere on the same level as the 'untermenschen', the same class of people the Third Reich had sought to eliminate. He would tell Sebastian, Schmidt decided, everything he knew about Rascher, without any urging, just in case he didn't get out of this as he expected. Pity that he couldn't tell him about the other two also. Especially Naumann. He had been the prime mover, the one responsible for his destitution.

Hot flashes of anger welled up from his belly and spread outwards in a molten stream. He had been safe in Argentina, secure in the airy, high-ceilinged apartment that faced on to a spacious park in the wealthy section of Rosario, 190 miles northwest of Buenos Aires. A maid and a butler – really a general factotum – attended to his every need. Funds came like clockwork from Switzerland. The SS took care of their own. Even the non-coms were set up in situations commensurate with their position, but the officer class – the élite, as was their God-given right – were placed in positions of trust, accompanied by the wealth, prestige and social standing that a superior person deems as natural as breathing. Now endowed with his new identity as Rudolph Werner – a Swiss national, the passport said – he slipped into his new life as if it were a second skin. They had made him a banker in a small, private bank which claimed to have its home office in Zürich. And that was a joke, because what he knew about banking would amount to the size of a pimple on a flea's ass. But he was smart, and he learned quickly, and it was no great trick to make investments into businesses with large earning potential if you had enough money, and he had plenty to play with.

He and Rascher, Naumann and Spitzweg, had all been taken out of Germany together and would form an integral part of the South American Connection, and eventually the network that would criss-cross the world, touching on all the major financial centres and secretly preparing for the time when the Nazis would rise again.

For five years he had done well, really well. He had used the bank's money wisely. It was stimulating, he had got a genuine kick out of investing in a broken-down business, chopping off the dead wood, and breathing a new life into the healthy core, until, at the end of the day, it flourished.

He stayed with the local businesses – grain, meat, hides, sugar and rum. By the end of his tenure, he had bought all of the distilleries in the area, modernized them, and put them under the control of one man, a local named Cardenas – not much education, but he possessed a native intelligence. He had put great trust in the man, soon to prove misplaced.

Schmidt reported to Naumann, his nominal superior, who was based in Buenos Aires. Naumann, of the four of them who had started out more or less equal as SS captains, had progressed the fastest, so that by the end of the war he had reached the rank of Oberführer, equivalent to the brigadier-general.

In addition to the commercial consideration, part of Naumann's brief was to survey locations in South America and prepare bases for high-up Nazis on the run. It was he who welcomed Dr Mengele when he arrived in Argentina, and he who procured a safe haven for him. It was he who solidified his own power base and held the reins with a grip of death, who, with his enormous capacity for work, sought out every avenue to increase his influence, and who never missed a turning, and was never waylaid, so that the armour with which he protected himself was built up, layer on layer. At the end of the day it would have been impervious to an atomic blast. It was he who became the pillar of rectitude, the self-appointed moral watchdog of his SS comrades, and it was he who toppled Schmidt in the dungpit.

It was such a small thing. Schmidt had been a participant in situations that were far worse. During the war, no one would have turned a hair at what he did. At worst, it would have been considered a minor indiscretion, the reaction to which would probably have been gales of laughter, a slap on the back, and a demand that he buy the next round of drinks, and that he should not be so silly as to get caught at it in the future.

And it was all because of the local distillery manager, the

ambitious bastard, who thought he saw a chance to further his career at Schmidt's expense.

But it had all started out innocently enough. Late one hot afternoon over his third rum punch, Schmidt had casually mentioned that he would enjoy something different in the way of ladies of the town. He was tired of the whores – no matter how expensive they were – and wished he could find something to renew his interest. Cardenas had suggested, slyly, that what the *jefe* needed was a young girl, a virgin, unsoiled, but willing to change that. Schmidt's interest perked up when the man said he knew just such a girl, and that it would be the crowning delight of his life to arrange a meeting for the *patrón.*

And so three evenings later, Schmidt paced the floor in the cottage he owned on the Paraná River, fifteen miles outside Rosario, as he waited for the girl in a state of high excitement. Cardenas brought her at last, stopped only long enough for Schmidt to register his ingratiating smile, and left without a word.

The girl was a beauty – large dark eyes and an olive skin, long black hair bound up with a ribbon, and a fresh young body, smooth skin, gentle curve of breast and hips, a tiny residue of baby fat; not surprising when Schmidt realized that she couldn't be more than fourteen.

He felt clumsy at first. He hadn't dealt with a child-woman for many years, not since they had been shipped into the concentration camp by the trainload, and where, totally at his own discretion, he could decide whether they lived or died, and in what manner either state would be manifested. This was a completely different situation. This girl was to be paid for the use of her body. She didn't have to beg for favours, beg for her life; she didn't have to show fear.

But she did; it was there in her eyes and in her every action. Her hands trembled, her lips quivered. He could hardly contain himself.

The old feeling was coming back to him in waves, and soon he would be inundated. It started in his loins and spread, so that he, too, trembled. Then he touched her, it was like an electric shock, a spark that arched through his body quicker than any bush fire. One moment he was caressing her cheek as she shrank away from him, the next he was tearing her clothes. And then she screamed, a continuous shriek that seemed to get louder and louder. It bounced and rebounced around the adobe walls of the room, and swamped the inside of his skull, filled him with a rage that overflowed in a bubbling mass so that he struck out at her, hit her again and again, and when she crumpled to the floor, he fell on top of her, forced an entry, and climaxed almost at once.

He lay there panting and gasping for breath, muttering to himself, anger slowly draining. He tried to rouse her, and then he had the sudden realization that he, or the gods themselves, would be unable to rouse her, because she was dead, and that she had probably been dead for the whole of their brief intercourse.

He panicked at first, paced up and down the room, jerked his head round as if to catch her pretending. Surely, she would get up, brush herself off, laugh and ask him if he didn't think she was a good actress and that she would now have her money, *por favor*, so that she could go back home and prepare herself for the next *gringo* she would have to please.

He had to get rid of the body, cover his tracks so that nobody would ever find out. Thank God there was no blood. He didn't need to clear that up as an extra complication.

He lifted her under the arms and dragged her outside. Solitude he had wanted, and solitude he had. There was no other habitation for at least a mile in any direction. Nobody around to have watched him with prying eyes, to go to the police. Nobody to hear those terrible screams, unless a passing fisherman . . . he looked up and down the river that fronted the cottage. His luck was in. Nobody. The river flowed peacefully along, the night air was scented with jasmine, the frogs croaked on the bank.

He dragged the girl, her heels trailing in the dusty path, to where he'd parked his new 1950 sea-green Packard with matching interior, of which he was so inordinately proud.

He opened the rear door and stuffed her in unceremoniously, anger and bile rising again in his throat when one limp leg slid off the seat to hang down beyond the running board. Schmidt kicked the leg savagely back inside and slammed the door.

He had no clear idea of what to do with the body; he only knew that he must dispose of it in a place where it wouldn't be discovered. He must be kept safe from exposure.

He had a thought and ran round the back of the house to

where a flimsy shed was used by the gardener, who came weekly in a vain attempt to tame what Schmidt laughingly called his garden. Maybe he had left some tools there. Again, his luck was in. Propped against one wall was a rusty rake with bent teeth, obviously discarded, and next to it, a shovel with only half a handle. Bad for gardening, perfect for him. He grabbed it and ran back to the car, sweat dripping down his face. He felt clammy all over.

The path that led to the house came out on a narrow rutted cart track that paralleled the river and eventually joined the main road to Rosario, a mile and a half further along. He pushed the Packard cautiously along in first gear. One part of his mind cried out for speed, but a more rational corner told him that the last thing in the world he wanted now was a broken axle.

The road, he knew from previous trips, fell away from the river for about half a mile, then angled in to where, at one point, only ten yards or so separated them.

A half-formed plan had finally crystallized. He knew that he would be wasting his time trying to dig into the ground anywhere near the house. It was stony, and at this time of the year – close to the high summer – baked hard. The spot along the river at which he stopped, on the other hand, had a high bank, and he remembered from a walk he had once taken, that there was an overhang that was the top lip of a hollowed-out section composed of loose loam, kept moist by the water table. And the river was lower at this time of year; he shouldn't have any problem digging into the side of the bank, placing the body in the cavity, and making it disappear for ever.

Schmidt slid down the bank to the water's edge and started digging. No light shone anywhere in the vicinity. A sliver of moon on the eastern horizon gave off a wan light, enhanced by the stars overhead. It was enough to see by. He dug deeply into the hole, casting the dirt to one side, sweat and dust streaking his face. At last he was satisfied, climbed back on to the road, wrenched the rear door open, dragged the girl by her feet over to the side of the bank, and rolled her down. He jumped down beside her in a fever, teeth chattering. He pushed the girl into the hole, tugged her into a foetal position until she fitted, pushed the hair over the face to cover the staring, accusing eyes. Then he shovelled the dirt on top of her – short, jerky strokes;

he didn't seem to have complete control over his limbs. At last it was finished. He threw the shovel into the middle of the river, turned, and fell to his knees on top of the make-shift grave.

With what he could only describe later as a touch of madness, he patted the dirt down with his palms, forcing it to congeal, smoothing it so that not a ripple remained. He sat back on his haunches, examined his work, felt satisfied.

He drove back to the cottage, stripped his clothes off as soon as he entered the door and, naked, padded to the bathroom, where he filled the tub with steaming water. He soaked for what seemed ages, the tension went little by little, he began to smile. No one would ever know. If Cardenas inquired about her, he would say that he drove her back to the city where she asked to be let off next to a café where she was to meet some of her friends. That was the last he had seen of her. Didn't come home? Too bad. The girls these days! What are they coming to? Probably ran off. After all, she had some money. Tell her family to look for her in Buenos Aires.

And that's the way it had been, at least for a while. The next day, Cardenas came to see him, carrying his obsequious smile like an offering, and inquired about the evening's activities. Schmidt told him that they had been quite satisfactory and that, afterwards, he had dropped the girl off in the city. Cardenas was back again the next day, looking worried. The girl's family had been on to him. Where was their daughter? Schmidt shrugged and told the very plausible story about money and the use of same by a peasant girl. He suggested Buenos Aires as the likely place to look. Nothing happened for a week. Cardenas came back again, looking grim, all trace of servility gone, belligerence in its stead.

'Dropped her in the city, did you, Señor Patrón?' inquired Cardenas. He made it sound like an insult. 'Then perhaps you can explain how it is that the girl was found buried about a half-mile down from your cottage, by a man with an inquisitive dog?'

Schmidt blanched the colour of ripe cauliflower and sat down as if someone had kicked him in the stomach.

Cardenas' eyes became very bright and knowing. He leered. 'I see,' he murmured. 'It is what I expected. The police have been told about the body. They are investigating. There will be much scandal. The family have blamed me. I do not like that.

But I have managed to satisfy them that I saw the girl for only a moment, and after that . . .' he shrugged, for emphasis. 'I have not mentioned your name at all.'

Some colour came back into Schmidt's face.

'But I have called the *patrón* in Buenos Aires to tell him the circumstances. You will understand, of course, señor, my duty is to the company. He is the head of the company. He was not pleased at my news. He will be arriving here this afternoon.'

Schmidt seemed to shrivel in the chair.

Naumann raged at him, the tirade lasting a full half-hour, and all the while Naumann stomped back and forth on the marble floors of the apartment. Schmidt's mind numbed under the onslaught so that eventually only key words and fragmentary phrases registered . . . 'intolerable' . . . 'animal' . . . 'crass stupidity' . . . 'depraved' . . . 'endangered the operation' . . . 'exposed everyone' . . . 'all vulnerable' . . . 'have to go' . . .

'Have to go' echoed and re-echoed inside Schmidt's skull. What was Naumann saying? That because of one momentary slip, one tiny mistake, they were throwing him out?

That was exactly what Naumann was saying. Schmidt was to leave Rosario immediately, leave the country, get off the continent. Where was he to go? Anywhere he damn well pleased, as long as it was away from the rest of them. As of this moment – and not one second longer – Schmidt was terminated, finished with his work, to be ignored by his comrade, kaput.

So Schmidt was unceremoniously escorted on to a boat leaving Buenos Aires the very next day. He was given enough time only to pack a few belongings and to take with him the cash he had on hand. Everything else was confiscated, peremptorily. That was his punishment and his sentence.

And when Schmidt reached Europe and attempted to contact other former members of the SS, he found that the word had already travelled ahead of him, the poison spread like thick treacle. He would receive no help from anyone.

Schmidt went back to Germany, knowing that it was risky and feeling that it was probably worth the risk. Things had cooled down a little, and the chances were that no one was actively seeking him. The real truth of the matter was that he had nowhere else to go.

And so he began the proverbial slide, gentle at first, but as the inertia caught up with him, the angle became more acute, and soon he was tumbling hell-for-leather, arms and legs waving metaphorically about, into the pit from which there was no return.

A thought sprang into the surface of his mind. 'Why did you take so long to come?' he said.

Sebastian paused in mid-stride, started again. 'I had to prepare,' he muttered. Sebastian's thoughts went back to all the years of preparation, all the things he had forced himself to learn, all the uncounted hours of training to gain expertise, many of them probably unnecessary, but you never knew. And then the time he spent putting his knowledge to the test, in real-life situations.

'I know where Rascher is,' Schmidt volunteered. 'Do you want me to tell you?'

Sebastian stopped pacing, body tense, shoulders hunched forward. 'Where?'

'I was having a schnapps about two years ago in a bar not far from here . . .'

'You saw him there?' Sebastian interrupted.

'No, no, no. I was sitting at the bar. The television was on. A news programme. There was an item from England at a race track called Ascot. It was an event called "Ladies' Day". Many, many ladies wearing strange hats.'

'So?'

'The camera came in, you know, close on this very beautiful girl, and then it pulled back a bit so you could see she was standing arm-in-arm with a man. It was Rascher.'

'Are you sure?'

'Positive. He had hardly changed. The only difference – he had a small moustache. I would recognize him anywhere. Older, of course, but really the same as I saw him years ago.'

'And?'

Schmidt shrugged. 'The announcer said that they were in the Royal Enclosure and that the girl was the daughter of Lord something, and that the gentleman with her was an owner of horses. I think he said he had one running that day. I don't remember. It was a shock to see Rascher and I stared.'

'What else?'

'Nothing else, that's it.'

'What do you mean, that's it? Certainly you must remember

something else? The girl's name? The name Rascher's using?'

Schmidt shook his head. 'No. Nothing. There's nothing else to tell you. It was Rascher.'

Sebastian took a long stride forward. It brought him right in front of Schmidt. He reached down and grabbed a fistful of shirt and pointed the silenced gun at a spot between Schmidt's eyes. 'More, you fucking Nazi son-of-a-bitch. I want more.' He shook Schmidt's heavy body like a rag doll.

Schmidt fell back and threw up his arms as if to ward off the blows that would come at any instant. That was when he had the opportunity as he had planned, to reach behind him, grope for the pot on the hot plate, find the handle and, all in one motion, throw the steaming soup into Sebastian's face.

Sebastian yelled, a combination of pain and surprise, let Schmidt go, dropped the gun, and clawed at his face where the tomato soup made him look like a victim of a massacre. Adrenalin coursed through Schmidt's veins. The old, tired body reacted like a sprinter's. Long-forgotten muscles tensed, hardened. He sprang at Sebastian, lips pulled back in a feral grimace, murder in his eyes. The gnarled hands went for Sebastian's throat, found it as he banged into him, and they both fell to the floor with a loud crash that shook the room. The fall knocked the breath out of Sebastian with a 'whoosh'. For a moment, he lay there dazed. Schmidt's crushing weight on top, Schmidt's hands trying to squeeze the life out of him. Then the long hours of practice took over, and the automatic reflexes. Sebastian rolled, shifted his two hundred pounds, gained the leverage needed to turn Schmidt over on his back with him on top. The heel of his hand shot out, and just like his father before him, he broke Schmidt's nose. The man screamed, let go of Sebastian's throat, swiped at him back-handed. He caught Sebastian off balance so that he fell over on his side. Sebastian went with the motion, executed a perfect back-roll and wound up on his feet in an attack stance. Schmidt dived for the gun, five feet away from him, reached it, grabbed it, started to point it in Sebastian's direction.

Sebastian's foot reached the radial bone before he had a chance to aim, broke the wrist. The gun went off with the soft plop of a silencer, the bullet tore into the wall. Sebastian bent over, grasped Schmidt's neck with his hands, lifted him to his feet, lifted him off his feet, muscles bulging, the long pent-up rage let loose. Schmidt's eyes rolled as the breath was being squeezed out of him, Sebastian shook him, so that he refocused, locked on to the other man's eyes, saw death reflected there.

'Thank you,' Sebastian hissed. 'I almost wasn't going to do it.'

Schmidt tried to scream, to speak, to say something, to groan. Nothing but a feeble croak came out.

The larynx was the first to go, crumpled beyond repair. Then the windpipe was crushed.

Sebastian held him upright long after it was necessary, long after Schmidt had given his final death-rattle. Schmidt's sphincter muscle relaxed and the smell as he soiled himself brought Sebastian back to his senses. He let go and Schmidt thumped on to the floor in an untidy heap.

Sebastian took a long, deep racking breath, steadied himself, moved over to the bed, took a corner of a dirty blanket, wiped his face. He touched the scalded places gingerly; nothing terrible, it would heal.

He retrieved the gun, unscrewed the silencer, put them both away in his jacket. He took out the note he had prepared from his pocket, unfolded it and laid it on Schmidt's chest. It read, 'December 12, 1940.' Underneath, four names were listed. 'Schmidt, Rascher, Naumann and Spitzweg.' Schmidt's name had a line drawn through it.

Sebastian took a last look and let himself out of the apartment.

Chapter Two

The taxi took the turn into the Hilton and stopped in front of the entrance. The doorman hastened over to help, but Sebastian beat him to it. He emerged from the cab, stood on the forecourt and looked about him, remained aloof and uninvolved as luggage was transferred from taxi to bellboy.

It was bleak this early December day, clouds covered the sky like a grey blanket, an icy wind whipped across Hyde Park, dodged between the cars on Park Lane and funnelled into the Hilton entranceway. Sebastian's face felt frozen. He touched it, an unconscious gesture. He had gone from Bremen to the apartment he kept on the Boulevard St Michel in Paris. He stayed in most of the time, reading, thinking, straying out only occasionally, an anonymous figure among the students of the Left Bank. It had taken him ten days for all the scald marks to disappear, but they were still tender and he felt them burn in patches as the cold wind touched him. He ignored it.

He paid the driver, followed his luggage into the hotel, registered under his own name, and was shown to his room.

He had chosen the Hilton as a place to stay because of its anonymity – the lifts were automatic, the staff indifferent to personal service. As far as they were concerned, he would be one of many faceless individuals. But there was one other reason why Sebastian had chosen a hotel in the heart of London, and why he had registered under his own name, reasons that had not fully surfaced to his conscious mind and that he might have denied if pressed. It was exciting. He had eliminated the first of the four men he sought and had left a note that would be like a beacon to those who knew. He had no delusions about the others. He felt sure that they were fully apprised of the situation, knew who he was, knew that he was after them. But even with an organization like Die Spinne as an adversary, it would take time to pin-point his whereabouts. It would take time to find out the history of one, Mark Sebastian. It would take time to get a picture so that they would know what to look for, and for that matter, where to look. Sebastian, sitting in his apartment in Paris, had made careful calculations, estimated that it would be close, that his appearance in London might coincide with his opponents having full knowledge of what and whom they were dealing with. It was a risk, dangerous in the extreme, and it made him feel alive. He wanted them to know. He wanted them to sweat.

The others could not know what Schmidt had told him, or for that matter, if he had anything to tell. There had been no contact between Schmidt and his erstwhile colleagues for more than two decades. Even if Schmidt had known that one of the others was a resident in London, it was three to one against Sebastian starting there.

Sebastian knew that the odds against all three of his quarry being situated in London were about a million to one. It was a hard and fast rule that members of the same network would locate themselves in different cities, often in different countries. It was essential for their safety, and necessary for their business. Sebastian's probings of the Die Spinne octopus had shown that their interests were multinational.

Sebastian felt that he was on pretty safe ground. It would be folly for the Germans to dismiss him entirely as a crank; revenge was a remarkably powerful opiate, but on the other hand, there was no reason to suppose that they would go to a complete alert status. Be watchful, be careful, don't be unconcerned; keep the panic button within reach, but don't hit it yet.

He sat down on the bed, took the newspaper from his attaché case. It was a copy of the *Hamburg Morgenpost*, dated 29 November, already folded back to the article he had read a dozen times. It was headed 'EX-NAZI FOUND STRANGLED TO DEATH'. Sebastian started to reread it.

'BREMEN, 29 NOVEMBER. The Chief of Detectives, Homicide Division, reported here today that after three days of intensive investigation, the man known as Rudolph Werner, found strangled on 26 November, was identified as Hermann Schmidt, a former Nazi SS officer, who was wanted as a suspected war criminal.

'The body was found by Schmidt's landlady on the morning of the 26th. The medical examiner estimated that the man had been dead for at least twelve hours. Schmidt's identity was determined from a set of fingerprints forwarded to the Central File.

'Schmidt was a major in the Totenkopfverbande, and was last known in 1945, where he was posted at Dachau Concentration Camp, where he allegedly participated in the murders of several hundred people. He was sought after by the War Crimes Commission, but dropped out of sight and his whereabouts was never discovered.

'Schmidt, 53, lived alone in a rooming house on Henbergen Strasse in Bremen, in reduced circumstances. He was employed by the Bremen Overseas Trading Corporation as a cleaner and temporary storeman. Little else is known about him, as neighbours who were questioned stated that he lived a solitary life and apparently had no friends.

'There are no clues as to the assailant, and the motive for the crime is unknown. Speculation among his neighbours is that it was done in a fit of drunken rage, or perhaps in an attempt to collect a debt.

'However, this paper has learned that a note was left by the murderer with the body, and that the police are withholding the contents.'

Sebastian put the paper back in the briefcase. He stripped off his clothes down to his shorts, went through his daily ritual – seventy-five finger-tip push-ups, a hundred squat thrusts, two hundred sit-ups; his breathing was easy when he finished. He went in to the bathroom, showered, dressed in a conservative grey suit and sombre tie, put on his overcoat and went out.

Reinhart Kessler read the same article on the morning of the 29th. He put the paper to one side of his mahogany desk, pushed his coffee cup away and sat back in his leather swivel chair. His gaze on the wood-panelled walls of his office was unfocused, his expression thoughtful.

Kessler was a suave, lean man in his early sixties, sharp-featured face, silvered hair combed smoothly back. A resident of Hamburg for forty years, he was a notable lawyer in the business fabric of the city. Adviser to chairmen of some of Hamburg's largest businesses, a reputation for incisiveness, a brilliant negotiator, a social necessity at a society function. He was other things also, which many of his clients – had they known – would have had to denounce in public, although they might have secretly approved. He was the lawyer for Die Spinne, The Web – the organization of and for the benefit of former members of the SS. Kessler was in touch with all the leaders of Die Spinne, in Germany and in all the countries where the members had been forced into exile. His primary responsibility was for the channelling of funds. Formerly, the money had been needed to smuggle Nazis out of Germany, relocate them – complete with new identities – in other countries, and set them up in business enterprises. Now, money was only ever needed for commercial ventures, and Kessler was the link by which the profits from these businesses were channelled into numbered Swiss accounts, or other designated tax havens, or straight into the pockets of ex-Nazis who were now high-ranking, respectable industrialists and politicians who were doing their best to run a 'free, democratic' West Germany.

His second responsibility, and only slightly less important, was to provide – through intermediaries – the adequate defence necessary for any former SS killers who were caught and on trial. In both respects, he was eminently successful.

Kessler remembered Schmidt and the circumstances around which Die Spinne had withdrawn its support. The man had then disappeared. For all practical purposes, he could have crawled into the woodwork. It had been more than twenty years since Kessler had heard of him.

Kessler picked up his private telephone and dialled police headquarters in Frankfurt, where a former SS officer – and a still-current member of Die Spinne – was a police superintendent.

The man had read the article and Kessler told him that he wanted to know the contents of the note. The answer came fifteen minutes later and Kessler copied the information on to a notepad. He put the phone down and frowned at what he had written. Then he called Rascher in London.

Sebastian drove his rented car away from the Hilton, circling Hyde Park Corner, heading up Pall Mall and then east to Fleet Street. He drove with the familiarity of a man who had spent enough time in London to know the city well. And, indeed, since his first trip at the age of eighteen, he had been back a dozen times – once spending six months in a one-bedroom flat in Chelsea, while he toiled away at perfecting his riding, dressage and show jumping, under the tutorage of a famous British rider of the thirties. Sebastian remembered it well, his teacher, a wiry little man with alert movements, had thought his ambition lay in becoming a showjumper of international repute. Sebastian did nothing to dissuade him from that idea, although his reasons were as far away from that as he could possibly get. The discipline of showjumping and dressage were just the final way to gain mastery over the art of riding. He sought for control. He would go to any ends to achieve it.

His first riding lesson was clear in his mind. The horse was an old sorrel gelding who looked down at Mark with ruminative eyes. It was all the same to him if he was ridden or left to gaze at the horizon. The lesson had come almost six months to the day after he had started speaking . . . again.

He was ten years old and in a private school in the Big Sur country of Northern California. It was a school that had been set up and run by a retired army colonel, and it was for the very rich and the very unruly. When the two factors coincided, a boy was sent to the school to learn discipline, to be trained to become 'a valuable member of society', to learn an unpampered existence, to eventually take his rightful place as a captain of industry. So, by definition, all the boys were the progeny of rich and influential people who were separated or divorced, or who simply did not want to take the time to be a parent. Mark Sebastian was the exception. Since 12 December 1940, at the tender age of four, the night his parents were murdered, he hadn't spoken a word.

He had been taken to the best psychiatrists, counsellors, healers, witch doctors – everything money could buy, but nothing broke through the silence. In fact, the practitioners of psychology were probably the worst, certainly the least sensitive. They tended to treat Mark as an inanimate object. They poked, prodded, theorized, invented ever more elaborate games to play with his psyche. No two psychologists agreed with each other. They argued long and hard, expounding ever more convoluted dialectic; convened seminars at which hundreds of cigarettes were smoked and copious amounts of coffee consumed. The only thing on which they agreed was that Mark Sebastian was a 'classic case', but whose classic? One psychologist was positive and pounded the table to bolster his convictions that Mark was the repository of induced schizophrenia; another opted for autism and waxed long and hot on the symptoms that had led him to that conclusion. A third was sure that it was a classic case of aphasia, a loss of speech, although it was pointed out that this condition usually resulted from a brain lesion, of which there was no evidence. Still another – and it was immediately noted that he was an exponent of a new and very radical branch of psychology – felt that Mark was a completely normal and healthy boy who just didn't feel like speaking, and that they should leave him alone, for eventually, when he was bored with this silence, he would come round. He was shouted down, dismissed as a lightweight, if not a feather brain, and suffered the ignominy of just being ignored. He responded by pouting.

Fortunately, there was plenty of money, enough so that Mark Sebastian would never have to work if he was unwilling or unable.

His father, Robert Sebastian, was a third generation native Californian, the product of a long line of pioneers. When the first Sebastian, in the 1850s, had realized that prospecting for gold was a fool's task, and that only the very few prospered, he turned his hand to providing supplies for those who would remain fools for the rest of their lives.

At first it was picks, shovels, sluice-boxes. Then he expanded into even more essential tools – rifles and handguns with which a prospector could protect himself from claim jumpers.

The business grew and the other Sebastians that came along were just as adept at making money as the first had been, so that by the time Robert Sebastian was old enough to have taken his rightful place as the head of the company, it was no longer necessary.

The Sebastian Arms Corporation manufactured high-quality hunting rifles and small arms in several calibres. They had also obtained lucrative military contracts and expanded into bazookas, machine guns, mortars and a dozen other items that would kill, blow up or vaporize.

Robert Sebastian had chosen public service as his career – as many of his contemporaries felt constrained to do – as a probable sop to their collective consciences. Sebastian became a career diplomat. He was bright, vigorous, energetic and tipped to go far in the political world, which was why he had been posted to the very sensitive position in Berlin. If he handled it well, it would be a great boost up the next rung of the ladder.

The only blot on his otherwise immaculate record was his choice of a wife. Within the confines of the White Anglo-Saxon Protestant society that young Robert almost exclusively inhabited, the idea of him taking off with a Jewish girl was shocking. Yes, they acknowledged that she was from a good family. Intelligent, even intellectual, certainly wealthy, but Jewish.

Robert had met her in Washington DC, where she had accompanied her father, a Chicago banker, on his trip to the White House. Franklin Delano Roosevelt, himself, had requested the presence of Morris Goldman. Goldman had a reputation as one of the most astute financial brains in the country, and Roosevelt, still in the midst of climbing out of the depths of the Depression, was looking for help from anyone he could get. It was also good politics. Goldman was a friend of Henry Morgenthau, the Secretary of the Treasury, and a Jew.

Robert and Natalie fell instantly, deeply, irrationally in love. Natalie's parents were just as anxious to dissuade her from marrying a gentile as Robert's were for him to dissolve his relationship with a Jewess. It was all to no avail. They were married, and a year later, Mark was born.

Mark was enrolled at the Gustavus Adolphus Academy, the military leader the colonel most admired, just after his ninth birthday. The instructors knew about his past history and tried hard to reach him, without results. The boy was obviously not an imbecile. He would listen, sometimes meet the teacher's eyes, albeit without expression, carry out simple tasks as he was instructed, but never a millimetre more. Without a specific instruction, he would sit for hours gazing, unblinking, into the distance, not sullen, but passive, completely impassive. Of course, the rowdier elements of the school picked on him, taunted him, roughed him up, when there was no instructor around. Mark accepted all this with extreme stoicism, allowed himself to be a punching-bag, never fought back, never changed expression.

The turning point was an accident of time and place. An instructor named Gerry Beaver, an ex-marine platoon sergeant, decided to give the boys some lessons in unarmed combat, jujitsu, at which he was an expert. Mark was in the group and, as usual, stood motionless at its fringe. He watched solemnly as boy after boy was shown the basic throws, as Beaver demonstrated the points of leverage.

One boy, particularly tall and skinny for his age, stepped forward for his instruction. Beaver used him to illustrate what could be done if he were attacked from behind. He turned the boy around, gripped him by the upper arm and half turned to his audience so that they could see exactly what he was doing.

A cloud passed over Mark's face. Something deep in his memory that had lain like a quiescent beast at the bottom of a black lagoon, shivered, shook itself, stirred. The monster's ugly head broached the oily surface of his memory, blood-red eyes peered myopically at its surroundings.

Mark's mouth fell open. His body went rigid. Beaver and the boy were being viewed at precisely the same angle with the exact juxtaposition of bodies as four-year-old Mark had seen the German holding his mother from the doorway.

An overpowering wave of nausea washed through him. It had the fetid stench of corruption. It burned his nostrils, sent messages through his nervous system. His extremities tingled, started to tremble.

Mark had forgotten to breathe, felt himself blacking out. He took a long shuddering breath. No one noticed. They were intent on the demonstration. Mark reached for, took a conscious grip on, self-control that he had exercised without knowing it. Little by little, starting from his toes, working up through his body, he relaxed. The trembling stopped. The severe traumatic spasm passed without notice.

Mark felt light-headed. Colours that had always seemed pastel and washed-out, brightened, became more vivid. He was aware of the air drawn into his nasal passages down to his lungs. A tiny glimmer of light kindled in his eyes.

Mark's unblinking stare was a source of consternation to the teachers. It was unnerving. The instructors had got into the habit of glancing at him and, as quickly, away. Beaver, too, followed this procedure, and was sharp enough to notice the interest. He beckoned to Mark and asked him if he'd like to learn. Mark came over, unhesitating, planted himself in front of Beaver, stared up at him. Beaver showed him the basic moves, how to fall, how to use an opponent's thrust to the best advantage. The boy was good, excellent, in fact. He learned quickly, an instruction never had to be repeated. He had the right build for it. Even at his young age, he had the sturdy frame of his father, the quick reflexes. The lessons became a passion to be practised all day and every day with only short breaks for meals. He and Beaver became inseparable, and one day, without warning, Mark spoke. Long sentences followed each other in a stream, as if they had been stored in a warehouse and were suddenly released for the Christmas rush. The catharsis was long in coming, and unaccompanied by screaming and crying. Just words, hundreds and thousands of them. Beaver never thought he would see the day when he would have to restrain himself from telling the kid to shut up.

Chapter Three

Sebastian squeezed into a parking space in one of the narrow roads off Fleet Street, checked the credentials that he would use that said he was Anthony Christie, journalist, reporter for the

Washington Post. The credentials were perfect, and so they should be, he had made them himself. He'd realized early on that the weakest link in his sort of quest was the ability to pass borders without question, the ability to be accepted as a person of his own choosing. The key was documentation. With the proper documents, anything was possible. He studied the various types of paper used – watermarks, inks, handwriting – and the way to disguise it, the photography necessary for identification photographs. A year in a school of graphics, and hours on his own in diligent practice, and he could forge papers that would stand up anywhere.

He went into the *Daily Express* building, made inquiries for the morgue where the newspaper files were held, and was directed to the second floor.

All he had to go on was the one clue Schmidt had given him. He had seen Rascher in the company of a socialite, the daughter of Lord something, at the races. The *Daily Express* printed the Hickey column in which all the exploits and social doings of débutantes and their escorts were faithfully recorded. It was a long shot, but perhaps the Hickey column had printed a picture of this particular girl in company with Rascher. Sebastian knew what Rascher looked like from the SS identification photo he had procured, and Schmidt had said that he still looked pretty much the same. If he got lucky, there would be a picture of the girl, resplendent in her Ascot hat, with Rascher beside her, and the paper should give the name by which he was now known.

He smiled at the librarian, introduced himself, showed his credentials.

And what, the white-haired lady wanted to know, could she and the *Express* do for the *Washington Post*?

Sebastian explained that he was on a swing through Europe for the paper and that his assignment was to unearth local eccentricities and package them for America, part of which would be 'silly season' stories designed to warm the hearts of chilly Washingtonians. Could he get all the papers relating to Royal Ascot for the last five years, 'as the people back home would love to read about the Royal Personages that attended – the stunning outfits, the bizarre millinery creations'.

The librarian assured him that nothing was simpler. She was back in ten minutes with a boxful of microfilm spools. Sebastian followed her to the projector, where she showed him how to use it, then left him.

Sebastian wasn't going to take any chances that Schmidt's memory had been faulty. The man had said two years ago. It could just as easily have been three or four. The thing that Sebastian was positive about was that Schmidt had told the truth about what he had seen. There had been that ring of sincerity, and something else, underlying it. Sebastian was convinced that Schmidt had felt no great love for the other three – wanted him to find them. Sebastian's mouth pursed into a tight little smile. 'Hermann Schmidt, *in memoriam*, you are about to get your wish.' He inserted the spool for June 1966, the first day of Royal Ascot that year. There was a lot about the races – the form that was expected of some of the favourite horses, the fact that Queen Elizabeth was due at the race track on Ladies' Day – nothing of particular interest. The Hickey column contained its usual society notes. On second thoughts, Sebastian decided that it was duller than usual, probably a slow day. He forwarded the spool to the next day's paper, much more of the same. He finally got to the paper that related to Ladies' Day, the one day during the meeting where each of the ladies in the Royal Enclosure attempted to outdo the other in what they wore, from the most elegant outfits to the most bizarre. Balmain, Balenciaga and Dior originals cheek by jowl with Mary Quant and King's Road antique market kitsch. But the hats received the most attention. There were several pictures of Mrs Shilling, an annual visitor noted for her zany creations, who wore a hat that was nothing more, and certainly nothing less, than a huge teapot, complete with a spout, handle and lid. There were other pictures also of more conventional ladies. Sebastian examined each in turn, but found no one that looked like his picture of Rascher. He made notes of all the ladies' names to see if they would re-occur. He scanned the rest of 1966, went on to the following year.

Ladies' Day, 1967, had pictures of many of the same women he had already seen. Mrs Shilling was again in evidence, this time in a three-foot-tall top hat with a bunny peeking out of the top. No Rascher. He read every word of the Hickey columns, paused each time a titled lady was mentioned, wrote it down. The columns were beginning to take on much of a sameness, lots of items about who Lady so-and-so was seeing, how the Duchess-of-something's daughter had decided to become a model or ride to hounds or devote her life to the care and attention of handicapped children; and the slightly *risqué* items about how the Countess 'W' was seen in the company of an internationally known roué, flying down to the South of France, or how the Honourable Priscilla had caught her mini skirt as she was climbing over a fence at Lord 'R's' houseparty and wasn't she embarrassed standing there half-naked in front of her peers. He went on to 1968.

He struck gold almost immediately. On the page that contained the pictures of the Ladies' Day fashion parade, Sebastian's eye, scanning quickly, passed over the photo in the lower left-hand corner, stopped abruptly, returned.

It was a full-length picture of a very beautiful girl in a floppy brimmed hat festooned with flowers and a mini dress that showed up light in black and white. Next to her, almost out of frame, was an older man in top hat and morning suit, shown in three-quarter profile, smiling at the girl. Sebastian's heart rate increased. He sat back, rubbed his eyes, calmed himself. He leaned forward, operated the projector controls to blow up the picture, until it filled the screen, then he took an envelope from his inside pocket, extracted the picture within, placed it alongside the newspaper picture.

Sebastian's picture, blown up to postcard size, showed Rascher serious, unsmiling, as an SS Colonel. He compared the photos. Although a score of years separated the ages of the two men, there was a striking resemblance. The shape of the eyes, slightly tilted at the corners, the snub nose, the set of the thin-lipped mouth, although the older man sported a narrow moustache. The chin that came almost to a point was rounded off at the apex.

The photo caption said that the girl was the Honourable Pamela Driscoll, daughter of Lord Driscoll. The man next to her was not identified. Sebastian cursed. He went through the rest of the pictures for that year, changed spools and flipped through the pages for 1969 and 1970, three more pictures of the girl, none of Rascher. Sebastian took a deep breath, let it out slowly. He went back to the beginning.

He referred to the list he'd made of all the titled ladies mentioned in the Hickey column. Pamela had one mention prior to 1968. It was for October 1967, and said that she, then aged twenty-two, had accompanied the heir to a beer fortune to a huge Hallowe'en ball held in Shropshire – innocuous and uninformative. He started in on the Hickey columns for 1968. A short paragraph in March said that Pamela Driscoll had been seen at an out-of-the-way restaurant with a wealthy industrialist/horse owner – a married man – and no name. Sebastian paused, pictured the words that Schmidt had uttered. 'The gentleman with her was an owner of horses. I think he said he had one running that day . . .'

He kept reading. An item in December 1968 said that Pamela Driscoll had flown to Barbados for a three-week holiday, ostensibly to visit friends, and a not-too-subtle hint that she had really gone to meet her married boyfriend, a relationship now of some ten months' standing.

1969 provided three mentions of the girl. Two were routine house parties where she was part of a crowd, the third, that she had been seen at Epsom for the Derby in the company of a horse owner whose horse was one of six given a chance to win the race – again, no name.

Sebastian stood up, stretched, took a walk around the chair. Here, at least, was another way to go. He could get the list of all the horses entered for the Derby, check the favourites to find out who their owners were. He decided to finish the Hickey columns for 1970 first, follow that clue to its logical end, curb his impatience. Deviation would be haphazard. He had waited this long, another hour wasn't going to make much difference. He sat down again.

1970 had only one further mention, that the girl, in company with five others, was to cruise the Greek Islands in August. All her companions, as described by Hickey, seemed to be of her age – a dead end.

Sebastian went back to the spool for 1969, turned to the day in June on which the Derby was run. There were twenty-two runners listed for the race and, as far as he could tell, other than two horses who were co-favourites at 13–8, a further nine horses were posted with odds up to 10–1, and therefore in with a chance. He made a list of all eleven, wrote the owners' names down alongside. As he expected, nobody with the name of Rascher, but that had been unlikely anyhow. At a glance, in fact, all the owners appeared to be English, Irish, Scottish, or at least of Anglo-Saxon extraction. There was a MacNab, a Lord

Harwell, an O'Sullivan, a Johnson, a Swift, a Nottingham, a McKenzie – not a foreigner in the bunch – at least at first glance.

Sebastian returned the microfilm to the librarian, requested a photostat of the page containing the picture of Pamela Driscoll and friend, and asked the librarian for anything she might have in her alphabetical listing for Lord Driscoll, Pamela Driscoll or whomever else constituted the family. The librarian said she would look to see if she had anything and suggested, in the meantime, that he look up the names in *Burke's Peerage* and *Who's Who.* She pointed to the section where the volumes were stored.

Sebastian went to the shelf, found the current *Burke's Peerage*, turned to 'D's'.

'Lord Charles Thomas Driscoll of Chadwick Hall, Battle, Sussex. Educ. Eton, Christchurch Coll. Oxford. Served in Second World War. 1939–45 Coldstream Guards. Rank of major. Member of HQ Staff British Red Cross, Order of St John.

'm. 7 May 1943, Cecilia Ramona Laura, 2nd daughter of late Sir Hilary Rowland Tyssen and has issue:

1 Pamela Ramona b. 1 June 1945
2 Philip Charles Thomas b. 12 November 1947'

Sebastian made notes, replaced the volume, took down *Who's Who*. First he thumbed the pages to Charles Thomas Driscoll and repeated the procedure. The entry read, 'Lord Charles Thomas Driscoll'.

There followed much of the same information as listed in *Burke's Peerage.* In addition, it listed him as a director of three companies, as a member of four clubs in St James's, and elicited the startling information that his hobby was collecting barbed wire.

Sebastian closed the book, replaced it on the shelf. He went back to the counter where the librarian awaited him. The woman exchanged the photostat of the page that he had requested for the five shillings' fee, and then handed him additional microfilm spools, along with a list of reference dates. He took everything back to the projector.

At that moment, Ernst Rascher was sitting not a mile away in his thickly carpeted, richly appointed office in Cornhill Street. He had come out from behind his Louis Quinze desk and settled into the button-back leather chesterfield sofa that took up most of one wall in the large room. He lounged, arms flung casually along the back, in his three-piece suit, Savile Row, tie by Hermes, head tilted towards the ceiling in direct line with an opulent crystal chandelier, French, circa 1790. One corner of the office overlooked the Royal Exchange that was noted for its ambulatory, statues, mural painting, and courtyard. The other corner looked down upon the pillared edifice of the Bank of England. But it was wasted on Rascher. He seldom bothered to reflect on anything historical that had no direct bearing on the here and now, his lifestyle, its continued success. And he was in just such a pensive mood. It probably had something to do with today's date, 7 December, the day that the Japanese had invaded Pearl Harbor and brought the United States into the war. The war was never far from his mind. It had nurtured him, formed and set in granite a personality that, prior to the conflict, had been ill-defined, wayward, meandering. The war had taught him what true power was and its manifold uses. He had acquired a taste for it that was now an addiction. His position as a high-ranking SS officer had ensured continuous influence, despite the fact that Germany had lost the war. From Rascher's point of view, it was only a minor setback, one that would eventually be rectified. Mistakes had been made, not to be repeated. Experience would see to that. The Führer had been brilliant, imbued with the gift of omniscience . . . perhaps a little excessive . . . some had said mad. But those were the heretics. Rascher still burned a candle at the altar in the cathedral of his mind – an inextinguishable flame. One shouldn't, couldn't chastise the Führer just because of his zeal. He had been a visionary and had worked hard – too hard? – long strenuous hours to make the dream come true. It had been too much for one man. Inevitably, the strain had told, caused the man to make mistakes. After all, he was only human – superhuman? And so was the view of mid-twentieth century history, according to Ernst Rascher.

Rascher leaned over to the coffee table, Italian Renaissance in marble landscape, *pietra dura* in lapis lazuli and mother-of-pearl from the Ducal Palace at Urbino, fifteenth century. The table stood on an Aubusson carpet in mauve and green. On the table was a silver tray that contained a four-piece silver tea service – Queen Anne. He took the teapot and poured a fragrant brew made from Lapsang Souchong into a Ming cup with its distinctive flowered pattern. Rascher was unaware that his choices of furniture, decorations, accoutrements, were unmatched – didn't necessarily complement each other – or that to a connoisseur, the *mélange* would be considered vulgar, the acquired vulgarity of the *nouveaux riches*. He cared only that they were expensive, in demand, and were the best one could get, coveted by experts, if not necessarily *in toto*. The pictures that covered his Regency-papered walls followed this format ideally. No attempt had been made to collect by artist, by school, or even by period, so that Rubens was hung next to a Corot, followed by a Jackson Pollock and original da Vinci drawings. He had installed an Adam fireplace, stacked with logs and surrounded by polished brass implements, but incapable of doing the job for which it was intended. There was no chimney. On the ornate mantel, in solitary splendour, stood an ormolu table clock with carved figures from the workshop of Ignaz Franz Platzer, circa 1765.

Rascher admired them unreservedly, knowing to the penny what each would fetch on the current market. These, of course, were the 'clean' ones, the ones he had been seen to collect from auctions and private galleries. There were others, many others, stacked like so much cordwood in the vault built into the basement of his house: paintings 'donated' by their unwilling owners during the war, stored in various secret caches, awaiting liberation when it had been safe. Rascher had collected them and kept them. After all, they were a hedge against inflation.

Rascher was doing well. He chided himself for being too modest. He was doing superbly. Not bad for the son of a minor civil servant from a small Westphalian town. And now there was this trouble. And after so many years. How could it come to haunt him now, when he was at the top of his form? The London director of the Swiss-based pharmaceutical firm with multi-national connections, owned and operated by former SS officers – a director of six other enterprises that ran the gamut from frozen food to oil – a member of the illicit operation that paralleled the legitimate ones and was hidden by them – the supply of dope. And there was the enterprise of which he was most proud. He was the owner of several magnificent thoroughbreds that won races steadily, enhancing the reputation he craved as an owner of international repute.

Rascher had been sitting in his office on the morning of the 29th when Kessler called from Hamburg and told him about the article.

Hermann Schmidt – he'd almost forgotten the man existed – had certainly not spared him a thought for more years than he cared to count. And now he was dead. Good, and so what? The 'so what' was embodied in the note left by the corpse – with his name on it and the date 12 December 1940. When Kessler told him about it, it meant nothing. He tried to think where he had been on that date and what he might have been doing. He got only as far as placing his location in Berlin. The rest was a blank.

He pondered the question for an hour – a painstaking reconstruction of old memories. He could place where he had been in November 1940 and January 1941, but 12 December? Then it came. He relived the scene in vivid detail as it flooded back. His hand stole down to his groin in an unconscious gesture. His subconscious remembered the painful kick he had received from that berserker. He felt a twinge and locked his thighs together, and shivered . . . What was the man's name?

His phone call woke Spitzweg. It was only 6.00 in the morning in New York. Spitzweg was testy over the intrusion into his sleep until Rascher told him about the murder of Schmidt and the note with their names on it. Then a tremor came into his voice. He sounded frightened.

'And that,' Rascher thought, 'was in character.' He felt a perverse joy at being the first to tell Spitzweg the bad news.

Two days elapsed before Spitzweg called with a progress report. He still sounded scared and he spoke fast, tripping over his words. He had been in constant communication, he said, with Naumann and the people in Germany, and they had narrowed down the assailant to one possible, the son of the murdered couple, Mark Sebastian, who had been four years old at the time of the débâcle. 'Naumann wants us to have a meeting in New York right away. He thinks it could be an isolated incident, but he doesn't want to take that chance. It must be isolated, don't you think, Ernst? After all, we haven't seen Schmidt for twenty years or more. He didn't know where we are or what we are doing.' His voice craved reassurance and Rascher was careful to squash the fragile comfort he sought.

'Ah, Max, don't forget that he knew many of our colleagues and could have found out. If it is this Mark Sebastian who is after us, Schmidt probably told him everything before he died.'

Rascher put a hand over the mouthpiece and chuckled as he heard an agonized 'oooh' escape from Spitzweg's lips.

Rascher flew to New York and the meeting was held in Spitzweg's penthouse, high atop Manhattan in the East Seventies. The meeting was inconclusive. It had been learned that Mark Sebastian had been a disturbed child for several years after the 'accident', but had apparently come out of it, attended college, travelled extensively. His present whereabouts were unknown, but further information was expected.

They discussed the significance of their three names on the note along with Schmidt's. The easiest interpretation was that Mark Sebastian sought revenge and wanted them to know it. He had eliminated Schmidt and, in theory, would be coming after them next. How he was to accomplish this was another question. There was no possibility, they decided, that Sebastian could have learned of their whereabouts from Schmidt. Since Schmidt's peremptory dismissal from the organization, there had been absolutely no contact. Naumann had a complete dossier by his side of Schmidt's life up to the day of his death. The man had slid further and further downhill until he had reached the status of a Skid-Row bum. The unanswerable question was, 'why now?' The man had to be in his mid-thirties. Why had he chosen this time to act? Was there something significant in the timing? Schmidt had been in Bremen for years. Was it possible that Sebastian had only just found that out? They decided that caution would be a good idea, but they were used to being cautious and this would not impose any extra burden.

Naumann changed the subject to a far more pleasant topic – how much money their enterprises were making. Pharmaceuticals were on the upswing. All the advertising that was pumped out about headaches, backaches, sinus conditions, diarrhoea or the reverse, was producing a generation of hypochondriacs.

Naumann philosophized that, due to this phenomenon which had been unforeseen, one could become extremely rich by conventional means. And with a wolfish grin, he commented on how nice it was to receive such a bonus. He was pleased to report that the importation of the South American cocaine – for which the pharmaceutical company provided such excellent cover – was doing extremely well, and that profits were estimated to be up more than 80 per cent over the previous year.

The rest of their legitimate enterprises were also doing well. Frozen food was showing a startling growth potential, the mortgage brokerage was doing landslide business and, at last count, their oil exploration company was bidding on twenty-three jobs and expected to land nearly half of them. 'Which brings me to Mexico,' Naumann said. 'If I can secure a concession, as I confidently expect to, all else will be as nothing in comparison. As you know, we are in a critical stage. The Imperial Petroleum Corporation has agreed to all my terms and is now standing by, waiting for me to deliver.'

'And do you think you will be able to?' Rascher asked. 'Is your man in Mexico behaving himself?'

Naumann answered the question with a trace of a sneer. 'Luis Francisco Montez is being a good little boy. He knows what will happen if he misbehaves. I think he will get his appointment as the Minister responsible for oil in the next few weeks, and then . . .'

They separated in good spirits.

On the flight back to London, Rascher – alone, without his associates to bolster his courage – felt his good cheer slowly drain away. It was fine to tease Spitzweg, and he had always derived pleasure from it, but this could be serious. It was fine to say nothing would happen; it was probably even correct to assume it, but Rascher decided a few basic precautions would be in order. It had been several years since he had felt constrained to look over his shoulder. Fear grasped for his bowels with bony fingers. What he needed was solace, something to assuage his fears. An evening with Pamela. He had neglected her lately. If truth be told, it was more of a backing-off process. An instinct that had never matured into a full-blown thought had warned him that their relationship had changed, subtly at first, so that it went unnoticed, but quicker in the last six months, so that the rift was now apparent.

Pamela was beautiful and Pamela was useful, and Rascher's ego would not allow him to believe that the disparity in their ages could bring a change in their relationship. He rationalized her increased aloofness as the restlessness of youth. He had always given her room to breathe – within certain limits. After all, he deserved to get his money's worth. The girl was not an inexpensive plaything, what with the flat in Belgravia, the clothing allowance – generous by any standards – and even the favours he'd done for her father. He'd procured a couple of directorships for the old boy – sinecures that wouldn't tax him unduly, and a good thing too, as Rascher privately believed that Lord Driscoll didn't have enough brains to fill an egg cup. And the old boy was grateful, embarrassingly so, because, quite simply, Lord Driscoll needed the money and looked on Rascher benevolently as his current saviour, a rôle Rascher guessed that others had occupied in the past. Never mind that he was fucking the man's daughter, a girl young enough to be his own offspring; and Lord Driscoll even managed to ignore the fact that Rascher was not an aristocrat, and worse, a foreigner.

The benefits to Rascher were great. He had a beautiful young girl who catered to him, whatever her motives, and he had an entrée into an enclave of society that would have been difficult for him to have reached under normal circumstances. Rascher never stopped to think of the reasons why; the nuances and subtleties would have escaped him anyhow. He saw himself as a direct, incisive man; everything could be construed in black and white. There was no question of marriage. After all, he was a married man, a good family man. Divorce would be unthinkable, although he despised the woman who had been his wife for twenty years. He didn't care a wit for her sensibilities, blunted as they must be after all this time, but the children, that was different. His fourteen-year-old son, Henry, who he always thought of as Heinrich, and little eleven-year-old Gretchen. They were what constituted his family, occupied his thoughts. They would be the recipients of his heritage, the heirs to his fortune, the leaders of the new Fourth Reich. He was careful how he nurtured this, satisfied himself with just planting seeds that would sprout at maturity. It wouldn't do for the children to act superior around their classmates. Better that they fitted in now, and were only gradually made aware that they were 'special'. He still had plenty of time to bring them around to his way of thinking. Let them be children now.

He'd installed them in the country, fifty miles from London, in a magnificent house with twenty acres of ground, and provided for all their needs. His wife had the help she wanted and was satisfied in her way, never complained when he spent the week in his London flat, and hardly chastised him when he skipped the weekends in the country. They had never had much to say to each other anyhow, and his only reason for going was to see Henry and Gretchen.

His thoughts turned to Pamela. His groin began to warm in the old familiar way, as it did every time he thought about her. It had been far too long. He resolved to talk to her about their differences. Whatever had caused her coolness couldn't be very serious. He would take her for a trip to the sun – perhaps to Barbados again.

Rascher put down the tea cup, refilled it, leaned back and watched the cloud of steam rise from the surface of the pale liquid. The bitch! She had rejected him from her bed on the skimpy pretext that she had to be up early in the morning for a photographic session, and she needed her beauty sleep, for God's sake. And hadn't he told her, time after time, that she didn't need to work, but just to be available. This try for independence – stupid, irrational. And she had talked back to him, mocking him. And when he disciplined her – no snip of a girl would speak to him that way – instead of remorse, compliance, she had been defiant, eyes blazing as her hand went to the cheek he had slapped, livid finger marks showing distinctly. And he warned her before he stormed out that this was only a mild beginning compared to what he could do. Of course, a whore like her could go out and become someone else's mistress. She would be all right. But her father . . . he would go out of his way to ruin the old bastard, cut off his credit, terminate his directorships; and what would happen to him then?

Rascher felt satisfied with himself. He had given her a few days to stew, and when he next called, he fully expected to see great changes. There had better be, or he would prove to her that he wasn't in the habit of making empty threats.

Rascher dismissed her from his mind and thought about Sebastian. Since his return, a photograph of Sebastian had been forwarded to him from New York. It was a picture from the college yearbook that showed a boy of nineteen or twenty, a full face photo, expressionless; nothing could be read from it. A more up-to-date picture had not yet been found. Rascher tried to guess what changes might have taken place in the intervening years. Sebastian would now be in his early thirties. Probably no marked changes.

And still no line on his whereabouts after Bremen. Even with all the resources at their command, they had been unable to find any trace of the man. But Rascher was confident that they would. In the meantime, he imported a bodyguard from New York – someone he could trust – a good German, the son of an SS sergeant who was on Spitzweg's payroll.

Rascher picked up the cup of tea, blew on it, sipped noisily.

Sebastian ran through the handful of cuttings on the Driscoll family. There wasn't much. There was an item from the financial section when Lord Driscoll was appointed to the board of a small electronics company. There was a general item on the House of Lords where Lord Driscoll, in company with a dozen other hereditary peers, was mentioned – unfavourably – as taking his place in the House when the mood suited him. The article was about non-contributors in the Government. There was an article – complete with fuzzy picture of Lord Driscoll standing in the driveway, with his house in the background, in Battle, Sussex, on the day in 1966, commemorating the nine hundredth anniversary of the Battle of Hastings when the Normans invaded. The picture of Lord Driscoll showed a tall, spare man with a supercilious expression on his thin face.

There were four items on Pamela Driscoll, all pictures with captions. They showed the girl modelling clothes, called her a model. As the pictures covered a three-year span, Sebastian guessed that she didn't work very hard at it. But the girl was beautiful. By chance, all four photos had been taken from different angles, and they all looked like her 'good side'. He returned the clippings, thanked the librarian and left the building. When he came out on the street, he was surprised to find that it was already dark. He looked at his watch, almost 5.00. He had worked straight through the day, without a break, without lunch, without noticing it.

He drove back to the Hilton, left the car with the attendant and went down to Trader Vic's in the basement. He sat himself down in a corner, ordered a Chivas Regal on the rocks, sipped it thoughtfully when it arrived. It was too late to try and find the girl today, and anyhow, as he allowed himself to relax, he realized how tired he was. Eight hours of non-stop concentration had left him drained. He decided on a solitary dinner in his room, some desultory TV-watching, and an early bed time.

Chapter Four

Sebastian was up at 7.00 a.m., did an hour of exercises that included karate manoeuvres, leg stretches, splits, waist rotation, kicks and jumps. He ordered breakfast from room service, shaved, showered and was dressed when it arrived. He laid out a dozen different vitamins to down with his orange juice. By the time he'd finished his second cup of coffee, he felt ready for whatever the day would bring him.

He looked in the London telephone directory first. No Pamela Driscoll. He wasn't disappointed, as he hadn't expected to find her that way. That would have been too easy. That left him the next alternative, the one he'd been sure he'd have to follow. Pamela Driscoll was a model, models have to have agents. He took the classified directory from the shelf of his bedside table, flipped the pages to model agencies. He ticked off the ones that had the biggest advertisements. He looked at his watch, a quarter to nine, still too early to call. He put on his windbreaker, went downstairs, left the hotel and walked up Park Lane towards Marble Arch. As long as he was on the move, time would seem to pass more quickly. He hardly noticed the bleak day and the lowering clouds. He returned to his room forty-five minutes later.

He dialled the first agency on his list, Annabel's, by name. 'Hello,' he said to the pleasant voice that greeted him. 'I'm Anthony Christie, a freelance photographer for *Harper's* magazine, New York. I'm here to do a fashion layout and I wanna use a model that I understand is with your agency.'

'Who's that?' the girl asked cheerfully.

'A girl called Pamela Driscoll.'

'Pamela Driscoll,' the girl repeated, sounding doubtful. 'I don't think she's with this agency, but I'll check. Would you hold the line, please.' She came back on thirty seconds later. 'No, I'm sorry, Mr Christie. She's not with this agency. Are you sure that it was Annabel's that you wanted?'

'Oh, hell,' very regretful, 'I thought it was, I must have been given the wrong information. You wouldn't know which agency she is with, would you?'

'No, I'm sorry, the name sort of rings a bell, but I'm afraid that I don't know.

'Well, thanks anyway, sorry to have bothered you.'

'That's all right, no bother. Call us again any time. Good-bye.'

Sebastian said good-bye and dialled the next agency on his list, Calendar Girls. He repeated the questions with the same result, except that the girl at the other end thought that she remembered Pamela Driscoll was with the Vanity Fair Agency. Sebastian thanked her and dialled.

'Yes,' the girl from the agency said. 'Pamela Driscoll was with us, but she left about two years ago. I think she went to Frazer's.'

Sebastian thanked her and called Frazer's. A lisping voice at the other end told Sebastian that Pamela Driscoll had indeed been with Frazer's but had left six months ago. 'A very flighty girl,' he added.

'Ah well,' Sebastian said in his most sympathetic voice. 'That's the nature of the business. These girls are just never reliable or grateful. You make a name for them and then they leave you.'

'Exactly what I tell my girls,' the man lisped excitedly. 'They just treat you like dirt, after I have given my life for them.'

'I know, I know,' said Sebastian philosophically. 'What can you do, except carry on? You wouldn't know where she went to, would you?'

'Oh, she went to Super Models. I told her she would get lost in the crowd there, they have so many girls, but she wouldn't listen.'

'They never do. Thanks very much for your help,' Sebastian said. 'You sound like a terrific guy to work for.'

He called Super Models, went through the now familiar introduction, said that he understood Pamela Driscoll was on their books and was rewarded with a 'Yes she is.'

Sebastian went into part two of the scenario he'd outlined. 'I saw a picture of her in New York and she looked like the girl I want to use for this layout. I hope she hasn't cut her hair.'

'No, she still has long hair. She looks incredibly good at the moment.'

'Glad to hear it.'

'When are you planning on shooting?'

'A day's booking on the tenth, so I hope she's free.'

'Just a moment, let me check the booking sheet' – pause for ten seconds – 'You're lucky, she's had a cancellation so she can do it.'

'Great, obviously I'd like to see her and her portfolio before I make it a definite booking. Will you arrange that for me? It would probably be easier if I came around to your agency.'

'Sure, that would be fine. When would you like to see her?'

'I think that it had better be as soon as possible, this afternoon maybe. I want to decide on the girl today, if I can; because of my schedule, I can't postpone the session on the tenth. I've got to fly out right after.'

'Well, I can call Pamela now and see if she can come in this afternoon. Where can I reach you?'

'Nowhere, I'm afraid. I'm calling you from someone's office and I'm just on my way out. Can I give you a bell back in about half an hour, when I get to my next appointment?'

'Fine, Mr Christie, I'll wait to hear from you.'

Sebastian thanked her and put the phone down. He looked at his watch, 10.25, almost a solid hour on the phone. He went down to the lobby, bought a *Time* magazine and a *Herald Tribune* from the newsstand, and returned to his room.

At 11.00 sharp, he put the paper down and called Super Models. 'Hi . It's Anthony Christie, any luck?'

'Yes, Mr Christie. Pamela can make it this afternoon. Would three-thirty suit you?'

'Hang on a sec, just let me check my appointment book.' Sebastian covered the mouthpiece for fifteen seconds. 'Yeah, three-thirty is great. See you then.'

Sebastian arrived on Brompton Road at five minutes to three, and found the Super Model Agency about midway between Harrods and the large Italian Renaissance-style church, the Brompton Oratory. The street was crowded with Christmas shoppers, most of whom seemed to be converging on Harrods department store. By the size of the lines of the people waiting to get in, it looked as if Harrods was giving things away. Sebastian knew better.

The agency was up one flight of stairs through a door that had an estate agency on one side and a sewing machine shop on the other. Sebastian sauntered past the place and stopped a half-dozen doors down in front of a jewellery shop. The day had already dimmed, sunset was scheduled for 3.48 that afternoon, and a cold wind was blowing from the north-east. Sebastian put up the collar of his sheepskin coat, put his hands in his pockets, walked back towards the agency.

At 3.25, as he was approaching the agency for the umpteenth time, he saw an orange Mini, with a sunflower painted on the roof, slow down and pull into the kerb a couple of doors from the agency. He slowed his walk even more, saw the car lights go out. The driver's door opened and a girl emerged clutching a large leather-bound book under one arm. Sebastian recognized her instantly. Her long blond hair hung down past her shoulders; her face, where the street light caught it, angles, planes, shadows, was better than any photograph. She wore a fox fur hat and coat to match, with high-heeled black leather boots that reached to her knee. She slammed the door, came around to the back of the car and crossed ten feet in front of Sebastian and into the door of the agency. She didn't even give him a glance.

Sebastian went for his car where he'd parked it on a double yellow line in the next side street. He tore the parking ticket off the windshield where it had been Sellotaped, crumpled it, tossed it into the gutter and slid in behind the wheel of the grey Volvo.

He edged the car into Brompton Road, turned left and found a parking space five cars behind the girl's Mini, and facing the same way.

He turned off the engine and the lights, leaned back on the seat, eyes glued to the door of the agency. The throng of shoppers had thinned somewhat. Sebastian reminded himself that it was tea-time and that many of the people were renewing themselves for a last frenzied rush before closing.

Sebastian's thoughts drifted back to Bremen and the encounter with the derelict who had once been the all-powerful Nazi, Hermann Schmidt. He hadn't really stopped to think until now about the chance circumstances that had him sitting in the heart of Knightsbridge, pursuing a trail that would lead him to the next man on his list, Ernst Rascher. It was an almost mystical chain of events that had brought him this far. He was beginning to feel the man's 'spoor'. Could he call it luck? He could, but he doubted it. From the start, when he stumbled on where Schmidt was living, it appeared to have a sort of inevitability about it.

Sebastian thought that he could trace it back to his fifteenth year. Before that time there was aimless drifting, a meandering between a choice of realities, one from his point of view, and others that were imposed upon him by instructors, relatives, well-wishers and busybodies imbued by their own sense of self-importance. Very little of it had been real, less remembered.

Sebastian plodded on like a sleepwalker through a swamp with no purpose in life, no resolve to do anything but to exist through another day.

Of course he was speaking again, although there is a vast difference between talking at somebody and communicating. Sebastian spoke just enough to get by while remaining untouched by the contact. His energies, such as they were, were entirely on a physical level. He threw himself into learning the techniques for self-defence until he was exhausted. His mental energies were enclosed in solitary confinement. He could have been a lone island in the middle of the Pacific. Knowledge soaked up in a vacuum with no external conduits.

He remembered thinking, 'What can I do with all these facts, they don't apply to anything.' 'They're meaningless.' And then afterwards, 'What am I doing here, why am I still alive?' 'What do I do with myself when I leave here, because I do have to leave some time?'

He had brief thoughts of suicide and even went so far as to list a number of methods he could use to accomplish it. But it was never a very serious thing. Something within him rejected the thought of suicide. He was unable to explain what it was but the thought of ending his life would make him break out in a cold sweat and would give him a gut ache that would last for hours.

Of all things it was a Shakespeare class that led him to taking his first tentative step on the road out of the labyrinth of his convoluted thoughts. It was the first link in the fate chain. He was supposed to have had an arts and crafts class at that time but an administration foul-up had landed him with Shakespeare instead and he was still too insular to make a fuss.

'Would I be sitting here in Knightsbridge right now,' Sebastian wondered, 'if it hadn't been for that screw-up. My whole life might have taken a different turn.'

Scholars have written that Shakespeare had an answer for everything, a turn of phrase to cover any eventuality, animal, vegetable, mineral. All you had to do was to look and something appropriate would jump out at you. Sebastian found the quote from *Othello.* The bard had written:

'Had all his hairs been lives,
My great revenge had stomach for them all.'

Young Mark Sebastian closed the book, keeping his finger between the two halves so as not to lose his place and he pondered the meaning of that line. Could his revenge be as terrible as that? Is that what he really wanted? An hour later, not noticing that his finger had gone numb from a lack of circulation, he decided that it could and that he did want it. He searched Shakespeare for other references and found from *The Merchant of Venice* that Shylock said:

'Hath not a Jew eyes? Hath not a Jew hands, organs, dimensions, senses, affections, passions? Fed with the same food, hurt with the same weapons, subject to the same diseases, healed by the same means, warmed and cooled by the same winter and summer, as a Christian is? If you prick us, do we not bleed? If you tickle us, do we not laugh? If you poison us, do we not die? And if you wrong us, shall we not revenge?'

The half of Sebastian that was Jewish found the quote particularly appropriate. The other half applauded and begged to be included. And from King Lear, he found in Act Two, scene four, that Lear proclaimed:

'I will have such revenges on you both,
That all the world shall – I will do such things –
What they are yet, I know not; but they shall be
The terrors of the earth.'

'The both', had become four, but Mark Sebastian wouldn't find that out for a long time. He cherished the quotes, they energized him in a way he thought impossible. He wanted to refer to them whenever the desire ebbed. He wanted them in plain sight, but where no one else would know what they were except him. A knotty problem for a fifteen-year-old who lived within the confines of a boys' school and who shared a cabin with three others. It was difficult to keep anything secret from all those inquisitive eyes, and if they saw what he was doing, they would laugh at him, ridicule him, the way they used to.

Sebastian guessed that this would no longer be the case, since the time his three most persistent tormentors – who went back to the days when he had been their silent punching-bag – had cornered him behind the recreation hall with the usual malicious mischief in mind. With three years of intensive training and self-defence behind him, the time had come to put it into practice. He blacked one boy's eye, put the second out of commission with a kick to the stomach, and broke the third's arm. From that point on, nobody bothered him and he was allowed to go his own way, keep silent if he felt like it.

Sebastian decided that he still didn't want to take any chances. Captain Midnight and his 'secret decoder' were very much in vogue then. There was much talk about how to pass messages without anyone knowing, the use of secret inks. When nothing else was at hand, Sebastian had learned that one of the best agents for use as 'invisible ink' was urine.

He used an empty milk carton, filled it from his own bladder and tried it out. It worked perfectly. He wrote the three quotes on a piece of blank paper with painstaking care, waited until the letters faded, but brought them back when he waved the paper over a candle.

He tacked the paper on the wall next to his bed and found that if he held a lighted match close, the quotes would come out clear and legible. He only did it when the other three boys were out of the cabin, felt secure that they had no idea that the paper was anything other than blank. Sebastian smiled at the reminiscence. He had kept his resolve. It drove him to acquire expertise in many areas.

There was that summer in 1968 when Paris was just recovering from 'going mad'. The debris from the riots in May was still in evidence, holes in the streets where paving stones had been prised up to hurl at the police, and the CRS, revolutionary slogans daubed on buildings, walls, sidewalks. Sebastian had kept out of it because he had felt it had nothing to do with him. He was intent on his own private conflict.

He was known then as Brian Weber, an alias he had concocted and could prove with authentic-looking papers. He had decided to enlist his services with a unit of mercenaries that he'd heard were going to fight for Biafra. It was a purposeful move on his part to get 'on-the-job training'. He had tried to enlist in the Arab/Israeli war the year before, but the six days it had lasted hadn't been long enough for him to get there, and he'd been too young for the Belgian Congo conflict.

He knew where a lot of the mercenaries hung out, a tawdry bar on the edge of Pigalle. They were a violent, suspicious lot, some former OAS types who were on the run from French Intelligence, some hard-core criminals who were finding life in France a little too hot, Foreign Legion deserters, a sprinkling of psychos from half a dozen countries who just liked to hurt or kill – preferably in that order, and the German.

He was known as Bosch by the others, a man in his late forties or early fifties, it was difficult to tell. His hair had gone iron grey, and he still maintained it in the style prescribed by the German High Command – short and neat. His face was thin and gaunt with a permanent tan that looked as if it had been acquired over many years under a hot desert sun. The eyes were dark and looked out on to the world unsmiling, as a stern headmaster might, who would brook no nonsense. The other features – nose, chin, mouth – were thin, angular. But the most striking features were the man's hands. They were elegant hands, the fingers long and tapered like a concert pianist.

He was civilized and educated, unlike the rest, and it was apparent that he commanded their respect. All of them, down to the most crude, addressed him with deference.

He always sat at a corner of the greasy bar on a stool that he fastidiously wiped before using, and he drank – continuously. As soon as one glass of the Armagnac he favoured was empty, the bartender would replace it with another.

The night that Sebastian walked in dressed in jeans, western shirt, leather jacket and loafers, about a dozen men were clustered around the bar telling stories and laughing uproariously. Sebastian paused by the door, prepared to advance into the room. The bar went silent, a dozen pairs of eyes swivelled towards him, glared with hostility. Sebastian took the scene in with a glance, the cluster of men almost directly in front of him; the lone man with the grey crewcut to his left; four dark-haired girls, who looked remarkably similar in dress and overdone cosmetics, sitting at a table to his right; five other unoccupied tables and chairs placed on the bare boards in the intervening space; the debris that had piled up at the base of the table legs; the fat candles on saucers that dripped thick globules of wax down the sides, encrusting the plates, spattering the tables; the jukebox with flashing lights on the right-hand wall that played a scratchy disc of a French *chanteuse*, accompanied by a concertina; the bartender just coming from the back room; tattered boxing posters on faded blue walls that were barely discernible through a heavy pall of smoke; the odour of new garlic and old sweat.

Sebastian walked to the bar, followed a path between tables, chose a space between the group of men to his right and the other man on a stool to his left.

'Cognac,' he told the bartender. He dropped a ten-franc note on the bar. The bartender took a nervous look at the group of men, poured the drink, set it down and took the money.

The men had begun muttering to themselves in low voices, getting louder. The words became discernible. There were cries of, 'Go on, Bear. Do it.'

The man called Bear detached himself from the group, took the few steps that brought him close to Sebastian, leaned an elbow on the bar, tilted his head, stared. Sebastian ignored the man, sipped his drink. He'd already sized him up with one swift glance.

Bear was perhaps an inch or so taller than Sebastian's 6 feet 2 inches, and considerably heavier. The round head was completely bald, the pig eyes, nose and mouth looked small and ridiculous within the folds of flesh, as if they had been popped in as an afterthought. Bear's belly looked like 'beer's belly'. It hung well over the belt of his dishevelled trousers and showed through the shirt where a couple of buttons had fallen off or had just given up. The man's chest was covered with a thick matting of cinnamon-coloured hair, as were the back of his hands, wrists and arms up to where they disappeared into the sleeves of his shirt.

'What are you doing here, pretty boy?' Bear growled like a bear with a Marseilles accent. 'We don't like nobody drinking here we don't know. You look like a fag to me, or maybe a *flic*. Get out of here before I mess up that pretty face of yours.'

Sebastian put his drink down, turned his head very slowly, met the man's eyes, held them. 'Fuck you,' he said.

Bear looked stunned that anyone would speak to him that way. The other men, sensing action, giggled, started to gather around, shouted encouragement.

From out of the corner of his eye, Sebastian was aware that the older man to his left watched the proceedings without a change of expression.

Bear recovered from his amazement, grabbed Sebastian's wrist as the first step of swinging him round. Sebastian reacted instantly, grabbed the man's hand where it held his wrist with his free hand, twisted his body slightly to the left, putting intolerable pressure on Bear's wrist joint, forcing him to his knees with a surprised yell of pain. Sebastian brought his foot up, planted it squarely in the middle of the man's chest, pushed off and let go at the same time. Bear landed on his rump with a crash that shook the floor. There was a stunned silence, then Bear, rubbing his wrist, rolled over, stood up clumsily, reached for a beer bottle on the bar, knocked the end off with a sharp crack on the edge of the wood, and faced Sebastian, holding the jagged piece of bottle in a line with his throat, where a swift upthrust could sever the jugular.

'You filthy fag, son-of-a-bitch, I'll cut your heart out,' he screamed in a high-pitched voice that sounded ridiculous coming from such a gross body.

Sebastian faced him loose, relaxed, a half-smile on his face. 'Well, come on then, you fat eunuch, or are you just gonna stand there and talk me to death?'

Bear opened his mouth and yowled with rage, his little eyes almost disappearing in his face. He lumbered forward, starting slow like a locomotive, picking up speed. The broken bottle started up in an arc, aimed at a point just under Sebastian's nose. Sebastian waited until it seemed he'd waited too long. Just as the bottle was about to reach the top of its arc and make contact, he moved. One moment he was there, the next he wasn't. He ducked under Bear's arm, grabbed the wrist, put his shoulder in the man's armpit, used Bear's own momentum, braced himself, and flipped the man over on to the top of one of the unoccupied tables. It collapsed like an accordion, splintering into matchwood with a resounding crash. In the silence that followed, Sebastian turned and picked up his drink, sipped it appreciatively.

A couple of the onlookers, making sure that they made a

wide circuit of Sebastian, went to help Bear up. He was groggy but fully conscious, still belligerent and even madder. He was just shaking off his helpers and about to charge when the grey-haired man, who had taken no part in the proceedings up until then, held up a restraining hand, waggled a slim forefinger. Bear stopped short as if someone had pulled a string.

The man put his hand down, addressed Sebastian in a monotone. 'What is your purpose in being here?' The voice was low, commanded attention, the French was fluent, the accent, Germanic.

'I understand you're recruiting mercenaries,' Sebastian replied in German. 'I'm applying.'

A slight flicker of the eyelids was the only reaction by the German at being spoken to in his own language. But he replied in kind, 'If this were the case, and I'm not saying that it is, why did you choose this place for, as you put it, your application?'

Sebastian shrugged. 'I heard it on the grapevine. It is not exactly a secret.'

'Perhaps not, but there are those not in total agreement with the role of a mercenary. They feel that trained men whose chosen career is fighting upset the balance of power, and they would dearly love to infiltrate such a unit so as to obviate its usefulness. How do I know that you were not sent by such persons. You do not fit the mould of . . . my other charges.' He tilted a chin towards the other men who watched with intense interest, heightened by not being able to understand the language.

Sebastian sipped his drink before answering. 'The easy answer is that you don't know, and you are unlikely to find out – but I haven't been sent.' Sebastian locked his gaze with the German, held it.

'The men call me Bosch,' the German said with a mirthless smile. 'The War continues to follow me wherever I go. We Germans are not loved. What is your name?'

'Brian Weber.'

'Weber,' Bosch repeated. He pronounced it 'Vaber' in the German way. 'A German name, but not your real name, of course'.

Sebastian shrugged again. 'It's real enough. I have a German background.' And that was the last time the subject was discussed, but from that moment on, Bosch thought of him and accepted him as a German.

Bosch led a unit of forty mercenaries into Biafra in August. Their contract was for six months, many of them would not live that long, others deserted. But Bosch and Sebastian and a handful of others lasted, came out the other end mentally scarred, if not physically.

By orders of Colonel Ojukwu, the Biafran leader, Bosch and his men were sent to stop the Nigerian army before they could reach the towns of Aba and Umuhia. The Second Division of the Nigerian army had just crossed the Imo River and expected to reach their objectives with ease. They were sadly mistaken. What the mercenaries and the trained Ibo tribesmen lacked in numbers and firepower, they made up for in expertise.

One of the mercenaries that Bosch brought with him was a saturnine Italian named Danelli, no intellectual, but a wizard with explosives and dynamite, which was the one thing they had in quantity. Sebastian became his pupil. Danelli made up mines that the Biafrans called the *ogbunigwe*. They were cone-shaped, with dynamite packed into the narrow end, and the rest stuffed with ball bearings, nails, stones, scrap iron and metal chips. The mine was placed at the foot of a tree to absorb the shock, the trumpet-shaped opening facing down the road towards the oncoming forces. When set off, it had a killing range of two hundred yards over a ninety-degree arc. The first time they used the mine, the Nigerian army walked down the road with no regard for cover. They looked like they were on their way to a Sunday picnic as they weaved from side to side, laughing and joking. Bosch, who observed them through his field glasses, said, 'I've seen it before, they're doped to the eyeballs.' And when the *ogbunigwe* went off, they didn't feel a thing, literally or figuratively.

But they kept coming in bigger numbers and with more hardware, so that Bosch's unit found themselves with the inevitable, fighting the losing action in slow retreat.

At a critical point in the campaign, Bosch went down with a recurring bout of malaria, and Sebastian, now his second-in-command, performed the double duty of tending the German and leading the company of mercenaries and about a thousand Ibos. He had never fought before, but had plenty of theory to fall back on. One of the disciplines he had sought to master was strategy and tactics. He'd read and reread Karl von Clausewitz's book *On War*, as well as the works of Generals Liddell-Hart and Fuller, and selected works by de Gaulle, Mao Tse Tung and Che Guevara, as well as the account of famous battles that started with Alexander and progressed through Skipio, Hannibal, Genghis Khan, Wellington, Frederick the Great and Patton. He found, as many had before him, that there was a vast gulf between theory and practice. None of the books and treatises could adequately describe what it was really like in hand-to-hand combat; how a sharpened bayonet went into a body, resistant at first, then sliding easily through the viscous matter; how a spurt of hot blood rose like a geyser, the sticky crimson fluid adhering to anything it touched, except where it was sucked in greedily by parched brown earth; how you could work up so much hate for someone you had never seen before; how your entire being was encapsulated in the second of time it took to make the contorted face in front of you disappear, silence the screaming mouth for ever.

And the most ironic part was, when Sebastian thought about it, that he had been rejected by the American army because of a punctured ear drum. It didn't hinder him at all. In less rational moments, he thought he might write his Congressman about it.

The mercenaries were surly, but took his orders anyhow. Bosch had appointed him as his surrogate, and Sebastian was a crack shot, and Sebastian could kick the shit out of anyone who wanted to argue. All in all, a happy combination of circumstances.

Sebastian found that he was good at the 'art of warfare'. It was like football. It started off with a set-piece situation, the ball was snapped, generally a messy exchange that resulted in a broken play, that in turn dictated that a little broken field-running was necessary to make yardage. The only difference was that you could wind up dead.

Bosch was delirious for most of the time, babbled incoherently, long rambling sentences. Occasionally a word or a snatch of a phrase would be comprehensible. Most of it seemed to be concerned with his role during the war as an officer on the Russian Front. He sweated and moaned, eyes open and unseeing, as he described the visions in a croak – deep drifts of snow stained in blood; burned-out tanks, skeletal against the stark landscape; charcoaled corpses; severed limbs, like a giant game of pick-up sticks, tossed casually on the snow – framed in pristine whiteness; torture and interrogations; maimed bodies in a communal pit, the SS officer in charge, smiling, enjoying his work.

'Hermann Schmidt,' Bosch said in a clear voice.

Sebastian, who had been slumped in wariness next to the German's cot, jerked upright as if he was electrified. Could it be 'his' Hermann Schmidt? It was a common enough name. But there was one additional factor that sent adrenalin coursing through his veins. He knew from the records that the Hermann Schmidt he sought had been on the Russian Front as part of the Einsatzgruppen Unit.

'Tell me about Hermann Schmidt,' Sebastian said.

Bosch didn't hear, or didn't understand, deep in his delirium.

'Tell me about Hermann Schmidt,' Sebastian repeated. He punctuated each word with a punch on the German's bicep. Bosch's eyes focused.

'I hate the bastard,' he hissed. 'He is an animal. I would like to kill him.'

His long elegant hands encircled an imaginary neck, wrung it. Bosch fell back on the pillow, exhausted. 'Children,' he mumbled. 'Killed them for sport – ripped bellies open.' He sat up seeing what was in his head, pointed a finger at the wall of the tent. Sweat poured off him. 'I see you, Hermann Schmidt. You will not get away this time.' He laughed; it sounded hysterical. 'Who broke your nose, Hermann Schmidt? I want to congratulate him, but why didn't he kill you? You are no German soldier. You are an embarrassment to the Fatherland. You are a mockery of a human being.'

'Where is he?' Sebastian interrupted. It came out in a harsh whisper, penetrating.

Bosch turned and looked at Sebastian. 'In Bremen, of course,' he said conversationally. 'He is in Bremen. I saw him by the docks and asked someone who he was. The fool has changed his name to Rudolph Werner. But I knew him anyway.'

He was so calm and rational it was eerie. Sebastian felt the hairs prickling at the nape of his neck. Bosch lowered himself on to the cot in slow motion, was instantly asleep.

Chapter Five

The girl came out of the agency. Sebastian looked at his watch – 4.40 – she'd waited over an hour. Her face was pinched with anger. She strode to her car with long strides, swinging her portfolio under her arm in cadence. She went to her car, snatched the door open, slid inside and slammed it. The engine started with a roar, the gears clashed, and the Mini shot out into the traffic, leaving a strip of rubber behind, and almost slamming into the side of a taxi. The cab driver honked and shook his fist. The girl gave him the finger.

Sebastian followed at a more leisurely pace, but kept the girl in sight, manoeuvring so that there were only two cars between them.

The light was red at the junction of Brompton Road and Sloane Street, where it ran into Knightsbridge, and Sebastian pulled into the other lane one car length behind. When the light changed, the girl shot forward and made an illegal right turn down Sloane Street. Sebastian, caught in the wrong lane, cursed under his breath, went straight ahead on to Knightsbridge, made a 'U' turn in front of a line of cars who honked at him, and then made a left to follow her. The girl was well ahead, brake lights just going on as she slowed marginally to make the left turn into Cadogan Place, where the Carlton Tower Hotel stood. Sebastian accelerated, screeched around the corner, and caught sight of the Mini a block ahead as it veered left. He turned into Motcomb Street, saw the girl turn ahead of him. He made the left into the narrow road, Kinnerton Street, and saw her car fifty yards ahead. He slowed down to maintain the distance between them.

The girl drove the Mini almost the entire length of the street, turned the car into a passageway just before its end. Sebastian slid into the kerb before the entrance, jumped out of the car, stuck his head around the corner. The girl had parked at the far end of the mews and was walking swiftly up a flight of stairs. Sebastian stepped into the passage as the girl disappeared around the corner. He could hear her booted heels as they stamped up the stone steps. He reached the inner courtyard just as the girl reappeared on the first landing. He ducked out of sight. The boots on the steps recommenced, this time a wooden sound. Sebastian peeked out, saw the girl going up a second flight of stairs. She emerged at the second floor, walked along a narrow balcony that brought her towards Sebastian, reached her door, opened it, went inside and slammed it hard.

Sebastian smiled. 'Temper, temper,' he murmured. Now, at least, he knew where the girl lived.

He had several options. He could wait for her to come out again, follow her to wherever she went, see what she did, the kind of people she did it with; or he could stake out the flat, waiting to see who came to visit. Maybe he would get lucky and Rascher himself would arrive. Or, he could wait until the girl left her apartment, make sure it was empty, discreetly let himself in and bug the place, including the telephone.

He chose to wait and see what developed, play it by ear. The other two ways were time-consuming and might never bear fruit. He couldn't be sure that the girl was even in contact with Rascher.

The pub on the corner opened at 5.30 and a sprinkling of people came out of their houses to use it. Other than that, the street, although just off the main road, was quiet and mostly unused. As the chill of evening drew in, Sebastian walked around to keep up his circulation. He walked into the passageway of the mews, looked up to the second floor flat. The lights were on, as they were in several other flats. The only sound that broke the silence was the cooing of pigeons.

Sebastian was prepared for a long wait and was surprised to hear a car engine fire-up in the mews as he approached it. He sprinted for his car, slid in behind the wheel, started his own engine. If it was the girl, he was going to be ready this time. He had the notion that she always drove like a maniac.

The orange Mini with the sunflower on top backed out of the passageway with a rush, squealed to a stop, turned, and went forward to the exit that would take it out on to the main road. Sebastian followed.

The girl took the scenic route through Belgravia that eventually brought her on to Hyde Park Corner. She circled the roundabout and entered Park Lane, turned into where there was a passageway for the traffic in the divided road, drove back the way she had come, and turned into the Hilton.

Sebastian was surprised, but he pulled in behind her, left his car with the attendant. The girl swept past him and down to Trader Vic's.

When Sebastian got downstairs, he saw the girl in the bar area greeting a man in his late twenties. She kissed him on both cheeks and they sat down at a table against the far wall. It was next to the table he had used on his previous visit and it was unoccupied. Sebastian took it.

The girl had her back half turned to him, facing her companion. She was speaking, her voice low and throaty, the sort of voice that carried across rooms.

'I'm so pissed off,' she said. 'I wasted a whole bloody afternoon at the agency waiting for some burk who wanted to see me for some layout, and the twit never turned up. And,' she emphasized, 'he never had the decency to call.' Her companion murmured something that Sebastian couldn't catch, but it sounded soothing.

The kimono-clad waitress came to take the orders for both tables, temporarily halting conversation. Sebastian ordered a Chivas on the rocks and heard the girl ask for a Zombie. He winced. He heard the man ask if she were crazy drinking something that potent.

'I feel like it,' she said petulantly. 'I may just sit here and get smashed.'

'Then you're going to have to do it without me, darling. I have to meet my wife in an hour. Why don't you come and have dinner with us?'

Pamela shook her head. 'Thanks anyway, but I'm not in the mood to make polite conversation. I'm feeling terribly uptight.'

'Why? Just because a nasty old photographer stood you up?'

'No, it's not that. That was just the last straw. It's other things. You know what I mean.'

'You mean the boyfriend's acting up again? I told you you were going to have trouble with him. What happened this time?'

The girl took a big swallow of her drink, made a face, took another. 'The bastard hit me.'

'Did you deserve it?'

'What a typically male chauvinist statement! No, I bloody well did not.'

'Then why don't you end it? You've been threatening to for ages.'

'It's not that simple.'

'Do you want to talk about it?'

Pamela set her glass down with a bang. It was empty.

'Jonathan, you're a marvellous friend, a wonderful photographer; a shrink you are not. No, I don't want to talk about it. I'll work it out by myself.' She softened, put her hand on Jonathan's arm. 'But thanks anyway for the offer, I appreciate it.' She signalled the waitress for another drink.

'Hadn't you better slow down,' Jonathan suggested gently. 'That stuff's lethal.'

'Good. It'll give me the courage to go and seduce someone.'

'How about me?'

Pamela smiled and shook her head. 'That wouldn't be much fun, I know you.'

As Sebastian listened, the conversation turned to more general topics – mutual friends, photographic sessions, who was doing what to whom. Another Zombie was consumed in the interim.

Jonathan checked his watch, said that he regretted having to leave, but he was going to be late, asked her again if she didn't want to join them. He received the same answer as before. Kissed the girl good-bye and left.

Pamela sat back squarely in her chair, surveyed the room. She toyed with her fourth Zombie, twisting the glass on the paper coaster. Her movements had slowed down, were more deliberate. She picked up the glass, held it to her lips, turned and looked at Sebastian for long moments, turned away, took a large swallow, put the glass down. She turned back to Sebastian. 'You,' she said.

Sebastian looked around, felt foolish doing it. 'Who me?'

'Well, of course, you.' The girl sounded belligerent and her words were just a little slurred. 'Do you see anyone else sitting there? I'm looking at you, aren't I? I'm not cross-eyed you know.' She tapped the space between her eyes with a forefinger.

Sebastian thought of, and rejected several answers to the outburst. He opted for a neutral, 'Yes?'

'Do you think I'm attractive? No, forget that, I know I'm attractive. Would you like to buy me a drink?' Sebastian started to speak, but she interrupted him. 'No, forget that, too, that's silly. That's just a roundabout way of what I really want to ask you. Would you like to go to bed with me?'

Sebastian realized for the first time in his adult life that he finally understood what was meant by 'being speechless'. He was aware of his mouth hanging open like some dumb yokel in the big city for the first time. It took a conscious effort to close it.

'Well?' the girl demanded. 'Are you just going to sit there, or answer my question? You're not queer are you?' she asked suspiciously.

Sebastian regained his poise. 'No and yes,' he said.

The girl took a moment to puzzle that out, her eyes screwed up in concentration. Then the light dawned. 'Oh, I see. No, you're not queer, and yes, you would like to. What are you, the strong, silent type? You're not big on sentences are you? You have my permission to speak, my man.' She made a regal gesture with her hand almost knocking over the glass in the process.

'Thank you.'

'That's not much better, but I'll forgive you. What's your name?'

Sebastian thought of several aliases he could use. Then he smiled. 'Mark Sebastian,' he said.

'I'm Pamela Driscoll.' She put out a hand and Sebastian took it. Her grip was firm. They shook gravely. 'How good are you at defending yourself?' The *non-sequitur* was surprising, but less so, and Sebastian fielded it with ease.

'Pretty good. Why do you ask?'

'Because if I take you to my place you may have to. I have this boyfriend and he's v-e-r-r-r-y jealous. You know why he's jealous?'

'Why?'

'I'm glad you asked me that. Because he's o-o-l-d.'

Sebastian's pulse raced with anticipation.

'He's old enough to be my father. Don't you think that's disgusting? My real father, my dear daddy, he doesn't think it's disgusting. Do you know why? Because Daddy is supported by this old bastard. He is using his one and only sweet little daughter as a means to get money. I am his meal ticket.' She looked momentarily confused. 'Does that make him a pimp, or me a whore, or both? Never mind, it doesn't matter, I'll figure it out later. He buys me things.'

'Who does?'

'My boyfriend, of course. Aren't you listening? He is v-e-e-r-r-y rich. He has more money than Croesus. Are you rich?'

Sebastian just smiled and the girl went on without seeming to expect an answer. 'He buys me clothes and he keeps me in a flat in Belgravia and he takes me on expensive holidays. He can be very generous when he wants to be. And he doesn't want me to work. He thinks that I should just sit around like some damn doll, all dressed up with nowhere to go, and wait until he calls. And you know something else, he's not even English.'

Sebastian's heart rate doubled, his throat felt dry. 'What is he then?'

'A German, for God's sake.' She mimicked a German accent. 'He is very precise, very military, very correct. He scolds me when I swear or do something that he doesn't consider lady-like. But he never hit me until a few days ago.' Her eyes blazed. 'He won't get away with that.'

Sebastian decided that it was a strategic time to change the subject. 'I'm staying in the hotel, shall we go up there?'

Pamela took another large swallow of the drink. 'Let's go.' She slid out from behind the table. Sebastian dropped some money on his table, stood up and took her arm just as she made a precarious wobble. He steadied her and they left the bar, went upstairs to the lobby and over to the lifts. The girl was silent on the ride up, and maintained it as they went into Sebastian's suite. She dropped her coat carelessly over the back of a chair.

Sebastian had been studying her on the way up. It was the first time he'd seen her up close and in good light. She was about 5 ft 7 in or 5 ft 8 in, he guessed, with a figure as good as her face, and her face was striking. Classic bone structure, high cheek bones, small turned-up nose, delicately arched eyebrows and long lashes that framed large green eyes with golden flecks in them, sensitive full-lipped mouth, a strong chin. The mini dress that she wore in defiance of the cold weather ended just below crotch level. The legs were long, perfectly shaped above the knee-high boots. Sebastian shook himself mentally, thrust his hidden desire into the background. 'Can I order you something?' he asked. 'Champagne maybe?'

The girl gave him a brief glance, dropped her head so that her blonde hair fell forward, brushed her cheeks. She clasped her hands in front of her. The situation seemed suddenly awkward, an air of tension pervaded the room.

'Maybe I shouldn't have come,' she said in a low voice. 'I think I've had too much to drink' – she paused – 'this will sound terribly corny, but I've never done anything like this before. I was just . . . very angry . . . and I . . . was sitting there . . . and you were next to me, and I thought you were cute. I know that it sounds like an excuse, but I think I should go.'

A layer of the permafrost that had enclosed Sebastian's emotions melted. He stepped forward, touched her cheek, a caress as light as a snowflake. The smoothness of her skin surprised him, thrilled him. The texture was soft, yielding, warm under his fingers. Gently he lifted her face; her eyes looked enormous, the pupils dilated, the green irises darker than a moment before. He saw despair there, desolation, and something he knew a lot about, loneliness. Her eyes brimmed with tears. He was moved. He leaned over and very gently kissed her. She resisted at first, and then tentatively kissed him back. She flung her arms around his neck, buried her head in his shoulder, sobbed quietly. He held her tight, wanted to comfort her, didn't know how. He thought of all the times when he was a boy when he felt as she did. Loneliness and despair and no one to comfort him, because when it was offered he had rejected it. And now that the situations were reversed, he didn't know how to cope with it, had no experience on which to draw, so he just held her, lost in the fragrance of her hair.

'Make love to me, Mark, please make love to me.'

He led her into the bedroom, left the lights out. She stood submissively, her head bowed as he unzipped her dress, helped her out of it. She wore no bra, her breasts were round, firm, nipples dark against the skin. He seated her on the bed, bent down and unzipped her boots, pulled them off, stood her up again. She seemed incapable of doing anything for herself. He slipped off her panties. He led her to the bed, drew back the covers, made her get in. She curled up into a foetal position. Sebastian undressed quickly, got into bed. She lay there shivering, still crying. He put his arms around her, giving her his warmth. At last she lay quiet.

He traced a pattern with his fingertips up her thigh, following the curve of her buttocks, to her waist, the hollow in the small of her back, up her spine. She shivered again, but this time not with cold. He kissed her, placed a hand on her breast, slid a thumb on to an erect nipple. She returned his kiss, tongue exploring. The taste was sweet; it stirred a memory in Sebastian that he couldn't pin down. She caressed the back of his neck, ran a hand down his arm, trailed her fingers across his stomach, stroked his penis. She began to writhe against him, slowly at first, hips rotating to an unheard rhythm, then quicker. Her breathing started to get ragged. She broke the kiss and gasped, 'Do it, Mark, do it.'

He rolled on top of her, went inside her. She wrapped her arms around him, closed her legs around his in a vice-like grip. She moaned softly to herself, but louder as their love-making became more violent. Beads of perspiration came out on her forehead. 'Yes, darling, yes,' came out in a strangled gasp, as they climaxed together.

They lay there for a long time, breathing slowing to normal, saying nothing. Sebastian remembered what the taste of the girl reminded him of. It was the time when he had gone to visit his grandparents in Los Angeles during summer vacation, when he was about thirteen, he thought. As a special treat, they'd taken him to Ocean Park, where all the amusement rides were. He'd experienced intense joy, and a little fear, whizzing down in a roller coaster, looking over the whole of Santa Monica from the top of the ferris wheel, the fine centrifugal force on the Whip. And all the things on which he'd gorged himself – snow cones, popcorn, cotton candy. The girl tasted like cotton candy, and he experienced the same sort of intense joy.

The second time they made love, it had an unhurried, timeless quality. The soft caresses, long languorous kisses, passion spread like honey, velvety, smooth, sweet, perfection sought after, reached in both their minds. Sebastian took the girl in as a total experience, absorbed her through his pores, everything else was blotted out – all his goals, forgotten for the moment in the cocoon that surrounded them. It was a first. They didn't talk, it hardly seemed necessary. The longing that each felt was recognized by the other. Touched, soothed, satisfied.

They slept huddled together. For the first time in a long time, Sebastian didn't dream.

Rascher had decided that he would pay the girl a surprise visit. His new Mercedes limousine purred up to the mews at

7.30, Erik, his bodyguard, doubling as driver. Rascher got out, entered the mews, went up two flights of stairs to Pamela's flat. The lights were out. He tried his key. He jiggled it. It didn't work. He knocked on the door, no answer. He gave the door a vicious kick, returned to the car.

He called the girl, off and on, until 2.00 in the morning. Still no answer. With a sinking feeling, he realized that the chances were she wasn't going to be home. The bitch! That was the last straw. Now he would fix her.

Sebastian and the girl woke at the same time, rubbed the sleep from their eyes, smiled at each other. They made love again.

Sebastian ordered breakfast while she showered. It came twenty minutes later as Sebastian came out of the bathroom in his robe. The waiter, who had seen it all before, never gave the pair of them a second glance. He set up the collapsible table, put the food on it from the trolley, accepted his tip and left.

They smiled a lot over the orange juice, bacon and eggs, toast. Conversation was desultory, the subject limited to the state of the weather, the difficulty of finding a taxi.

A cloud passed over the girl's face. Sebastian was quick to pick it up. 'What's the matter?'

Pamela toyed with her cup of coffee. 'Oh, nothing. It's just that I've realized it's back to reality time.'

'How do you mean?'

'Well, in the cold light of day, I've still got the same problems that I had last night.'

'You mean the boyfriend?' he prompted.

Pamela nodded, disconsolate. 'I don't know how to get out from under. I really want to, but it's not that easy. My father's tied in – did I say that last night? – and besides that, he's vindictive. He won't let go easily.'

'Tell me about him.'

'Oh, he's in his fifties. Does that shock you?' Sebastian just smiled. 'He can be very nice when he wants to, when things are going his way. He hates to be contradicted.'

'What does he do?'

'Oh, I don't know,' she answered vaguely. 'Something in the City. He runs a few companies. He's very rich.'

'How did you meet him?'

'Oh, at Epsom.'

'You mean the race track?'

'Is there anything else at Epsom?'

Sebastian shrugged. 'How would I know? I'm a stranger in your country, remember.'

'Well, there isn't. I went to the Derby, it must have been about three years ago, with a lot of people. Do you know anything about the Derby?'

Sebastian shook his head.

'Well, it's very traditional. Groups of people rent charabancs, you know those double-decker buses that are open on top, and they bring in food and lots of drink, and you spend the day, as the PR releases say, "in convivial companionship". It's a good excuse to get tiddly, and lose money on the gee-gees. Well, anyway, the boy that I was with was the son of a viscount from Cornwall. He's never worked a day in his life, and as long as Daddy's money holds out, he never will. He has a part interest in some horses with some of his chums and he wanted to go talk to the trainer in the owner's enclosure, so I went with him.'

'Who's that?' Sebastian asked.

'Oh, a man named Trevor Willis, you wouldn't know him. Well, we found him at the bar talking to another man and he introduced us.'

'And who was he?' Sebastian asked, trying to keep his voice neutral.

'His name is Ernest Swift, sounds English or Irish, doesn't he, but he's German, speaks English with an accent. I asked him about it once and he said his name in German was too difficult to pronounce, so when he came to live here, he Anglicized it.'

Sebastian visualized the list of owners he'd checked off from the newspaper files. He remembered a Swift, the owner of a horse called Boomerang. A smile twitched at the corners of his mouth. He should have guessed. Krauts never had much imagination. Swift in German is *rasch,* close enough to Rascher, and Ernest for Ernst. He felt a great weight drop away. This was going to be a marvellous day. The girl interrupted his reverie, didn't notice his withdrawn look.

'I could see that immediately he liked me. No, that's such a banal word. I mean fancied me. And I have to admit that I was flattered. He has excellent manners, real Olde Worlde charm, the kind you don't find in the group of people that I know. And he exuded money, had a huge diamond ring on his little finger. Actually, I thought it was a bit garish, but what the hell, it was big, three carats anyway. And he had a terrific tailor. Not one of those rented jobs for him. You know they wear morning coats, striped trousers and top hats for the Derby?'

Sebastian nodded.

'Well, the boy I was with got into a deep conversation with his trainer and Ernest gave me a glass of champagne and . . . flattered the hell out of me. Said that I was the most beautiful girl he'd seen in a lifetime, begged the honour of escorting me to dinner at a place of my choosing and damn the expense. And it just sort of happened from there. He's very large on presents, and I think I was very greedy. I mean, after all, it was easier than working. So one thing led to another, now he thinks he owns me. He bought my father.'

Sebastian nodded sympathetically.

'Listen . . . I don't suppose . . .' she looked hopeful, 'that you are planning on staying in London. I mean, I know you are staying in a hotel and that you'll probably go back to America. How long will you . . . ?' she trailed off.

Now Sebastian thought of all the answers he could give her. He had them off pat, well practised, and glib with it. Pick a number, and right before your eyes you get – an instant alias, complete with a tightly woven, entirely credible pack of lies.

Very gently, he said, 'I'll have to go soon.' He sounded regretful, and that was easy because he felt that way.

'Oh, well,' Pamela said. The heartiness and the smile with it were forced. 'It was fun while it lasted, maybe I'll see you around some time.'

'I'm not leaving yet. My business is going to keep me here for a while and . . . I would really like to see you while I'm here. I mean a lot. You might even get sick of me.'

The girl thought about that, shook her head. 'I don't think so, but I'm glad of the opportunity to find out.'

'Great,' Sebastian sounded enthusiastic, and that was also easy, because he was. 'I've got a full day ahead of me, got a lot of work to do. How about tonight, will you have dinner with me?'

'I can't think of anything I'd rather do. What time?'

'Well, supposing I pick you up about seven-thirty, that'll give us time for a couple of drinks in a "quaint pub" that you're going to find for me, then we'll go to eat. Oh, yeah, I almost forgot. I don't know where you live,' he lied.

Pamela wrote down her address and telephone number on a piece of paper, gave him directions. They kissed at the door and she was gone.

Sebastian closed the door, the smile faded. For sure he had a full day ahead of him, time that would be fully occupied with finding out all he could about one, Ernest Swift. He sat down at the table, poured himself another cup of coffee. He tried to work out how to get the fastest results. He could, of course, fall back on his journalist credentials, go back to the *Express* or one of the other papers, research the files. But that was too slow and he rejected it. There was a quicker way. It was a way that he didn't particularly want to use because it would involve other people. He'd every intention of playing this whole thing solo. It was safer, and not only for him. Anyone that he contacted could become a target. He was playing for keeps and had no doubt that the other side was also. It was going to get rough, and some innocent bystanders might get hurt. But the speed factor decided him.

Chapter Six

The Sebastian Arms Corporation had its main office in Los Angeles and branches in six other countries, one of which was England. The factory and warehouse were in Birmingham, the offices and showroom in London.

Sebastian put in a call to the company, asked for the managing director, identified himself. Roger Webster came on the line.

'Mark?' he sounded surprised.

'I cannot tell a lie.'

Webster was effusive. 'When did you get in? What are you doing here?'

'Hang on a second, Roger. One question at a time.' Sebastian smiled in spite of himself. Roger Webster had been one of his father's oldest friends and had taken a genuine interest in Mark, the boy, as he had grown up. They had established a warm relationship and Webster was one of the very few whom Sebastian called on the rare occasion when he felt he needed advice. Now he was paunchy and balding and on his third wife, but still had the same enthusiasm that carried him from crack salesman to head of European operations.

'I only just got in. I've got a little job to do.'

'Oh, yeah? What are you working at this week?' Webster laughed and Sebastian joined him.

'Aren't you ever gonna let up on me, Roger? I'll settle down one of these days. I keep telling you I'm a late starter.'

'Late starter,' Webster snorted. 'If you wait much longer, you'll make Grandma Moses look like a juvenile delinquent.'

'OK, OK, I give up. I'll become respectable – right after I finish this.'

'Sure, I believe you. You are going to come and have dinner with Claire and me, right?'

'Well,' Sebastian hedged. 'I'd like to, but I'm a little pressed for time. You see, I promised to do a check on a guy for some-one, and I've got to get back to the States.'

'You're like a goddam Scarlet Pimpernel. Now we see you, now we don't. OK, what can I do for you, I know you want something.'

'Roger,' he said with mock shock, 'you do me an injustice – but I could use a little favour.'

'OK, what is it?'

'Can you find out whatever you can about a guy named Ernest Swift?'

'Hang on, let me write it down.'

'OK? He's in his fifties, something big in the City, I don't know what. From what I can gather, he's lived here for quite a while. He's not English, German I think.'

'And what exactly do you want to know?'

'Everything. The kind of business he's in, where he hangs out, habits, routines. You know, the usual when you're working up a profile.'

The profile was one of the safeguards that the Sebastian Arms Corporation, and all the other arms companies em-ployed to get them off the hook, just in case the proverbial shit

hit the fan. Many potential clients for arms were of dubious character and background. In order for legitimate arms companies to operate with Government sanction, they had to prove that the end user of the weapons, for whom they had to issue a certificate, was strictly legitimate. The penalty for making a mistake was severe; Governments could be extremely heavy-handed.

Webster retained a company who specialized in making discreet inquiries, and who compiled their findings into a complete dossier.

'Can you tell your people to step on this, Roger. I'm in a kind of hurry with this one.'

'OK, Mark. Where can I reach you, if I have to?'

'At the Hilton.'

'I'll tell them to extra-special step on it. Call me at home this evening. I don't suppose there's any point in asking you why you need it.'

'A favour for a friend.'

'Bullshit. But I won't press you.'

'Thanks a million, Roger. Talk to you later, huh?'

The next order of business was to find out about Trevor Willis, the trainer that Rascher employed for his horses. He would be able to provide another facet of the man's personality. He looked up the number for the Jockey Club, called them, and asked for Willis's location and phone number. He received a prompt reply and dialled the number he was given.

A musical voice at the other end in an accent that Sebastian identified as Yorkshire, said that he was Trevor Willis. Sebastian decided to be 'broad American', straight out of the Midwest and twice as ingenuous.

'Mr Willis, you have been recommended to me as a very fine trainer. I'm just buying some horses here and I'm looking to find me the right place to stable them. I think you could be the right place.'

'Well, thank you,' Willis was obviously flattered. 'May I ask who recommended me, Mr . . . ?'

'Oh, didn't I say? Well, pardon me. George Osborne is my name, from Columbus, Ohio, greatest little town in the whole Midwest. Ever been there, Mr Willis?'

'Can't say that I have, Mr Osborne.'

'Well, if you ever get the chance, you must come and visit

me. You want to know how I know about you. Well, I wanna tell you that you shouldn't be so modest. Everybody knows about you. Some of my friends at Churchill Downs and Belmont were telling me how good you were with horses. If you don't mind, I'd like to come out and take a look at your stables.'

Willis, in a very respectful voice, said, 'That would be my pleasure, Mr Osborne. When would you like to come?'

'Oh, I thought that I could drive out today. Is that all right?'

'Perfectly. You know that the flat racing season is over for the moment, so there's not much on. It will be a privilege to see you and show you around. Would you like to stop for lunch?'

'That's mighty generous of you, I'd be much obliged.'

'I will look forward to it.' Willis gave him detailed directions to the stables.

Sebastian decided that he'd better dress for the part he'd created for himself. He carried around several items of wardrobe and an assortment of props – to fit, vary or alter one of a dozen different personalities that he wished to effect. He had taken dramatic lessons from an actor's studio in New York, paying particular attention to 'the method' by which he could easily get into a part and maintain it. He acquired the knowledge and a facility for make-up during a season of summer stock in New England. At the end of what amounted to a short flirtation with acting, he felt confident enough to check off that item on the list that he had compiled while still a student at the Gustavus Adolphus Academy. He'd even kept the same list. The original fifteen items in a round boyish scrawl, that contained such skills as: swimming, horseback riding, and fencing. They were the stuff of which boyhood fantasies are created. When dealing with villains, one never knew when it might be necessary to plunge into a castle moat, or encourage the trusty steed to jump the abyss, or to practise Errol Flynn-like swordsmanship; up and down staircases, on top of tables, or swinging from chandeliers. Learning how to do cartwheels and somersaults was mandatory and he was very proud when he accomplished his first handstand. The list had been amended and added to many times, and as it grew, so did the handwriting change to concise, forceful letters, a formed personality. It was like the genesis to manhood.

He chose a tweed jacket with leather elbow patches, grey flannel trousers and suede boots, and a trilby hat – the image that every good Englishman should have of what every good Midwesterner should look like when in England. He added a pair of glasses – clear lenses and horn-rimmed frames – and a well-used briar pipe and tobacco pouch.

He collected his car from the garage and drove towards Surrey.

Trevor Willis was a short, wiry, energetic man, with a cheerful countenance, a spider web of lines etched into his face. He greeted Sebastian at the top of the long circular gravel drive that led up to the house. As it was getting close to lunch time, he suggested that they should have a drink and a chat first, eat, and inspect the place afterwards. Sebastian agreed.

Willis took him into his solidly built red brick house and poured him a liberal scotch. He apologized for his family not being there, they were away visiting relatives, but they would be amply looked after by the housekeeper. Sebastian told him that he wasn't to go to any trouble on his account.

'No trouble at all, Mr Osborne. It's part of the daily routine. Tell me, how many horses were you thinking of stabling?'

'Well, I thought I'd start out slow, not more than a half-dozen or so.'

Willis's eyes widened. 'You mean that you may build it up from there?'

'Most assuredly. When I go into something, it's never half-baked. I'll tell you what, you convince me that you're the right trainer and this is the right stable, and you can have the whole string. I'm aiming for about two dozen.'

Willis was very impressed. 'Well, I'll do my best.'

Lunch consisted of home-made pâté, shepherd's pie with brussel sprouts, and apple pie for dessert, served with a very good bottle of Beaujolais Villages. Conversation was polite, and, for the most part, stayed near the surface. Sebastian's response to the question of what business he was in, was that he owned a machine tool company in Columbus, and had branched out into horses a couple of years earlier. Willis accepted it without reservation and, as the meal progressed, he warmed up and regaled Sebastian with 'horsey stories', great races, champion thoroughbreds, eccentric jockeys. When lunch was finished, they went to inspect the facilities.

The stables were about a hundred yards from the house.

They were modern concrete cubicles that occupied three sides of a quadrangle. The tack room was over on one side with the feed storage unit next to it.

They started on the left-hand line of stalls. Willis turned on the lights so that Sebastian could peer inside at the 'happy horses'. He commented on how clean and shipshape everything looked.

'Tell me, Mr Willis, do all these horses belong to individual owners?'

'Most do,' Willis replied. 'Except for two. One of the gentlemen owns four horses and the other, seven.'

'Oh? Who might they be. I might know them.'

'One's called John McKenzie and the other Ernest Swift.'

'Ernest Swift, that rings a bell. Let me think. I remember, isn't he the owner of a horse called Boomerang?'

'He's the one. I'm Boomerang's trainer. He's right over there.' He pointed diagonally across the quadrangle to where a grey stallion stared back placidly. 'Came in second in the Derby, you know, and he's won several races. Putting him out to stud next year.'

'Sure don't know what's wrong with my memory. It must be your excellent lunch. A friend of mine in Kentucky told me to look up Ernest Swift when I got here. He said he has several fine horses he might be willing to sell. And you're sure the right man to tell me if that's true.'

'Oh, he has a fine string of horses, I'll show them to you by and by. Sell?' Willis shrugged. He looked doubtful. 'He might be willing.'

'And what sort of a man is he? I like to know who I'm dealing with. I don't mind paying top dollar, but I always make sure I get my money's worth.'

Willis thought about it for a long moment. A horse whinnied. 'Well,' he began cautiously, 'he seems a nice enough chap. He's a foreign gentleman, you know. I can't honestly say I know a lot more about him than that. He has something to do with a big pharmaceutical company; comes down here every now and then to look at the horses.'

Sebastian grinned. 'You mean he doesn't know a lot about them?'

'I didn't actually say that,' Willis protested. 'He comes to all the big races, seems to enjoy it.'

'You're a very tactful man, Mr Willis. I like that. But I also like to call a spade a spade. I'm sure the arrangement suits you. Keeps another meddling owner out of your hair, huh? I should warn you, I do know my horses.'

Willis acknowledged the statement with a nod and a smile. 'Suits me.'

'Good, I'm glad we understand each other. Tell me, what's he like personally, I'd like to hear your impressions.'

Willis took off his cloth cap, scratched his thinning hair. 'I don't know if I should really be talking to you about him. He's a client you know.'

'Oh, come on,' Sebastian cajoled, 'I'm not asking you to tell me any secrets. Just what the man's like. Does he have a bad temper, for example?'

A cloud passed over Willis's face, his cheeks reddened. 'Funny you should ask me that.' He looked Sebastian square in the eye. 'You know about him then? Your friend told you, I bet.'

Sebastian remained nonchalant, put his hands in his pockets. 'Oh, he didn't tell me much, said he could fly off the handle.' Sebastian took a stab in the dark. 'But he said he's got a bad habit of doing it with people who can't argue back.'

'True enough,' Willis muttered. He jammed the cap back on his head. 'He came out here one day to look at his horses and I had to go into the house for a minute to answer a phone call. Well, I'd just finished when I heard shouting outside, and so I came running. Seems that one of the lads who brought a horse out for inspection got him too close to a mess bucket, and it tipped over and one drop, mind you I'm not exaggerating, one drop got on the man's shoe. I thought he was going to murder the lad – shouting, screaming. I hate to think what would have happened if I hadn't come along. He insisted that I sack the boy, said that he'd remove all his horses if I didn't.'

'And did you?'

Willis smiled with genuine pleasure. 'For about five minutes – until he left. I just have the lad stay out of sight if I know he's coming round now.'

Sebastian shook his head. 'Sounds like a nasty customer if he's riled. I'll have to remember that. Show me his horses, will you. I'd like to have a look at what I may be buying.'

Sebastian left an hour later with a promise to contact Willis in the very near future. His watch read 4.30 as he pulled out on to the road for London.

Chapter Seven

By the dashboard clock, a precision-made instrument, it was precisely 4.31 as Rascher's Mercedes slid to a halt outside the mews in Kinnerton Street. He waited until Erik shut off the engine and opened the door for him.

'Shall I wait here, sir?'

Rascher hesitated. 'No, come with me.'

Erik locked the car and followed Rascher into the mews and up the two flights of stairs to Pamela's flat.

Pamela had spent the morning at her agent's, lunched with two girlfriends at a fashionable Italian restaurant on the Fulham road, where she couldn't contain her excitement about her evening with Sebastian. 'Mister Right' had a habit of cropping up in 'all-girls-together' conversations. Usually it was one girl or another who had just found hers and changed him for another one by the next luncheon, proving that several wrongs still make a right. Pamela had been an observer up till now, and her friends were pleased that she had finally decided to play the game. They were only a teeny bit jealous, neither of them had anything current about which to brag.

Pamela was leafing through a magazine when she saw the silhouettes of two people pass by her curtained window and heard the knock. She had a sinking feeling in the pit of her stomach and a premonition of what was to come. She was pretty sure that she knew who it was. She opened the door and stepped back to admit Rascher and Erik without a word of greeting. They followed her into the lounge. Pamela sat down in a corner of the sofa, curled her feet under her, stared at Rascher with an expressionless face. Rascher removed his bowler, handed it to Erik, who placed it on a table in the hall.

Rascher began mildly. 'My key didn't fit.'

'I changed the locks.'

'*Ach so?*' Rascher towered above her, hands on hips, the beginnings of a sneer on his face. Erik crossed his arms and leaned his back against the doorjamb.

Rascher spoke in a quiet monotone. 'Why did you do that?'

Pamela fumbled for a cigarette on the table next to her, lit it with hands that trembled a little. She inhaled deeply, expelled the smoke in a rush.

'Because I didn't want you to come in when you felt like it.' More defiantly, she continued, 'I don't want you to come in. I would rather not see you again. I don't like being slapped.'

Rascher slid off his overcoat, tossed it on to a chair, removed close-fitting kid gloves, one finger at a time. He closed his hand around the pair, tapped his other palm with the leather fingers. 'I see,' he said. 'It is to be over – just like that.'

He looked around the brightly decorated room at the patterned pale pink sofa, the softly draped curtains shaded to match, cream walls and chairs, white carpet, rose-coloured cushions, a standing lamp with frilly beige shade, little porcelain figures on the mantelpiece, a ticking china clock, draped tables. He waved an arm that took in the whole of the room. 'And how do you expect to afford all this?' He turned back and looked hard at her. 'And all those pretty clothes . . . and you are forgetting your father. What is he going to do?'

Pamela took on a mulish expression. 'It's about time he took care of himself . . . without help. And as for the other things, I can do without them if I have to. But I have no intention of doing without them. I can work, you know. I've had to turn down jobs because you wanted me to be somewhere. Well, I don't have to do that now.'

'Ah, now I do see. The pretty girl who makes money from her looks. Many people would pay to see her.' He leaned over and grasped her chin between a thumb and a forefinger. Pamela wanted to move away but she was fascinated by his eyes as he stared at her – like a rabbit mesmerized by approaching headlights. 'Beautiful, isn't she, Erik? Everyone should see such a face.' Erik grunted.

Very deliberately, as he held her with his eyes, he lifted his other hand and struck her across the face with the gloves.

'You bitch,' he hissed.

The girl gasped in surprise and tried to jerk away, but Rascher hemmed her in with his knees on the edge of the sofa, pressed his body close over her, grabbed her by the hair, used the gloves once, twice, three times, forward and back across her cheeks, raising welts.

'I'm not good enough for you any more, huh?' The words came out in a strangled, high-pitched shout. He pressed his face close enough for her to smell the pungent odour of mint on his breath. 'You whore, you're fucking someone else, aren't you? Who is it, I want to know?'

The girl raised her arms in an attempt to fend off the blows. Her cigarette went spinning across the carpet, lay smouldering. She sobbed and screamed, tried to kick him without success.

'Who is it?' He had her by the neck of her dress, shook her violently. 'Who is it?'

With overpowering desire to hurt him, she screamed more in defiance than fright, 'He is a real man, not a limp-dicked Kraut!'

Rascher punched her in the face, catching her just under the eye, her head snapped back, bounced off the wall. 'You son-of-a-bitch,' she hissed.

She went for his eyes, missed, raked his cheek with her nails. Rascher struck at her again, the blow glanced off her forearm. She struggled to keep away from his fists.

'If he were here now, he'd kill you,' she grated through clenched teeth.

Rascher thought that was so comical that he momentarily stopped his assault. 'And who is this hero?'

'His name is Mark Sebastian, and I'll make sure that you meet him.'

Rascher froze in the position he was in, one knee on the sofa, bent at the waist, right arm raised to strike. Erik snapped to attention. The tableau lasted for a full five seconds.

'Who did you say?'

The girl, uncomprehending, looked from one to the other. She punched Rascher in the stomach. 'Mark Sebastian, Mark Sebastian.'

Rascher's breath partially went out of him, but he recovered quickly, grabbed the girl by her hair, stood up, forced her to her feet. He nodded to Erik who came behind the girl, grabbed her arms, pinned them behind her back.

Rascher's voice was strangely calm, the more menacing for

it. 'I want to know where he is. You will tell me or I'm going to hurt you.'

Pamela looked up at him and for the first time felt frightened. She didn't understand what was going on, but knew that somehow she'd made a big mistake. 'Go to hell, you bastard.' She tried to kick him, missed, hit the telephone table instead. The instrument teetered on the edge of the table, fell with a loud clang.

Rascher punched her hard in the stomach. The breath went out of her as she cried out in pain. Erik held her up, preventing her from doubling over. 'Where is he?' Rascher shouted. Pamela's chest heaved and she took a deep racking breath. She straightened up, gasping. That's when she spat in his face, and that's when Rascher went crazy.

Erik, solid and taciturn, held her as Rascher laid into her with crashing fists. Pamela tried to scream, tried to get out of the way, it was no use. She tasted blood where her lip was split. Rascher pummelled her unmercifully, and only stopped when her head lolled to one side, obviously unconscious.

Rascher was breathing hard when he nodded to Erik, who let her go. She slid to the floor, lay in a heap. Rascher grabbed his coat, put it on, jammed the gloves into a pocket, stalked to the door. Erik followed, picking up the bowler on the way. Rascher opened the door and had the presence of mind to stop for a moment. He looked into the mews, listened for anyone who might be there – nothing. All the windows in the other flats remained blank. Either no one had heard, or pretended that they hadn't. Rascher left the flat, Erik close behind.

Rascher sat silent and white-faced in the back of the Mercedes as Erik drove him away from Kinnerton Street and, at his curt command, back to his flat. He clamped his mouth shut to stop his teeth from chattering, his shoulders were hunched forward, hands clasped tight so that the muscles knotted, the veins standing out in bold relief. One leg twitched involuntarily.

The encounter had left him shaken, far more than he'd want Erik to see, far more than he dared admit to himself. He was scared silly, his stomach doing flip-flops. He felt his bowels loosen and managed to hold on to them only after an extreme effort. The veneer of well-being that he'd built up over the years, cracked and fell away in brittle pieces. He felt naked and vulnerable.

He had a vivid memory of the last time he'd felt that way, so frightened that nausea threatened to overwhelm him and make him spew his guts out in the muddy ditch where he lay hidden with his comrades. The shame of it would have been unbearable. But he had been saved that embarrassment – just. The Dornier bomber had landed on the crater-pocked airfield, and had taken him and his friends to safety in literally split seconds ahead of the advancing Russians. So close had it been that bullets from the angry Reds had weaved a pattern through the fuselage, one bullet passing a millimetre from Rascher's ear. That had been only the beginning of the danger-filled route. It took him first to Rome, where a Bishop at the Vatican got him forged papers to his next destination, then to the Middle East, Syria, and from there to the safety of South America. He could recall the panic at will.

The Mercedes came to a halt in Grosvenor Square, and Rascher bolted from it without waiting for Erik. He shouted over his shoulder for Erik to park the car and come up to the apartment, then opened the entrance door to the building with a bang, and hurried to the elevator.

He placed a person-to-person call to Spitzweg in New York before he took off his hat and coat, then dropped them carelessly on the floor and paced back and forth in front of the windows that looked on to Grosvenor Square, while he waited. He caught glimpses of the American Embassy as he passed the windows, on his route back and forth along the thick-piled carpet, fragmentary pictures of lighted windows that housed sombrely dressed civil servants, the Stars and Stripes fluttering atop the flagpole as the wind shipped at it, but he saw none of it.

When the phone rang, he ran for it, picked it up. The operator informed him that his party was not available, as he was out to lunch. Was there anyone else that he wished to speak to? Rascher cursed under his breath and looked at his watch. 5.15 p.m. Was it possible that only forty-five minutes had elapsed since he had first entered the girl's flat. It was possible, and that meant that it was 12.15 p.m. in New York, and Spitzweg always went out for lunch early.

'I will speak with his secretary,' he shouted into the phone.

He was dimly aware that Erik had let himself into the apartment and had retired to a corner of the room, expressionless, awaiting orders, 'like a good dog', thought Rascher, 'like a good, dumb dog'.

The operator came back on the line to tell him that the secretary was also out to lunch. Rascher gripped the phone hard enough to whiten all his knuckles, shut his mouth so tight that the scream of rage was unable to escape. He tried counting. He'd heard that was a good way to calm down. 'Eins, zwei, drei . . .' it was working, '. . . neun, zehn.' He gave the operator Naumann's number in Los Angeles; it would be 9.15 in the morning there. The operator said that she would call him back. He slammed the phone down.

Rascher lit a cigarette with shaking hands, sat down, tried to relax, couldn't, stood up again. When the phone rang, even though he was expecting it, his body made a convulsive jerk.

The operator told him that the party with whom he wished to speak was not there. Was there anyone . . . ? 'The secretary,' he shouted.

The secretary was unable to tell him where her boss was, but that he was expected within the hour.

'He must call me immediately.' Rascher spaced the words out so that each syllable was emphasized. 'It is urgent.'

The flow of adrenalin had left him weak. His energy spent, he replaced the phone in the cradle with a soft click.

Erik spoke up from his corner. 'Do you have any orders for me, sir? Do you want me to go back to the girl's apartment and wait for Sebastian? I could overpower him and bring him here.'

'And what,' Rascher raged, 'do you expect me to do with an unconscious man in the middle of Mayfair, you imbecile? I want him eliminated, but not with the police knocking at my door two seconds later. This is not New York, you know. And what if he doesn't go back there? What if he comes here, and I am alone, unprotected?'

'What would you like me to do then, sir?' Erik replied in a flat monotone.

'Do? I'd like you to do nothing. Just stand there in your corner and keep quiet. Things are difficult enough without having to listen to your moronic observations.' Rascher stubbed out his cigarette, lit another. He snapped his fingers at Erik. 'Bring me a Scotch, neat. Make it a large one.'

Rascher grabbed the glass from Erik, spilling some on the carpet. He took a large gulp, then another.

Chapter Eight

Sebastian arrived back at the Hilton at a few minutes before 6.00, left the car with the attendant, went into the lobby. There were no messages for him and he went upstairs. He showered, changed his clothes, tried to call Pamela, a busy signal. He checked his watch: 6.30. She was probably on the phone to a girlfriend. He tried another couple of times over the next forty-five minutes, still busy. He frowned, that was one long conversation. He left the hotel, picked up his car, drove to Kinnerton Street.

He went up the stairs to her flat, two at a time, passed the curtained windows; strange the room was dark. He knocked on the door. No answer. He knocked again. He was puzzled. A little warning bell went off in his head. Something was wrong. What? He turned, looked out on the mews. Lights burning in all the flats, the muted sounds of a television programme, two pigeons cooing at each other. He turned back to the door, knocked again, still nothing. He went over to the window, tried to peer in. It was useless, the curtains were close-fitting and the flat was completely dark. He thought he heard a noise from inside, put his ear to the window. He heard something, couldn't identify it. It sounded a little like the mewling of an injured animal. He had a presentiment of impending disaster. He moved back to the door, examined the lock. Easy, a simple Yale. He took the plastic strip that he always carried with him out of his pocket, slipped it in the crack of the door, slipped the lock.

He entered the dark hallway, the sound he'd heard louder now. He found the lounge, it was almost pitch black. He fumbled for a switch on the wall, found it, turned it on. The overhead light came on, revealing the room in disorder, the telephone off the hook. Pamela was on the floor. He stood stock-still, felt his heart miss a beat. His breath came out slowly between his teeth. 'Jesus Christ,' he whispered.

He went to the girl, knelt down beside her. Pamela was a mess. Both eyes were swollen and purpling, one brow split, blood trickling on to the white carpet. One cheek was bruised and double its size, the other had red welts imprinted on it. Her lips were split and torn, rivulets of congealed blood down both corners of her mouth. Her hair was a tangled mess, small clumps of it lay on the carpet. One arm was broken, a bone showing very white through the skin. Sebastian put a hand on her forehead. It was hot and sweaty. Miraculously, her nose had escaped the assault, but her breathing was ragged. She was doubled over in a foetal position, her good arm holding her stomach.

Sebastian sat back on his heels, knowing what to do, not knowing what to do. He debated whether to call an ambulance or take her to a hospital himself, it was only a block away. Moving her could be dangerous, might cause permanent harm, but then speed was another factor. He decided to risk it.

For five seconds, he allowed himself the luxury of his emotions, let them sweep over him. He had never felt rage or hate in such intensity. Now they were both there, white hot. For the first time, his vendetta became three-dimensional, had flesh on the bones, was really personal.

He lifted her very gently, careful to avoid putting strain on the broken arm. She moaned, cried a little. He murmured soothingly to her and she quietened. He took her into the hallway, put her down on the carpet without jarring her. He found a coat in the closet, covered her with it. He opened the door behind him, took measured steps down the stairs and out to where his car was parked. A couple of people were just coming out of the pub. They glanced at Sebastian and the girl, looked away. Sebastian laid her on the back seat of the car. She moaned again, her eyes flickered open. She looked like she was about to scream, then she focused, recognized Sebastian, started to cry.

'It's all right, darling,' he soothed. 'I'm here and we'll get you fixed up real quick.'

'I didn't tell them,' she croaked.

Sebastian didn't understand. 'Didn't tell them what?'

'Where you were . . . he wants you.'

'Don't talk now, darling, you can tell me later.'

Pamela said weakly, 'No, now. I told them your name. He seemed to know you – he hates you – I think he's scared of you.'

'That's okay. No more now. I'm going to get you to the hospital.'

Sebastian went around to the driver's side, got in. 'So,' he thought, 'the bastard knows who I am and that I'm here. Good. This time it's going to be a pleasure.' Grimly, he started the car, drove it carefully and slowly to the hospital.

There were the usual endless questions in the emergency room. Sebastian told the simple story, and, for the most part, held to the truth. 'He was a friend of the girl, who had come to visit, and had found her in this state. Obviously, she'd been assaulted. And no, he didn't know who the attacker was. The girl had been unable to say anything.' He gave his name as Brian Weber, and a fake address in Chelsea.

The examining doctor clucked over her, shook his head. 'It's pretty bad, I don't know what the extent of the injuries are without a complete examination. She might have internal injuries. I won't know that for a while yet.'

Sebastian said he'd call in a couple of hours, and he left the hospital, despite the protests from the matron. This was a police matter, and he'd have to be interviewed. Sebastian said that he would, but that he had something urgent to do first, and would be back.

He drove away from the hospital, and back to the Hilton. All his responses were automatic, the shifting of the gears, the brake applied at the right time, the observation of traffic. Anger had given way to cold rage. Tendrils of hate entwined themselves around his brain, numbing his perception, freezing emotions. Through it all, his presence of mind persisted. The watcher still watched, the survival instinct operated at maximum efficiency.

He swung in behind the Hilton, parked in a narrow street. He went in through the back entrance, wary, careful. The girl had said she hadn't told them where he was, had made a point of impressing that on him before she lapsed into unconsciousness. He was fairly sure they couldn't know he was at the Hilton, unless they struck lucky, or were clairvoyant. He dismissed both possibilities. His alarm system was intact, and no warning bells had gone off, but he was still careful.

He paused at the entrance to the lobby, searched the room, his eyes flicking from person to person. No danger there. He waited for an elevator door to open, stepped in quickly. He approached his room with the same caution, no one in the hallway. He stopped in front of his door, paused to listen before he inserted the key. Nothing.

The suite was as he had left it. He packed his suitcase with quick, rapid movements, loaded his toiletries into his airline bag, finished in five minutes. He called down to the reception desk, asked them to get his bill ready as he was checking out now.

Five minutes later, he was back out on the street, loaded the cases into the car and drove off.

He drove down to South Kensington where rows of modestly priced hotels serviced the package tour trade. He picked one at random that had a vacancy sign, checked in under his Anthony Christie alias. He barely glanced at the room which was as nondescript as the hotel. He picked up the phone and dialled Roger Webster's home number.

It took six cigarettes and two glasses of Scotch before the phone rang.

'What is so urgent?' Naumann asked Rascher. 'You have news of Sebastian?'

Rascher forced a laugh. 'Yes, news. That is good.' His hand went to his cheek where Pamela's fingernails had raked parallel furrows. 'Yes, I have news. He knows who I am and where I am. For all I know he may be outside my door now, waiting for me.'

There was a long silence on the line. 'How did he find out?'

'What difference does that make?' Rascher sounded on the edge of hysteria. 'He knows, he knows.'

Naumann contrived to sound both petulant and commanding. 'Well, what am I supposed to do about it? I'm six thousand miles away, so I am unable to hold your hand. May I remind you, my dear Ernst, that it is only one man we are talking about, not Patton's entire third army. You have resources, do you not? You have Erik, do you not? Eliminate him. As far as I'm concerned, this Sebastian is only a minor annoyance. I am far too busy . . . we are far too busy to let one individual get in the way. Our project in Mexico, as you are aware, is at a very delicate stage. I need to focus my entire concentration on that. You are blowing this whole thing out of proportion.'

'I am doing no such thing. You can be as complacent as you like, sitting in the sunshine. It is not you he is after.'

'Perhaps not,' Naumann replied laconically. 'But if I am to believe you, he soon will be. And so, my dear Ernst, it is up to you to stop him.'

'I need more help. I don't even know what he looks like.'

In the silence that followed, Rascher could hear Naumann breathing, echoey over the long distance line, then the sound of pages turning. 'I have no new information on the man. There do not seem to be any more pictures available. There's only one more thing that I can give you. The family company, the Sebastian Arms Corporation, has an office in London. The managing director is a man by the name of Roger Webster. He was a friend of Sebastian's father, and we understand that he and this Mark Sebastian are close. He might contact Webster. Perhaps you should speak to Webster and see what you can find out . . . and I strongly urge that you do it in a way so as not to draw attention to yourself.'

'I do not need your advice about interrogation,' Rascher said coldly.

The image of himself as Standartenführer Rascher of Einsatzgruppe A, glowed brightly in his mind. Had he not been promoted because of his interrogation techniques? Because of his ability to weed out elements inimical to the Reich? The Führer had said, when referring to the conquered Russian territories, 'The whole vast area must be pacified as quickly as possible – and the best way to do that is to shoot anyone who so much as looks like giving trouble.' And he followed the directive to the letter. From Kowno to Lithuania, to the Ukraine, Southern Russia and the province of Bialystock, communists, guerrillas, gypsies, mental defectives, Armenians, prisoners of war, and Jews. All had been shot, especially the Jews – men, women and children. Thousands had died. Had he not personally been responsible for hundreds, walking up and down the ranks of those people, those anthropoids, using his

Mauser so that it was red hot to the touch by the end. Who was this Naumann, to talk to him like that?'

Naumann's reply was soft and menacing. 'You are overstepping yourself, Ernst. I will forgive it, as you are under stress. Do not forget who is in command.'

Rascher coloured, half murmured an apology, but Naumann had already put down the phone.

Rascher recovered quickly from the blunder he'd made with Naumann. The fact was that Naumann was sitting six thousand miles away, and he was in the front line, and Naumann had said that he expected him to take care of the situation. He would . . . in his own way.

The organization maintained contacts with a certain number of villains. Respectability was a nice word, and provided the proper framework to accomplish a number of things, but it stopped short in certain cases. Rascher had used muscle before to make a point.

He called the man he knew as Jack, who had performed well on previous jobs. The man was available and willing to start at once. Rascher instructed him to bring one other man, and that both should come armed. He demurred when asked the nature of the job, and said that he would explain later.

Next, he called the organization's 'fixer'. Alfred Drake was retained by the company as a sort of upper class factotum, supernumerary *par excellence*. He had enough social standing and political clout to act as a lobbyist, public relations man, expender of largesse to deserving or not-so-deserving individuals, and general oiler of rusty gears. He would know the Sebastian Arms Corporation and Roger Webster, and if he didn't, he would know where to find out.

Drake did know Webster, and after a couple of minutes delay while he used his other phone, he was able to come up with the man's address and phone number. He also supplied Rascher with Webster's description and general history from his own personal knowledge. Drake had one other exemplary quality. He never asked questions. Rascher thanked him and hung up.

Jack, and a man he introduced as Jimmy, arrived a half-hour later. They were remarkably similar in appearance, blunt-featured heads set on squat, powerful bodies. They were even dressed the same, black trousers and roll-necked sweaters, patterned tweed jackets. Dante's version of the Bobbsey Twins. Jack affirmed that they were armed, and asked what they were expected to do. Rascher's big problem was that he wasn't sure. 'Protection,' he said, 'my protection. There's someone I want to find . . . and I want to find him before he finds me. We will leave in a minute. I'll be right back.'

Rascher left the two men and Erik to eye each other with suspicion, and went into his bedroom. He slid aside the Italian Renaissance painting of the Madonna and Child, by an artist whose name he could never remember, although he knew what the painting was worth, and worked the combination on his wall safe. He took out the soft chamois leather bag that fitted into one corner of the safe. He fingered the leather before opening the snaps. It always gave him a warm, confident feeling, knowing what lay inside. If he had been able to articulate it, he might have said sensual. He opened the bag and took out the Mauser pistol that had been with him throughout the war, and that had gone everywhere with him. He took it by the grip, hefted it, pointed the barrel at the window, sighted down it at an imaginary target.

It was a large, brutal weapon, almost a foot long, three pounds in weight, and shot 7.63 mm steel-jacketed bullets, with enough muzzle velocity to stop anything human. He checked the ten-round magazine, set the selector switch to automatic fire, set it on safety, put the pistol into the pocket of his overcoat, then rejoined the others.

Rascher ordered Erik to take them to Webster's house in the London suburb of Richmond. Jimmy sat up front to act as navigator, Jack in the back. Rascher huddled in one corner of the Mercedes, face frozen into immobility, withdrawn from the others. They kept their conversation to terse sentences involved with the best way to reach their destination.

Rascher had a good reason for isolating himself. He had no clear idea of what he was going to do, and was trying to think it through. Contacting Webster was, at best, a long shot. Sebastian, to date, had been the complete lone wolf. There was no reason to suppose that he would change the pattern he had established. Rascher acknowledged with rare insight that it was a mark of how insecure he felt – scared was a better word – that he had chosen this direction, grasping at straws.

He tried to think of the approach he would make. How could he get Sebastian's whereabouts from Webster and make it appear innocent. How could he justify rolling up in a Mercedes with three men, who were obviously heavies to the least discerning of persons. How could he make Webster tell him anything, if he resented the questions and baulked at answering. He wavered, his indecision affecting his body temperature, alternately bringing him out in chills and sweats. And then he was there in the right street and, as it turned out, the decision was taken out of his hands. Animal instinct took over.

Roger Webster had lived in Europe for eight years. In the third of those years, he had finally given up the American habit of dining early. He couldn't fight City Hall for ever. He'd even come to enjoy eating later in the evening – no earlier than 9.00 p.m. – and had established a routine of sorts. When no social obligations made demands on his time, he would arrive home from the office at around 6.30 and drink exactly two martinis prepared for him by his latest adoring wife; she was a divorcee, although only a one-time loser. She was plump and attractive and, with no children to worry about, they could devote much time to each other. Their relationship was comfortable and very affectionate. When they finished discussing the day they'd had, she would leave him to read the evening papers while she prepared the meal, and a quarter of an hour before it was ready, Webster would put his papers aside and take the dog for a walk.

Webster was just coming back to the house, the Irish Setter having done what it had to, and now straining at the leash, when the black Mercedes rolled past them and came to a stop. Webster noticed it without paying any special attention, noted that it was a limousine, that the outlines of four men could be seen through the tinted windows. He was just walking past when the rear door on his side opened.

Rascher saw the man and the dog as the car entered the road and slowed down looking for addresses. The man exactly fitted the description he'd been given of Webster. Decision flashed like summer lightning. To hell with being careful. To hell with Naumann, the pompous bastard.

'That's the man . . . I want him . . . in the car.'

Jack nodded, Jimmy grunted from the front seat. They both took out coshes. The car came to a stop, Rascher opened his door and stepped out. Jack and Jimmy waited for a couple of beats and then also got out, went around the back of the car and behind Webster.

'Roger Webster?' Rascher asked.

Webster stopped, and the dog stopped, pulled up by the leash. He looked back at his master, annoyed, but it was a momentary annoyance. He wagged his tail. Webster looked at the man who had addressed him, took in the cashmere overcoat, bowler hat, noted the foreign accent. He saw the other two men get out of the car, walk around behind him. He thought nothing of it. 'Yes?' he said, interrogatively.

'Are you the Roger Webster who is acquainted with a man named Mark Sebastian? I must reach him urgently.'

Webster looked puzzled, frowned. 'Well, he's supposed to call me later. Why? Is there something wrong?'

Rascher's mouth twisted into a thin smile. 'Not yet, but there soon will be.' He nodded to the other two men behind Webster.

Webster finally realized that he might be in some personal danger and opened his mouth to speak, half turning at the same time. He was far too late. Jack's cosh caught him behind the ear and he would have crumpled to the pavement if Jack hadn't held him up. The leash dropped out of his hand, and the Irish setter started barking furiously.

'Shut that fucking dog up,' Rascher hissed.

Jimmy grabbed the dog by the collar and hit it over the head with his cosh. The setter was cut off in mid-bark. It fell to the ground, yelped weakly.

'In the back,' Rascher ordered.

Jack and Jimmy bundled the inert form of Webster into the back seat. Rascher got in beside him. Jack resumed his seat on the other side, Jimmy jumped into the front, Erik pulled away.

They drove in silence for a block. 'Do you think anyone saw us?' Rascher said.

'I don't think so,' Erik answered. 'The street was empty, and it all happened pretty fast.'

Rascher smiled, he was happy.

Then Erik asked, 'Where to, sir?'

Rascher's sense of euphoria deflated. Now that he had him, now what? He thought of all the places he could take Webster to question him, and dismissed them one by one. They were all too public. That was the problem of living in a democratic country. The government objected to private citizens being interrogated against their will. Rascher had a sudden brainstorm. 'The stables,' he shouted.

Erik glanced over his shoulder. 'Where, sir?'

'The training stables where my horses are kept. We're only twenty minutes away from there.'

'Won't there be someone there?' Erik asked. He was careful to keep his voice neutral.

'Of course, there will be,' Rascher snapped. 'The trainer is there, but I happen to know that he is on his own, and he has only one other boy looking after the horses who lives there. You,' he jerked his thumb at Jack, 'and your friend,' he pointed his chin at Jimmy, 'will go and knock on his door. When he answers it you will overpower him, bind and gag him, and put him out of the way. Do not be any rougher than you have to. I still want him to train my horses.' Rascher tittered. 'Then do the same with the stable boy. I am sure it is obvious that I do not wish to be seen by either of them.'

Erik stopped the car on the road before the driveway that led up to Trevor Willis's house. Rascher checked Webster. He was just coming round, and when Jack and Jimmy got out of the car, he slumped over on to the vacated part of the seat.

Jack and Jimmy returned in ten minutes. It had gone off without a hitch. Erik drove into the driveway and stopped before the house. They dragged Webster in.

Chapter Nine

The phone rang only once after Sebastian had completed dialling. It was picked up, but there was only silence on the line. 'Hello,' Sebastian said. 'Hello. Is that you, Roger?'

The voice that answered whispered, 'Who's that?'

Sebastian's scalp prickled. 'Roger? . . . Claire?'

The voice that answered, whispered, 'Who's that?'

'It's Mark Sebastian. What's the matter?'

'Oh, my God.' The woman said something else, but it was garbled, run together, lost in a welter of hysterical crying.

'Claire,' Sebastian rapped out. 'Calm down, tell me what happened.'

She made a couple of false starts, finally got the words out, they tumbled over each other. 'I was making dinner – Roger was walking the dog – he was late – looked out the window to see if I could see him coming – saw the dog lying on the side-walk – no Roger – I ran to the dog – he'd been hit over the head – he was hurt – I carried him inside – then the phone rang just a few minutes ago – a man said they had Roger and if I wanted to see him alive again, I had to do exactly as they say – no police – they said you were going to call – they said I had to get a phone number from you – where you can be reached – they said they'd call back in an hour. Oh, Mark, they said they'd kill Roger.' She started crying again, deep racking sobs.

Sebastian let her go without interrupting. His mind raced with where? when? and how? It was a useless exercise. There was nothing he could do. He felt impotent. 'Claire,' he repeated the name again, breaking in on her crying, getting her attention at last. 'Claire, I'm going to make you a promise. I solemnly swear that I'll bring Roger back home to you alive and in good health. Do you believe me?' Long pause.

'Yes,' she whispered.

'Good. Now listen to me. I'm going to hang up. I'll call you back in five minutes and give you the phone number where they can reach me. OK?'

'OK.'

'Fine. Call you in five minutes.'

He grabbed his jacket and went out. Sebastian had noticed a café at the corner of the street and headed for it. It was a small, cheerful room with wooden tables and chairs, and, judging from the clientele, a student hangout. He spotted the telephone at the back where a narrow passageway led to the toilets. He went over to it, placed his call. 'Claire, it's me. Here's the number to give them.' He read the number off the dial, '370-6498. OK, you got it? I'll be here waiting for them. Now you just relax and don't worry. I made you a promise and I always keep my promises.' He said good-bye because there was nothing else to say, hung up, went over to the table closest to the phone, sat down. He ordered coffee from the teenage waitress, sipped at it automatically when it arrived, kept an eye on the phone.

He restrained himself from doing anything when a bearded

youth, dressed in a frilly yellow shirt and red velvet trousers, went to use the phone. Sebastian checked his watch: 9.40. They would be calling Claire back around 10.00. Sebastian decided that he couldn't take any chances that they would be that accurate. He stood up, went over to where the boy was chatting on the phone.

'Excuse me,' Sebastian began. 'I'm expecting a very important phone call. Would you mind cutting it short.'

The kid looked at him with hostility, told the party he was speaking to, 'Hang on a tick,' then looked at Sebastian. 'Fuck you, mate. Get yourself another phone. This is public, you know.'

Sebastian took a deep breath, let it out in a long sigh. His eyes went opaque, his mouth smiled. The kid, whom he judged to be about nineteen, was Sebastian's height, and about forty pounds lighter in weight.

In a very soft voice, Sebastian said, 'If you are not off the phone in thirty seconds, I'm going to break both your arms and twist your head off your shoulders. Please believe me. I'm not kidding.'

The kid looked at Sebastian's face and believed. He turned the colour of putty. 'I'll call you back later, mate ' he said into the phone, and then hung up.

'Thank you. You made a very wise decision.'

The kid laughed nervously, said, 'Sure, any time. I didn't know it was that important.' Then he sidled past Sebastian and went back to rejoin his friends at his table. Sebastian resumed his seat.

He looked at his watch when the phone rang: 10.02. It told him something about his adversary. He was precise. He strode to the phone, answered it.

'Mr Sebastian?' the accented voice asked.

'Yeah.'

'I have a friend of yours here. If you wish to see him alive again, you will do exactly as I say.'

'What do you want?'

'I think we should have a little talk . . . a quiet talk . . . about why you are bothering me. It is a nuisance, you know. We must put a stop to it. I do not like being harassed. But I am a generous man. I'm willing to believe that you are under some sort of misconception about me. We can perhaps clear it up when we meet, then go our separate ways. I am not looking for trouble.'

'What about Roger Webster?'

'Oh, he's here with me. He is . . . shall we call him, an insurance policy. I want an end to all this rancour now, and Mr Webster is here to make sure you will be sensible about it.'

'How is he?'

'Oh. Very well.'

'How do I know that?'

Rascher laughed; it was a harsh sound. 'Nothing simpler, my dear Mr Sebastian. I will put him on the telephone and you can speak to him yourself.'

There was a pause, then a familiar voice came on the line. 'Mark, is that you?'

'Are you all right, Roger?'

'Yeah, yeah, OK.'

'I'll see you soon. Just take it easy and don't do anything dumb.'

'Don't come . . .' The rest of the sentence was cut off as the phone was jerked away from Webster, and Rascher came back on the line.

'I think that is quite enough, Mr Sebastian. As you can see, your friend is quite healthy, and if you want him to stay that way, you will come and see me at once.'

'Where?' Sebastian asked in a flat voice.

'There is a place in Surrey where we can talk without being disturbed.' Sebastian experienced sudden exhilaration. Could he really be at the training stables? 'There are some training stables.' He gave Sebastian explicit directions. 'And don't be long. As you are in London, I estimate that it would not take you longer than an hour to find this place. I will give you an extra ten minutes because of your unfamiliarity with the countryside. But that is it. That would make it . . . let's call it eleven twenty-five. If you are not here by that time, I'm afraid something drastic is going to happen to Mr Webster. Need I say, do not bother to call the police. We will be watching. If anyone other than you arrives, Webster is a dead man. And I am assuming that you have the good sense not to do anything so rash, such as trying to take me by surprise with a gun. That would be just as fatal. Have I made myself quite clear?'

'You'd better take good care of him, Rascher. This is between you and me.'

'Agreed.'

Sebastian hung up. He raced back to the hotel, ignoring the people on the street who gave him peculiar glances. He took the stairs two at a time to his room. His brain had been working at the same pace, and he knew exactly what he had to do, and the Lord also knew that wasn't much. He had decided against bringing any weapons with him from France other than the throwing knife that lay concealed in a special compartment in his briefcase, which he felt was just innocuous enough to pass muster, in case he'd been stopped at Customs. He had intended to make an inspection of the Sebastian Arms Corporation, and take a gun from the stockpile, with or without Roger's permission. It was a little late for that now. He would have to improvise. He went to the bathroom door, put both hands on the knob, turned it and then exerted all two hundred pounds worth of his strength. The metal protested, then yielded, the knob twisted off in his hands. He took a pair of socks from his suitcase, put the door knob inside one sock, then that into the other. He tied the ends into a knot. He hefted it. It was makeshift, but it would have to do. He slipped the knife into its sheath from the briefcase, and fastened it on to his right calf. Just one more thing to do before he left. It had been weighing on his mind throughout the waiting period, but because of the current crisis, he had pushed the anxiety he felt into a remote corner.

He dialled the hospital, tried to curb his impatience as he waited to be put through to the casualty department. He told the nurse he was Pamela Driscoll's brother and had just heard about her accident. What condition was she in? The nurse said that she would check. He reached for a notepad on the table, scribbled something, tore off the sheet, put it in his pocket. She was away for a full two minutes, each seeming like an hour. The latest report was that the girl was bruised and battered and had a broken arm, but it was still too early to tell if there were any further complications. Sebastian thanked her, jammed the phone back on its cradle, and sped out of the room.

Traffic was light on the way out of town, and Sebastian kept pretty much to the speed limit, this was no time to attract the attention of cruising cops. As he had made the trip to Trevor Willis's stables so recently, he barely had to slow down for the right roads. They were still etched in his memory. He knew from the previous trip that the stables were situated about a mile and a half down a narrow, two-lane road that ran off the auxiliary motorway on which he was travelling. He had noticed, without paying much attention to it at the time, that the country road, which was called Waterfield Lane, started to curve sharply eastward just past the Willis property. He felt that it was a good bet that Waterfield Lane described an arc and rejoined the motorway further on. If he was right, he could take the second turning and come on to the stables from the back. It would give him the edge he needed.

He went past Waterfield Lane without slowing down, just in case someone was posted there to watch for him, and exited off the motorway at the next turning. He slowed the car down to ten miles an hour, switched the headlight on to high beam. The road ran straight as far as he could see. He pressed on doggedly. He'd covered almost two miles, according to the mileage counter, before the road started curving to the left. He stopped the car, shut off the lights. The darkness enveloped him. It was almost completely black. No moon showed through the heavy cloud layer, and the spill of light that was always part of an urban sprawl was absent in this remote part of Surrey. The luminous dial of his watch said 10.55. He had made good time and had a half-hour to get into position. He estimated the distance around the turn that would take him to the back of the stables was about a quarter of a mile. He turned his parking lights on, moved the car another three hundred yards, and pulled off on the side of the road. He got out and started jogging towards the stables, keeping to the middle of the road. It was 11.10 when he caught sight of the lights that were Trevor Willis's house.

The lounge that the five men occupied had become oppressive, at least as far as Webster was concerned. At another time, he might have appreciated the beamed ceiling, the polished parquet flooring, the wine-red throw rugs, the pictures in lithographs of jockeys and horses that crowded the walls. He could take no pleasure in the antique furniture and comfortable chairs. He was depressed that everything seemed to be working out for this German. And he still didn't know what it was all about.

Still groggy from the blow on the head, he had watched from

the car as the man they called Jack had gone to the front door, and when the trainer had opened it, invited himself in with his drawn gun. In five minutes he was out of the house, rousted the stable boy from his quarters and prodded the scared kid ahead of him to join the trainer.

When Rascher replaced the phone, he was smiling. He turned to where Webster had been pushed into a chair, beamed at him.

Webster looked back boldly. 'I don't see anything funny.'

Rascher laughed. It took hold of him, and in a moment it seemed like the funniest thing that had ever happened. He howled, holding his sides. He made a vain attempt to stop himself, but it only made him laugh harder. Eventually, he calmed down. 'I know,' he said between giggles, 'you're going to tell me that I can't get away with this. Please save me your clichés, because I can.' And that started him off again.

Erik caught Jack's eye, shrugged, remained impassive.

As the time dragged by, Rascher became more serious. He walked over to the fireplace, warmed his hands in front of the cedar logs, became absorbed in the flames. The clock on the mantel read 10.30. Rascher spun on his heel. 'Erik, go to the front of the driveway. Watch for him and keep out of sight.'

'What do you want me to do when he comes?'

'Just follow behind him. Make sure there are no tricks.'

Erik nodded and went out of the door.

'What do you want us to do, guv?' Jack asked.

'You stay in here. When he comes through that door, grab him and frisk him.'

Jack nodded assent, folded his arms across his chest and leaned against the wall.

The tension was building and Rascher wasn't equal to it, because ten minutes later, he changed his mind on how he wanted to deploy his troops, and it was all because the lounge in which they were sitting seemed to be getting smaller, while the windows seemed to increase in size. Rascher started to worry about the windows. He tugged the curtains together so that nothing could be seen from the outside, then opened them wide so that he wouldn't miss anyone who might sneak up on him. He sent Jack to do a circuit around the house, then dispatched Jimmy to ask Erik if he had seen anything. Eleven o'clock came and not a sign of Sebastian. All of a sudden the house was too confining and Rascher couldn't stay in there for a moment longer. He pulled Webster up from his seat and prodded him towards the door, checked to see that the ropes that bound his hands behind his back were in place.

'I'm a target in here,' Rascher said to no one in particular. 'We're going outside, Jack. I will choose the ground where we meet, not Sebastian.'

Jack said, 'Sure,' and winked at Jimmy.

Rascher put on his overcoat, took out the Mauser from his pocket, rechecked it, took off the safety catch. He waved the pistol at Webster. 'Let's go.'

Webster's fears had long passed and he was very much in control of himself. He didn't look the courageous type, but appearances are deceiving, and he could recognize paranoia as well as anyone. He tried to engage Rascher in conversation, tried to find out what it was all about, and was answered either in monosyllables, or a long diatribe about how an individual could not be left alone but was continually hounded – even though that individual was innocent of any crime, had spotless white hands and even loved babies. Webster watched the mounting tension with care. An opening might present itself, and then . . .

Rascher had Webster by the arm as they went outside the door, and jerked to a halt on the threshold. He peered out to where the stable area lay in complete darkness. 'Jack, go to the trainer. Find out where the light switches are.'

Jack went to where Willis was tied up in a back bedroom, got the information and found the switch box in the laundry room by the back door. He turned them on. The lights illuminated the whole quadrangle of the stable block. A horse whinnied, irritated at being wakened. Rascher marched Webster over to the stables, Jack and Jimmy trailing behind.

The stable area formed three sides of a rectangle, the short open side nearest to the house and driveway. There was space for ten stalls at the far end, and two rows of twenty stalls on either side. The buildings were whitewashed concrete, the stall doors in black gloss paint, giving it a sort of chequerboard appearance. Immediately to the right was the tack room, separated from the stalls by a narrow passage. There were passageways at the other ends also.

Rascher stopped in what he estimated was the middle of the rectangle, told Webster to stand there where he could be seen by Sebastian. He ordered Jack to stand in the walkway between the tack room and the stalls, and sent Jimmy to the far end of the stalls where he was to secrete himself in that passageway and keep his gun trained on Sebastian all the time. Rascher took up a position behind Webster, using him as a shield. He looked at his watch; it was 11.15.

Chapter Ten

Sebastian turned the corner in the road and saw the house. He estimated that it was about two hundred yards south of his position. He flitted across the road on silent rubber-soled shoes, and came to the white-painted wooden railings that enclosed the property. They showed up as a pale glimmer in the darkness. He slipped through the rails and stumbled as the ground dipped. He caught himself and came up on to the grass. He cut across the paddock that took him at right angles to the house and to a position behind the stable block.

The blackness was Stygian and he felt his way cautiously, trying to keep in a straight line. Just as he was coming up to where he thought the stable block might be, the floodlights went on and lit the whole area. Sebastian threw himself flat and lay still. The ground was hard and cold, the winter grass wet with frost. It seeped through his clothes. In a few seconds, he could see four men walk from the house to the stable area. He recognized Webster immediately, and Rascher holding his arm. The other two, he had never seen before.

The four men were cut off from his sight as they passed in front of the tack room and into the stable area. Sebastian took advantage of the situation and crawled forward on elbows and knees. He stayed down in case there were others.

He crawled on, until he came abreast of the walkway between the tack room and the stalls, then stopped, observed. One of the heavy-set men he had seen was now in the passageway with his back to him. Sebastian began to crawl again, this time angling towards the back of the stalls. He came up against the wall. He could hear the occupant of the stall move around.

The horse gave a soft whinny, he hoped it would go unnoticed. He held his breath, straining to listen. Everything seemed OK. He went on, hugging the wall, stopped just before the walkway. He got to his knees – stood up. He made his breathing as shallow as possible, was able to see the condensation of his breath in the overspill of light. He held his breath so that there would be no tell-tale signs, peeked around the corner of the wall.

The other heavy-set man was five feet away, back turned, a gun pointed in the direction from which Sebastian was expected to come.

Sebastian ducked away, put his back against the wall, thought of what to do next. He glanced at his watch: 11.19. Rascher had set the deadline at 11.25. Sebastian was sure the German would stick to the timetable – it was in character. So, thinking had to be put aside. It was time to act.

Sebastian reached into his pocket, pulled out his door-knob blackjack, took a firm grip on the knotted sock. He turned round, stepped into the passageway, froze to see if there was any reaction; there was none. The man kept his broad back to him, gun pointed ahead. The man shifted his feet, scratched his head with his free hand. Sebastian took advantage of the noise to take a step forward. Two more would do it. He lifted his foot very slowly, made the step, set his foot down without a sound. He rehearsed the next movements in his mind. Step forward, raise his right arm, bring the cosh down on the man's head. He did it just like that. He was prepared for the sound that the blackjack made like a boxer hitting a heavy bag, but unprepared for how loud it sounded in the confined space. The man crumpled without a murmur.

Sebastian made a dive for the gun, caught it just before it hit the cement path. The man fell backwards on to him, momentarily pinning him to the ground. He eased the body off him, laying the man down as gently as a baby. He stood up from his squatting position.

Rascher's irritated voice floated across the quadrangle. 'Do you have to make so much noise? He's not supposed to know you're here.' No reply. Pause. 'Is everything all right?'

Sebastian grunted an affirmative.

'Then just remain quiet,' Rascher said petulantly.

Sebastian bent down and checked on the man. He was

breathing easily and looked like he'd be out for quite a long time.

He stood up, cat-footed to the back of the walkway, peered round the corner – all clear. He checked the pistol. It was an old Smith and Wesson .38 calibre revolver, the kind known as a Police Special. It was fully loaded.

He transferred the revolver to his left hand, used the right to keep in contact with the stable wall as he approached the other walkway. He had to take the other man out, also without making a sound. At first sign of trouble, he knew Rascher would kill Webster without hesitation. He would have to figure out a way to catch Rascher unawares.

He came to the walkway, peered around the corner. The man, his back to him, looked relaxed. One hand held a gun; he'd propped himself up against the wall with the other. One leg was crossed over the other. Just like a Sunday outing. The man wasn't expecting trouble.

Sebastian reversed the gun so that he held it by the barrel, took a deep breath, let it out slowly. He stepped into the passageway, intending to take this man out as he had the other. He took the first step, noiseless, then the second.

A tiny fragment of glass, invisible in the half-light, crushed under his weight with a brittle tinkle. Sebastian's arm had just reached the top of its arc and was starting down when Jack, alerted by the noise, spun around.

Sebastian's blow missed its mark, caught Jack on the juncture between shoulder-blade and collar-bone. Then several things happened at once.

Jack let out a loud grunt of pain and surprise. The nerve that Sebastian had inadvertently struck, spasmed in a reflex action; Jack's finger jerked the trigger. The bullet hit the wall, ricocheted off, spun the gun from Sebastian's hand. Rascher shouted; Sebastian registered the reversion to German. He disregarded his fingers that tingled from the shock – no time for anything fancy. He launched himself at Jack, hit him with his shoulder just below the breast-bone – his other arm knocking away the gun. The force of his lunge carried both men out into the stable concourse.

Sebastian had an impression – too busy for more than that – of Rascher swinging Webster around by his collar, waving his pistol wildly.

The two men hit the ground hard. The gun struck the cement, discharged another shot that hit the top of the stable block and whined away into the night. The gun skittered across the paving, clanged to a halt against a stall door ten feet away. The horses whinnied in panic in their dark stalls, closed for the night, kicked hooves against walls and doors, the noise rising in intensity from all sides of the stable block.

Rascher raised his pistol, taking aim at Sebastian.

Sebastian chopped down on Jack's bull neck with all his strength. There was the sharp crack of broken vertebrae, Jack gagging; Sebastian rolled away, just as Rascher's first shot rammed into the space he'd vacated. It hit Jack in the belly. The man screamed.

Sebastian somersaulted, landed on the balls of his feet. He could see everything. It was like a slow motion ballet – Rascher pointing the Mauser in his direction – face screwed up, gash of mouth working – German curses spewing from it.

Rascher held Webster in front of him, the tip of his gun barrel resting on Webster's shoulder. Sebastion could see the knuckles whiten as Rascher pressed the trigger. Webster kicked behind him, rammed his shoulder into Rascher's chest. The gun went off on automatic fire. Webster let out a yell of pain, as the bullets seared a line across his shoulder. Sebastian tried to leap out of the way, was just too late. The heavy Mauser, thrown off line by Webster's sudden move, was pointing towards the ground, the slugs streamed out, the muzzle velocity raising the barrel skyward. A bullet caught Sebastian in the thigh, another in the fleshy part of the waist, a third scoring a line just under his armpit.

The bullets were physical blows. They caught Sebastian in mid-leap, turned him sideways. His momentum carried him into the other two men. Webster was like the meat in a sandwich as Sebastian landed, the three of them tumbled to the ground. There was sudden quiet as the Mauser ran out of bullets. Webster tried to roll out of the way. Sebastian's fists crashed into the German's face, punched again and again. He heard Webster's urgent voice calling him as through a haze. He paused, rolled over, saw Erik running towards them, gun in hand. He grabbed the Mauser, pointed it, pulled the trigger, realized at once that it was empty. No time to think, Sebastian threw the gun at Erik in a deliberate, high arc. Erik paused for a moment to watch its flight, prepared to duck out of the way. That was his last mistake.

Sebastian's throwing-knife came away from where it was strapped to his calf, and was in flight in one fluid movement, too quick to follow. The knife thunked into Erik's chest, burying itself three inches deep. Erik's look of surprise was almost comical. He spread his arms wide, as if in supplication, then dropped on his face, forcing the knife in, up to the hilt. Sebastian lay gasping.

'Mark,' the voice was sharp. Webster was on his side, pushing up on his elbow, trying to struggle to his knees. He teetered, almost fell back, gained his balance. 'Mark, how bad are you hurt?'

Sebastian lifted his head. It felt like it weighed a ton, it pounded like a thousand tiny blacksmiths working at their forges in his brain. He glanced down at his wounds. The entire left side of his body was bloody. Drops, looking bright vermilion in the floodlights, fell in a steady stream on to the concrete. He raised his left arm, tested it gingerly. Intact, but the armpit stung like hell. He probed the wound with his other hand. The bullet had cleaved a clean line out of his jacket and had etched a path into his skin two layers deep. Painful, but not terminal. The other two bullets had passed right through flesh. The wounds bled profusely, but no bones had been broken and nothing vital had been hit. He'd have to staunch the bleeding before he became too weak. 'I'm all right, I'm all right.' His tongue felt dry as dust, seemed too thick for his mouth.

He looked over at Rascher who lay on his back, knees drawn up protectively. His face was pulpy, a bloody mask, his breathing stertorous.

Sebastian pushed himself up, got to his feet with an effort. His mind was still in overdrive, sorting out priorities. First things first; he had to take care of his wounds and needed Webster's help, the ropes had to be cut. He limped over to where Erik lay face down on the concrete, rolled him over on to his back, tried to pull the knife out – it was stuck fast. He put a foot on Erik's chest, wrenched the blade free, it came reluctantly with a great sucking sound.

He cut the ropes that bound Roger's hands, slipped the knife back in its sheath. 'How's the shoulder, Roger?'

'Like they say in the movies, it's just a scratch,' Webster said straight-faced. 'Let's take a look at you.'

Webster ripped away the trouser leg, exposing the wound. He used Sebastian's handkerchief and his own to bind it. Sebastian winced. Webster mumbled under his breath as he worked. He tore off a piece of Jack's shirt, used it as a pad, pressed it against the waist, held it in place with the tie he'd retrieved from Erik's body. Then he sat down on the ground, mopped his sweating face with his sleeve. 'What a mess. I haven't seen so much blood since Anzio. What do we do now? You need a doctor . . . and these guys,' he gestured at the bodies strewn around, 'it looks like a fucking slaughter house.'

'We got another problem. We've got to get out of here fast before the cops come. Somebody's bound to have heard the shooting – sounds carry in the country. Look, my car is parked just up the road, the key's in the ignition. Are you fit enough to get it and drive up to the house? I can't move too far on this leg.'

'What about them? Are you just going to leave them here?'

'What do you want me to do? Take them with us?'

'I guess not,' Webster said doubtfully. 'Jesus Christ,' he exploded, 'it looks like World War Three.'

'Yeah, well just be thankful that we won it.'

'What about . . . ?'

'No more questions now. I'll tell you everything when we get out of here. Go.'

'Ah, shit! OK. I'm going. Where's the goddam car?'

Sebastian showed him where to cut in behind the house and through the fence that would take him to the car. Webster ambled off in a curious rolling gait, weaving a path around Jack and Erik. Sebastian watched until he'd disappeared into the gloom, then turned to Rascher. 'Thank you, Roger,' he said under his breath. 'I didn't want you to see this.' He stooped and grabbed Rascher by the shirt front, dragged him to his feet, pushed him against one of the stall doors.

Rascher was groggy, his head hung down on his chest. He lifted his head in mild protest when Sebastian slammed him into the wall. Sebastian slapped his face back and forth, back and forth, snapping the head back. The horse in the stall reacted, gave a terrified whinny, kicked at the door. The stink of sweat and horse manure and fear lay heavy in the enclosure. Rascher's fear had its own distinct smell.

'Stop, stop,' he rasped through broken teeth.

Sebastian took out his knife, grabbed Rascher's hair with his free hand, banged his head against the wall, held the knife-point to his throat. 'Now, you son-of-a-bitch, you're going to tell me where Spitzweg and Naumann are.'

Rascher's eyes jerked open, terror was mirrored in the pin-point pupils. 'I'll tell you anything you want, but don't kill me. I can give you money. I have many treasures. They're yours. Whatever you want. Tell me,' he blubbered.

'Spitzweg and Naumann.'

'You'll let me live if I tell you, won't you?'

Sebastian exerted pressure on the knife, a bead of blood blossomed at the point. Rascher screamed, a high-pitched female scream.

'Spitzweg and Naumann,' Sebastian said.

'Spitzweg's in New York and Naumann's in Los Angeles.'

'What names are they using?'

'Spitzweg's called Spicer now.'

'And where do I find him?'

'He has a penthouse on the corner of Seventy-sixth and Lexington. And Naumann,' he said without prompting, 'has made his name Newman and he's in Beverly Hills, somewhere near to the hotel, on Carolyn Drive, I don't know the address, it's in the phone book.

'Thank you, Herr Rascher.'

'I've told you what you want to know. Now just let me go. I won't make any more trouble for you, I promise.'

'No, you won't – or for a girl called Pamela Driscoll, who's lying, battered, in a hospital where you put her, with a broken arm and maybe internal injuries; and my parents – remember the people you murdered? Wherever they are, they might rest a little easier, and I am going to do your trainer a favour; he's tired of you, too. You just aren't very lovable, Ernst.' Sebastian reached over and unbolted the top half of a stall door. The horse inside was frightened, wild-eyed, and careened about the stall. Sebastian tightened his grip on Rascher's shirt. 'I think we'll leave it up to Boomerang, he's your horse, let's see what he thinks.'

Sebastian unbolted the bottom half of the stall, opened it and gave Rascher a violent shove inside, slammed the door behind him. Rascher screamed, 'Nooooo.' The horse, already frightened, went berserk. The thoroughbred bucked, plunged, lashed out at the unwanted visitor. The hoofs struck bones, shattered them.

The screams diminished, stopped. Rascher's lifeless body lay on the stall floor. Wisps of hay matted with blood clung to his face.

Sebastian watched, impassive, as inscrutable as a Mandarin. He wedged the note he'd scribbled in the hotel into the door slot, then turned away. Roger had just driven up to the house.

Chapter Eleven

Claire Webster had got over her panic and fright with remarkable speed, Sebastian thought. She fussed over the two men with a zeal of which Florence Nightingale would have approved. Sebastian had vetoed any suggestion of going to a doctor, overrode all Webster's objections. And, although he felt weak from loss of blood, and shock was setting in, he remained adamant throughout the ride to Webster's home. Webster finally, recognizing an immovable object, capitulated. And so Claire was enlisted to perform the services necessary for sterilizing the wounds and bandaging them.

Sebastian marvelled that she didn't even ask any questions. In fact, Claire was burning up with curiosity, but exercised iron control until she could get Roger on his own. When no one was looking, she licked dry lips. She was scared to death of the consequences. Would the police come round, and if they did, how would she handle it? She reached for, found, and held on to her normal stability. It calmed her.

She cleaned her husband's shoulder wound, spread on antiseptic cream and a light bandage.

'How's it feel?' Sebastian asked.

Webster shrugged with his good shoulder. 'Did you ever play tug-of-war when you were a kid? You know, ten little monsters on either side, scrambling and pulling like it's coming up to the end of the world? Then the little bastard in front of you slips, and the rope where you got it over your shoulder takes out a big hunk of skin. That's the way it feels. What about you?'

One of the Mauser's slugs had gouged a hole out of the fleshy part of the thigh, leaving an exit wound twice the size of the spot where the bullet had entered. Another three inches to the left and the femur would have been shattered. 'Lucky,' Sebastian muttered, and took a large swig out of the glass of neat whisky.

'Yeah, lucky,' Webster agreed. 'Still and all, you're not going to be doing any dancing on that leg for a while, pal. And from what I can tell, your waistline's about an inch smaller. Goddam it, you need a doctor.'

'I told you, no doctor. I just got to find somewhere to rest for a while.'

Webster threw up his hands in disgust. 'Oh, Jesus! What am I getting into? A few hours ago, I was a law-abiding citizen with a nice uncomplicated life. All of a sudden, there's enough dead guys around to make a mortician smile, and I'm breaking every law in the book by ignoring it.'

Sebastian was contrite. 'I'm really sorry, Roger. I'll be out of your hair in a few minutes. You and Claire will be safe. There's nothing to connect you with . . . what happened.'

'The hell, you say. You're not going anywhere. You're not moving until that leg heals, and if you try, I'm going to break your other one.

'And I'll help him,' Claire added. 'We're involved whether you like it or not.' She examined her handiwork, was satisfied. 'I'll go make some coffee and sandwiches, you both look like you need them.

Sebastian smiled. He felt it freeze on his face. Funny things were happening in his stomach. He swallowed hard, almost rid himself of the lump that had arisen in his throat. Those walls that he had built up for years to protect his solitude were in danger of being breached. He cleared his throat. 'Look, I know that you mean every word you say . . . and I appreciate it . . . more than I ever thought I could, but we're going to have to make a few changes.' He put a hand out to stop Webster's protest. 'It's not safe for me to stay here, or for you to have me.'

'I thought you told us we couldn't be connected,' Webster said aggressively.

'And I believe it.' Sebastian replied with more conviction than he felt. 'But let's be realistic. Rascher found you, and that means somebody else could. If I'm not here, you can tell them that you haven't seen me in ages.'

'And what if they try what Rascher pulled?'

'No way. They're going to have to be very careful. Rascher did it because he was desperate and reverted to his old SS methods. I don't think the others would be that dumb. They spent a lot of years building up an aura of respectability, and they're not going to blow it because of a single thorn in their side. And I'll tell you something else, if Rascher had survived instead of me, they would have got rid of him, dumped him down the nearest sewer. He reacted like a maniac, he could have ruined it for all of them. And the first rule of the neo-Nazi is the same as the old guard – chop off the dead branches and cut your losses.'

Webster shook his head, looking mystified. 'I'm beginning to feel like Alice through the looking-glass. Here I am calmly talking about murder, Al Capone-style carnage, Nazi-killers, secret organizations, as if I were discussing the weather. Are you crazy, and is it catching, because I think I am too.'

'I didn't mean for you to get stuck in the middle.'

'Well, I am and I don't much like it. I mean that I sat in the car on the way back here while you explained what was going on, and I don't understand a damn thing. It's Loony Tune time. All of a sudden, this kid, who I've seen grow up, is fighting a holy war, committing international mayhem, for parents you never even knew. I always thought you were a sensitive kid – quiet maybe, reserved is probably a better word, and all the time you have this shit churning around inside of you. I thought that when you went off to Japan to study with a karate master, OK, the kid wants to become an expert at something. And when you did your acting bit and became a make-up expert, and learned to fly and parachute and all those other things, I thought, well, the kid's restless. He's had a tough start in life and he doesn't really know what he wants to do, so he's trying a little bit of everything, and one day he'll come out of it and settle down – and all the time it was for a purpose. What floors me is that I was completely wrong as anyone has ever been.'

'You don't know the half of it.'

'And that's what really worries me. How long has this been

going on? How far back was it when you decided that this was your mission in life?'

'A long way.'

'Christ!' Webster turned away, walked to the bar at the far end of the room, poured himself a brandy. He took a large swallow, wrinkled his nose as the amber liquid burned its way down into his stomach. He turned back to Sebastian, gesticulating with the glass. 'Just answer me one thing. Are you doing all this because your mother was Jewish? I still don't understand the reason.'

Sebastian shook his head. 'Hell, it's sometimes hard for me to get hold of all of it. Well, Jewish . . . ? My mother was Jewish, so officially I am, but it really has nothing to do with it . . . or almost nothing. Sure, I feel an empathy with the six million Jews killed. What person in his right mind doesn't? But it really has nothing to do with the ethnic side of it. You know, when I wasn't talking and no one could get through to me about anything, that included religion also. Afterwards, there were some half-hearted attempts to get me interested in it, and I was pretty forceful in rejecting them. To a kid who got a start like I did, it all seems pretty ridiculous to try to convince me that there was some higher purpose for what happened.'

'OK, OK, you have explained that,' Webster said. 'I still can't pretend that I understand.' He paused. 'I don't suppose there's any way to stop you from this madness? You're going to go on, aren't you?'

Sebastian nodded.

'What about the cops? If you know who these guys are, why don't you have them arrested? Take it through the courts, you got proof.'

Sebastian gave a derisive laugh. 'Fat chance of them doing anything. They just walk away.'

There was a silence in the room as Webster continued to shake his head. A car with noisy tappets passed by outside. Webster looked nervously at the curtained window. 'I can't help you, Mark, you know that, don't you? I don't believe in what you're doing. It's not right. You can't take on the whole world by yourself. All that's going to happen is that you're going to get yourself killed.'

'But you're not going to try and stop me.' Sebastian made it a statement.

Webster lifted the glass to his mouth, a deliberate movement to give him time to think. He sipped more brandy, hardly tasted it. He shook his head. 'No, I'm not going to try and stop you. It wouldn't be any use. You've unleashed a juggernaut. You have to put on the brakes by yourself. I'm not going to give you all that crap about paying for it later, but somebody's going to collect their dues.'

Sebastian stood up, limped to the window. A spasm of pain went through his leg. He paled, wiped off a bead of perspiration that appeared in an instant. He put his weight on his good leg, peeked through the curtain at the street. Empty and quiet. He started talking to Webster in a low voice, without turning around. 'I know you don't understand, Rog. I wouldn't expect you to. But I'm going to try to explain, because I feel that I owe it to you. And one of the reasons is that you are almost the only one who treated me like a person instead of a porcelain doll . . . or a freak.

'My first real memories start when I was about eight years old.' Sebastian turned to face Webster, leaned on the window sill. 'Can you imagine that? Nothing until eight years, or practically nothing. Just hazy memories, fragmented pictures, like when you come into a dark room after being out in the sunshine, and you have after-images, pinpoints of light that form the outlines of something, and you want to reach out and touch them but they disappear before you can get near them. That was me, a child zombie, breathing, eating, sleeping because I didn't have to think about it. That's how it was – with one exception. There was one clear memory, one that I wished I didn't have. It was there all the time. I didn't have to reach for it. It stood next to me like a Siamese twin, in my dreams, too. I suppose you can guess what that memory is. I was never rid of it, never have been able to get rid of it, only push it away in a corner. It lurks there like a toothache, ready to grab at you, and ready to make you aware of its presence when you lose your concentration. It's a vivid picture, replays itself like a tired, old film. Four men in uniform, a man, a woman, blood.

'One day – and I remember that well – I was sitting in my room at my aunt and uncle's house in Newport Beach, staring into space. One second, blank, the next, that scene in front of me – big – three-dimensional, in living colour. But there was one difference. This time I was like an outsider, watching a drama as it unfolded. In one corner was this little punk kid staring with his fist in his mouth, scared shitless. That was me, that kid. The first time I'd ever seen it from that perspective. And I cried. And that was also a first, because I'd never cried before.

'From that day on, I started taking notice of things around me. I still wasn't speaking, but I listened and learned . . . and I remembered. I could see the faces of those four Germans, clearly . . . I recognized them immediately when I traced them through the hospital records in Berlin and used the names to get pictures.

'Pretty soon I was sent to that school in Big Sur, a school devoted to rich, undisciplined freaks, and I was the freakiest. I was put into a cabin with several other boys, because they thought that, with company my own age, I'd come out of myself, start speaking, start joining the human race. I didn't. I withdrew even further. And then there were my roommates. Wonderful little children. They took great delight in tormenting me. It got to be quite a ritual. They enjoyed their little game, and God knows, in that isolated area, it was the only game in town. I remember one night after lights out, they decided that they were going to try to get me to speak, or die in the attempt, and the method that they used was inspirational. Wrestling was very popular on television, and how better to practise holds than on a dummy. They figured they'd make me give in, and I'd start speaking. So they jumped me and tried in succession, hammer locks, step-over, toe holds, head locks, chokes, the Indian death lock; well, anyway, you get the picture. Gorgeous George would have been proud of them. But I kept my mouth shut. Even when the pain was so excruciating that I wanted to scream. I bit my lip until the blood ran down my throat. But I didn't give them the satisfaction of hearing a sound out of me. I think they finally got scared and gave up.

'It was right after that, that one of the teachers started to demonstrate jujitsu. Something happened when he was demonstrating. I won't tell you what it was, it's still too personal. I don't want to talk about it. But after that, all of a sudden, everything was very clear. I could see what I wanted to do. I could see my whole life laid out in front of me like a four-lane highway. I wanted to be the best at jujitsu first, and then anything that would get me bigger, stronger, faster. And I started with the tormentors nearest to me; those punks were just for practice, because I knew that eventually I would go after those four Germans who killed my parents. What they did was responsible for the life I was leading. And only after that was taken care of, would I be released from – what would you call it – maybe purgatory.'

Chapter Twelve

It was an hour before the sleepy village constable grumblingly consented to leave his warm bed to investigate the report by a persistent caller concerning what sounded like machine-gun fire, and another hour before the constable, checking on all the properties in the vicinity, drove into Trevor Willis's driveway and rolled up to the house. To his everlasting credit, he determined, quick as a flash, that something had to be wrong. All the lights were on in the house, and the stable area was floodlit. When he went to investigate, he went rigid with the horror of what he saw.

Another hour elapsed before the murder squad was in full swing, flash bulbs popping, Willis and the stable lad being interrogated.

Everything was as Sebastian had left it, with one exception. Jimmy had regained consciousness, took one long look at what had happened, and ran like hell, taking the Mercedes with him and abandoning it in the West End of London, where it was found the next day. Jimmy was never found.

It was Willis who, more concerned with his horses than dead men, discovered Rascher's battered body in Boomerang's stall, and who was able to make an identification for the police.

The Press went back to their papers and wrote the story for the early morning edition, also, as was common practice, putting it on the news wires, so that people in New York and Los Angeles knew about the 'massacre' before the people in Britain had had their first morning cup of tea.

Spitzweg was just finishing dinner at Twenty-One with a well-cushioned redhead, when his chauffeur, who heard it on a news broadcast, ran in to tell him. Spitzweg blanched to the colour of the oysters with which he had started his meal, thrust twenty dollars into the redhead's hand for the cab fare, and ran out, making a bee-line for his apartment.

He found Naumann at his home in Beverly Hills and told him what he knew, which wasn't much. After a ten-second silence and a muttered curse, Naumann was back on balance and ready to take charge. 'I never should have left it to that fool,' Naumann said to Spitzweg, who made an affirmative throat-clearing sound; he was unable to get any words out.

'The time has obviously come to take this Sebastian seriously. I thought at first that he was just a lunatic, but he has proved to be far more resourceful than that. The two questions that present themselves for an immediate answer are, does he know who we are and where to find us? And there is a third question. What are we going to do about it?'

'Well,' Spitzweg began.

But Naumann didn't wait for him, as the question was purely rhetorical. 'I'm sure that the answers to the first two questions are yes, and yes. That means that we must protect ourselves and take immediate counter-measures. I have forgotten how to look over my shoulder, and have no desire to re-acquire the habit. We must have a meeting at once, I will expect you here lunchtime tomorrow.'

'At the office?'

'No, the house; that will be more private.'

Sebastian fell into an exhausted sleep. His leg ached, his waist, his whole body ached, and despite all his protests, Webster and his wife helped him into their guest bedroom and undressed him, and put him to bed. The last thing Sebastian did before passing out was to extract a promise from Webster to wake him at the crack of dawn and get him out of the house to a 'safe place'. Webster crossed his fingers when he made the promise.

Sebastian clawed his way up from the depths of sleep, blinked a couple of times, had no idea where he was – then memory flooded back. He tried to sit up, suppressed a groan. His leg had stiffened up and the pain in his side was like a stiletto being twisted. He broke into a sweat, was bathed in it, fell back on the pillow breathing hard. A wave of nausea came and went and he struggled up on one elbow, looked at his watch. It read

1.35. He looked at it unbelievingly, held it to his ear to hear if it was running. A chink in the curtains showed that it was full daylight. He was trying to struggle out of bed when the door opened.

'How are you feeling?' Webster asked.

Sebastian tried to reply, croaked something unintelligible. Angry, he licked dry lips, cleared his throat, 'Are you crazy, Roger? It's the middle of the fucking afternoon. I should have been out of here hours ago.'

Webster only smiled at the outburst, remained reasonable. 'And where did you think you were going to go, looking like you do? Maybe you didn't notice, but your clothes were caked in blood and, just in case I have to remind you, there isn't any way of fitting you into this man's clothes.' Webster pointed to his short rotund figure. 'Now,' Webster continued as if he was talking to a child, 'one of us has to do some thinking around here, and I've elected myself.'

Sebastian glared, then flopped back on to the pillow in resignation. 'OK, boss. What next?'

Webster beamed, 'I'm glad you're seeing the light. I've been busy while you've been getting your beauty sleep. As you know, I'm not without connections ...'

Sebastian shut his eyes and groaned. 'Oh, Jesus, Rog, don't be so goddam pompous. I'm at your mercy.'

'As I was saying,' Webster continued pompously, 'I'm not without connections. I got on the phone first thing this morning and called this guy I know who's in Italy for the next couple of months. I rented his apartment in Chelsea right near the Thames. It's enough out of the way so that nobody will bother you.'

'What did you tell him?' Sebastian asked sharply.

'Take it easy. Just that a business acquaintance of mine is in town for a few weeks and hates hotels. As long as you don't wreck the place, he won't ask you any questions. And I have some other good news.'

Sebastian felt suddenly nauseated. He swallowed hard to keep the bile down. His reply was dull. 'What's that?'

'I thought that you'd be more interested than that,' Webster chided him. 'Remember a girl named Pamela Driscoll?'

Sebastian's eyes snapped open. 'What about her?'

'That's better. She's fine. Well, she's got a broken arm and bruises, but nothing more serious than that. The hospital said that they'd probably let her go tomorrow.'

Sebastian realized that he was holding his breath, let it out slowly. He smiled for the first time in a long time. Tension eased.

'Now,' Webster said. 'Where were you staying? I'll get your clothes and check you out. Then we'll go on to the apartment.'

Sebastian told him, and Webster headed for the door, then turned back. 'Oh yeah, I almost forgot to tell you. Our little escapade is front page news.'

Sebastian's mind started to function. He was alert in an instant. 'What did they say?'

'Lots of stuff about an international crime syndicate, a Mafia shoot-out, a power struggle among the gang leaders, take your pick. You can read it for yourself.' He was back in ten seconds, dumped a stack of paper on the bed. 'I'll be back as soon as I can.'

Four hours later, Sebastian was moved to the house in Chelsea, had had his bandages changed, wounds cleaned properly and had been given antibiotics and a tetanus shot, and was now sleeping peacefully. Webster indeed had connections. One of them led to a doctor who was a Polish immigrant and a former inmate of one of Hitler's concentration camps. One mention of Nazis was enough for him to treat the patient without asking questions.

Chapter Thirteen

Naumann had been very busy in the sixteen hours since Spitzweg's phone call. He had made calls of his own to colleagues in different parts of the world, all of whom were connected in some part of his business, and many who stood to benefit directly from the successful completion of Mexican oil leases. He related the problem of Sebastian, asked for advice on how to handle it. Opinions differed, but the consensus opted for solving the problem on a personal basis. Naumann thought there was no point in mincing his words. Murder was what he was talking about, and what he needed was the best man to do the job. As he was dealing with an unknown quantity, what he required was part oracle, part bloodhound and two parts killer.

Three of the people he called told him that they had heard of a man called Youngblood, who seemed to fit Naumann's requirements in all particulars. A man in San Francisco named Mizelli was the person through whom the arrangements were made. Naumann called Mizelli.

The flat voice at the other end of the phone wanted to know how Naumann had heard of Youngblood, and how he knew where to call. Naumann mentioned a name that seemed to satisfy the man. Mizelli asked what was required, 'in general terms only', and Naumann answered, 'A removal.'

Mizelli said that Youngblood was expensive, to which Naumann offered no response, and – after a pause – told Naumann bluntly that he would have to be checked out, and if everything was okay, then Youngblood would call him in the morning.

Naumann made a last call to Darrell Bradshaw, who acted as fixer and trouble-shooter for the Imperial Petroleum Corporation, IMPETCO. He requested that Bradshaw, through his extensive contacts, find out all he could about a man named Robert Youngblood, and get the information to him at once. He was evasive about the reason, but stated that it was vital and that the Mexican oil deal might hinge on it. He also asked Bradshaw to come and see him at lunchtime the next day. Bradshaw hesitated, then agreed.

The dossier on Youngblood came in late the next morning. There wasn't much, but what there was was impressive.

Youngblood was thirty-four, the same age as Sebastian. Naumann noted that he had been at UCLA at the same time as Sebastian. Could he have known him? That would be too much to hope for.

Youngblood did his graduate work at Berkeley, then enlisted in the Green Berets, which Naumann knew to be one of the toughest units America had to offer. He passed with flying colours, was shipped to Vietnam as one of the first 'advisers', where Youngblood's psychological training was utilized. He was detailed to handle interrogations of Vietcong prisoners, and – in parallel – learned the rudiments of behaviour modification – brainwashing. He became an expert. The file said that he was an excellent linguist, soon fluent in Vietnamese, Cantonese and Mandarin. As his proficiency increased, his services became more and more sought after by the brass. His judgements rapidly took on the tenor of pronouncements, and that was when the first deviant streak became apparent.

There was a note that Youngblood's requests for transfer to an action unit were repeatedly denied, and a note of an official reprimand when Youngblood absented himself from the interrogation room to go off, of his own volition, on 'search and destroy' missions, and continued to do so with a flagrant disregard for authority. He chalked up several personal kills, and was allowed to get away with it because the other area of his expertise was so highly prized. The rest of the information on Youngblood was negative, a condition of which Naumann approved. Since his discharge, he had come back to California where he was based, but seemed inclined to travel. He disappeared for periods of time, anything from a week to a month, destinations unknown. He had no visible means of support other than occasional advisory jobs for police departments who wanted psychological profiles on criminals.

Youngblood was sorting through a considerable array of winter sports gear – boots, parkas, gloves – when the call from Mizelli came in. He told him of the call he had received. 'The guy's name is Carl Newman, at least that's what he calls himself.'

'So who is he?'

'A Kraut. My contacts tell me he is an old line Nazi whose real name is Naumann. There is still a warrant out for him as a war criminal.'

'H-m,' Youngblood said. 'Why don't we turn him in? Maybe there's a reward.'

'Very funny. Ho-fucking-ho,' Mizelli said. 'If there was a reward, it wouldn't keep you in cigarettes for a month. This cat's talking big bread and he sounds scared. I think you could jack it up to damn near what you liked.'

'Well . . . I don't know. I'm going skiing.'

'C'mon, Bobby, damn it. I've been up half the goddam night getting this information.'

'Aw, poor baby. Little Diddums is tired and cranky. You are still gonna get only twenty per cent – *if* I take it.'

'Shit, at least talk to the guy.'

'OK, OK, give me the number.' Youngblood wrote it down.

Youngblood had to wait a minute while the man who answered the phone with, 'Mr Newman's residence,' transferred the call. He identified himself, noted the slight German accent of 'Mr Newman', who acknowledged that the call had been expected and how pleased he was that it had been so prompt. Youngblood agreed to the German's request for a lunchtime meeting.

He opened the sliding glass door that led to the patio and pool area, stepped outside, sniffing the air. He wondered who the target was.

It was a crisp December morning, but the sun shone brightly and the haze that usually covered over his view of the Hollywood Hills was absent. He slipped out of his Japanese kimono, dropped it on the ground, and plunged naked into the pool. The icy water took away his breath, and he stroked ferociously to get his circulation going. A dozen lengths of the pool was enough to work up a warm glow, and he emerged, dripping water all the way to the bathroom, where he immersed himself in a hot shower.

At that moment, Spitzweg was in the company Lear jet winging his way westward, and landed at noon, Los Angeles time.

Another black Mercedes (old habits are hard to break) rolled noiselessly up the winding roads to the heights above Beverly Hills. Spitzweg sat in the back by himself, a bodyguard and chauffeur up front. The car came to a stop just inside the entrance driveway to a house with a massive iron gate flanked by stone pillars. The electric windows slid down, and the chauffeur thumbed the call button on the entrance phone to the left of the driveway. He identified himself and, a moment later, the gates swung back on silent oiled hinges. The Mercedes followed the driveway around a curve to the front of the mansion that could be suitably described as being built in Hollywood baroque. It was a massive structure of three floors, and had been constructed to the specifications of a cowboy star of the silent screen. The talkies arrived simultaneously with the star's departure – his voice sounded like a girl's – and the house had been sold, and subsequently changed hands to a number of eccentrics, until Naumann had purchased it. He'd left the façade as it was – gargoyled roof, dormer windows, and copies of Lancier lions, rampant, who stood guard on either side of a huge, intricately carved double door with a domed stained glass transom. He had gutted the inside and refurbished all the rooms with a different motif, so that you could go from Japanese silk screens and Tatami mats to American colonial to French provincial, all done in individual good taste, but taken as a whole it had the mustiness and oppression of a private museum or a time capsule.

A rigid-faced butler opened the door to Spitzweg and led him across marble floors past the giant room to the left that was known as the ballroom and down a long hallway that led to a patio at the back of the house. Naumann, who was staring at the green and purple hills that disappeared into the smog, turned, gave Spitzweg a perfunctory handshake, and waved him to a seat at the round glass table that stood in the middle of the patio.

Two men were already seated there. One, a man in his fifties, with a sombre expression on his ruddy face, Spitzweg recognized as Darrel Bradshaw. Bradshaw's grey suit, black tie, grey crewcut and full lower lip that gave him the look of a petulant baby, was in sharp contrast to the other man. Spitzweg judged him to be in his late twenties or early thirties, although there seemed to be wisdom beyond those years in the wide-spaced grey eyes and the hint of sardonic amusement in the slight twist of the thin mouth. His brown hair was thick, and long enough to classify him – in Spitzweg's mind – as a hippy, and his manner of dress did nothing to dispel that evaluation – jeans and sneakers, pink satin shirt, a peace symbol on a gold chain, and a string of brightly coloured beads hung around his neck, leather jacket thrown carelessly over the shoulders.

'This is Robert Youngblood,' Naumann said, 'and you know Bradshaw.'

Spitzweg shook hands in turn, firm from Bradshaw, languid from Youngblood. The light pressure from the limp hand repelled him.

'You can call me Bobby,' Youngblood drawled. 'Robert is a guy my mama calls her husband.'

Spitzweg watched Youngblood without expression, turned to Naumann for an explanation.

Naumann smoothed out non-existent wrinkles from his beautifully tailored Italian-cut suit, adjusted the knife-sharp crease in his trousers so that they hung exactly right on his long legs – just touching the top of highly polished black shoes. He smiled, exposing a double row of faultless caps. The blue eyes crinkled in the corners, the cheeks creased in just the right spot to give him a rugged appearance. Even the scar that ran from the base of his left ear to the corner of his mouth had a certain amount of charm. The white line stood out, prominent in the tanned face, and gave him a piratical look, but an avuncular one. A small dimple appeared in the firm chin. With a gesture Spitzweg had come to know well over the years, Naumann passed a hand over a full head of black hair, down greying side-burns, clipped to perfection. As usual, every hair was already in place. Not for the first time, Spitzweg thought that he looked as if he had just stepped from the pages of *Esquire*, and his envy flared. He cast a quick surreptitious glance down at his own body. The years had not been quite as kind to him. He was running to fat; a paunch that had been created under the auspices of good food and drink, hung over his belt. Without touching them, he could feel the jowels that sagged on either side of his pudgy face, knew the pouches of flesh beneath the pale, watery blue eyes that stared just a little myopically at him in the mirror every morning.

Naumann cut into his reverie. 'Robert Youngblood,' he emphasized the formal name, leaving no one in doubt as to what he thought of a grown man calling himself Bobby, nor was he entirely able to suppress the general disapproval he felt for the man, 'is here at my invitation.'

Spitzweg looked from Naumann to Youngblood, remained wordless. Naumann used the pause to take out a gold cigarette case, extract a cigarette, light it with a matching Cartier lighter. He inhaled, squinted as a wisp of smoke curled into his eyes, exhaled in slow motion. 'Doctor Youngblood,' one corner of his mouth quirked into a smile, 'yes, Doctor Youngblood, despite his appearance, has a PhD in psychology and is a leading authority on stress factors and behaviour modification.' Spitzweg blinked. 'Yes, when we grew up there were simpler terms for such things. Today everything must be in a sugar coating to be palatable. Never mind, eh, it means the same thing. Our good doctor has had the good fortune to have the opportunity to put his theories into practice in Vietnam, where no one is calling him a criminal.' The statement was delivered in a bland conversational tone. Spitzweg was sure that he was the only one who caught the tinge of bitterness. 'And further to his release from the army, he has been able to put his talents to work in private practice. He is consulted by many police departments when they want a psychological profile of a wanted felon. His speciality is the killer.' Spitzweg took a quick glance at Youngblood, who casually crossed one leg over the other. His sardonic amusement was now very evident.

'*Ach so*,' Spitzweg exclaimed, reverting to the German.

'That is why I have obtained Doctor Youngblood's services . . . at considerable expense. He is aware of our problem and assures me that everything that is told to him will remain in strictest confidence.'

'He knows,' Spitzweg hesitated, 'how much?'

Naumann turned to Youngblood, looked directly at him as he spoke. 'He knows that there is a man trying to kill us and that we cannot deal with him in the conventional way. No police action. I'm already feeling the repercussion's of Swift's death. I had a Los Angeles police lieutenant here this morning asking questions about our late colleague.'

'How did they . . . ?'

'Scotland Yard passed on the information. As we are officers in the same company, they were under the misconception that I could shed some light on the reason for the tragedy. Of course, I told them I knew nothing, was as shocked and mystified as they were. But we are getting off the track. What I am telling you is that I want no recurrence of police interest. Doctor Youngblood has other talents which he is willing to put at our disposal, he . . .'

Bradshaw, who had contrived to be both petulant and sour at the same time, lifted a meaty hand. 'Hang on a minute, Carl,' he cut in. His voice had the quality of a rasp and rumbled across the patio, 'All I'm interested in is the goddam oil leases and Mexican politicians. I don't want to know about all this other shit. What you're talking about sounds as if it is none of my business. So tell me what you want from me, and let me get the hell out of here.'

'Just your support,' Naumann clipped the words. 'You and IMPETCO are involved, whether you like it or not. We have a business agreement; we are tied together. Publicity will hurt you more than me, and I can ill afford it. Now I am trying to do something about it. If your stomach is too delicate to listen to details, then by all means get out. But be under no illusions. My health is of prime importance to you. Without me, there is no deal. Do you understand?'

Bradshaw's ruddy complexion went even redder. 'Yeah, I understand and will support you in the deal, but I still don't want any part of this other shit. You're talking about murder,' and he gestured at Youngblood. 'And it looks to me like you're bringing in some crazy hippy to do the job. I don't wanna know about it, and I don't want to know him.' He lumbered to his feet and headed for the door. 'I'll be in touch,' he said.

Youngblood recrossed his legs, took out cigarette papers and grass from his shirt pocket, rolled a joint with deft fingers. He lit it with a kitchen match that he struck on the sole of his shoe, took a deep drag, held it for a long time. The silence stretched out as Spitzweg and Naumann watched him with a fascination reserved for a creature viewed through a microscope. Somewhere in the distance a lawn mower started up and putt-putted its way through someone's lawn, the sound alternately louder and softer as the waves bounced off the surrounding hills; the smell of new mown grass wafted in on the breeze.

'He sure do run off at the mouth,' Youngblood drawled in pure country boy which he wasn't. 'Back in 'Nam, they would have called him a chickenshit mother-fucker, and more'n likely he would have wound up getting shot in the back.'

'I'm sure that's fascinating,' Naumann was icy. 'I am, however, not interested in your observations. I find your cracker-barrel philosophy tedious, and your southern accent ludicrous. I happen to know that you are not from the South and have never spent any time there. I would also prefer that you save your vulgarities for those small-minded individuals who would appreciate it. I do not. They are out of place here. I have engaged you because of a very serious situation. Please treat it that way.'

Youngblood was unabashed. 'Yassah, boss!' he said. He hardened. 'Let's talk about bread and who the target is.'

'How much do you want for your services?'

'Two hundred and fifty big ones – one hundred grand in front, and the balance when I complete the job. Get the money to Mizelli.'

Spitzweg was staggered. 'A quarter of a million dollars?'

'The cost of living has gone up,' Youngblood said straight-faced, 'and dying too.'

Spitzweg turned to Naumann, sure that the man was going to erupt into one of his towering rages. He was surprised to see Naumann remain the soul of impassivity.

'That's a lot of money,' Naumann said. It was a very mild statement. 'I will expect a great deal for that price . . . all right, I agree.'

Youngblood nodded, the wry smile in place. 'Who do you want hit?'

'His name is Mark Sebastian.'

It was Youngblood's turn to be surprised. The smile disappeared, the eyes widened, the mouth opened and shut.

Naumann pressed on with a tight-lipped smile. He was delighted with the reaction. 'You know him then?'

'Yeah,' Youngblood muttered. He straightened up from the slouch, stared hard at Naumann. 'A long time ago. Why him, what's he done?'

Naumann's face became a mask. 'That's irrelevant. He's trying to kill us and I want him eliminated. That's all you have to know. Can you do it or not?'

Youngblood leaned back on the chair, tilted his head up to where interlaced latticework formed the ceiling. 'Yeah, I can do it.'

All of a sudden the money was secondary. He felt strangely drawn to Sebastian. He remembered him from college, a man to whom everything came easily, but a driven man. Youngblood was jealous of his prowess as an athlete, respected his capabilities as a student. Sebastian would prove to be a worthy adversary, a challenge for which he felt a deep need.

'Tell me what you know about Sebastian,' Naumann demanded. 'I want to get, what would you call it, a feel for the man.'

Youngblood gazed out into the landscaped garden. A faraway look came into his eyes. Spitzweg took a seat, watched Youngblood intently.

'I first noticed Sebastian in my sophomore year,' he crushed the joint under his heel. His accent had shifted north of the Mason-Dixon line. 'We had a couple of classes together. I think I noticed him in particular, because he always seemed so self-contained, and at nineteen that's a hell of a thing to be. He was a big, good-looking kid and had a lot of the girls creaming in their drawers to get to him, but he didn't pay them no mind.' Youngblood smiled and looked almost apologetic at reverting to the southern dialect. 'I'd think, "Hey boy, you got all that quail hot after your body and you carry on like they're not even there." So I decided that he was a fag, and that made me feel better, although I knew, deep down, it wasn't true. He just didn't give a damn, and I could understand that even less. I tried to start a conversation with him once or twice, but that didn't get me no further than a flea jump. He'd be as polite as hell, answer questions like a gentleman, but you had the feeling it was like penetrating the polar cap with a toothpick. You were frozen out, nicely, but the deep freeze. He was distant. Man, I wanna tell you that the Milky Way seemed closer.

'Then, in his junior year, he joined the football team. He was a walk on. Nobody knew he could play. Fact is, there was a story going around about how he got on the team. Seems like he walked up to the coach before practice one day and said, "Coach, I'm here because I'm going to be your starting linebacker when the season begins," and the coach, who'd heard it all before and was as sceptical as hell, said, "Oh, yeah, son? That's darn right nice of you. I really don't know how we would have managed to field a team if you hadn't turned up," and Sebastian is supposed to have said, straight-faced and completely serious, "I understand, Coach. I'm glad that I'm going to get the opportunity to save your job for you." ' Youngblood broke off the story to guffaw at the memory. 'Well, I hear tell that the coach almost had an apoplectic fit. And when he recovered, he sent Sebastian in to play with the third and fourth stringers, and gave instructions to the Varsity for them to run him over. Well, on the first play from scrimmage, the tailback comes off tackle with the fullback leading interference, heading straight for Sebastian. I hear tell he pushed the fullback out of the way like you move a coffee cup without thinking about it, and hit that tailback with such a vicious tackle that he was laid up for a week. The coach couldn't believe his eyes, and sent another couple of players right at him. And each time, the same thing happened.

'And sure enough, come the opening game, there was Sebastian as a starting linebacker. He made All-Conference and a couple of the All-American polls. I'm telling you all this, 'cos here's the really curious thing; no, freaky is a better word. At the end of the season, Sebastian just up and quit. No reason, no nothing. I hear the coach pleaded with him, I guess begged him is a better way to put it, to come back for the good of the team, for his own immortal soul and all that crap. But he was like the Rock of Gibraltar. I hear he said, "Thanks, Coach, I enjoyed playing football for you, and now I don't want to do it any more." And when the coach, madder'n hell by this time, asked why he did it in the first place, Sebastian seemed surprised and answered, just to prove he could, and now that there was no question about it, there seemed no point in continuing. Like I said, a loner. And that's why he's going to be tough to stop. That's something I learned in 'Nam. A guy who's completely independent has very few weaknesses you can exploit. Don't get me wrong. I'm not saying "no weaknesses", but if there are any, they won't be very apparent. But that's what you got me here for, huh?'

There was a long silence when Youngblood had finished. Spitzweg had the feeling that he had been mesmerized. He had tried so hard to put the memory of the incident in Berlin out of his mind, had almost succeeded. And all these years he was going about his business, a boy named Mark Sebastian was growing up and planning to kill them all. He looked down at his hand resting on the table, the fingers tapping a rhythmic tattoo. He hadn't realized it. He closed his hand into a fist and put it in his lap.

Naumann patted his head lightly, looking for stray hairs. Found none. 'And how do you propose to get him?'

Youngblood raised a hand, let it flop with a thack on to his thigh. He shrugged. 'I could outline it for you, but I think better on a full stomach and you promised me lunch.'

Naumann went to the call button at the side of the door, pressed it, and when the butler arrived, told him to bring lunch.

When Naumann had finished his explanation of what he knew about Rascher's death, the rest of the meal was consumed in silence, broken only when Youngblood commented on how ripe the avocado was and what a good vinaigrette sauce, and what an excellent sole meunière, and what a distinguished bottle of Montrachet they were drinking. Youngblood finished his fresh strawberries flown in from Hawaii, and sat back with his coffee cup and saucer balanced on one palm. He closed the slim file about Sebastian's activities since college. 'Well, I've been thinking about it, and the one idea that makes sense to me is that we set a trap for him.'

'And what,' Naumann asked sarcastically, 'do you propose to use as bait?'

Youngblood's teeth flashed into a smile. 'Why, you of course, and your buddy here.' He gestured at Spitzweg.

'I don't find that very amusing,' Naumann said, 'and I hoped you had something more to offer than an asinine suggestion. I'm not used to sitting and waiting for a killer to get me when he feels like it. I want him now. We will take the initiative.'

'You mean like a blitzkrieg. I'm afraid that went out with padded shoulders and ration books. We'll have to try to think of something a teeny bit more subtle . . . unless you think it's time for the Fourth Reich to rise from the ashes.'

Naumann flushed to his hair line and his voice was unsteady, barely controlled. It never crossed his mind that Youngblood had made a reference to his past. It slipped by. He confirmed it with his outburst. 'Do you mock me or the organization I stand for. You know nothing about it. We have survived in spite of the most intensive witch-hunt in history, and when we are ready, the world will know about it.'

'Sure you will. And I can see the day when all you fat cats will get off your duffs and take over the world . . . but I don't think I'll hold my breath until it happens.'

'It is unfortunate you feel such repugnance for us,' Naumann snapped. 'I can't imagine why you accepted this commission.'

Youngblood gave a short bark of a laugh. 'Why? That's real easy. A quarter of a million smackers. I am strictly apolitical. The bullets in my gun got no causes engraved on them. They are as neutral as death. One lump of flesh is very much like another. If it makes you happy to run around in fancy uniforms and jack boots, shaking swagger sticks and giving orders, then, hey, good luck to you, pal. Whatever turns you on. Me, I'm just a craftsman, you know, an artist. Nobody's going to come and see my stuff hanging in a gallery and nobody's going to remember me when I'm gone. But I'll know what I did. Now there's a job to do and I know how to do it. You don't like it, great. Get someone else. I'll take a walk.'

Naumann bit off an angry retort and stifled the urge to

throttle the despicable, smirking individual in front of him. The problem was that much of what Youngblood said was true, and he had only just seen it. Youngblood had made a jagged rent in the fabric of his dream for the future, and when he peered cautiously in, he realized there were things he hadn't wanted to see, others he'd conveniently forgotten.

He'd spoken to Reinhart Kessler, the paymaster in Hamburg, requested help from within the organization, was regretfully told that none was available. Oh, Kessler had made excuses about the lack of manpower, that recruitment was difficult, that the existing personnel was engaged elsewhere on the organization's behalf, but really he could read between the lines. The organization was moribund, and its members choking on the excesses. The old-line Nazis who shared his dreams were all his contemporaries. They didn't want trouble any more. They had become wealthy and comfortable and filled with sloth. They were every bit of the 'fat cats', as Youngblood had accurately depicted them. And so he was stuck with this insolent young man to do a job he'd forgotten how to do, perhaps had no will to do. That didn't bear thinking about.

It took but fractions of a second for all these thoughts to be sifted and for Naumann to reach a conclusion. He was wound up tight as a bowstring but kept his voice mild. 'What do you want us to do?'

If Youngblood felt any exultation from his victory, he didn't betray it by the blink of an eye. The expression remained the same – sardonic.

'Sebastian's got it all his own way at the moment. He's got you running scared, and he can afford to take his time, sit back, pick his spot. And you got no link to him, well maybe this Webster character, but I doubt it. That's tenuous at best.'

Naumann watched and listened with sharp interest, took note of how Youngblood went from Harvard English to swamp southern in one breath, wondered what personalities were fighting for supremacy in him, and which one would win. If nothing else, he was sure there was something deviant about the man, what the doctors would call a flawed personality. Naumann speculated that Youngblood had entered psychology for only one reason, to find out who he was, and he doubted that he'd made that discovery.

'If Webster knows anything, he sure won't be talking. I guess maybe I could shake his tree a little and see what comes down, but I'm pretty sure that would be a waste of time. First of all, it would start a few too many ripples, and secondly, I just don't believe that Sebastian would confide in him anyway. So we're going to have to make him come to you, through a prepared channel, so he'll pop up just where we expect him. There's a lot of work to do, a lot of things to go over. I'll lay it out for you as simply as possible. It's like mathematics. If you balance the equations, you come up with the solution. Let's call you and your buddy there "A" and "B", and Sebastian is "X", the unknown quantity. Now, his equation is "X" minus "A" and "B" equals "W". That's "W" for winner take all. And the way you'd like to see it balanced is "AB" minus "X" equals "W". We take all the steps that lead to that answer. We want to make Sebastian predictable. We do that by taking away his options. I'll give you a simple example. If there are three ways, for instance, to approach this house, we make two of them secure, so secure that it would be out of the question to use them; take them right out of the picture, and the third way we make easy. At least, that's the way it looks to an outsider. Like one of those fancy mousetraps where there's only one way to come in that looks really safe, and there's a big, fat lump of cheese at the other end waiting to be gobbled, then . . .' Youngblood made a chopping motion with his hand, 'let the guillotine fly, Mother, and watch that the blood don't get into your blueberry muffins.'

'Very picturesque,' Naumann said. 'How do you propose to apply this to Sebastian?'

Youngblood gulped down the coffee that had gone cold. He made a face, set the cup and saucer down on the table. 'I need a lot of information from you, your habits – nasty or otherwise – your movements for the next couple of months.'

'I don't see why,' Naumann said stiffly. 'All my movements have to do with my business and are no concern of yours.'

'As a matter of fact,' Youngblood replied laconically, 'I don't give a shit about your business, and I don't even care if you fuck pigs for fun. I listen to everything with a purely clinical ear. Hippocratic oath and all that. Your perversions are safe with me, but I've got to know about them to get to Sebastian, 'cos you know he's going to find them out.'

Spitzweg made a strangled noise in his throat, looked fearfully at Naumann, but Naumann remained stoic. Perhaps the line of his jaw hardened a little. It was difficult to tell.

'I will be very busy for the next few months,' Naumann said evenly, 'and much of the time, I will be travelling back and forth between here and Mexico.'

'Tsk, tsk,' Youngblood shook his head ruefully. 'That's too bad. That sure do make you vulnerable. But what the hell,' he brightened, 'if he gets you before I get him, I don't collect the rest of my bread.'

Naumann had finally passed beyond rising to the bait. He set his teeth, kept his mouth shut. Youngblood looked at his watch, a gold Piaget that looked out of place with the way he was dressed. 'Two forty-five,' he announced. 'If you have anything else planned for this afternoon, you'd better cancel it. Time's a-wastin' and you can bet your sweet ass that Sebastian ain't just lying around.'

That, however, was exactly what Sebastian was doing at that precise moment, without a single thought as to how he was going to reach his next objective – the elimination of Spitzweg and Naumann. But Youngblood wasn't to know that, and proceeded like the good professional he was.

The next three hours were a painful experience for Spitzweg and Naumann. Youngblood questioned them minutely about anything they might do more than once, and therefore constitute a discernible pattern. Like a surgeon, he probed for the smallest details. At the end of the ordeal, he was satisfied that he had enough to start with; the Germans just had had enough.

'What will you do now?' Naumann asked.

'I've been toying with the idea of going over to London to find out what I can for myself.'

Spitzweg looked scared. 'But what if he comes here in the meantime?'

'Well, I can't rule that out. But I don't think you have anything to worry about. He knows it's going to be even tougher from here on in. You know,' he mused, 'it's almost like he's waving a flag and saying, "Here I am and I'm coming ready or not."' Spitzweg gave Naumann a surreptitious glance. 'It's going to take him a while to spy out the land, and I'll only be gone three or four days at the most. So in the meantime, you just lie low, go out to Malibu or somewhere, and rent a room in a hotel. As long as LA don't fall into the sea, you should be perfectly safe, and I'll be back before you know it.' Youngblood stood up, nodded to both of them with his sardonic smile, and walked out without another word.

Spitzweg took out a silk handkerchief and mopped his brow. Although it was a pleasant seventy degrees out, his face streamed with sweat. '*Gott im Himmel*. What have we got ourselves into? I feel like I'm in the hands of a maniac. The whole world has gone topsy-turvy. Nothing is like it was. And just a month ago I allowed myself the luxury of thinking that things could not be better, a fatal mistake. One should not tempt the gods. I'm getting too old for this, Carl. I have a sick feeling in the pit of my stomach. I have to tell you, I'm scared.'

Naumann curled his lip in contempt, then abruptly it went, adding years in a heartbeat of time. He weighed what Spitzweg had said, adding a bit to one side of the scales, then the other, until they balanced. He realized, if he allowed himself to, he, too, would feel scared. He thrust the unfamiliar emotion away with a violent shove. 'He would make a good officer for the Gestapo.'

'*Ja*,' Spitzweg exclaimed. 'Exactly. He knows too much about us.'

Naumann traced the path of the scar with a fingertip. 'He knows too much about us,' he echoed under his breath, 'and when Sebastian is dead, Youngblood will follow him.'

Chapter Fourteen

Sebastian had it rough for three days. The transfer from Webster's house to the flat in Chelsea was an agony. Every bump in the road seemed to have his name on it. The apartment was up a flight of stairs. A deep mahogany door with brass door knocker opened into the two-bedroom flat that had white rugs, leather furniture and paintings of storm-lashed coastlines in gilt frames. Sebastian barely noticed it, as, aided by the support of Webster's arm, he was led to the master bedroom, undressed and put to bed.

A high temperature raged through his body, waxing and waning so that Sebastian was only ever on the edge of consciousness. Time and events blurred in his fogged brain. Faces faded in and out: Webster; his wife, Claire; the Polish doctor; and once or twice he thought he remembered seeing Pamela, but couldn't separate the dream from the reality.

On the fourth day, he awoke, his brain clear, his lips and throat dry as dust, his body weak. He blinked once or twice and tried to focus in the darkened room. He could see that it was daylight, as the weak December sun brightened the orange curtains that covered the window in the places where the folds were least evident. He could see the tall outlines of a wardrobe in one corner, the squat girth of a low dresser with a rectangular mirror next to it. His fingers felt the cool sheet beneath them. Tentatively he stretched out his hand towards the end of the bed, and, unable to find where it stopped, determined that he lay in solitary splendour on a king-size bed.

He felt for the injured leg, gingerly touched the bandages, probed for the double-holed wound. He gritted his teeth in expectation of a sharp pain, was almost disappointed when it didn't happen. There was only a dull ache that pounded in a slow, steady rhythm to the beat of his heart, like far distant African drums that are more felt than heard.

The bandage for his waist went completely around his middle. That wound had a special pain of its own. His chest felt stiff from the effort of his muscles that continued to work his lungs while ignoring the pain.

He felt dejected, more depressed than he could recall. For the first time in his life, he felt his body had let him down. He was an invalid, unable to make it do what he wanted. He was just lying there staring at the ceiling when the door opened and Webster peered in. 'Ah, back in the land of the living. How're you feeling?'

'Like an elephant kicked me.'

'Well,' Webster said cheerfully, 'that would probably have had the same result.' He walked over to the window and pulled back the curtains. The sunlight slanted in, illuminating the oyster-coloured walls, creating deep patches of shadow outside the shafts of light. Sebastian judged by the angle of the sun that it was mid-afternoon. He began to take more interest in his surroundings. He looked at Webster's smiling face. 'Well, you don't look any the worse for wear.'

Webster laughed. 'Maybe I should get shot more often. It's given me a whole new slant on things. When you get that near to dying, you start to realize how unimportant some things are that you've placed a high value on, and how really important the simple things are, like breathing. And as far as my sex life is concerned, Claire tells me that I'm acting like a love-sick teenager.'

Sebastian groaned, turned his head, saw the carafe of water and tumbler that stood on the bedside table. He started to reach for it, but Webster beat him to it, poured a glass and handed it to him. He gulped it down thirstily. 'When's the last time I ate?'

'A while ago.'

'That's what I thought. I can't take philosophy on an empty stomach. I think I'm hungry enough to eat a cow – whole!'

'Now I know you're getting better. I'll go rustle you up something.' Webster left the room.

Sebastian had resumed his scrutiny of the ceiling when the door opened five minutes later. He turned his head, caught his breath. Pamela entered the room, balancing a tray on one hand. She kicked the door shut with her foot. She smiled at him, and – despite the bruises under her eyes that had gone yellow, the lip that was still slightly puffed in one corner that made her mouth look as if it were curled into a prurient leer, and the cast on her broken arm that was held up by a sling – he thought she looked wonderful. His spirits lifted with a noticeable lurch. 'Looks like you've been through the wars, kid,' he said with wry amusement.

'Well, you don't exactly look like you're ready to enter the Mister Universe contest, yourself.' They laughed, holding each other's eyes, and even though the wound in his waist protested with a sharp stab of pain, he continued. She put the tray down awkwardly on the bed, and he took her hand in both of his. She bent over and kissed him lightly on the forehead.

They talked for the next hour. Pamela brought him up to date on what had happened to her, the events that had put her into the hospital, and what had gone on since she had left. Sebastian filled her in with as much as he thought she should know, leaving out the details. The memories were painful. He could feel her hand tensing in his as the story unfolded. What he gently reminded her of at the end was that it was all over. The food lay forgotten.

*

Youngblood breezed through London Airport. His plane, with a strong tail wind, had landed half an hour early on the direct flight from Los Angeles, and at that time of the morning – 6.15 – there wasn't a lot of other traffic around. Not that many people came to England in mid-December anyway. His plane had been less than half full, and the passengers and Customs people, who looked both sleepy and bored, waved him through with barely a glance. Part of the reason was that he didn't stand out. He'd traded his jeans and frilly shirts for a conventional sports coat and slacks, turtle-neck sweater and Gucci loafers.

It was still full night as the taxi raced down the M4 Motorway and on into central London. The street lights gleamed in the frigid air, making pools of light that intersected each other, making the main roads bright enough so that only the side lights were necessary for driving. There was a surprising amount of traffic, milk floats, Post Office vans, early morning motorists driving like zombies.

Youngblood sat back on the comfortable seat and stretched his legs, letting his mind run free. He thought over the events that had brought him to London at this time. It was his nature, since he'd become independently wealthy, to play it by ear. He never knew from one day to the next what he might be doing, preferred it that way. The one exception was the ski trip to Aspen. He had planned to get there two days before Christmas and stay long enough to take him a few days past New Year. It was another test he'd set for himself. He had every intention of skiing each mountain in the vicinity by day, and fucking every clean-limbed lady by night. It was a gargantuan task, but he felt up to it. Now he might not get the chance because of this new assignment.

He thought back to his first meeting with Naumann. A butler had opened the door to him and led him down the long hallway where Naumann was waiting. On the way, he'd caught a glimpse of a middle-aged woman through a half-open door, which closed silently as he passed. In fact, the whole house was silent, unnaturally so. There were none of the noises associated with modern California living. No radio, TV, records. Even the butler who preceded him stepped along as if he were walking on eggs.

He was impressed with the air of authority that Naumann exuded. He had come to rely on his snap analyses of people, and they very seldom let him down. He took in the suave man with the impeccable suit and tie whose height made him look elegant. He noted the manicured fingernails, the handsome face, the immaculate hairstyle, the prominent scar. He wondered about it.

He was introduced to Darrel Bradshaw, who gave him a perfunctory handshake without making any attempt to rise from his chair, and recognized the look of disapproval in the man's eyes. Youngblood smiled to himself. He'd worn his hippy clothes for the meeting, knowing that they provoked strong reactions in the so-called straight businessmen. He wore them for a purpose. When you attacked a man at the foundation of his morality, the façade crumbled, and he exposed his personality much quicker than usual. Youngblood liked that also. It gave him an edge. He told himself that was also the reason why he slipped into his 'good old boy' southern drawl. It made people angry. They felt they were being patronized. And that was part of it, but not all. Sometimes he just couldn't help himself. He'd hung around with too many shit-kickers in 'Nam, and the dialect had rubbed off. But it served a purpose, and he used it.

Youngblood was pleased that his target was Sebastian. He had wanted to know him, but had not been allowed the chance. Sebastian had kept him, like all the others, at arm's length. Sebastian was an impressive figure – strong, silent, self-sufficient – and represented everything that Youngblood, in his youth, thought he wanted to be. He knew there was a danger that his impressions of Sebastian were magnified with the passing of years, but he doubted it. If anything, they were understated. This would be a real test of skill, his analytical powers, his cunning.

The first time, he hadn't needed any. He had been in Saigon for a couple of days of rest and relaxation. One evening, he was sipping a beer at the long bar at the Continental Hotel, and struck up a conversation with the man next to him, a Belgian. He found out that the man represented a company that supplied cement for many of the constructions the Americans were building at a rapid rate. The Belgian complained bitterly that one sale he was trying to complete, worth several millions in dollars, was being held up by one man, a Vietnamese civil servant, and that he'd tried everything, including the usual bribes, but the man had refused and the Belgian thought he knew why.

He'd heard from other businessmen that this very same civil servant had obstructed other deals. There was a persistent rumour that he was a Vietcong supporter, and this was the way he could gum up the works.

Youngblood asked him why he didn't take it up with the authorities, if that was the case. The Belgian was bitter. There was no proof, he said. Without it, the Americans would let him keep his job. It was politic to support the local Vietnamese.

The Belgian said he would give a lot to see him removed. Youngblood asked idly, 'How much is a lot?' The Belgian's gaze sharpened through the alcoholic fog, and he suggested, trying to remain diffident, that the removal of that kind of obstruction might be worth $10,000. They settled on $15,000, and the next day a certain Vietnamese civil servant was found knifed to death in an alley, not an uncommon occurrence in wartime Saigon.

The Belgian gloated over his success, and related the method by which he had achieved it to other business associates. It started as a trickle and became a steady flow, as one by one they beat a path to Youngblood's door. Youngblood's method of solving their business problems had the advantage of simplicity, and it was permanent. It cost them money – the price had gone up to $25,000 – but it saved them months of frustration. The red tape was cut with surgical precision. It was worth the money.

Youngblood's protection was the languid manner he effected. The men he dealt with found it hard to equate this with the underlying menace they felt in his presence, but it scared them, and it kept their mouths shut.

Youngblood built up a nest egg of almost a quarter million dollars when he decided to quit Saigon. His instinct for survival told him that he had just about outstayed his welcome in Vietnam. It was time to move on. He took his discharge and left for the States with enough money to keep him comfortable for a very long time, and a reputation that could get him more whenever he wanted it.

There was the usual bottle-neck around Hyde Park Corner, and it was ten minutes before the taxi driver was able to get around and into the forecourt of the Dorchester Hotel.

Youngblood flopped down on the couch in his suite after he had dismissed the bell hop. He crossed his legs at the ankles, lit a cigarette and puffed contentedly, one arm behind his head. It was too early to do anything but relax and drink the strong Dorchester coffee that would arrive in a few minutes. The last time he'd stayed at the hotel had been two years earlier, when for a period of a week, he'd stalked an unsuspecting quarry through the streets of London – watching, observing, gathering the knowledge he needed.

It was a curious assignment, curious in that the man he was to hit was the Belgian who had originally hired him in Saigon, the very same man who had started him off on his new profession.

The Belgian had been a naughty boy: he'd neglected to pay a certain powerful individual who had cleared the way for him to make his lucrative deals. The man, understandably miffed, chose to teach the Belgian a lesson, a permanent one, and coincidentally an object lesson for anyone else who contemplated a double-cross.

Youngblood recognized the irony of the situation and viewed it with a certain wry amusement. He had long ceased to be surprised by anything that humans did to each other, and business was business.

He considered and rejected several methods he could employ for the Belgian's demise. His brief was that it should look like an accident. He finally decided on one fool-proof method where there would be no witnesses and no way of determining what had happened.

The Belgian flew his own plane, a twin-engined Cessna, that he had flown in from Antwerp and kept in a hangar at Heathrow.

It was a ridiculously simple matter for Youngblood, dressed as a mechanic, to gain entry to a plane with his tool box in which were six pounds of plastic explosive and a detonator, procured from his employer. He attached the bomb to the altimeter and set it to go off at eight thousand feet, which would be approximately in the middle of the English Channel.

He'd watched from the spectator's gallery as the plane took off. There was only an inch of space, buried on page forty-one of the newspaper, that was devoted to the disappearance of the aircraft. He spent an extra five days in London doing nothing more than enjoying himself. He haunted the King's Road – fertile ground for mini-skirted lovelies who were 'duck soup' for his easy smile, charm and good looks, and who just adored going to clubs and expensive restaurants, and ultimately to his bed.

Youngblood had no special plans about Sebastian. Purposely, he had left it that way. He looked on it as a fact-finding trip. If there were any facts to find, well and good; if not, he still hadn't lost anything. It wouldn't change his basic strategy.

Privately, he was convinced that he was wasting his time. The trail was days cold, and Sebastian wouldn't be hanging around congratulating himself on a job well done, because it wasn't. He would most certainly, wherever he took himself, be planning the next step.

The one thing that nagged at Youngblood was the inescapable fact that the job had been messy. Not only was Rascher dead, but two others also. Certainly they were his bodyguards, and probably had to be eliminated in order to get to Rascher. But there was something decidedly wrong about the whole set-up. It had the appearance of being a setpiece battle, lots of open space with no close neighbours, the owner of the place and his employee tied up and kept out of the way, the stable block area as the killing ground. It didn't take too much imagination to think of it as a fort, Rascher and his troops defending, Sebastian the lone attacker.

But that didn't make sense and postulated more questions than there were answers. Why was Rascher defending a piece of ground in a lonely part of Surrey? What inducement had he used to lure Sebastian there? For that matter, how had he made contact with Sebastian? And finally, how did he manage to so thoroughly mess it up that he wound up as a candidate for a breaker's yard?

Youngblood tried to place himself inside Sebastian's skin, made a clumsy attempt to use the same thought processes, and gave it up as futile. He had too little information. He knew he was dealing with a paranoid who was as inexorable in his pursuit as a creeping glacier. Again, there were too many questions to go any further than that. For example, what had triggered Sebastian to go into action now, so many years after the event? Why hadn't he started ten years earlier?

Youngblood dismissed the train of thought. He would probably never know, as the chances of a cosy face-to-face chat were slim and none. And he thought that was a shame, because he liked to know about the people he was going to kill. It made it somehow neater that way, a package wrapped in gaily coloured paper and finished off with tinsel and ribbon. He felt close to his victims, felt the delight when they smiled, remorse when they hurt.

The first one hadn't been that way. It was a butcher's job. A quick flash of a knife in the alley and it was all over, and he'd hated it. Not because of the killing. Existence in 'Nam and membership of the Green Berets had taught him that life was cheap and, at best, transitory. He'd hated it because he hadn't known the man, he hadn't had the chance to care for him as a person.

Sebastian was different. He knew Sebastian, his employers didn't. But how much did he really know? – Sebastian was an enigma and he longed to know more.

Youngblood called Rascher's office at 9.00 and asked for a Mr Lichfield, whom he had been told was Rascher's assistant. He made an appointment to come round in an hour.

He dressed for his foray into the City of London in a pearl-grey silk suit, dark Hermes tie, black shoes and a charcoal cashmere topcoat.

Lichfield looked exactly as he sounded on the phone – fussy, a mixture of subservience to superiors and arrogance when he could get away with it. He had thinning, mouse-coloured hair, a pinched face, a prim mouth and a prominent Adam's apple. He had been instructed by Mr Newman, he said, to show Mr Youngblood anything he wanted to see, and offer him any assistance necessary. It was clear that he disapproved of these instructions.

When Youngblood was shown into Rascher's office, he paused inside the doorway and just stared around him. The mixture of styles offended him, the blatant garishness clanged like a cracked bell. He admired the pieces individually, was unable to understand how anyone with the least degree of sensibility could shove them all together in the same room.

He went to sit behind Rascher's desk and was given a set of keys by Lichfield, which he said would open all the drawers, and in addition, there were the keys to the flat in Mayfair.

Youngblood went through the appointment book, starting with the beginning of November and working forward page by page. The appointments looked innocent enough, almost all different with just an occasional repeater. There was an exception. Several times during the month of November and the beginning of December, Rascher had pencilled in the letter 'P' at varying times of the day, lunchtimes once or twice a week, dinnertimes with the same frequency, the occasional weekend. Youngblood went back a further three months, and the same pattern was repeated. He asked Lichfield, who was sitting across from him chewing a nail, who 'P' stood for. Lichfield shrugged and said that he wasn't privy to such information, but believed that it was a young lady. He had caught a glimpse of her once in the outer office as Rascher escorted her to lunch.

Youngblood opened all the drawers and went through them one by one. In the bottom left-hand drawer, under a stack of *Business Week* magazines, he slid out an eight-by-ten glossy picture of a lovely blonde girl. He studied the face and decided that she would make a welcome addition to his bed. An inscription read, 'All my love, Pamela.' At least 'P' was explained. He wondered what had become of the girl, and how, if at all, she would fit in. He showed the picture to Lichfield, who confirmed that it was the girl he had seen. He rolled the picture loosely, and slipped it into his topcoat pocket. There was nothing else of interest in the drawers.

Youngblood took a taxi to the Mayfair flat and stopped for a brief conversation with the porter before going upstairs. He told the man that he'd been sent by the head office in America to go through Rascher's effects. He asked about visitors to the flat, but the porter was vague about arrivals and departures. Youngblood suspected that he spent a lot of time dozing in his cubby hole. He showed the man the picture of Pamela and recognition dawned in his dull eyes. He informed Youngblood that he had seen the girl on a half-dozen occasions over the last year, but didn't know anything about her or where she lived. Youngblood went up to the flat.

The apartment was silent and empty and already smelled of disuse. All the windows were closed and the air was stale. He examined the place minutely, looking for – he didn't know what.

When he reached the bedroom, he found the wall safe almost at once. It was locked, but that wouldn't present any great obstacle. It was a simple mechanism and Youngblood was a practised hand. He timed himself. It took him only thirteen minutes to work the combination. He reached inside, drew out a metal box and the object next to it – a velvet-wrapped bundle. He put the items on the bed, unfolded the velvet package first.

He knew in an instant why he'd come to London. As usual, his instincts had been infallible. One by one he lifted the framed pictures that had been so carefully wrapped. Most of them were portraits of Napoleon. He recognized them at once as miniatures by Jean Baptiste Isabey, who had painted numerous portraits of the Emperor. They were paintings that had supposedly been lost during the war. Youngblood's knowledge of art was considerable. He had always been interested in it, and when his fortunes increased, he started buying as an investment. He didn't consider himself an expert, but he was only a step or two from it, and so his guess about the miniatures was an educated one.

He opened the metal box with anticipation and wasn't disappointed. It looked like Rascher had squirrelled away several portable treasures as his own investment – against discovery.

The contents of the leather bag, when he undid the draw strings and spilled them on to the bed, glittered in a shaft of sunlight. He ran his fingers through the gems, smoothing out the pile so that they were all separated. Diamonds, blue-white, and all of three carats or more; deep-red rubies; emeralds; black star sapphires. The rest of the box contained sheaves of stamps, which he assumed were valuable – he was no expert – and bearer bonds that, when he made the exchange from Swiss francs, were worth about three hundred thousand dollars. There was also a sheet of paper with a neatly typed row of numbers, against which were various Swiss banks and recognition codes. Numbered accounts? He thought so. He folded the paper, put it in his inside breast pocket. He scooped up the gems, returned them to their bag and replaced them in the box. He sat down on the bed and lit a cigarette. He tingled all over, his forehead had broken out in beads of sweat. He tried to think the thing through. Would anybody but Rascher know of his secret horde? He doubted it, or else he would never have been given the keys to his flat and been allowed in on his own. Therefore, if nobody knew about them, by right of discovery, they were his. All of a sudden he felt very well disposed towards Rascher, and towards Sebastian, because he was directly responsible for this unexpected inheritance.

Youngblood found a bag in the kitchen, put his bundles in it, left the flat and the building without seeing the porter, and caught a cab for the Dorchester.

He felt better when he had all the items deposited in a safe in the Dorchester's strong-room. He found he couldn't get the smile off his face. Actually it was more of an ear-to-ear grin. He tried to control himself, but the muscles wouldn't go back into position. And so the taxi driver and everyone in the hotel, employees and guests alike, were treated to the American with the foolish grin on his face.

It was lunchtime and he felt like celebrating. He chortled his way into the dining room, and through eight ounces of caviar, a whole Chateaubriand, and the best bottle of Dom Perignon they had in the place. He left a lavish tip and almost skipped up to the room. At least, it felt like his feet hadn't touched the ground.

He changed into a blazer and slacks, replaced the tie with an Ascot, took his Aquascutum raincoat and went back out. This, he decided, was 'his day', and when the cards were running, you went for broke. If he was ever going to get a line on Sebastian, this was going to be the time.

He directed the taxi to take him to a pub he knew to be frequented by all the Fleet Street regulars. He, like Sebastian, knew the value of pretending to be a journalist. He was constantly amazed at what people told him because they thought he was going to write about it.

It was just after 2.00 when he entered the pub, and it was in full swing. The 'babble level' was high enough to hurt his eardrums. He shoved his way through to the bar, ordered a double whisky and then turned to the two men next to him, who were engaged in a conversation about the relative merits of bombing Vietnam into submission. He asked them what they wanted to drink and, when they looked at him like he'd just flown in from Mars on a tricycle, he laughed and told them he was celebrating on this, his 'lucky day' – a relative had died and left a substantial inheritance – not too far from the truth. They accepted the drinks and introduced themselves as reporters from the *Sunday Mirror*. Youngblood told them that he'd been sent in by *Newsweek* to do a follow-up story on those guys who were shot at the stable in Surrey. His editor thought that it sounded like a Mafia hit; had they heard anything more about it? The two journalists looked at each other, shrugged, and said, 'What the hell?' as *Newsweek* wasn't in direct competition with them. They could tell him what they had just found out and were saving for the Sunday edition. They'd heard from a police contact that, when the lab reports came back, one sample of blood on the ground hadn't matched any of the victims'. Conclusion: either there was a fourth guy who'd been wounded and got away, or the guy who'd done the shooting had been hit.

Youngblood kept the smile on his face although it felt frozen, and he did a lot of nodding. 'Hey, that's great stuff,' he said, and he meant it. He had that feeling again, certain knowledge without anything concrete to back it up. Sebastian had been wounded. He was sure of it. And that meant that he was probably still in England.

On a whim, he left the pub, found the nearest Hertz agency, rented a car – nice unobtrusive Vauxhall Victor, checked his route on a map and drove to Webster's office. He drove around for ten minutes looking for a parking space, finally found a vacant meter. His luck was still in, the entrance to the building was thirty feet ahead and he was on a one-way street, and the large parking lot, which had to be the one Webster would use, was also in front of him on the next corner.

Youngblood walked slowly past the building, then retraced his steps, entered. He walked over to the directory board as the porter looked on incuriously. The Sebastian Arms Corporation was listed in Room 718, and underneath it read 'Roger Webster – Managing Director'.

He re-entered the street and walked down a block, until he found a café with a pay telephone. He looked up the number for the Sebastian Arms Corporation, dialled it and told the girl who answered that he wanted to speak to Roger Webster. 'Kevin O'Reilly,' was the response to the girl's question of who was calling. A man came on the line and identified himself as Webster.

'Mr Webster,' Youngblood began in an Irish accent that jumped back and forth across the border at almost every syllable, 'I represent some people who want to purchase a large quantity of arms.'

Webster was non-committal. 'Oh, yes?'

'That's the truth,' Youngblood continued. 'They're willing to pay cash, I mean a lot of cash. The extra is so that they don't have to get involved with a lot of paperwork. Nobody likes that, do they?'

'Mister Oh-Ri-ley,' Webster enunciated every syllable and his tone was as frosty as liquid oxygen, 'the Sebastian Arms Corporation is a highly legitimate company. We don't do business that way. Good-day.' The connection was severed.

Youngblood put his own phone down with a smile. It was such a dumb trick and it worked every time. Now that he knew Webster was in, he would wait.

Webster came out of the building at 5.00, part of a stream of secretaries and executives. Youngblood recognized him from the picture in *Fortune* magazine that Naumann had provided. He started the car, let it idle, watched Webster, who paused at the kerb, looked up and down the street with quick jerks of his head, then turned towards the parking lot.

Webster walked the block to pick up his car, trying to notice everybody, and feeling foolish about it. Sebastian had tried to get him to stay away from the Chelsea flat, and when Webster baulked and remained resolutely obstinate, Sebastian tried to impress the basic rules of security on him. He tried to give him a crash course in surveillance techniques, how to spot a tail, how to lose one. Webster was attentive, nodded and agreed to follow all the rules. He was unable to tell Sebastian that he thought the whole thing sounded like melodramatic clap-trap. He remembered the danger he'd been in, and like any solid citizen who had few personal experiences with the seamier side of life, dismissed it as a once in a lifetime proposition. Nothing like that could happen twice.

Still, he did try to follow Sebastian's instructions. He found that he was staring at people and averted his eyes guiltily when they stared back. How was he expected to recognize anyone who seemed to have a special interest in him? They all looked like normal everyday people going about their business. He felt ridiculous at the way he was acting, and each succeeding day his watchfulnes decreased. If it hadn't happened by now, it wasn't going to. So he never noticed the car that followed him all the way to the flat in Chelsea.

Webster eased his two-year-old Aston Martin into a parking space, careful to avoid scratching the car. Youngblood had seen him slow down and pulled into the kerb fifty yards back. Webster got out of the car, did his little act jerking his head from side to side to see who was on the street. It looked very comical from where Youngblood sat.

As Webster went up the steps to the building and entered it, Youngblood moved the car closer. He was just in time to see a light go on in the first floor apartment, and a moment later, Webster passing by the window. There was barely enough time for that to register when another car pulled up and a small, bearded man headed for the building with a bag in his hand, and a few seconds later he, too, passed in front of the window.

Youngblood got out and shut the door softly behind him, went over to where the elderly Morris was parked. One glance at the windshield confirmed his hunch about the man and the bag he was carrying. In the lower left-hand corner was a sticker that said 'Doctor' and the permission to park anywhere. Youngblood returned to his car, lit a cigarette and tried to figure out how serious Sebastian's injuries could be, when there was a doctor making a house call. He was now convinced that Sebastian had been wounded in the shoot-out. He was in the middle of puzzling it all out when the entrance door to the building opened and a girl came down the steps and into the street. Her face was illuminated by the street lights, and Youngblood straightened up to take a good look, but he didn't need one. He recognized her immediately as the girl whose picture he had found in Rascher's desk, the girl named Pamela.

Everything fell into place for Youngblood at that moment, the presence of the girl at the apartment where he now knew Sebastian to be, the cast on her arm, the pale bruises on her face. He couldn't be sure of everything, and he could write a dozen scenarios with slightly altered story lines, but they would all come down to the same conclusion. Somehow Sebastian had met the girl, an obvious way to get to Rascher, and somehow Rascher had found out about it. That the Nazi had beaten her up, broken her arm, was a certainty. Perhaps the girl had been the bait to lure Sebastian into the Surrey countryside. Whatever lever Rascher had used, Youngblood was as sure as night follows day, that it had happened that way. Sebastian's wounds had probably resulted because of spur-of-the-moment improvisation. He wouldn't have had any time to plan, and Rascher wouldn't have given him any. The fact that Sebastian won, despite all the odds against him, came as no surprise to Youngblood. From what he already knew of the man, he was tough, capable, able to think on his feet.

There was a breathless moment of time as all the facts and conjectures were fed in, played ping-pong in his brain cells and came to rest in the front of his mind with the word 'decision' written in big, fat letters. Youngblood could take him out whenever he wanted. One call to Naumann would get him a weapon. He supposed that it wouldn't be too difficult to get the 9 mm Ingram which he'd used before, although he personally preferred the Uzi. But he was pretty sure that using an Israeli gun wouldn't sit too well with Naumann.

It would be a simple matter to break into the apartment and catch Sebastian unawares. And if there was anyone else there, well, that was too bad. He calculated. He could have the job finished by tomorrow, collect his fee, go off on his ski trip, which had begun to look doubtful.

Skiing set off a whole new train of thought. It was high on his list of priorities, something that he really wanted to do. He hadn't intended to take on any assignments until after his return from Aspen, but this one had looked too good to pass up. It wasn't the money, it was the challenge. He finally had a chance to come to grips with an adversary who had his level of expertise.

If he went ahead with his plans, it would be too easy. There wasn't any fun in winning, and little skill needed when the other guy was lying flat on his back. He would be disappointed, and knew that he would regret it for the rest of his life. He needed the stimulus, and if he went ahead as planned, he would just be cheating himself. Maybe there was another way.

He had it in a flash, and the beauty of it was so startling that he burst out laughing. He knew what to do now. He rolled down the window, tossed the butt out, started the car, and drove to the Dorchester.

Youngblood caught the night flight to Zürich, checked into the Dolder Grand, went to bed, sleeping the sleep of the just, and rose early.

He was no stranger to Zürich. It was the best place to lose large amounts of unaccountable cash, and provided the most anonymous way of doing it. His numbered account had been in operation for five years, and the bank was his first stop. He rented a safety deposit box and put in the pictures, gems and bearer bonds.

He chose a small bank from the list of accounts he'd found in Rascher's safe, and went in warily. As it transpired, there was nothing to worry about, and his caution evaporated, replaced by euphoria. The prune-faced clerk never gave him a second glance after he filled out a slip with the account number and proper signature, but returned in moments, with the current statement of the account written in neatly on the piece of paper. Youngblood kept his face neutral, but his stomach did a flip-flop when he saw the figure, three hundred and eighty thousand Swiss francs. He wrote out a withdrawal slip for two hundred thousand, asked to be given large denomination notes, and stuffed the bills in his pocket. He left the bank with his heart beating hard. It had been very easy, and he'd made an instant decision about the withdrawal. There was a better than even chance that Rascher was the only one who knew about these particular accounts, but why take chances. Maybe his wife knew about them. He doubted it. It was more likely that the other two Germans knew about the accounts and just hadn't thought about liberating the money, as they had more pressing concerns. What was obvious was that he just couldn't leave the money sitting there, and he didn't think his withdrawal would attract any special attention to him. If he found out that it was safe, he would go back for the rest of it. In the meantime, he had a full day's work ahead of him.

He stopped in the first luggage shop he could find and bought a briefcase. He transferred the money from his pocket to the case and went to the next bank on the list.

Twelve banks on the list. He had visited them all. The least amount in any account was one hundred and twenty-five thousand francs, the most, in excess of one and a half million. He had withdrawn approximately half the money from all the accounts, except the biggest one, where he had satisfied himself with a withdrawal of three hundred and fifty thousand. He was still afraid to draw too much attention to himself. He deposited all the notes into his own account and made his way back to the hotel.

It was below freezing, and the wind that gusted down the narrow street and whipped the branches of the horse chestnut trees made it seem colder. It was even worse in the open squares. Rush-hour was on, and every taxi he saw was occupied, so he plodded on through dirty snow that had turned to slush in places, black ice in others. He arrived at the hotel just before 6.00 and went to the bar for something to get rid of the chill, and to think.

It was a smallish room as bars go, dimly lit and cosy. Some sort of dark wood panelled the walls, a real fire with real wood crackled in the grate. Most of the tables were taken, almost exclusively by men. Swiss businessmen looking very uniform with short haircuts, dark suits and ties, bending elbows rhythmically with tumbler-size glasses. All conversation seemed to be conducted in gutteral Swiss–German.

Youngblood took an unoccupied table for two in the corner, seated himself on the banquette that faced the room, and ordered a double Scotch when the waiter hurried over. He just had time to take off his overcoat when it arrived. He grabbed the glass, took a large swallow, and let the spirit burn its way down.

He relaxed and thought of the events of the day. There had been no time to do that until now. He had felt under intense pressure, going from bank to bank, withdrawing money under the scrutiny of dour Swiss tellers, always afraid that they would challenge him. None had. He searched for an analogy, and found it in the animal kingdom. His mouth twisted into a smile. He was like a goddam squirrel, foraging in bountiful lands, and returning the horde to his own hidey-hole for a rainy-day.

The point was that when he added it all up – the money in the accounts, the paintings, the gems and the bearer bonds, he was well and truly a goddam millionaire in good old American greenbacks. He could tell the two Krauts to take a flying fuck on a leprous llama. He didn't need their bread.

He thought of all the things he could do, all the dreams and fantasies he'd nurtured over the years that had been relegated to some unspecified future time. Like buying a Land Rover, and driving the whole length of Africa from north to south, taking four months to do it. Or having his own boat, at least a sixty-footer, and floating among the South Sea islands, staying as long as he wanted on a Pacific paradise, sailing away when the mood took him. He would never have to work another day in his life. He could retire from his 'trade' and just disappear.

He became aware that his glass was empty of whisky, a solitary ice cube tinkling against the side, as he moved his hand. The level of conversation from the other patrons broke through his concentration, intruded into his consciousness. He countered with an almost inaudible, 'shit'. He spotted the red-coated waiter, who hovered expectantly near the doorway, caught his eye, signalled for another drink with upraised glass. He lit a cigarette, and sighed the smoke out through pursed lips.

It was a terrific dream. The only problem with it was that he would be bored to death. He might as well dig a hole and pull it in after him, for all the pleasure he would get out of just enjoying himself.

So the Sebastian assignment would still be on. Maybe after it was over he would think again.

Chapter Fifteen

On the plane back to Los Angeles, Youngblood did a lot of staring out of the window. There was very little to be seen at 35,000 feet, and cloud-cover ensured that even major landmarks would be obscured. So when, at odd times during the flight, Youngblood began to giggle for no apparent reason, the very straight executive-type sitting next to him edged further away at each outburst. Eventually he got the stewardess to change his seat.

They met in Naumann's office on top of the bank building in Wilshire Boulevard in Beverly Hills, a suave Naumann looking as ice-cool as his eyes, a nervous Spitzweg fidgeting on the edge of his seat, and Youngblood in a beige suit and open-necked turquoise shirt, looking like a Hollywood PR man.

'Well,' Naumann demanded. 'What did you find?' Spitzweg looked eager and hopeful, waiting for the answer.

'What I expected. Nothing.'

Spitzweg was crestfallen. His face crumpled. He looked as if he was going to cry.

'There is no trace of Sebastian. My guess is that he is already here.'

Spitzweg took a nervous glance over his shoulder as if he expected Sebastian to come flying in through the window.

'Didn't you find out anything?' Naumann persisted. He pressed on without waiting for an answer. 'I have alerted my organization, and they are putting as many men on to it as they can spare to locate Sebastian. Nothing yet. I told them to leave his office and apartment to you so that no clues would be disturbed.'

Youngblood masked the sudden rush of warm gratitude he felt for Naumann. His worst fears were allayed at one stroke. It was apparent that Naumann was so concerned, that he had not even thought about what Rascher might have hidden away . . . where he could find it. It was even probable that Naumann didn't know about Rascher's secret banking arrangements or the other items. Certainly, he would have expected Rascher to have made arrangements, that would be normal, and just as normal for Rascher to have kept it to himself. If his beneficiaries didn't bitch, and Youngblood thought that probably meant his wife, then Naumann would never know. And if she did complain, well so what. No one could prove that he had anything to do with it. He thought of the money he had left in Rascher's accounts, and promised himself to make those withdrawals at the earliest opportunity.

'I didn't find anything. I went through his office and apartment from top to bottom. If your buddy knew anything about Sebastian, he sure as hell didn't write it down.'

Youngblood managed to keep his face straight, but the twinkle in his eye would have been a dead giveaway. Naumann was too agitated to see it. 'I've had the devil's own time trying to smooth things out. I've had the police on to me again, and Scotland Yard sent over their man.'

'What did you tell them?'

'As plausible a story as I could manage under the circumstances. I suggested that Rascher and his driver were kidnapped and were being held for ransom, and that my dear colleague died heroically in a vain attempt to free himself from his captors. He managed to get one, that explains the third body, and was killed for his trouble. Fortunately, the trainer – what was his name, Willis? – never saw him and was unable to contradict my version of the story.'

'Ah, but your speech about lawlessness in Britain was a masterpiece,' Spitzweg said, mopping his face with a handkerchief.

Naumann glared at Spitzweg with contempt. 'My speech

didn't cover several points. I doubt that it even confused the issue for very long. Those officers were not stupid. Didn't you notice how the Scotland Yard inspector looked at me? He was mocking me. He knew I was lying when I made that self-righteous speech. The only reason that he allowed me to get away with it was because he couldn't prove it.'

'What did they know?' Youngblood asked.

'They knew enough to ask awkward questions. They hinted at a conspiracy involving me. I have never felt so vulnerable. I didn't like it.'

'Bet your ass, you didn't – when you're used to being on the other end.' That was a random thought from Youngblood. He left it unspoken.

'It was the inspector from Scotland Yard who did most of the talking. He asked me if I knew why Swift had gone to the stables in the middle of the night and why there was a Mauser pistol lying on the ground that had this very same Swift's fingerprints all over it. I said it was completely beyond me. And then he wanted to know how long I had known this Mr Swift, a German gentleman, he said, wasn't he? But not a German name. I told him we had known each other for many years because, of course, we were officers in the same corporation. It was at this point that he became impertinent. He said, "You're a German also, sir, aren't you? Did you meet in your home country?" And when I told him no, that I was Swiss and we had met there, he had the audacity to raise an eyebrow and say, "Oh, really?"'

Naumann was fidgety. He moved backwards and forwards on the seat, swivelling it to emphasize a point. The more he talked, the angrier he became, face colouring. He shot out of the chair and started pacing, hands clasped behind his back. His footfalls made no sound on the thick pile carpet as he stalked around the large office like a caged leopard. 'Then he went on to the third man who was killed. He had been identified as some fellow called Jack Poggins, an enforcer who hired himself out to provide protection and collect debts with menaces, as he put it. He said it was unlikely that he would go in for kidnapping. It was out of his line. And so the obvious conclusion to that bit of information was that this Poggins was hired by my friend, Swift, and did I know why he should require the services of such a person. I said that whatever he concluded, it was highly unlikely that my colleague would hire a crook, and that the whole catastrophe was a mystery to me, and I was terribly distressed about it. That is when he springs his question to catch me out. Did I know about the note found on the body?'

Youngblood cut in on the rambling dissertation. 'A note? What note? What did it say?'

'The same as the first time. There were four names on it and a date. Two of the names were crossed out, Schmidt and Rascher.'

'The first time? Schmidt?'

Naumann sighed. He returned to his chair and sat down heavily, folded his hands in front of him, rested them on the desk. The interlocked fingers twitched. With a deliberate movement, he separated his hands, reached into his breast pocket and withdrew a cigarette case. He flipped it open. The top made a dull thud as it landed on the leather pad; it was the only sound in the room. The gold case was shiny and warm against the hickory brown leather. He took out a cigarette, held it between thumb and forefinger, tapped an end on the desk, lit it with a lighter in a crystal cube. 'There was another one – before this. A few weeks ago – someone we knew – our names were on that note also.'

'And you never told me,' Youngblood chided gently.

'There was no need. You were hired for a specific job and I told you as much as I deemed necessary. You already know more about us than I care for.'

'Well, I probably know more than I care for – except that you seem to have left out something important. Tell me about this guy, Schmidt.'

Naumann told him what he knew about the incident in Bremen, and said that they had known Schmidt during the war and for a few years afterwards, but that he had then dropped out of sight and was never heard of again until he turned up dead.

'What's the connection?' Youngblood asked.

Naumann flushed, he was angry, 'That Sebastian is a misguided maniac. He blames four of us for the death of his parents. Now he is trying to kill us all.'

It was easy for Naumann to think of it in those terms. He had convinced himself that it was Robert Sebastian's fault for coming home when he did, reacting like he did. If guilt were to be found, it would be placed squarely on Sebastian's shoulders. He viewed the whole thing as a distressing accident for which he felt no responsibility. Blood drained from Spitzweg's face. It turned the colour of putty. He managed to look appalled.

Youngblood listened in silence, reading between the lines. And there was plenty to be read there. He guessed that all the doors on these particular memories had been kept locked and bolted for a good number of years. It certainly explained a lot about Sebastian. He thought of him as he knew him in college, the one he envied. He could see him now from a totally new perspective. It was like watching a puppet show where all the painted dolls were dressed in magnificent costumes, talking and reacting to each other without hesitation, and then sneaking backstage while the show was still in progress to see – with horror – that not everything was as it appeared – that the puppets, perfect in dress and action, were being manipulated by a couple of balding old men with warts, unshaven faces, foreheads slicked with sweat, ragged shirts and dirty jeans.

He tried to remember his brief conversations with Sebastian, re-evaluate them in the light of his new knowledge.

Naumann shifted in his chair, stubbed out the cigarette in a large glass ashtray, lit another. 'I told them, of course, that I hadn't any idea of what the note was. Rascher's name was listed as that, not Swift . . . and the rest of the names aren't the ones used today. I'm sure that the Scotland Yard man didn't believe a word of it, but that's his problem. He won't be able to prove it.' There was a long pause. 'That's it. Rascher was a fool. The last time I spoke to him he sounded hysterical, like an old woman. It coloured his judgement and got him killed. I cannot understand how one man, this Sebastian, was able to kill three others and disappear into thin air.'

'Perhaps because he's good,' Youngblood said softly.

'What?'

'Maybe because he's a professional. I don't suppose that that crossed your mind.'

Naumann's face underwent a range of expressions. 'A professional.' It was a new thought and an uncomfortable one. He opened the left-hand bottom drawer of his desk, took out a green folder, set it on the desk in front of him, opened it. From where he sat, Youngblood could see that there were three or four closely typed sheets of paper, clipped together. Naumann ran a finger down the top sheet as he read, flipped it over and followed the same procedure for the rest of the pages. He refolded the pages, closed the folder, rested the palm of his hand on the top of it. He stared with unfocused eyes across the room, hummed softly to himself, then, 'A professional,' he said. 'Yes, very possible. And the question certainly must be asked . . . is this his chosen occupation – or has he trained himself . . . for us?'

Naumann picked up the folder and handed it across the desk to Youngblood. 'This is additional information on Sebastian. There are still many gaps but, in the light of your suggestion, a certain pattern emerges. Read it.'

Youngblood opened the folder and placed it on his lap. The first page was concerned with a summation of Sebastian's early life. Youngblood knew most of it from the earlier dossier, but this was an expanded version. The investigator had interviewed Gerry Beaver, who was still an instructor at the school, and had traced three of the boys who had been Sebastian's classmates. Beaver had recalled for the investigator how Sebastian had never spoken a word until he had reached the age of ten. And then how he had mysteriously begun to speak in unending streams of words. Beaver had never known what had triggered the change, and was so gratified that he never questioned it. It was almost as if Sebastian had been two different people – uninterested, listless, malleable, while he was silent, and keen, dedicated, at times almost truculent in his eagerness, afterwards. Sebastian had thrown himself into every project with reckless abandon, as if he knew how much time he had lost and was making up for it. He sopped up knowledge like a sponge and set out to acquire skills with complete concentration and devotion to detail. He had started with jujitsu, and at the end of three years had learned everything Beaver could teach him. He proved to be an excellent athlete and became outstanding at football, basketball and baseball, although he never seemed able to learn the team concept. He never depended on his teammates for support, in fact, actively rejected it. His teams won, but he was never accepted into its camaraderie. He remained aloof and unreachable, but was evidently respected. As one of his classmates related ruefully, that was probably because he could back it up. He told the investigator how he and two others had started a deliberate fight with Sebastian, and how he wound up with a broken arm for his trouble.

Sebastian excelled at individual sports, fencing and shooting in particular. As the head of the Gustavus Adolphus Academy was an old military man, he encouraged his charges to learn the skills that had been so much a part of his own life. Sebastian would bang away for as long as he would be allowed on the shooting range, and became a crack shot with both rifle and pistol.

The academic side of his life received just as much attention. He studied hard for every subject he took. Youngblood noted that after only a year of French and German, both of which languages were taken simultaneously, Sebastian had amazed his instructors by being very nearly fluent in both, and showed that he also had an excellent ear for accents.

Youngblood turned the page. Half of it listed Sebastian's other accomplishments at the Academy. Straight A's in maths, science and literature. In fact, straight A's in everything he had set his hand to. He left the Academy at seventeen and enrolled at UCLA.

That brought Youngblood on to more familiar ground and he read with interest how the boy he had envied breezed through college, making the Dean's list, making everything he tried for. The investigator had been thorough and reported how Sebastian had been rushed by practically every fraternity on campus, and how he had rejected them all, preferring to remain on his own. He had maintained an apartment in Westwood Village, near to the university. There was a parenthetical note from the investigator about how Sebastian's monthly allowance from a trust fund had permitted him to do anything he wanted. The apartment was an expensive one for a student, and he also ran a new Olds convertible.

Sebastian's personal life during this period was sketchy. The investigator editorialized that the reason for this was that Sebastian kept himself to himself. He was unable to find anyone with whom he had associated for any length of time, or for that matter, any girl with whom he had had an affair, no matter how brief. There were whispers that Sebastian had entertained girls on a fairly regular basis, but he had not been able to confirm that.

Youngblood stopped reading and lost himself in thought,

oblivious to Naumann and Spitzweg, who watched him intently. He tried to reconstruct in his mind all the times he had seen Sebastian on and off campus, whether or not any other person entered the picture. His visualizations flitted from the football field to the bookshop on Westwood Boulevard, to the Bruin film theatre to the local hamburger hangout. He had a clear picture of Sebastian, but he was always on his own. He remembered the Olds convertible. It was a metallic blue and had whitewall tyres and was another thing he envied about Sebastian. He could see no one else in the car.

The dossier continued with the rest of Sebastian's college activities, and was careful to note that he had never joined any club, association, service organization or even any regular social gathering. The paragraph ended with Sebastian's graduation, a Bachelor's in Psychology.

Youngblood paused again. That was how they'd met. They had many of the same classes. He had wondered at the time what Sebastian was going to do after graduation. He could easily have gone on for his PhD. He had a four-point grade average and every instructor in the place rooting for him. Youngblood had once overheard two of his professors discussing Sebastian. One had told the other that the boy was the smartest student he'd ever had and that he could go on to great things. There was absolute agreement. Youngblood remembered his anger when he listened to the conversation. Sebastian here stating that he had kept up his lessons in martial arts while he had to work his ass off to achieve lesser results. Now he knew why Sebastian had not pursued a further degree. He glanced at Naumann, who was lighting another cigarette. Now he understood a lot of things about what motivated him.

According to the investigator, the new graduate went off to England, where he spent several months learning the finer points of horsemanship, with only one side trip during the period. Sebastian competed at Bisley and won two trophies for pistol shooting and small bore rifles.

From there he went to New York where he enrolled in the Actors' Studio and spent the next couple of years going to school and appearing in various theatrical productions.

Sebastian spent the time he wasn't acting enrolled in another school that taught him printing and graphic art. Youngblood raised an eyebrow.

From New York, the investigator had traced him to Japan where he lived for three years at Kyoto. There was another note here stating that he had kept up his lessons in martial arts while in university, where he had switched to karate and judo. The three years in Japan were spent with a karate master, where he achieved a fourth degree black belt.

He returned to Los Angeles in 1963 and was resident for a year, working briefly for the family company and two other jobs not specified, then left suddenly for Europe. The next four years were like a travel agency's dream come true. Sebastian began his odyssey in Paris and went from there to most of the countries in Europe, Asia and Africa. The investigator had lost track on several occasions but had always managed to pick it up again. It appeared that the longest Sebastian stayed anywhere was three weeks, most often a shorter period. Then in early 1968, the investigator lost him in Brussels, this time for good. The period between then and the time he turned up in Bremen was a blank. Youngblood closed the folder and smiled.

'Interesting,' he said.

'Well, what are we supposed to do now? What kind of man are we dealing with?'

'I'll answer both of those, but I'll take your last question first.' Youngblood chuckled. 'I don't think you are going to like what I'm going to tell you. You gotta understand that I'm trying to do a psychoanalysis on somebody I only knew casually and haven't seen for years, so there might be a couple of things that are wrong, but nothing basic, and this,' he tapped the folder with a fingernail, 'confirms it. We're dealing with a paranoid, but in a special sense of the word. This is a man with an obsession. From all the clues provided by the dossier, and based on my personal contact, Sebastian is a guy with only one thing in mind – revenge. Other than that, he's an essentially normal human being. I guess we could argue for hours about what "normal" means, but for now let's take it in the accepted sense of the word, that is, well adjusted without any marked mental aberrations that we know about. He's a man with a mission, a zealot without any of the religious hang-ups. He is a loner, but not a sociopath. He participates in normal social intercourse when he wants to. My guess is that his emotional stability is way above average. He's trained himself for it. Once he'd made up his mind, it would be difficult to make him change it. He'd have to be absolutely convinced that he was wrong and would require twenty-four carat proof. You want more?'

Naumann looked down his nose at Youngblood with disdain. 'It appears as if this paragon of manhood impresses you enough for it to be termed as a love affair.'

Youngblood's mouth lifted into its sardonic smile. 'I said that you wouldn't like it.'

'Let us discuss more practical matters. What are you going to do about it? What are we supposed to be doing in the meantime?'

Youngblood let the question hang. He took a cigarette out of the pack he had in his jacket pocket and lit it with a Zippo that had a Marine Corps insignia embossed on it. He squinted through the smoke at Naumann. The man with the matinée idol face and livid scar stared back at him. 'The pompous, arrogant asshole,' Youngblood thought. The contempt for these Nazis that he'd felt at first meeting, ran deep enough to break through to China. He realized the vaunted organization of ex-Nazis was nothing but a bunch of old men, toothless and ineffectual. They were whiners. He couldn't imagine how men like these had at one time been in a position to conquer the world. For the first time, he had a clear idea of why his services had been sought and why they hadn't quibbled over the exorbitant fee he had demanded. Naumann knew – maybe wouldn't admit – but knew that his organization was incapable of doing the job. He found himself rooting for Sebastian. That was a dangerous thought.

'Well, I'll tell you,' Youngblood said, 'you and the other one,' he indicated Spitzweg, 'if you stay here, you'll be like sitting ducks. Sebastian's got all the advantages. He knows where you are and you don't know when he's coming. So I want you to disappear for a couple of weeks. You're a big man in Mexico, right? Go to Acapulco or Puerta Vallarta. Take a house out of the way and stay in it. There should be plenty to keep you busy – sunshine, *margaritas*, hot-eyed *señoritas*.'

'And what are you going to do?' Naumann's tone was acid.

'Me? I'm going to be here. Well, I don't mean in the house, but near by.' He slipped into his drawl. 'Just awaitin' and a watchin'. I've got to assume that Sebastian follows a pattern.

Looks like he reconnoitres his ground real well. He thinks he's a fox hunting the chickens. He'll stalk them real good and pounce when he's ready. Except that the chickens won't be in the coop, and what he's going to find instead is old farmer Brown with a double barrelled shotgun, who's going to blow his fucking head off.'

'Where will you be?'

'Don' worry about it. Around. I'll see him before he sees me and that'll be the last thing he ever sees.'

Spitzweg looked at Naumann with pleading in his eyes. 'What do you think, Carl, sounds good, doesn't it?'

Naumann let a full half-minute elapse. He stood up and walked to the window, gazed down at the traffic crawling along Wilshire Boulevard fifteen floors below. 'All right,' he agreed grudgingly, 'I can't think of anything better, and I might be able to utilize the time profitably. How will I contact you?'

Youngblood's reply was bland. 'You won't. This is field work, man. I'm not going to be near a phone. You leave me a number where I can contact you, and I'll call every couple of days to let you know what's happening.'

'How long do you think we'll have to be there?' Spitzweg asked.

'Well, shit, I don't know. As long as it takes. Couldn't be more than two or three weeks.'

Youngblood chuckled to himself all the way down in the elevator, received a terse message from Naumann the following day with a number in Acapulco. Two days after that, he left for Aspen.

True to his word, every couple of days, Youngblood called the number in Acapulco and reported to Naumann that there was nothing to report. Once he made the call while sitting on the side of his bed – the phone in one hand, the other cradling the bare breast of an athletic co-ed from Brigham Young University – and thought there was nothing so wild as a devout Mormon. And a couple of days later, he lay on his back talking to Naumann, while a girl who looked so much like Lolita that it made him ache with desire every time he turned his eyes on her, held his cock in her mouth, soft curtain of hair covering her face and spread all over his belly as she serviced him. When she pushed the hair aside and looked at him with those big blue eyes that sparkled with mischief, he came right in the middle of telling Naumann how much he was on the job.

And so the New Year came and went, with the tension mounting daily for Naumann, Spitzweg almost in a state of nervous collapse, and for Youngblood in perfect bliss.

Chapter Sixteen

It was a blissful period for Sebastian also. At least it had started out that way.

It began with Webster saying, 'See, a week's gone by and not a hint of trouble, and I guarantee you if anyone had been interested in me I would have spotted him in a second.'

Sebastian was distracted. 'Sure, sure,' he said. He was hobbling around the lounge exercising his leg. Every time he put pressure on it, a shooting pain travelled from his toes to his shoulder, but he gritted his teeth and continued. A fine cold sweat broke out on his forehead.

The lounge was compact and was a typical example of the room in a building planned by a conspiracy of modern architecture, box-like. It had plaster walls that the owner had painted pale coral and low ceilings covered with some sort of accoustical tile that was supposed to deaden the noise that came from the neighbours above, but never did. A thick white carpet ran from wall to wall. It made pacing very difficult and exercise almost impossible.

Sebastian had to keep close to the wall, passing the doorway to the bedroom, then make a sharp left at the corner where he had to squeeze behind the brown leather couch with stainless steel arms and legs to the next corner, left again, avoiding a television set that sat in front of the window, then circling behind a matching leather chair in the corner, and in front of an oval teak table with a lamp on it, being careful to avoid the wire, then behind the second chair, and back to where he started.

He stopped and glared at Webster. 'Rog, I'm starting to go

stir-crazy. Do you know how many times I've made that walk?' Webster shook his head. 'I don't either, but one helluva lot of times. I know every crack that the painters missed in this room, and where the cleaning lady piles up the dust in the corner behind the couch. I've gotta get out of here.'

'That's what I was going to tell you,' Webster said. 'A friend of mine just lent me his cottage in Buckinghamshire. He's going off skiing for a month.'

'You sure have a lot of friends,' Sebastian said acidly, 'this place, Buckinghamshire . . .'

'Hey, I know people, don't knock it. You'll love this cottage, it's right on the river, between Henley and Marlow.'

Sebastian thought about it. 'When do we leave?'

'How about tonight?'

Sebastian smiled, hobbled over and clapped Webster on the back. 'Now you're talking, Rog. Does Pamela know?'

'No, I thought you'd like to tell her.' Sebastian told her when she came in later. She was delighted, hugged him with her one good arm, and set about packing what they would need.

The first few days were fine. Sebastian was getting used to the cottage which he thought of as 'cute'. A slanting tiled roof sat on top of the red brick house that was built in the Tudor style, although he was sure that it had been constructed in the last twenty years. The rooms were small, but there were wooden beams and a fireplace, and a French window gave out on to a flagstone path that sloped down to a small boathouse, where the Thames meandered in both directions. Sebastian took walks, aided by a cane and went further each day. Finally, he threw the cane away and forced himself to put pressure on his injured leg. The muscles protested and tightened up from the abuse, but Pamela was there to ease the pain with liniments, and to take his mind off it in other ways. She was a talented bed partner and could do things with her pelvis and tongue that were graphically described in barrack room ballads or were the subject of locker-room gossip.

How had she achieved such expertise? Sebastian wondered. Was she really an experienced courtesan or an enthusiastic amateur? It was difficult to tell in the privacy of the bedroom and more so out of it. Sebastian felt that he was constantly kept off balance, whether by design or not . . . Pamela treated him like a king, a baby, an invalid. She was submissive and dominant by turns, desirous and giving. Sebastian remembered the stories he had read about mythical succubus, who sucked out the life juices and spirit of a man, leaving him without resolve, eventually leaving an empty husk. It left him vaguely unsettled.

Pamela was taking over, and it was obvious that she took on situations where she lacked experience. Every time he made a mild protest, she pouted.

Sebastian wondered if the attitude was because of her relationship with Rascher. What was it she had said at their first meeting at Trader Vic's? – 'he thinks that I should just sit around like some damn doll, all dressed up with nowhere to go and wait until he calls'. Obviously Rascher had been very much in control. What was this then – the classic form of rebellion? He pondered the question. If she had been kept under the German's thumb for all those years she would be ready to break out. 'And I've been elected,' though Sebastian ruefully.

He wondered if she ever thought about Rascher. By unspoken agreement they had never talked about the German's death, although the papers had been full of it and television had played it up big. She'd never asked him what had happened in the Surrey countryside, or how everyone had come to be there or what part he had played in the massacre. Sebastian wondered if she had any feelings about Rascher or ever had, whether she felt any remorse.

Out with the old, in with the new. Sebastian chided himself for being too hard on the girl. He admitted, grudgingly, that perhaps that line of thinking was just a subterfuge to lead him away from the real heart of the matter, his feelings for Pamela. The thoughts slid away like quicksilver and found a deep burrow. 'What's really bugging me,' he thought dishonestly, 'is all this taking-over crap.'

There was Christmas Day, for example, when the Websters came down for lunch. Fortunately, they were early enough for Claire Webster to save a series of culinary blunders from becoming a total disaster. Even then, the turkey was dry and the stuffing watery.

Sebastian shrugged helplessly at Webster. He had more than enough time on his hands and had offered to take on the cooking, but Pamela had turned the suggestion down flat. Cooking, she maintained, was *her* job, and the kitchen was no place for a man. Even with only one good arm, she stressed with implied martyrdom, she could handle it. What was a man supposed to know about cooking? – a remark that Sebastian thought was peculiarly sexist, as he happened to be a gourmet cook, and had tried to tell her so. She took no notice.

He started to do some light jogging. He kept his thoughts on other things. It helped to keep the pain at bay, but it was also disturbing.

He began to have doubts about his relationship with Pamela. He had never lived with a girl before, never had the desire to. He was not in the habit of sharing his problems and emotions with another human being, especially a female. He was a dedicated loner and no woman had ever broken through the barrier. Many had tried, but his philosophy about women up till now was that they were soft, cuddly, smelled good, and provided an outlet for certain physical needs. He was an attractive man, and in the past he had had women of all shapes and descriptions throwing themselves at him.

Especially the time when he was doing his theatrical bit, studying in New York and doing summer stock in New England. Aspiring actresses, many of them beautiful, had been neatly side-stepped when their amorous advances had become too blatant. Many times they were rejected out of hand, so that Sebastian was ultimately labelled a cold, unfeeling bastard who was also probably a fag. He hadn't minced the tag, but continued as he always had, using women to acquire yet another skill.

He remembered the first time in vivid colours and textures. He had just turned fifteen and was almost six feet tall, and his frame had filled out to one hundred and seventy pounds of muscle.

He was a little surprised when a light olive-skinned boy, with terminal acne, sidled up to him one day at the school cafeteria and asked, in true gangster fashion out of the side of his mouth, if he'd like to 'bang this broad'. It was set up for that night after lights out, when the two of them would meet the girl at her house, about a mile from the school. Sebastian was surprised, because the boy, whose name was Freddy, was in another cabin and in the two years he'd been there, he doubted that more than a couple of dozen words had been exchanged. But he thought it over. He thought of asking, 'Why me?', but refrained and instead thought about being fifteen and a virgin. Was it so terrible? Could he wait until he was sixteen, or even seventeen? He could, but why bother? Here was an opportunity for an experience, one that might elude him for some indeterminate time. And he might as well take advantage of it while he could. So he agreed to go.

Lights out was at 10.30, and in another half-hour, Sebastian could hear the deep breathing of his roommates. He eased out of bed, dressed quietly, and tiptoed out of the door.

The cabin was tenth in line of a double row of fifteen that was separated by a cement walkway. He slipped around to the back to where there was a narrow dirt path between the cabins and a wood, and soft-footed his way to cabin number four, counting as he went by trailing a finger on the weathered timbers. There was just enough light to see by, where the moon filtered through the trees. It was deathly quiet. Even the wind that usually sighed in the branches was still. He found Freddy waiting and nervous. The boy put a finger to his lips, showed Sebastian the flashlight he was holding, and nodded for him to follow.

They came out in the open and flitted like wraiths to the protection of the classroom building, gave the teachers' quarters a wide berth, and arrived at the south gate without mishap. They climbed the fence and turned west along the road that would eventually meet with the Pacific Ocean.

The road was pitch black, the white dividing line showing faintly in the moonlight as it ran between stands of old elms and chestnuts and the occasional house. When they were far enough from the school, Freddy switched on the flashlight and kept its wavering beam pointed at the ground a few feet in front of him. It was eerie being out like that at night. Small sounds of scuttering things were all that he could hear, and a chorus of crickets, and Freddy's nervous breathing that sounded asthmatic. Once they heard a car and hid behind a tree, shaking until it had passed and gone out of sight.

The road turned north in a gentle curve and then to the west again. At the beginning of the turn, Freddy pointed to a house. It was a narrow frame house, only two windows wide, that was set a few feet back from the road. It was hard to tell in the dark, but the house looked dilapidated and the windows, beyond which a small light burned, were scalloped in dust.

'This is it,' Freddy whispered, and Sebastian whispered back because it seemed the right thing to do.

'Do we go in?'

'Yeah, yeah. Her old man's going to be gone all night. She is going to be there on her own.'

'OK,' Mark said, 'let's go.'

Freddy licked his lips. 'You first, huh?'

'Naw, you know her, not me.'

'Yeah, but you're bigger than I am.'

'So what,' Mark said exasperated. 'Are we going to fight her or fuck her? Come on.'

He pulled a reluctant Freddy by the sleeve and marched him up to the front door, finally realizing why he had been asked to come along. Freddy was scared and wanted somebody big enough to fight his battles, if there were any.

'Knock,' Mark whispered.

Freddy raised a tentative hand and gave the door a light double tap. They waited for ten seconds before the door was opened a crack. An eye peered at them through the space, then the door was flung open wide.

Sebastian hadn't known what to expect, hadn't questioned Freddy about what the girl was like, so he experienced a sinking feeling and something approaching bitter disappointment when he saw her. She did not resemble any of the pin-up pictures that the boys had carefully hidden away. The girl was scrawny, with mouse-coloured hair in tangles. She had close-set eyes of a muddy colour and eyebrows so fine that they were almost invisible. Her nose was sharp and her mouth small. There was a large gap in her front teeth, and she looked bored. She had on a faded, ill-fitting sleeveless dress from which skinny arms protruded. Her legs were bare and her dirty feet were encased in scuffed sandals. Sebastian guessed that she was seventeen or eighteen, but she had a world-weary look which made her appear much older. She glanced at Freddy without much interest, gave Sebastian an appraising look, then turned away without a word and went into the room. Freddy pushed Mark in ahead of him and shut the door.

'Hey, Laverne, how are you doing?' Freddy said, in a high nervous voice. 'This is my buddy, Mark.'

The girl had seated herself on a fold-up bed covered by an old army blanket. The metal frame gleamed dully in the light of a naked bulb hanging from the ceiling. She arranged herself, ankles crossed, knees wide apart, skirt to mid-thigh. She gave Sebastian a gap-toothed grin.

'You're cute,' she said.

Mark pushed his cheek out with his tongue, put his hands in his pockets. The girl was not wearing pants, and he could see up her skinny shanks where a tangle of dark hair covered her crotch. He was in some confusion and looked away guiltily, unconsciously registering the rest of the room. That only brought him a little time, as there was not much to it. The floor was linoleum covered, a faded pattern of blue and white squares. A rough wood table with a greasy top stood in the middle of the room with two straight-backed chairs pushed carelessly near it. Angled in one corner was a big, lumpy armchair covered in some kind of sacking material, and next to it, a spindly table on which stood an old-fashioned radio. It was large and dome-shaped, and he could read the trademark, PHILCO, in capital letters. On the floor, next to a pile of dirty clothes, was an old black ceramic telephone pushed close to the wall. It was an early type with a circular base, tall trunk and mouthpiece, and a separate cone-shaped earpiece nestled on a hook. The room was chilly even though a kerosene heater laboured to take the edge off. It was a losing battle. There was more smell than heat.

Freddy giggled. It stuck in his throat and made him cough. 'Yeah, cute,' he said, 'that's why I brought him along.' He started over to where the girl sat.

'Uh, uh,' she said. 'Him first.'

'C'mon, Laverne,' Freddy whined, 'I'm the one that knows you – he's just with me.'

Laverne set her mouth in a stubborn line. 'Him first,' she repeated, 'or I don't do it.'

'Aw, shit!'

'You wait in there,' she pointed to a door with her chin.

Freddy shuffled his feet, appeared indecisive and looked at Mark, then back to Laverne.

'Well?' she said.

'OK, OK, I'm going.' Freddy went through the doorway. 'Where's the fucking light switch?'

'On the wall, you little turd,' Laverne said sweetly.

Freddy grumbled, swore under his breath, groped on the wall and found the switch.

'C'mon over and sit down.' Laverne patted the bed next to her. Sebastian had been rooted to the spot during the inspection and the exchange, and it was with some reluctance that he propelled himself forward and over to the bed. He sat down gingerly next to her. The girl put her hand on his thigh and he flinched. His heart was beating fast and he was breathing in quick, shallow gulps. She patted his leg and slid her hand to the top of his thigh.

'Don't be nervous. This is your first time, huh? Don't worry, Laverne will show you what to do.'

Mark tried to calm himself. He was aware of all sorts of sensations; the girl's hand on his leg, the swelling in his groin where the blood pulsed, and a warmth that was spreading through his body, the girl's breath on his cheek as she spoke to him, the smell of her cheap perfume.

She leaned over and started to unbutton his shirt. Mark felt he should protest, but didn't know what to say. He was more embarrassed than he could ever remember, and the warmth that had spread throughout his entire body had coloured his face a deep, rosy red. He kept his hands locked in his lap and sat as rigid as a statue, while Laverne flipped open one button at a time, making small snuffling sounds as she did it, brushing his cheek with her lips, blowing in his ear, slipping her hand into the opened front of his shirt and caressing his bare chest.

Mark fixed his eyes on the far wall where a calendar provided by Borden Dairies, pictured a pastoral scene. He concentrated on the cow with a stupid grinning face and a large udder. The legend ran 'Happy cows give happy milk'. He was only dimly aware that Laverne was tugging the shirt from his back, separating his hands that were in a death grip, pulling one sleeve, then the other from his arms. She pushed him down on the bed, unbuckled his belt, undid his trousers, took them off his unprotesting body, along with sneakers, socks and shorts.

'My, my, what a big boy you are.'

She tossed the clothes carelessly on the floor and stood up, and with a dramatic gesture, reached for the hem of her skirt with both hands, and in one motion, pulled it over her head, dangling the dress from one finger as a stripper would, and letting it drop in a heap on the floor. Mark squinted through half-closed lids at the girl posing naked for him, chest thrown back, arms akimbo, hands placed on the skinny hips with the fingers pointing towards the floor, one leg in front of the other, knee slightly bent in the classic model pose. Mark noticed three things: the triangle of matted hair, the belly-button – distended on one side, so that it looked like a kidney bean – the absence of swelling where the breasts should be, although the nipples were huge and stiffly erect.

Mark closed his eyes, he could hear his heart drumming in his chest and the girl breathing hard. Then he felt her hands as they trickled up his legs and encircled his penis. Then something warm and wet closed around the head. He opened one eye and peeked, saw the top of the girl's head pressed close to his body. Then an overpowering urge came over him, a rush of warmth, he clenched his fists, stiffened, gasped and climaxed. The girl made gurgling sounds, half-choking. He was deeply ashamed. He had never known such despondency before. He had completely lost control, and the only thing he could think about was how, when the story got out, all the other boys would laugh at him behind his back.

Laverne, on the other hand, didn't seem distressed at all. She stayed where she was and continued to make lapping sounds that reminded Mark of a dog with a bowl of water. He kept his eyes squeezed shut. Eventually, she stopped, took her mouth away, then put her hand on his belly. 'That's all right, baby, that was good. It will be even better next time.'

Mark opened his eyes in surprise. 'Was it really . . . OK?'

'Sure, baby, we'll do it again in a little while.'

Mark looked down at himself. His penis had gone soft and shrivelled. He put his legs together to hide it, rolled off the bed, grabbed his clothes from the floor and padded across to the doorway and into the room where Freddy was waiting.

'How was it?' Freddy whispered, eyes wide.

Mark shrugged. 'Not bad,' he said diffidently, 'I might even try it again.'

'Wow! I'm going to get mine.'

'Yeah, you do that. Where's the bathroom?'

Freddy pointed to a door covered by a distorted mirror, and scampered into the other room.

Sebastian was afraid he would catch something. He wasn't

sure how diseases were transmitted, and he hadn't brought any rubbers with him, but someone had told him soap and water would protect him. He took a shower, standing in a rusty tub, thinking about his experience. He hardly noticed the trickle of lukewarm water, but kept looking down at his symbol of manhood. He washed it thoroughly and rewashed it. Eventually he stopped the water, dried himself with a scrap of torn towel, dressed, and sauntered nonchalantly into the other room. He was surprised to see Freddy clad in a pair of boxer shorts, making a phone call. Laverne lay flat on her back on the bed, legs spread wide. She opened her eyes when she heard Sebastian come in.

'Come here, baby.'

Mark was nervous again but he walked over. She reached out a hand and grabbed him by the belt and pulled him down next to her. 'Why have you got your clothes on?' She sounded angry. Mark was stuck for an answer and his throat had gone dry once more, so he said nothing. Laverne started pulling at his buttons and his belt. He stopped her before she tore anything and did it himself. Then he lay down next to her . . . and, wonder of wonders, he had another erection.

This time she guided him into her, began to girate her pelvis, started to moan. The moans got louder and louder and Mark looked around nervously. He worried about the neighbours or passing strangers, and the thought went through his mind – what would he do if the police were called? He could hear the dialogue in his head. 'Hello, police? There's a woman being murdered in a house about a mile from the school. Come quick!' But there was nothing. Only Freddy squatting in the corner, watching intently. A lot of time seemed to pass before Mark once more felt that overpowering urge and the rush of warmth as if his body was going to explode, and then it was all over and he lay panting. Laverne was making purring sounds deep in her throat. Next thing he was aware of was Freddy tapping him on the back and saying, 'It's my turn.' Mark rolled off, took another shower and when he came out this time, he was surprised to see three other boys from the school in the room. They grinned foolishly at him and said, 'Hi!' and, 'How's it going?' And they clapped each other on the back and shoved each other playfully and acted like comedians by overacting and doing prat falls and doing a lot of giggling, and taking their turn with Laverne. In a half-hour, another dozen boys had shown up and the room was beginning to look like a locker room before a football game. It certainly smelled like one. And all the time, Laverne lay on her back and smiled and shouted, 'More!' and moaned loudly, sometimes going right up the register so that it came out as a piercing scream.

Mark and Freddy and four others cavorted down the middle of the road on the way back to school. It was two in the morning and quite deserted. They giggled and whistled and made ribald comments like, 'That was the best piece of ass I ever had,' which was answered by, 'That was the only piece of ass you ever had!' and, 'Did you get a load of Bobby's dick, you needed a pair of tweezers to find it!' And 'Did you see her move her tail? I bet she could win a jitterbug contest lying down!' which was followed by a chorus of groans.

Mark took Freddy aside. 'How did they all know to turn up?' he asked.

Freddy grinned, showing his crooked front teeth, and skipped a couple of steps in his exuberance. 'Oh, I set it up, man. Stew,' he indicated one of the boys who was doing a fair imitation of Laverne's moans to raucous laughter, 'was hiding behind the administration building; he was waiting for my signal. I let the phone ring once, then put it down. Then he let everybody know that the coast was clear. What did you think? Fantastic, huh? And we can do it any time we like.'

'Sure,' Mark said mechanically, 'fantastic.' He knew it had not been 'fantastic', but when he thought about it, he was damn glad he had done it. It was like a lot of skills he was trying to acquire. You have to start somewhere.

Chapter Seventeen

Naumann was moving quickly, as quickly as he dared; part of it was because he was beginning to feel the urgency of the Mexican project. It was getting close to the deadline and to the point where it would either reach fruition, or founder hopelessly, millions – possibly even billions – of dollars would be made, or five years of planning would go down the drain along with the three and a half million dollar investment. The project was delicately poised on a line the width of a razor blade, able to tip in either direction. On the plus side, he had the geological reports which had been done in secret. They stated in unequivocal terms that there were oil reserves in the billions of barrels, that the area surveyed in the Gulf of Campeche was unknown to the Mexican government, and that they had no plans to explore that area in the foreseeable future. The geologists were his own, good Germans who could keep their mouths shut, and he had taken those reports to parley them into a lucrative deal with IMPETCO. They had confirmed the reports with their own geologists, and had drawn up an agreement that said they would do the work and pay a nominal royalty on every barrel of oil produced. They had agreed for only one reason, because Naumann had a hole card, and it was an ace. Naumann had the man who was to become the next government minister responsible for oil exploration, and who might even be the next president of Mexico.

Naumann had the man in his pocket, owned him lock, stock and oil barrel. It was a relationship he had nurtured for several years, right back to 1955 in fact, when Naumann built a chemical factory that would export pharmaceutical products all over the world. He built the factory near Tampico, the principal sea port on the state of Nueva Leon, and Luis Francisco Montez was the municipal governor for the region. He was young, in his late twenties. He was tall for a Mexican – over six feet – with wavy hair, a flashing smile and very knowing eyes. He had thanked Herr Naumann profusely for having the wisdom and the social awareness to bring his factory to a depressed area and therefore able to offer the opportunity of employment to hundreds of poor Mexicans. The fact that Naumann had received encouragement from the Mexican government in the form of a large subsidy, accompanied by huge tax benefits, remained tactfully unsaid.

Naumann spotted Montez at once as a man who was going places. He did a discreet check of the man's background and found Montez to be of a good, but impoverished family who had scrimped to give their son a good education. He was a graduate of the University of Mexico in Mexico City, and he had done two years post-graduate work at Stanford in California, graduating with a Master's Degree in political science. Montez and his family had the additional advantage of being known as avid supporters of the PRI (Institutional Revolutionary Party), the party in power, and, *de facto*, the only political party in Mexico.

The PRI was the result of the civil war and bloodshed that occurred during the second decade of the century. The rebels, led in factions by Pancho Villa in Chihuahua, Alvaro Obregon in Sonora; Venustiano Carranza in Coahuila, and Emiliano Zapata in the mountains of the south, deposed the dictator, Diaz, and sent him into exile.

Obregon emerged as a leader of a loose alliance and became President of Mexico in 1920, when he instituted several land reforms and a constitutional government based on the United States. He was succeeded by his friend, Plutarco Calles, in 1924, and would have had a second term as president in 1928, but was assassinated by a religious fanatic before he could take office. Emilio Portes Gil filled the vacancy, but the real power behind the throne was still Calles, and it was he who was responsible for forming the early equivalent of the PRI in 1929. He had the ability to unite all factions under one roof, agrarian, military and ecclesiastical, and the party consolidated and remained in power from that time on – the president being elected by an overwhelming majority, which was not unusual, as he was almost always the only candidate.

When young Luis came back with his degree, it was natural for him to receive a political appointment. He started in the Yucatan as a coordinator between the inhabitants of the region and the Federal Government, and in two short years, was promoted to take charge of the region in Nueva Leon, which encompassed Tampico.

Naumann was a little surprised at first, but was then gratified to find such a political sophisticate in the hinterland, instead of the home-grown peasant.

Normally an outsider would have been resented, shunned, and even ostracized, but not Montez. He had a facility for ingratiating himself into every stratum of society. He could talk to the peasants in their own language and did not stand on ceremony, or he could be remarkably formal with the pompous elements who expected it.

Naumann was no stranger to power and the acquisition of it.

He could see, with complete clarity, the man who had his eyes fixed firmly on the brass ring. Montez was his kind of man because he understood ambition. Ambition meant giving and accepting favours, and accepting favours meant manipulation.

Naumann started slowly. He intimated that he could drop a word in the right quarters that would be of great benefit to Montez. He kept it low-key and was, in fact, as good as his word, so that eventually many of the right people in Mexico City knew who Luis Francisco Montez was. As the accolades multiplied, it seemed certain that he was destined to rise to great heights.

Naumann had done some homework on the Montez family and, through a contact, found out that they were in financial difficulties before young Luis knew.

It was a simple matter to draw the worried young man into a conversation about his family problems, and even easier to press financial aid on him as a 'friend', but no strings attached, of course, and not to worry about the repayment.

From there it was a small step until the Montez family became dependent on the largesse from Naumann, and once Luis got used to wearing the mantle of a 'bought man', the German knew that he had him.

Many perks followed. Montez exhorted the workers to greater efforts of production, and Naumann made sure that he received his share of the profits that resulted. He opened a Swiss bank account for Montez and kept to himself that the 'magnanimous gesture' was documented, and that the papers were in a safety deposit box, ready for use if necessary.

A Swiss account for a government official was about as illegal as anything could be in Mexico, a more heinous transgression than deflowering your best friend's sister.

Montez rose steadily through the ranks so that now he was on the brink of being appointed to the Ministry in charge of the very critical area of oil exploration. There was a growing faction in the party who wanted him for president. They were becoming vocal in their praise for Montez, and it was part of their function to advise the president on his successor. By tradition, the incumbent president made the final choice, and it was rumoured that President Ordaz was seriously considering Montez as his replacement. The election was only a year away, time enough for Montez to consolidate his power base, make more friends and influence even more people. All the better for Naumann, as Naumann saw it.

It would soon be time to call in the one big favour he wanted from Montez – to grant oil exploration rights in the Gulf of Campeche to IMPETCO. Under normal circumstances, it was perfectly legitimate to grant these rights to an outside company.

PEMMEX, the Mexican government oil monopoly, did not have the money or technology to do the drilling themselves, and would ordinarily put an area out for bids. If the wells came in, PEMMEX would cream off the profits from the top and eventually take control of the entire field, but there was always the continuing royalty to the company which did the initial exploration and drilling.

In this case, the geological reports looked so good, the reserves so staggering, that even a small royalty would be enough to buy and sell countries.

Montez, as the minister in charge, would make the ultimate decision as to which company would receive the exploration rights. It was Naumann's job to make sure he made the right decision. There would be no open bidding this time. Naumann felt reasonably secure about the granting of rights to IMPETCO slipping by without attracting undue attention. No other company was interested in the area, as it was rated 'low priority' and 'small potential' and so, were unlikely to squawk when IMPETCO went to work. If anything, the other companies would probably be thankful that they were not pressured into throwing a lot of dollars into an area where there was such a small chance of return. All of them had to do this at times. It was the *quid pro quo* the Mexican government demanded for granting the rights to high potential areas.

The one difficulty that remained was Montez himself. Naumann was not a stupid man and not the least bit insensitive. He knew Mexicans and the value they placed on formality. They were touchy, volatile, and likely to self-destruct if they were not treated with what they considered to be proper respect. Naumann thought they had a hugely over-developed sense of national identity, they were suspicious of strangers and were extremely resentful of anyone they thought had slighted them or had been condescending. They could harbour the resentment for as long as it took for the day America would need oil and Mexico would have it to sell, and would make demands commensurate with the iniquities they felt they had suffered at the hands of their neighbours to the north.

Naumann kept his negotiations with Montez in perspective. No hard line here – it could be a disaster. He would have to proceed with the delicate touch of a brain surgeon, and a gentle reminder of all past favours, a casual injection about Swiss bank account was all that was needed. Montez was a man in his forties going places. If the scales of naïvety had been present in his youth, they had dropped away some time ago.

Naumann made good use of his enforced stay in Mexico. As long as he had to be there, he would squeeze as much benefit as he could from the surroundings, good to the last drop.

He felt secure in his villa that nestled in the mountains behind Acapulco, and he entertained high-ranking Mexicans in regal style. The pool was in constant use, the rum drinks – garnished with fresh fruits – flowed, a smile was always in place. The approaches to the villa were guarded by his own men, and he rarely ventured down into the town to explore the pleasures of Caleta or Los Hornos Beach, or to watch the divers risk their lives at La Perla.

He made two trips to Mexico City in his private Cessna, once to pay a courtesy call on a government official who had always proved to be a fountain of information – he had nothing earth-shaking to report. He went to visit Montez on the other trip. Naumann induced him to leave the work that occupied him most of his waking hours and fly back with him to Acapulco for a couple of days. It was a good move. He got Montez on his own and in the relaxing atmosphere of the hot sun and a cold drink, found out that things were going well and that Montez confidently expected to be appointed to the Ministry within two months.

Spitzweg hung around on the fringe with a doleful look. He contributed nothing to the public relations exercise, and in fact looked so mournful that he put a damper on the festivities whenever he appeared, so that finally Naumann had to order him to stay in the house. He complied without demur and even seemed thankful that he could hide away in his darkened room.

The only sour note in the symphony of conviviality was Youngblood's negative reports. Naumann looked forward to each time that Youngblood would call, hoping for some good news about Sebastian. Good news would mean that he had been found. Excellent news would mean that he was dead. Each time his hopes were dashed. Youngblood had nothing to report, and Naumann went into a funk that lasted for several hours and made him unbearable to be with.

The only person who would brave his wrath was his wife. She was used to his moods and used to being ignored, which she returned with interest. They had not had much to say to each other for many years and she was indifferent to his swings of temperament, and always maintained an aura of rock-steady calm. Acapulco was very like Los Angeles or New York or Hamburg or Nome, Alaska. Naumann always took her with him, always maintained the man and wife charade they played. He did not know why, and would have been unable to articulate it if asked. His strict upbringing had taught him that husbands and wives stay together for ever, despite a lack of communication, despite a sense of loathing, despite anything. He was inflexible on the subject, but it was his very inflexibility that had propelled him to his position of power.

Back in the days when he was still a Hauptsturmführer in the SS, and theoretically on an equal footing with all his friends who were also Hauptsturmführers, it was obvious even then that he would outstrip them all, go further, achieve more, take charge.

He had reached the rank of Oberführer, equivalent to a brigadier-general in the US Army, by being incisive, tenacious, and at times even showing flashes of brilliance. He also knew how to follow orders and hitch his wagon to a rising star. He angled for and manoeuvred himself into a position on Reinhard Heydrich's staff, and when Heydrich was appointed Deputy-Protector of Bohemia and Moravia in 1941, Naumann went along as an intelligence officer. Heydrich took a liking to the ambitious young man and invested him with more and more authority, so that eventually he was made personal adjutant and promoted to Sturmbaumführer (major). Heydrich found that he could count on Naumann to execute his orders to the letter and, with excess zeal, sometimes exceed them.

When Heydrich was shot by Czech patriots on the Dresden–Prague road which led down to the Toja Bridge, and died a few days later of gangrene, Naumann took personal charge of the reprisal. He and his men descended on the little mining village of Lidice, whose sandstone and red-roofed houses nestled on a hillside around a Baroque church. The Gestapo had informed, wrongly, that the village had harboured Heydrich's killers.

All the men in the village were rounded up and shot – one hundred and ninety of them. All the women were sent to the concentration camp at Ravensbruck, and the children dispersed among German families, many never to be heard of again.

Naumann was rewarded for his 'devotion to duty', and promoted again and sent to the Russian front in charge of one of the Einsatzgruppen. These were the groups that went in with the soldiers and whose specific function was to weed out any of the disruptive elements left in the vulnerable rear. This meant interrogation, torture, and eventual elimination of left-wingers, churchmen and Jews.

Torture was commonplace, innovative and inventive, several steps ahead of the Spanish Inquisition. Sometimes, when Naumann wanted to find out something, or had a particularly recalcitrant subject, he would hang him by the nose. It could take many hours for a man to die that way, plenty of time to think about loosening his tongue. Naumann would leave the man to reflect on meeting his Maker. That was inevitable, but it could be either quick or done the hard way. He would go and have his dinner, sometimes bringing his dessert back with him, finishing it with relish while he watched the dying man.

He would use food in other ways also. A prisoner would be fed on salty fish and salt water, then brought in promptly at 7.00 each morning when Naumann was having his breakfast, drinking his coffee, carelessly emptying a tumbler of water back into the pitcher. If the prisoner refused to talk, he was taken back to his cell and fed more salt fish and water. Always just before he expired from thirst, he would tell Naumann what he wanted to know.

There were other bloodier, more violent ways, also. A well-applied electric shock to the testicles; the old stand-by, extracting fingernails with a pair of forceps; and the old Chinese torture of a thousand tiny cuts on the back so that the recipient would be unable to move a muscle without experiencing excruciating pain.

There were many other methods when he tired of these. He did his work so well that he became an Oberführer in 1944, and was sent to France to take charge of all the Einsatzgruppen.

At the end of the war, his name was known and he was

branded as a war criminal, and a search was instituted to find him. But he had laid his escape plans well, and Die Spinne had him out of the country far ahead of his pursuers.

So he started his new life in South America, financed by Nazi money deposited in Swiss banks, and found that his talent for organization applied to business also.

The first time he returned to Germany was in 1950. It was a must visit. He had to see people relating to his business, but he really wanted to see the Fatherland again.

He entered the country with a great deal of trepidation. What if he was spotted, arrested and tried? He knew he would be provided with an excellent defence. The best legal brains were at his disposal and money was no object. But it would seriously hinder his activities, and he valued his freedom above all else.

He need not have worried. No one paid any attention to him. The occupation forces were concerned with the administration of a country in a rebuilding programme. Many ex-Nazis had been installed as the managing directors of some of Germany's biggest companies. Many of them had their old jobs back. Naumann was just another German returning to his country, and, as far as the Allies were concerned, insignificant.

The New Year in Acapulco came and went in the usual way – whistles, horns and drunken Mexicans weaving their way among the more sedate tourists. Naumann was getting more and more irritable, and Spitzweg – Spitzweg was almost a basket case. He had all his meals taken to his room and hardly ever emerged except when he had to go to the bathroom, and then he was a furtive figure, scrambling between doors.

By pure force of will, Naumann lasted another two weeks. Then he had had enough. To hell with it! He was finished hiding like a rat in a sewer. He told Spitzweg he was going and that he could damn well do what he wanted. Spitzweg decided that the only thing worse than being a target, was being alone and being a target. They took the plane back to Los Angeles.

Chapter Eighteen

Sebastian had his blow-up with Pamela at about the same time Naumann was landing in Los Angeles. It had been brewing for quite a while. He could pinpoint it to New Year's Eve. He and Pamela drove up to London to meet the Websters in an out-of-the-way restaurant. It had been Roger's idea to stay away from the mainstream because he was still nervous about Sebastian being seen. Sebastian acquiesced because it was easier. He knew full well that if anyone was seriously trying to find him, they would still do it by tailing Webster, hoping that they would be led to him. Sebastian could not tell Webster that because the man was inordinately proud of his new-found skill of spotting a tail, and Sebastian let him dream on. But this time he was prepared. Webster had procured for him against his better judgement the Walter PPK Automatic that he preferred. He tried to argue Sebastian out of it, but it was to no avail.

The restaurant was French and so was the champagne. Much more of that was consumed than food, which was a shame, because it was excellent.

Pamela only toyed with her coquille St Jacques and filet de boeuf en croute, while she downed copious amounts of Louis Roederer Crystal, 1961, and the more she drank, the more incoherent she became. Eventually, she got the weepies and she attacked Sebastian, using the Websters as a springboard. 'Isn't it terrible,' she directed a third-person question to the Websters, 'that a man who one gives one's heart to, doesn't respond in any way, or even try to, and don't you think it's awful when one's emotions are played with?' And reversing her course, 'If one wants to do something for someone and that someone won't let you . . . what do you think of that?'

The Websters looked embarrassed and tried to change the subject, but Pamela pressed on doggedly. Sebastian alternated between wanting to find a hole in which to hide and doing something violent to Pamela, like breaking her other arm. He did neither, but just sat with his jaw clamped so tight that the muscles ached. He tried to make allowances for the undoubted fact that the girl had had too much to drink, but how far could you go along that particular path without bumping your shins. That old proverb, *in vino veritas*, was accurate enough, as he knew from other drinkers' past indiscretions. In the States, he reflected that it would be called 'kidding on the square'. Pamela had tried an approach with a touch of levity, but it was brittle and forced and enough of her real feelings and resentment came through loud and clear.

Sebastian came to the difficult conclusion that Pamela was spoiled, selfish, used to getting things her own way, used to dominating her male companions. Rascher had been the exception, but of course there had been an axe to grind there, at least that's the way Pamela told it. 'I did it for my father,' she maintained with so much sincerity Sebastian was positive she believed it.

In many ways he wasn't even sure he liked her. Her contempt, which she wore like a cloak, rubbed him the wrong way.

But 'like' was not what it was all about. He'd often read that one could feel intense dislike for somebody and still love that person. He was familiar with dislike and its range of intensities. Love was a complete stranger.

The drive back to the country was accomplished in silence. Pamela seemed penitent and glanced at him out of the corner of her eyes, silently imploring him to forgive her. Sebastian pretended that he didn't see. He didn't trust himself to speak because he knew, once he got started and took on a full head of steam, that he would say things he might later regret. He stayed on his side of the bed that night and feigned sleep when Pamela put out a tentative hand in her attempt to heal the rift. Eventually she gave up.

It took two days for things to get back on an even keel, but even then they were not quite right. A truce was declared, but it was a wary one. Everything that happened was a little larger than life. They were over-polite to each other and over-solicitous for each other's feelings, unwilling to tread accidentally on an exposed nerve. It resembled that old comedy routine about entering a room, 'After you,' 'No, after you,' 'No, after you, I insist.'

Sebastian jogged a little further every day. His leg was coming on fine, and, in fact, healing better than he had dared hope, but he had always recovered from injuries quickly. He had banged a knee up once in football practice and the doctor had said it was serious enough to sideline him for at least three weeks. But he was in the game that weekend astounding everyone with his rapid recovery. His other wounds did not bother him at all.

His mind was always occupied on these runs, but not where he wanted it. He wanted to think about the two Germans that were left, Spitzweg and Naumann, to make plans for their demise, to exorcise final demons. He had never thought beyond that. His life after 'the mission' was a black, swirling mist, impenetrable. He had always refused to contemplate what came after. He shied away from it deliberately. But he didn't have even the luxury of thinking about the unthinkable, because every time he tried to concentrate on his next moves, the thoughts slipped out of the groove and Pamela intruded.

He had never felt so indecisive. Everything had been clear and in focus before her, and if the future was not completely mapped out, at least the terrain was charted.

His thoughts about Pamela were in turmoil. He was grateful to her for more than one reason. She had not told Rascher where he was – although she easily could have – and she had given herself to him in body and mind without reservations. And he was the heel of heels because he could not accept it . . . or wouldn't.

He tried in vain to sort out gratitude from love. They seemed hopelessly intertwined and the present state of his psyche made them impossible to unravel. He sought for the words to express what he really felt for the girl, but failed miserably. He had no experience on which to draw. No one had ever come that close. He intellectualized that it was the circumstances that made it that way, but all the rational thought in the world would not help to find a way out of the maze. Pamela was looking for a commitment and he already had a commitment. It occupied all the spaces and did not allow for a duality of purpose. Ambiguity could be fatal, and even – at the very best – it would obfuscate the way he had to choose his options, sometimes they required a lightning decision, and the slightest hesitation could mean failure and death – his death.

Perhaps it had been a subconscious imperative to look for a spark to set him off. He was walking across the lounge to the kitchen. His leg was tired from jogging and he made a slight stumble. Pamela, who was five feet away at the time, rushed over to support him. He shook her off. 'Goddam it, I'm not a goddam cripple! Leave me alone. I don't need any help. You are smothering the life out of me.'

Pamela looked so hurt at his outburst that he almost relented and apologized, but he was beyond the point of no return.

'I can't stand it any more. You are treating me like a fucking infant! I can't do anything without you helping. Well, I want to tell you something, lady. I have been wiping my own ass for a lot of years now, and I am not about to change for you or anybody!'

Pamela was taken aback by the fury of his onslaught, and cowered away from him as if he had used physical blows. Her eyes brimmed with tears. 'I was only trying to help you,' she said. It came out as part of a sob.

'And I'm trying to tell you that I'm tired of being helped. There are some things I like to do for myself.'

'But I thought you wanted me to help.' She was sobbing loudly now, the words came out between snuffles.

'I want you to be you, and I want you to let me be me. Stop clinging.'

'But I want to do anything you want me to do.'

'That's what I am talking about. Goddam it, you're just a spoiled brat who's playing a role because you think it looks good. From what you have told me, you have spent all of your adult life depending on someone or somebody for everything, and you've got some crazy idea that you should demand some kind of payment for being available – and that you have got to pay it back double. You spread it as thick as molasses, and I'm feeling stuck fast.'

Sebastian paused to catch his breath and then softened when he saw the girl's face. 'You've got to leave me to myself sometimes. I need privacy, and sometimes I feel like I'm wearing you like a second skin.'

Pamela sat down on the floor, more like collapsed, and began crying in earnest.

'Oh, shit,' Sebastian muttered. He paced around the room, waiting for her to stop or even pause, but the floodgates were well and truly open. Finally, he said he was sorry and that he hadn't really meant to hurt her, but that he was on edge and restless and had to be by himself . . . and had to move on.

When she stopped crying, Sebastian sat down on the floor

next to her. When she started talking she was hesitant, but there was a difference. The cloying attitude was gone, replaced by something more direct. Self-esteem had surfaced. For the first time, they had a conversation like two intelligent consenting adults. For the first time, Sebastian felt that he was getting through to her, that she understood what motivated him, that he was uncertain about the future and that he had no idea if they could make it together or would want to.

She finally understood he was going to leave and why, and did a lot of growing up in the time it took for the minute hand to make one complete circuit.

It was the first time their lovemaking was unselfish. The passion was still there, and the one element that had been missing had been added, mutual respect.

Sebastian left the next day. He made no promises, but that didn't seem necessary any more. Pamela touched his shoulder as he turned to go and whispered, 'I love you.'

Sebastian stopped and turned back. 'Me too,' he said. He got in the car and drove away.

Part Two

Chapter Nineteen

Sebastian finally reached New York on 17 January. He had taken a roundabout route to get there because he did not put it past Naumann to have contacts in the Immigration Department, and they might have been alerted to watch for him if he flew straight into Kennedy Airport.

So he flew to Toronto instead, using his Anthony Christie passport, rented a car and drove to Detroit, with the minimal halt at the Canadian border and disinterested Customs officials. He took the first flight he could get that landed at Newark, New Jersey, where he felt secure from prying eyes. Hardly anyone flew into Newark any more. Even then, he took precautions. He put on the same horn-rimmed glasses he had worn on the visit to the trainer, combed his hair differently, added a slight touch of grey to his temples and drew in a few wrinkles with a make-up pencil. It added on ten years to his age, and he felt confident that he would go unrecognized.

He chose a hotel with the same care, opting for the City Squire on Seventh Avenue, because it was one of the more anonymous hotels in town. Once he checked in, no one at the desk gave him a second glance, and the elevators were automatic.

He went out on to Seventh Avenue and headed up town. It was 4.00 in the afternoon on a dull dismal day. Besides that, it was freezing. The sidewalks were cleared of snow from the storm the week before, but it had just been pushed to the kerb and was piled there in banks. Ice had formed in patches on the pavement from where water had dripped down the sides of the building during a brief thaw and made puddles. They looked blotchy from the dirt that had been ground into them, as if the sidewalks had caught some terrible disease and the prognosis for the blight was unhopeful. The pedestrians were huddled deep into overcoats to get as much protection as they could from the wind that whistled straight down the street, hard enough to knife through any material.

Sebastian hardly noticed. He felt good, alert and ready for action. It was great to be moving again. The enforced hiatus had got to him a lot more than he had realized, and now that he was actually back in the hunt, the cloud that had dulled his brain without him even realizing it, had lifted.

He stopped in at the Stage Delicatessen for a corned beef sandwich and a cup of coffee. He sat down at a table in a corner, intent on the problems ahead. The voice saying, 'whadda you want?,' jarred him back to the present. There was something familiar about that voice. Sebastian looked up and smiled. The years rolled back when he saw the old waiter with the stringy white hair through which great patches of pink scalp showed. The man looked at Sebastian with bird-like interest, alert brown eyes magnified by gold-rimmed glasses.

'Moish,' Sebastian remembered.

'I tell all you young people who come in here regular, call me Moish.'

Sebastian gave his order and watched the old waiter walk away. 'Moish, you look exactly the same,' he decided. 'Well, maybe you're a little more bent, but you still walk like a penguin with sore feet, and I bet you still snap at all the kids that come in here from acting classes, and forget to charge them when they look hungry, and don't have enough money to eat.

'I wonder if you remember me. I wonder if you recognize me. You never did miss much. You could always spot an actor from ten miles off. Here I am sitting with an old face and I bet it didn't fool you at all. I saw you glance at my hands. Not a liver spot in sight.'

Sebastian let himself drift back to the season of Summer Stock he did at The Eastern Mountain Playhouse in North Conway, New Hampshire. Those had been moderately happy times, he had almost managed to forget what drove him, so involved was he in the parts he played.

The season had started with Sandy Wilson's *The Boyfriend.* He had played the lead, Tony, and had given a credible if somewhat wooden performance. The fine tuning on his 'sensitivity' was a touch out of kilter. However he had sung 'I Could Be

Happy With You, If You Could Be Happy With Me', and 'All I Want Is A Room In Bloomsbury' in a passable baritone.

He'd next played George in *Our Town*, and the high point of that was that Thornton Wilder had come to watch their performance and later had come backstage to compliment the cast.

Next had come the role of Antipholus of Syracuse, in *The Comedy of Errors*, and then, Chance Wayne in *Sweet Bird of Youth*.

The role of Chance had proved conclusively to the rest of the cast that Sebastian was weird, strange, and possessed an aberrant personality. Their judgement as to his sanity had come about this way: Sebastian was playing opposite a middle-aged film star doing the role of Princess Cosmonophlous. The lady, who had been a universal heartthrob in the thirties and forties, and who was now settling into older parts with dignity and a great deal of talent, had come to do the Summer Stock season in order to 'recharge her batteries' prior to starting a major motion picture in the fall. Her producer and director had come up from New York to see her performance as a matter of courtesy. Their prime motivation was to discuss script changes on the upcoming film.

When they saw Sebastian, they did a collective and harmonized 'flip'. They had been searching for six months for someone new to play the male lead in the film. Sebastian was exactly right; 'perfect' they enthused.

They offered him a contract on the spot and were unbelieving when he turned it down flat. No amount of cajoling would change his mind, and they finally left, defeated, disgruntled, and unable to understand why. Sebastian's refusal cut right to the core of their virility. From that time on, all their power trips would have a little less meaning. They had run into a mountain, and had come away bloodied.

Sebastian was secretly amused and made no attempt to explain himself to anybody in the company. They all gave him a little more distance after that.

That was alright by him; he used the time to improve other skills.

He spent hours with Jack Clarke, the make-up man who had come up from Boston to instruct the cast in one of the most important tools of their trade. Sebastian learned how a pencil line alone could often be more effective than heavy grease paint in changing appearances. Clarke also expounded on his theories of posture, small gestures and minor characteristics, and how they could transform a person into a new entity. Sebastian listened and learned.

He used his free time to practise rock-climbing on Cathedral Ledge, a steep, almost vertical in places, rock, from which most people came to the top the easy way and practised their repelling manoeuvres. He climbed it from the bottom.

Sebastian worked steadily through the sandwich, drank two cups of coffee, and left a five-dollar tip for Moish, who looked at him in amazement and who, possibly for the first time in his life, was speechless.

Sebastian grabbed a passing cab and took it to 7th and Lexington, a block from where Spitzweg lived.

He walked with careful, measured steps down Lexington Avenue and reached out with a conscious attempt for a 'feel' of Spitzweg. He could see the building on the next corner and craned his neck to look at the windows of the penthouse apartment. They looked like black rectangles from his angle. They told him nothing.

Spitzweg had arrived in New York the day before. It had taken every ounce of will he possessed to get him to leave the safety of Naumann's house – where he had locked himself in a bedroom – and get on the plane for New York. Plainly he was terrified. His legs turned to jelly every time he thought of the 'assassin' lurking out there somewhere to take his life. And his thoughts were like spaghetti, jumbled in a mess of circuits and connections that led to a central core – his fear of Sebastian. He had not had a constructive thought since the news of Rascher's death had been brought to him at the restaurant. His health had suffered. He was pallid and was positive that he had palpitations of the heart. He sweated a lot, seemed unable to keep the palms of his hands dry and was having constant headaches, so that not even the brand of aspirin that his own company marketed was having an effect any more. If news of that leaked out to his rivals, he would be the laughing stock of the business. The slogan for the product was 'The aspirin that will stop a headache in its tracks.'

He had to go to New York. He had searched in vain for a way in which to get out of the trip, but it was impossible to avoid. A genuine emergency had arisen, in the business sense.

Spitzweg had many failings, but there was one area in which he shone. He was a salesman, sometimes referred to by envious rivals as a super salesman. It came easily to him. He genuinely liked people, and really believed his products were the best. His enthusiasm was completely sincere and, because of that, contagious, so that there were buyers who refused to deal with anyone else, and were so adamant in their refusal that they would more likely buy a product from another company than deal with a surrogate.

He had been away for four weeks now, and one buyer whose order meant sales in excess of $10,000,000 in the next year, had grown tired of excuses about Spitzweg's absence, and had threatened to walk out if Spitzweg did not show. Panic calls from the New York office had caught up with him in California, the context of which was that the ultimatum was serious and that Spitzweg had to put in an appearance. He had flatly refused; he claimed that herds of wild elephants would find it impossible to drag him one inch away from that resolve. But in the end, it proved unnecessary to make such a test. Naumann proved to be more formidable than an entire herd, all by himself. If there was anything to be learned from all this, it was that Spitzweg was more afraid of Naumann than Sebastian.

Naumann did throw Spitzweg a small bone. He agreed to send Youngblood with him to act as bodyguard. It wasn't purely out of kindness that he did it. There was an ulterior motive behind every move he made. There was a fifty-fifty chance that Sebastian would show up first in New York. After all, why not? It was closer than California by three thousand miles and was the next logical place for Sebastian to visit, and Sebastian seemed like a methodical man. He seemed like a tidal wave. He knew that eventually he would get there. Naumann was starting to get a fix on Sebastian. He reasoned that if Rascher had revealed the whereabouts of both he and Spitzweg, and he was in no doubt about that, then Sebastian would go to New York first. It was tidier.

Of course, the plan had been that there would be no one in New York for Sebastian to find, and that when he arrived in Los Angeles, he and Spitzweg would present a united front, on ground of their own choosing with their troops deployed in optimum positions. Naumann realized that he had been kidding himself. Spitzweg was worse than useless.

He was glad it had worked out this way. It would be much better for him. If Sebastian was in New York looking for blood, then Spitzweg would make an excellent sacrificial lamb. If Spitzweg were killed, he would know exactly when to expect Sebastian, advantage to him. In the meantime, he would protect himself very adequately while Youngblood was away. He would just have to be careful. The four men who guarded him had been recruited through a contact of Reinhart Kessler's in Los Angeles. He had been assured that they were professional and dedicated to the job. They were perhaps a little devoid of imagination, but who needed a genius as a watchdog.

Naumann was beginning to have his doubts about the flamboyant Youngblood. So far he had produced nothing but promises. If this was genius at work, he would take the plodder every time. He equivocated. As long as he was protected, and he would be, he might as well let Youngblood get on with it. He was cautious not to underestimate the man and he could afford to be generous. It was not costing him any more.

Spitzweg sat next to the window in the first-class section of the Boeing 747. He stared moodily at the landscape of Los Angeles that spread out beneath him as the plane lifted. His attempts at conversation with Youngblood, who sat next to him, were stillborn. The answers were monosyllabic and, as Spitzweg searched Youngblood's face for any sign of compassion, all he could see was that ubiquitous, sardonic smile, lips curved in contempt, the eyes unblinking. Spitzweg shuddered inwardly. He had seen that reptilian look before, but never when he felt like he was the supposed dinner.

Spitzweg made a mumbled excuse, pushed past Youngblood and went up the spiral staircase to the lounge. He took a table by himself and ordered a brandy from a too-cheerful hostess. He sipped enough of the drink to wet his lips, ran his tongue over them, and concentrated on the sting imparted to his taste buds. He found that he needed something on which to concentrate, to take his mind off his troubles. Otherwise, he would brood and sink into a black depression, from which he sometimes thought he would never emerge.

As usual, he concluded with a sigh, he was a victim of circumstances. As far back as he could remember, when he was engaged in his brave attempts to be accepted as 'one of the boys', invariably he would be swept along in a fast-running stream like so much flotsam and jetsam, and before he knew it – before he could even protest – he was doing something for which he felt no conviction. It was usually something with which he disagreed violently, but his overpowering fear of being excluded, ostracized, always prevented him from doing anything but complying.

He had joined the Nazi party because of it. He had seen the Austrian housepainter ranting and raving, his face contorted, and privately thought that the man was a maniac, that his promises were extravagant, his solutions ludicrous, and his histrionics positively Wagnerian. But he didn't dare express his opinion. All his 'friends', the members of his peer group, were caught up in the euphoric fervour that Hitler engendered, and it was much easier to go along with them.

He had joined the SS for the same reason. He wasn't even good SS material. He was the antithesis of the tall, blue-eyed, Aryan demi-god. He was under-sized, had always been a little dumpy, and his dark brown hair was wavy. But he was an Aryan – he could prove it. He was accepted reluctantly and just scraped through, primarily because of the help he received from his 'friends', Schmidt, Rascher and Naumann. Deep down, he knew that they were stringing him along, kept him around because he was good for laughs, the club mascot, the company buffoon. Like always, he went along with it, his need for acceptance far over-shadowing any convictions he might have had. He craved respect, sought ways to achieve it, always fell short by at least a factor of ten. But he kept on trying.

That is how he found himself in the *Bierkeller* that fateful night when Rascher had suggested that the four of them go along and check on the papers of one, Natalie Sebastian, Jewess, just for fun. When he thought back, he believed that he had had a presentiment that things would go wrong, but of course he said nothing. They would only have laughed at him and would have accused him of being a coward.

And when it had gone that stage further and the woman had been attacked and raped, he had contrived to stay on the fringe, so scared that his knees trembled, and had participated in the minimum amount he could get away with, so that he would not later be reviled with their contempt.

He was sure in his own mind that he would have found a way to avoid raping the woman when his turn came. As it turned out, he never had the opportunity to make an excuse. He was struck dumb when Robert Sebastian crashed in and attacked with a fury that he had never seen before or since.

He could see the man clearly now, thirty years after the event. He would have killed them all if Naumann hadn't shot him.

He was the only one who had escaped unscathed, and when he took the other three to the hospital, they had left it to him to explain why they were in such a state. He extemporized, the flow of adrenalin making him fluent, and was more surprised than anyone when his story was accepted without question. He said that they had gone to check the papers of a Jew, ostensibly true, and that a gang of them had jumped them from behind, and that although they had got away, several serious wounds had been inflicted, and that they would think twice about doing it again.

Nobody cared about the Jews, and it was an unwritten law, not yet official, that anything could be done to them without fear of consequences. The only reproof the three injured Nazis received was how they could have allowed themselves to be injured at all by Jews. Everyone knew the Jews were completely incapable as fighters. It was Naumann who had spoken up, as the gash in his cheek was being stitched. He confirmed the sneak attack and vowed that in future, he for one, would deal very harshly with the Jews. Spitzweg had believed him.

As the war progressed, the first flush of victory gave rise to even more grandiose expectations. The table of organization lengthened, proliferated. The other three went into branches of the SS that would ensure them of quick promotion, where the jobs were nastier and the rewards greater. Spitzweg, at last, made a conscious decision, based on certain knowledge, that he hadn't the stomach for those sorts of jobs.

He was assigned to Amsgruppe B, which was responsible for supplying the troops, and specifically B-1, which dealt with general supplies. He spent the war in relative obscurity, and was happy about it. He was well insulated from the horror stories that drifted in about what was going on in the concentration camps, and the similar exploits carried on by the Einsatzgruppen, for which Naumann was responsible.

He spent the war in ignorant bliss, concerned only with how many pairs of size seven boots were shipped out as distinct from size ten, and how many pairs of shorts should be accompanied by what quantity of undershirts.

It was only towards the end of the war, when Naumann reappeared in Berlin after withdrawing from Paris, that his bubble of security burst with a loud bang. Naumann could see the eventual outcome. It was inevitable, and one didn't have to drop a rock on his head to demonstrate to him that the Germans had lost the war.

As early as January 1945 he was already planning his escape. He could see it if Hitler couldn't; Hitler would not listen to reason, or was past the point of being able to. Naumann found like-minded individuals who planned to get out, intact in mind and body, and with plenty of currency to start over again in another place.

Naumann was sure of being branded a war criminal and convinced Spitzweg that everyone in the SS would be tagged with the same label. He painted such a gloomy picture of arrest, internment and imprisonment, that Spitzweg begged to be allowed to come along.

He sighed deeply. It was loud enough to attract the air hostess's attention. She looked at him inquiringly. A victim of circumstances again. If he hadn't been so stupid, he would have been living a comfortable, pleasant life back in Germany – probably a sales director of some company and without the stresses and pressures he was under now. And no one would be trying to kill him. That wasn't entirely accurate because Sebastian still held him responsible, but at least he would not be connected with the others. And he had an irrational belief that he would have been untouchable on his own.

Where would he be now? He dreamed about a house in Munich with a large garden covered in flowers, and a cottage on Lake Tergensee, where he could keep his boat. Perhaps . . . it was even possible that his wife might still be alive.

He had met her in 1943, and was married to her four weeks after they had first caught sight of each other. He had loved her as he had never loved anyone. When Naumann had scared him so badly, he communicated his panic to her, so that she, too, agreed they should leave the country.

It wasn't until three years after the war that he realized how stupid he had been, that he had never had any need to leave. By that time it was too late. He was well entrenched in South

America, part of the company financed by SS money that Naumann ran, too late to uproot himself again and start over.

Of course, he had been back to Germany many times. He discovered on the first trip, with no surprise at all, that he was free to come and go as he pleased. Nobody was looking for him. He felt very foolish with his passport that said he was William Spicer.

The Spitzwegs had three children in four years, two girls and a boy. It was a handful coping with three kids of approximately the same age, but they managed it cheerfully and when they moved to the States he was finally happy. He had his family and a house in Connecticut and an excellent position, and everything was coming up roses. It did for a while.

His wife had felt tired for a long time before she paid a visit to the doctor, She went through a battery of tests, and the verdict . . . Spitzweg remembered the verdict; it was the worst day of his life. Terminal cancer.

It had been more than five years since his wife had died and he still hadn't got over it. He threw himself into his work because there didn't seem much else to do. The children were taken care of, grown up and gone away – one daughter married with a child of her own, the other two at college. He felt very sorry for himself.

Youngblood was already walking east down 76th Street. He was coming from Park Avenue, where he had done some shopping, and was returning to the apartment to leave his packages before he went off to pick up Spitzweg at his office downtown.

He was just approaching Lexington when he saw the man crossing 76th. There was something very familiar about him. At first glance he didn't seem to be anyone Youngblood knew. At the distance he first spotted him, about seventy-five feet, the man appeared to be in his mid-forties, greying temples showed underneath the hat, and he wore glasses, but there was something naggingly familiar about the walk, somebody else had walked that way, fluidity of movement, relaxed, with more than a hint of spring-like tension that could be launched in an instant. Youngblood stared at the profile. Then his heart thumped – Sebastian!

He paused on the kerb, momentarily undecided, then the lights turned green and he made up his mind.

Sebastian was strolling past the building, head turned towards the entrance, when he felt the hand on his arm, heard his name called. 'Mark.'

Sebastian froze in mid-stride. His first reaction was to whip round and see who it was and then either to tell the man he was mistaken or hit him hard and fast and run like hell. He did neither. He felt short of breath, wanted to gasp in a lungful of air, but didn't. Slowly he turned his head.

'Mark Sebastian, it *is* you, isn't it? Remember me? Bobby Youngblood, your buddy from UCLA.'

Sebastian forced a smile, his face felt stiff. Thoughts all jumbled together, ran through his head. 'Of all the dumb, fucking luck,' and 'It doesn't mean a thing,' and 'How the hell did he recognize me?' and 'I won't be able to bluff him.' 'Bobby,' Sebastian said, a little more heartily than intended. He took Youngblood's extended hand and shook it. 'Of all the people to run into on a cold day in New York. What the hell are you doing here?'

'Oh, a little of this and a little of that. I have some people to see, and while I was here I thought I would do some post-Christmas shopping.' He indicated the package he held. 'But I tell you that I'm going to get out of this dump as soon as I can. Give me that LA sunshine every time. But what are you doing here? What have you been doing all this time? I haven't seen you for years. On second thoughts, don't tell me now. Let's get out of this cold, man.' He exaggerated a shiver and said, 'Brrrr! There's a bar half a block down – let me buy you a drink.'

Sebastian's immediate thought was to make an excuse and head the other way. He hesitated. That would make Youngblood even more curious. And what harm could it do? He hadn't seen the guy in years. 'Sure,' he said.

They seated themselves in the corner booth of the almost deserted bar. The only other customer was perched on a stool nursing a beer in morose silence. The bartender brought over the drinks himself after Youngblood called out the order, then went back to doing what bartenders usually do when nothing else interests them – polishing glasses.

'It's really great to see you, Mark,' Youngblood said effusively. The two glasses of Scotch touched in salute and both men took a big swallow.

'When did you start wearing glasses?' Youngblood asked. 'You used to be able to see like a hawk.'

'Old age,' Sebastian answered easily, 'it's creeping up on me.'

'Ah shit, we're the same age, man, and how about that grey hair?'

Sebastian had thought about lying, but decided not to. It would be better to stick pretty close to the truth, and if he dropped the odd double entendre or two, who would know but him? It might be fun to put Bobby on.

He remembered Youngblood well. He had been a skinny kid in college. He had always tried to be friendly and to hang around where Sebastian was. He knew it had been a form of hero worship. Youngblood used to show up for football practice and cheer him on, and he had always tried to get close to him, asking a whole lot of dumb transparent questions that had to do with the work in the classes they shared. He never felt any resentment towards Youngblood, but he had never encouraged him either.

'I guess I will have to tell you my secret,' Sebastian said, and touched the grey sideburns. 'It washes out.'

'No kidding!'

'Honest Injun.'

'Then . . . why?'

'Well, it's like this. I was trying to see if I could tail someone without them noticing me, and I thought a disguise would help to get me in the mood.'

'No shit? Why the hell would you want to do that?'

'Oh, you probably wouldn't know that, after college, I went into acting.'

'Oh yeah?' Youngblood said. 'No, I didn't know that. Is this some kind of role you're playing?'

'Give the man a Kewpie doll. Yeah, I got a part in a film playing this middle-aged guy who's tracking down a bunch of nasty old Nazis who did some pretty mean things to some friends of his. He knocks them off one by one.'

'Wow!' Youngblood exclaimed. 'A real live movie star! When are you going to do it?'

'Oh, the shooting has already started,' Sebastian said placidly. Youngblood smiled his sardonic smile but Sebastian was not looking at him.

'And what happens to this guy in the end?'

Sebastian shrugged. 'I'm not sure. Would you believe that the end of the script hasn't been written yet?'

'That doesn't sound very professional.'

Sebastian took another swallow of the Scotch. 'Maybe not, but that's the way it works sometimes. This is a story with a lot of possible endings.'

Youngblood lit a cigarette and blew an idle smoke ring. 'I wouldn't mind having a crack at writing that kind of a script some day. I have a lot of ideas how that sort of thing should work. I mean, take this character you're playing, for example. He can't just go around knocking guys off without a lot of people getting pissed off at him. So when they find out who's doing the killing they're going to gang up on him. Right? They've got to get him in the end.'

'You think so?' Sebastian asked. There was genuine interest in the question. 'I hadn't really thought of it that way. Why should a whole lot of people concern themselves over one guy? He is hardly significant enough to attract so much attention. Let's face it, there are murders happening every day of the year, probably one in progress as we're sitting here. Why should two or three more stir so many people up like you suggest?'

'Well,' Youngblood said judiciously, 'it would depend a lot on who these guys are that you're bumping off. Now I don't know the story, but let's suppose that the – what shall we call them, the victims? – were rich and powerful with a lot of influence. Nazis, you said, didn't you? As far as I know, all those Nazis stick together. They all belong to the same organization, don't they?'

'Maybe,' Sebastian admitted. 'And you think they would bring in the organization?'

'Well, it figures, doesn't it? They're not just going to stand by and say, "Go to it, pal, we didn't need those bums anyway." Well, if I was them, I would hire someone, a real pro, to go after this killer.'

That's an interesting thought,' Sebastian mused. 'You're giving me a lot of ideas on how to finish the script. I'm glad I ran into you. You're giving me a fresh viewpoint. Let me ask you another. This pro, what kind do you think they would hire?'

'Hmm, let me think. I have got to ask you one first. Do they know the killer?'

'Well, at this stage of the story, nobody knows for sure, but I would say yes, they've identified him.'

'Well, in that case, it's simple. I would try to hire a guy who knew him in the past. That way, this hit man has a pretty good idea of who he is stalking and can maybe guess at what the guy is going to do next. Do you think that's too much of a coincidence?'

Sebastian smiled. 'It could be a little far-fetched. I don't think this man had friends who turned out to be hit men.'

Youngblood sighed, his expression mournful. 'Ah well, I guess I was never meant to be a script writer.' He brightened. 'I suppose I'll just have to stick to shrinking heads.'

'You mean you went on with all that bullshit psychology?' Sebastian said, surprised.

'Aw, don't say it like that, Mark. I couldn't think of anything better to do. The bread is good, the time is my own and I'm making them crazier than they're making me. All in all, a very nice life for someone who is devoutly lazy. I like being a dilettante, it suits me.'

Sebastian laughed. 'And I always thought you were a serious student.'

'Who, me?' The statement came out so incredulous that Sebastian redoubled his laughter.

He left the bar a few minutes later explaining that he had an appointment to keep. He promised Youngblood that he would look him up if he ever got to California and was careful to say that he doubted if he would be there in the near future. Youngblood commented on how it was a funny old world and that he had a feeling that their paths would cross sooner than Sebastian expected. Youngblood shook hands warmly and watched as Sebastian left the bar, a more than usual sardonic smile on his face.

He left the bar a few minutes later. He stood just inside the doorway and scanned both sides of the street in both directions. Sebastian was nowhere in sight.

He stepped to the kerb, hailed a passing taxi and gave an address on Park Avenue where Spitzweg's office was.

He was already a half-hour late from his appointed time to pick up Spitzweg, and he knew that the little German would be fretful and worried. Youngblood had every intention of raising tension another notch. He composed his face into a doleful mask as he was escorted into Spitzweg's office.

The little man jumped up from behind his desk as soon as he saw Youngblood and asked excitedly where he had been and why he was late, and said that he thought something had happened to him.

Youngblood never replied, just waited until Spitzweg ran down. He stood, impassive, in the middle of the office, his contrived expression intact so that it was practically unreadable. One would have to look very hard to see the twinkle deep in the grey eyes.

Spitzweg finally ran out of words. He finished with a minor expletive and sputtered to a halt. Youngblood still said nothing, and Spitzweg watched him with mounting alarm.

'What's the matter?' he croaked. 'It's something bad, isn't it? You have bad news, I can tell.'

Youngblood made one brief nod.

'What is it?' Spitzweg asked, fear putting a tremor in his voice. He looked on the verge of tears.

'I saw Sebastian.'

'Oh, my God,' Spitzweg moaned. He crumpled into a chair.

'He was looking for you,' said Youngblood in a soft voice, enjoying himself immensely.

'How do you know?' Spitzweg asked. It was a barely audible whisper.

'Because I saw him standing in front of your apartment building.'

Spitzweg gave a cry of despair and buried his head in his arms. His voice was muffled and high-pitched. 'He is going to kill me, I know he is going to kill me!'

'That is a reasonable conclusion,' Youngblood agreed. 'Maybe you'd better not go back to your pad, huh?'

Spitzweg's head jerked up and he stared at Youngblood with a stricken face. 'Go back? I'm not going to go near the place! You've got to save me, you've got to get me out of here.'

'Sure, sure,' Youngblood soothed. 'But we will do this right, we'll make an orderly retreat. You send one of your gofers here to go pack your stuff up – mine too, then we'll go catch a plane for LA.'

'Yes, yes,' Spitzweg agreed, lunging for his intercom button and nearly falling off his chair in his eagerness.

Spitzweg spent nearly the whole trip to the airport looking out of the rear window of the limousine with fearful glances and darting eyes. He fidgeted constantly. It wasn't until the plane was high over Manhattan, nose pointing westward, that Spitzweg fell back into his seat in exhaustion. Youngblood chuckled to himself and raised his glass of champagne in a silent toast.

It took Sebastian the whole of the following day to determine that Spitzweg had been in New York and seemed to have left town suddenly. His office was unable to tell him when he would be returning, and offered the sales director as an able replacement. Sebastian demurred, saying that he preferred to deal with Mr Spicer directly and would call back. He took a flight from La Guardia to Chicago and changed planes for Los Angeles.

Chapter Twenty

The argument had been going on unabated for twenty minutes. Youngblood sat in one corner of the patio at Naumann's house, a position where he could see the hills and background and the spray from the lawn sprinklers that reflected silver in the late afternoon sun. Youngblood had his head tilted on one side, chin cupped in one hand, eyes behind wrap-around sunglasses, opened to mere slits.

The voices in the background smoothed out from sharp-edged consonants to the low drone that retreated further into the distance as his mind concentrated on sunshine, sandy beaches, luscious female bodies.

Youngblood at first was amused by the argument, even a bit surprised. The little fat German, Spitzweg, was actually standing up for himself, talking back to Naumann, making him angrier with every word. It was obvious that Naumann was unused to being contradicted by anybody. His face was engorged with blood, the scar standing out white and angry.

Spitzweg had been badly shaken by Youngblood's revelation that Sebastian had indeed turned up in New York, and there could be only one reason for that. Naumann had shown such callous disregard for his fears that something snapped in Spitzweg, and for the first time in his life he confronted the man, unwilling to accept his condescension and adamant that his suggestions at least be listened to and weighed, if not acted upon.

It was this attitude that really angered Naumann so that he shouted, and was taken by surprise when Spitzweg shouted back. Spitzweg, he declared, had seen enough of hit men, quasi-legal bodyguards and ridiculous subterfuge. His life was in danger and it was time to call in the authorities, starting with the police and ending with the FBI or the CIA if necessary.

He reminded Naumann that as far as he was concerned, he was a law-abiding citizen and entitled to the protection of appointed authority. His life was in danger, his stability in tatters, and he refused to go on any longer without something being done, and that if Naumann was not going to do anything about it, he would go himself.

Naumann vented his anger on the little man, accusing him of being cowardly and stupid. He put even more emphasis into his anger than usual because it had already been thwarted that day. The previous target had been Youngblood, whom he accused of not doing the job for which he was hired. How, he wanted to know, could Youngblood have spotted Sebastian and done nothing about it? He had let a perfectly good opportunity slip through his fingers. An unsuspecting Sebastian would have been eliminated with one bullet and that would have been the end of it. Youngblood's reply had been bland, was the perfect protection for the anger directed at him. The point of attack was blunted and easily turned aside. He reminded Naumann that when he had seen Sebastian, it was daylight, and even in New York it was frowned upon to kill someone in broad daylight. It made escape so much more difficult, and Youngblood had every intention of getting away with his assassination.

And why hadn't he followed Sebastian and done away with him at some more discreet location? To which Youngblood replied that, unfortunately, he had been caught up in one of the interminable Manhattan traffic jams through which Sebastian's taxi had zigged when his own had zagged.

Naumann's reply was to snarl about incompetence, at which

Youngblood had smiled and offered to resign. That shut Naumann up temporarily, and when he was ready to begin again, Spitzweg started in.

The decision of what to do was suspended, and, for the next two days, an uneasy truce prevailed until a certain event occurred which prompted action.

Sebastian drove slowly west on Sunset Boulevard in his rented Camaro. He was enjoying the drive through Brentwood and Pacific Palisades. The car handled well on the curving road that led to the beach. He had the window down, an elbow on the frame, steering the car one-handed with competent ease. He hummed tunelessly under his breath as he squinted into the sun. A warm breeze floated in through the window. It was fifty degrees warmer than New York.

For a while, all thoughts of Nazis and revenge were gone from his mind, replaced by a smiling Pamela – the new Pamela. He conjured up scenes of the two of them strolling hand in hand on the Santa Monica Pier, revisiting the amusement park that had been the scene of one of his happiest memories – getting a cotton candy – just to see if it really did remind him of Pamela. The daydream shifted to the two of them sailing to Catalina Island, watched over by a beneficent sun, and then making languid love on the deck in a soft purple-tinged twilight while the little boat rocked gently at its moorings. Then another shift as he escorted Pamela around the wonders of California, she looking up in awe at the giant redwood trees and the beauties of the Big Sur country. He might even stop and show her the school he went to.

He turned north on Pacific Coast Highway and drove for several miles up the coast, turning off alongside a line of houses that were a few hundred yards short of the Malibu Colony.

The houses, about twenty in all, were woodframe and stucco, and the side of one was flush to the next, so they appeared to be in an unbroken line. The only way you could tell they were individual units was that they were all painted in different colours reflecting the personality of their owners, so that they ranged from a subtle summery beige to a hideous green that Sebastian always thought of as the colour of pigeon pucky. One could tell a lot about the people who lived there by the way they painted their houses. He, too, had stayed in character. He had opted for a neutral shade of brown that the sun had bleached to a sand colour.

Access to the house was through a wooden gate, down a flight of stairs, along a flagstoned path and through a door – where Sebastian had to stoop – that was either the front or the back of the house, depending on your point of view. The other side of the house faced an isolated strip of beach that he liked to call his own – and it was, by virtue of its inaccessibility to the public.

He had owned the house for more than ten years now. It was one of the few purchases he had made when he had come of age, and the trust fund had reverted to him. The bulk of the money remained untouched.

Even then he had been cautious. The house had been purchased through a corporation, and nowhere in the deeds did his name appear. It was a completely safe retreat. All the bills, electricity, gas, phone, taxes, were paid through a bank. His neighbours knew him as Anthony Christie, but he seldom saw them. Nobody lived in Malibu all the year round, but used the place as a summer home or a location for an occasional weekend orgy.

Sebastian had not occupied the place for three years, but was confident that it would be as secure as he had last seen it. That was not an idle optimism, but was the price you paid for a valuable piece of real estate. A security company made regular inspections to make sure the premises remained untainted.

Not that Sebastian was worried about anyone breaking in. If a burglar had gained access, he would have found it unprofitable. Sebastian kept only the minimum of articles around for living – cane furniture, a bed, a dresser, a few clothes, fewer utensils, some basic toilet articles. That was all that was visible. There were far more interesting items contained in the house which he felt confident would remain undetected even with the most careful scrutiny.

Underneath the bed, if you knew how, a section of the floorboards could be prised up, but that would only reveal a stone floor. When the slab of stone was lifted, a concrete recess that resembled a small bunker would be revealed.

Sebastian had done the work himself – dug out the pit, poured the concrete, fitted the covering. It had been worth the effort. There he kept things that he might need in an emergency. It was part of his advance planning for the day when he might need some or all of them to further his reason for being. He had never thought of it as foolish, had never stopped to think of it that way. Even when he had not known where the Germans were, had no clear idea of how to find them, and was unsure when he would be ready to begin the search, still the point of his objective was focused. He was prepared.

The bunker contained an arsenal: half a dozen hand guns wrapped in protective coverings, four rifles in similar covering, telescopic sights, ammunition, plastic explosive, primers and detonators, wire, electric tape, lengths of nylon rope, a selection of tools, a make-up kit, wigs and other props, three sets of false identification.

Sebastian checked his cache as soon as he got in the house. It was as he had left it. He took the Walther from its hiding-place, unwrapped it, stripped it down, cleaned it, put it back together and loaded it. He slipped it into a shoulder holster, put the harness on, put the silencer into his pocket and sealed the bunker.

Sebastian was up early the next morning. He peered through the sliding glass door that looked out on to the ocean. The water was invisible, as was practically everything else more than twenty feet from him. The fog that was common in January blanketed everything in a dirty grey. Sebastian shivered.

He showered, shaved and dressed quickly. The coffee was just perking as he stepped into the kitchen. Ten minutes later, he eased the Camaro out on to the Pacific Coast Highway and drove back into town through the swirling mist that was patchy now.

He sat in traffic on Wilshire Boulevard. He was grateful for the early morning rush. It gave him a chance to study the building on the corner of Wilshire and Beverly Drive that he knew was where Naumann had his office.

Sebastian reached the corner in another five minutes and turned right, seeing immediately as he did so the entrance to the underground parking for the building. On impulse, he made a quick signal and swung the car through an open space in the traffic and down the ramp into the building. He took a parking ticket from the attendant. A big electric clock on the wall read 8.32. He eased the Camaro forward and followed the traffic aisle where it turned left. The sign above him had an arrow pointing to the right, indicating parking reserved for persons who paid by the month and occupants of the building. The arrow to the left pointed out the area where anyone else could park. Sebastian saw a space that afforded him a good view of the reserved parking area. He backed the Camaro into the slot and shut off the engine. He opened the door and got into the back seat, closing the door behind him. He hunched down so that he could see without being seen, and waited.

Cars came in a steady stream and parked. Executives with briefcases who looked like bankers (the building was owned by a bank), California types who were casually dressed and who were probably theatrical agents, public relations men, or a new breed of hip lawyer, marched through to the elevators.

The black Mercedes limousine arrived at 9.24 by Sebastian's watch. He could see five men in the car, two in the front and three in the back. The car stopped and let out its passengers before parking. The man next to the driver jumped out and came around the front of the car to stand next to the rear door. It was opened from the inside, and another man stepped out and positioned himself next to the rear bumper. Both the men were dressed in sober suits and ties, and were young and fit. They had one more similarity. Both pairs of eyes darted from place to place looking at everything. The man by the bumper swept his gaze towards the Camaro, paused for a moment, went past. Sebastian hunched down deeper into the seat.

A short, rotund man with grey unkempt hair, two sections of which stood up like wings, emerged from the car. He stood and looked around him. He blinked rapidly. He bounced on the balls of his feet.

The last passenger alighted from the car, pushing the short man out of his way with a muttered word that Sebastian couldn't catch. He was tall and elegant-looking and Sebastian knew him at once. The scar showed clearly on his cheek. Sebastian smiled grimly to himself.

The door was slammed shut and the four men headed for the elevators. The driver eased the car into the parking space, got out, made a great show of checking to see if all the doors were locked, then he, too, went towards the elevator. Sebastian sat and waited and watched. Around noon, an idea came to him. It was so wild that he dismissed it at first, but it stole back like a cat burglar and he let it gain prominence.

It was none the less wild for thinking about it, and it was so off-the-wall that it had a sort of childish appeal. He examined it from all angles, thought about the consequences and the possible ramifications. All the while, he kept an eye on the area within his field of vision. After 10.00, there was very little activity in the section reserved for resident parkers. There were a lot of comings and goings in the other section, and around a quarter to one, there was increased activity from people, presumably going out for lunch.

Sebastian waited until 1.30, made up his mind, got back into the driver's seat and then drove out of the building.

He made it back to Malibu in thirty-five minutes – that included a brief stop at a drugstore – had the bunker opened in another couple of minutes and busied himself with the contents. He worked carefully and completed his work in a half-hour. He took just a few more minutes to put on a brown wig and steel-rimmed glasses, grab a pair of grease-stained overalls that he kept stashed in the closet for when he worked on the car, and left.

The electric clock above the parking attendant's head read a minute before 3.30 when he drove back in to the building. There was a slot open about four spaces down from his original space and he backed into it, shutting off the engine.

The Mercedes was still as he had left it, and none of the five men who had arrived in the car were in sight.

Sebastian pretended to busy himself with something on the seat next to him as three men walked by on their way to the elevator. They never glanced in his direction. He got out of the car and quickly slipped into his overalls. He touched the wig to make sure it was still in place. Satisfied, he took the tool-kit containing the objects he had been working on and boldly walked across to the Mercedes. He started with the front wheel on the driver's side, took the three ounces of plastic explosive into which a primer had been inserted, put in the detonator with the connecting wire and taped it just under the fender. He slid the wire under the front bumper and left it there. He made up a second package and taped it under the rear fender on the driver's side. Two middle-aged women came towards him from the elevator talking to each other. Sebastian started to whistle, fiddle with the tools that he had brought, keeping his head down until they had passed. From the corner of his eye he could see that they glanced at him incuriously, without a pause in their conversation.

He took the trailing wire which he had purposely left longer, and taped it underneath the body of the car until it, too, rested on the ground next to the first wire. He went round to the other two fenders and pushed the wires to the front.

There was about a foot and a half of space between the Mercedes grill and a cement wall. Sebastian gathered the four wires and twisted them together. He took a pair of surgical gloves from the tool-box and put them on. From a pocket, he took out a small photographer's time clock, the type used in a darkroom. He taped the wires to the alarm bell. Then he took out the flat 9-volt battery he had bought at the drugstore and wired one terminal also to the bell. He sweated a little, as he always did when handling explosives. The other terminal, he wired to the bell-clapper. The timer had been set for ten minutes. When that point was reached, it would set off the alarm, and the clapper meeting the bell would complete the circuit, followed – a micro-second later – by an explosion. The clock was started by employing a simple lever that had an up and down motion. When the lever was pushed up, the clock started, when down, it stopped. It was now in its off position. Sebastian reached underneath the front bumper and taped the clock and battery to it. One last thing to do. A piece of wire was taped to the start lever, the other end to the ground where the wall and floor met. Sebastian tested it. As the clock was facing forward, the slightest tension on the wire would pull the lever up and start it.

Sebastian picked up his tool-box and strolled back to his car. He put it on the floor in the back, stripped off his overalls and tossed them in there also. He glanced at his watch as he got in behind the wheel. The whole job had taken just over ten minutes. Sebastian drove out of the building, turned left on Beverly Drive, and left again four doors down – into the parking lot of the Hamburger Hamlet. He went into the restaurant and straight to the restroom. He washed his hands thoroughly, made sure the wig was still set right and went out to the bar. It was just on 4.00, and he had no idea when Naumann might leave his office. He certainly did not want to miss anything, but he decided to risk it. He sat down at the bar and ordered a drink.

He left a quarter of an hour later and positioned the Camaro so that it faced the street in the first slot on the parking lot. It had been occupied before. He went out to the sidewalk and leaned against a convenient lamppost, gazing contemplatively towards the underground garage. He shifted his position several times over the next hour, and was leaning on the lamppost with one hand when the Mercedes poked its nose out of the garage entrance.

He dashed for his car, had it started in seconds and squealed out of the parking lot, turning right on Beverly Drive. The Mercedes was at the corner, stopped for a red light. When Sebastian stopped, he was the seventh car behind it.

He reviewed the actions of the Mercedes driver in his mind. Most probably the man had been the first in the car and had backed it out of the space without embarking the passengers. Then he would have to stop, wait for the other four men to get in, and take his turn to leave the garage. As it was now quitting time, other cars had preceded him. So, Sebastian estimated, three to four minutes had elapsed since the timer started.

The lights changed and the Mercedes went straight ahead up Beverly Drive. Sebastian followed – just beating the lights as they were changing. He was now fifth in line, and the convoy moved at a sedate pace through Beverly Hills, pausing for a minute where the lights held them up at Santa Monica Boulevard, then on again. Another car had turned off, and Sebastian moved up a notch. He kept glancing at his watch, trying to estimate when it was all going to happen, finally giving up in disgust.

The cars reached Sunset Boulevard where, again, the lights were red. The traffic on Sunset was heavy in both directions. There was a hold-up in the west-bound lane, as several of the cars paused to turn off into the Beverly Hills Hotel that stood in the northwest corner. It was cocktail time at the Polo Lounge.

The lights changed and the Mercedes, second in line, started off. As the car reached the exact centre of Sunset Boulevard, there was a flash of light and a loud bang. The car seemed to settle exactly where it was. All four tyres had blown, and the car rested on its hubs. There were shouts and screams and honkings from all directions. Sebastian joined in with enthusiasm.

Spitzweg let out a loud, piercing scream and fainted. Naumann blanched the colour of sour milk and reached for his heart, which seemed to have stopped. The other three men sat in stunned silence, dazed. Then all hell broke loose.

The driver screamed, 'Let me out of here!', wrenched the door open and bolted, followed closely by the two bodyguards. Naumann remained stiff and shaking. Spitzweg had slumped on the seat and was moaning.

It seemed only seconds before the wailing of sirens was heard and three police cars converged on the scene, screeching to a halt, causing a traffic tangle which would eventually back up for miles.

Chapter Twenty-one

Naumann caught a glimpse of his reflection in the window before he turned away. He still looked pale and drawn, and his flesh crawled and prickled every time he thought of the explosion. It could have been the end, but it wasn't.

The police lieutenant was talking to him. He dragged his mind back from the dark abyss and tried to concentrate. 'What was that? I didn't hear.'

The lieutenant patiently repeated the question. 'Do you have any idea who might want to blow up your car?' It was about the tenth time he had asked the question.

Naumann felt his fury rising. He had been sitting and watching that imperturbable face for an hour and a half now. 'Yes,' he wanted to scream, 'I know exactly who did it and when I find him I will kill him.'

Naumann checked himself, brought his temper under control. 'No,' he said coldly, 'no, as I keep telling you, I have no idea. That's certainly your job – to find out who did it.'

The man across the desk sat and gazed at him with an expression of mild reproof. He was a beefy man, large-boned and, judging from the tan, an outdoor type. He had deceptively mild brown eyes that at once seemed to convey compassion and the idea that he had heard it all before, so that there was no point in lying. 'People just don't go around blowing up cars for no reason. There is usually . . .'

'How is my colleague?' Naumann interrupted. 'Have you heard anything?'

Lieutenant Helder nodded. 'He was in deep shock but is resting comfortably now. He is under sedation and should probably sleep until morning.'

Naumann thanked the powers that be for that small mercy.

There was a knock on the door and a patrolman entered. He held out a sheaf of papers to Lieutenant Helder and left.

Naumann lit another cigarette.

The lieutenant flipped through the papers, one after the other, paused when he came to a passage that interested him, and on through until he had skimmed them all. He piled them neatly together and put them at the edge of his blotter. Naumann looked at him inquiringly.

'That was the bomb squad's report. Very interesting.'

Naumann kept silent. The lieutenant reached into his breast pocket and extracted a short, fat cigar. He rolled it in his fingers, sniffed it, then took a kitchen match from a box on his desk, flicked it alight with his thumb nail, and lit the cigar, turning it so that it burned evenly. His face was enveloped in a cloud of smoke for a few seconds.

Naumann couldn't stand it any more. 'Well?' he demanded.

'Well,' the lieutenant considered, 'the bomber didn't intend to kill you.'

'What?' Naumann exploded in a fury. 'The car blows up and you say he didn't intend to kill me?'

'He?' the lieutenant inquired.

'He, she, what does it matter? If that is your clumsy attempt to catch me out, you are making a big mistake, I know nothing.'

Helder shrugged. 'Like I said, it doesn't look like he intended to kill you. According to the report, there was just enough plastic explosive to blow the tyres. The bomb was pretty crude, but effective. The explosive was placed just underneath the fenders so that the force of the blast was directed towards the tyres. It was set off by a photographic timer that was taped underneath the front bumper. It's not even damaged. It was set to go off ten minutes after the timer was started.'

'But how did he know when . . . ?'

'The timer has an on/off lever. He probably rigged some sort of trip wire. I guess that when we go and investigate where you parked your car, we will find it.'

'You have this timer. Will that help you to find out who did it?'

Lieutenant Helder swivelled his chair around and put his feet on the desk. 'I doubt it. It is a pretty standard item. You can pick one up at almost any dime store, hardware store, photographic supplier. And he probably used gloves. There are no prints on it.'

'So where do we go from here?'

'A very good question, sir. There's not a lot of roads open – unless you can think of somebody who is trying to get at you.'

'Well, I can't.' Naumann stubbed out his cigarette viciously. 'Lieutenant, I am extremely tired. This whole affair has left me drained. I want to go home.'

Helder swung his feet off the desk and swivelled back to face Naumann. He stared intently, the brown eyes harder now. 'Sure I can arrange for someone to drive you, but tell me one thing before you go. If you don't know who the guy is who did it, how come you got bodyguards?'

Naumann gaped; the question caught him by surprise. His mouth shut with an audible snap. 'What do you mean, bodyguards? They are . . . business associates.'

'Oh yeah? Bullshit, Mr Newman. You have been waltzing me around the block ever since you came in here. I know a bodyguard when I see one. They are just hoods in custom-made clothes. All I got to do is scratch the surface to find a greasy punk underneath. What do you want to bet that they have a record, Mr Newman? So I ask you again. Why the protection?'

'How dare you talk to me like that?' Naumann spluttered. 'I will have you fired for your impudence.'

Helder's lined face creased into a wry smile. He spread his hands. 'Be my guest, the Commissioner's door is always open. Don't forget to tell him how I violated your civil rights. He gets very uptight about things like that. And at the same time, you might explain to him why you are being uncooperative when I'm trying to do my job and find out who blew up your car. I want to tell you something about Beverly Hills. We got some peculiar customers here. We have this idea, which you probably think unreasonable, that our residents have the right to live in safety, that they have the freedom to move around without worrying about things blowing up in their faces . . . and we even keep the streets clean.'

Naumann was about to retort but thought better of it. 'If there is nothing else, I want to go home.'

Helder picked up his internal phone and asked the policeman who answered to have Mr Newman driven home. Naumann stood up and left the office without another word. Helder watched him go with an expression of contemplation. He puffed on the cigar, drummed his fingers on the desk, then reached for his phone and dialled an internal number.

'Hello, Mac,' Helder said. 'That guy Newman, has just left here. Yeah, the one with the car bomb. There's something here that smells worse than last week's jockstrap. This guy is about as innocent a victim as Atilla The Hun. I want him thoroughly investigated. Here's the dope. He is the head of a pharmaceutical company called Forsche-Brandt. They have offices on Wilshire Boulevard. It is supposed to be a Swiss company, and he tells me that they have branches in other cities like New York. Check through Interpol and see what you can pick up. This guy, Newman, is a Kraut by the way. Just for fun, check with immigration and see what they know about him. There are also three other guys, their names are . . .' He checked his notes and read out the names to Sergeant George MacIntosh. 'See if they got a record. And there's one more guy – he's at Mount Sinai under sedation. The doc says he won't come out of it until tomorrow morning. I want to talk to him before anyone else does. Put a man on him, and let me know as soon as I can go over there. That's it for now . . . yeah, I know everything is closed. Get on it first thing tomorrow.'

Sebastian sat on a cane chair that faced the ocean. The picture window was wide open and a chilly breeze streamed in. The sound of the surf was a dull roar. Sebastian hardly noticed. He was lost in thought. It revolved around compulsions. What made him do what he did? Did he really have a death wish? If not, then he must be crazy. On reflection, it was a dumb stunt to blow up the car, maybe the dumbest one he had ever pulled, and for what? 'For your ego,' the inner voice said, 'just to prove how clever you are.' Sebastian agreed with the voice.

In one stroke, he had lowered the ante enough so that everybody could play. But, Sebastian argued with himself, that would mean that the quality of his game would have to be elevated to a pinnacle of excellence . . . if he was going to win.

He remembered the conversation he had had with Bobby Youngblood, something about everybody ganging up on him once they found out who it was. Sebastian considered. Maybe that conversation had been the subconscious trigger. Did he really want everyone to know who it was? Was he just a thrill-seeker in search of notoriety?

The whole quest seemed suddenly distorted out of all proportion. What seemed certain was that the trail that he was using to stalk his quarry, where he hoped to prod them into a dead-end by virtue of the panic he engendered, would now be strewn with an increased number of obstacles. It was likely that he would encounter a camouflaged pit, and he would have to be very careful or he'd fall in. The police would investigate as a matter of course. It was anyone's guess how far they would go. Probably, that would depend on how satisfied they were with Naumann's story. He was sure the German would tell them anything but the truth, and how convincing can you be when your car is blown up? There are only so many red herrings in a barrel.

He wondered what Pamela would think about his sudden departure from sanity. 'Assuming I'm sane in the first place,' he thought. He realized that that was almost an original thought. He had never seriously considered the question of his sanity before. In the early days, all his thoughts had been fragmented and had led nowhere. They had been like isolated threads, left dangling in a vacuum. And afterwards, when he decided his life had a purpose, there had never been any time to dwell on his rationality. He had been far too busy learning, acquiring skills.

He longed to talk to Pamela about it. He longed to touch her smooth skin, stroke her hair. He wanted her to understand about Naumann and Spitzweg and why it was so important for him to continue right to the end.

He pictured the words in his mind and his lips tried to form the explanation, but it wouldn't come. He felt as inarticulate as a mute. There was an explanation; there had to be one.

He felt the rightness of it, but he'd never be able to explain it to Pamela. She wouldn't understand. She didn't have references. She didn't know Naumann and Spitzweg, had barely known Rascher.

One person who would understand was Naumann himself.

Naumann was the one he could depend on to do something. He was sure that he had badly shaken the Nazi. He must have felt smug surrounded by his bodyguards, and it would be a great shock to have his security shattered, to see how vulnerable he really was. He would certainly be the one to escalate the situation. Probably, Sebastian estimated, he would abandon his defensive posture and go on to the attack.

Another part of Youngblood's conversation came back to him. Would Naumann hire a pro to get him? It was possible, even likely, but there would be more, much more.

Sebastian felt his excitement rising. The shit was about to hit the fan, and he had encouraged it. He was beginning to get a hold on a corner of a revelation. He could not see it yet, but it would come. He knew it had to do with him as a person, an entity. He knew it had everything to do with what motivated him. He tried to coax it from the shadows, praying for it to emerge, and afraid that it would.

His fear was multi-level, the primordial fear of being revealed to himself as a naked savage, the irrational fear that, once confronted, he would be unable to perform, and the ultimate fear that the entire point of his quest was meaningless, that it meant nothing because nobody cared, he foremost. The agony of such a disappointment would be unbearable, to discover that his whole existence was as worthless as a single amoeba in an entire ocean. Who was he doing it for, if not for himself? Surely not for his dead parents whom he never really knew, certainly not to avenge the genocide of a people to which one half of him belonged. His head began to ache intolerably.

Naumann paced his lounge, the one decorated in Danish modern – slingback chairs, low angular couches, blond wood tables. His shoes rang hollowly on the parquet flooring. His mouth was set in a snarl, his eyes narrowed, the scar danced as the muscles in his cheek worked, the well-groomed hair was dishevelled. He felt like Oberführer Naumann again. He issued orders to the driver and two bodyguards. The one who had stayed in the house was to remain there, one was to position himself by the front gate and turn back all the reporters that were trying to get a story from him. The other was to recruit six more men who were to report immediately, when they would be assigned their tasks. The driver was to go to Mount Sinai and supervise the transfer of the sedated Spitzweg to a private hospital in Santa Monica. Naumann had guessed correctly that the police lieutenant would want to interrogate Spitzweg about the explosion as soon as he woke up, and in order to circumvent this, had arranged for the transfer as soon as he reached home. Naumann was positive that Spitzweg had finally been pushed over the edge by the explosion and would blab everything to the police. That would not do.

Naumann saved a special burst of venom for Youngblood, who sat, unconcerned, in a corner of the room.

'If you had been doing your job,' he spat out, 'this wouldn't have happened. He could have killed me. He is playing with me, and right under your nose.'

'Hey, man, you didn't hire me to guard your body, that's what you've got all those gorillas for. And the bottom line is, he didn't kill you; if he wanted to he could have done it easily. He is just trying to scare the shit out of you, panic you. And it looks like he's done a pretty good job of it.'

Naumann stopped pacing. He admitted to himself he was in a panic. He hadn't been thinking straight since the explosion. That damn smug Youngblood is right again. He could have killed me, but he didn't – why? Does he just want to torment me? Does he want me face to face like Schmidt and Rascher? That, of course, must be it. 'You will have it that way, Sebastian,' he shook a mental fist at his adversary.

'And maybe that explosion was a good thing,' Youngblood continued laconically. 'It tells me something – Sebastian's getting cocky.'

'He's starting to think he's invincible, otherwise he wouldn't have pulled such a dumb stunt. All it did was attract attention and put you on the alert. It should make my job a hell of a lot easier.'

Naumann's fury returned in a rush. His rage boiled over. 'And while you were working on it, he sneaks right in. Do you realize what has happened? The police are now in the picture. Every hope I had of keeping this matter quiet is now shattered. You should have been with me, you might have seen him. There was no need for all of this.'

Youngblood gave an eloquent shrug. 'I told you why I didn't want to be with you. If the man sees me it's all over. I'll lose the advantage, and I guarantee he'll recognize me. He ain't no dummy. He sees me with you, sticks two and two together and comes up with a big fat four. And, anyhow, I couldn't be in two places at once. I've been busy.'

'Doing what? Masturbating on Hollywood Boulevard?'

Youngblood's eyes flickered and took on a dangerous glint. Naumann turned away. The moment passed.

'As a matter of fact', Youngblood said, 'I found out what airport Sebastian came through . . . and the car that he rented.'

Naumann's head snapped round and he gave Youngblood a searching look. 'How did you do that?'

'I hit all the agencies with the picture I got. I saw that the girl at Avis recognized him, but she was kind of hesitant to tell me about it. So I told her I was a private detective who is on the trail of this bad guy who is cheating on his wife and, just like that,' he snapped his fingers, 'she gave it to me. He's driving around in a brown Camero, licence number FRT 142.'

'*Ach*, so if we find the car, we find him.'

'Good thinking, Batman. The only problem is that there is a hell of a lot of cars out there. How do you think we are going to find it without the cops doing it for us?'

Naumann thought about it. 'Perhaps I might know a way. It is time for certain people, who have done nothing so far, to help.'

It was 1.00 in the morning in Dallas when the phone woke Darrell Bradshaw out of a sound sleep. 'Yeah,' Bradshaw mumbled.

His wife said anxiously, 'Who is it?'

'Oh, Carl,' Bradshaw said, a little more awake. 'What the hell is so goddam important you have to wake me in the middle of the night?'

There followed a stream of invective that made Bradshaw sit up and flush angrily. He covered the mouthpiece.

'It's for me,' he told his wife. 'Go back to sleep.'

'Yeah, yeah,' Bradshaw said. 'I told you that we wouldn't get involved with . . .'

Naumann cut him off. Bradshaw listened for a while. 'Call Stingley now?' Bradshaw's voice rose several decibels. 'You must be nuts! The esteemed president of our company don't take kindly to being woken up this time of the morning.' Bradshaw listened for a few seconds. 'The hell I will, I'll call him when the sun starts shining.' There was another pause for listening. Bradshaw's face got redder.

'No, you can't have the number,' he shouted. 'I understand the urgency and it will keep until morning . . . get me fired?' Bradshaw broke into harsh laughter. 'Well, I'll tell you what, buster, if you think you can, then you go right ahead . . . yeah, yeah, I know what the deal is worth. Yeah, we want to do it . . .' A dangerous note crept into Bradshaw's voice. 'I don't advise you to go shopping it around, Mr Newman. For openers, I don't think you will find anyone else who is interested. And secondly, that would make us mad. You understand? I'll call Stingley in the morning and get back to you.' Bradshaw slammed down the phone.

Naumann pushed the receiver away from his ear, held it at arm's length, then very softly replaced it on the cradle. His temples bulged with suppressed fury. He felt as if he would burst – if not in a thousand little pieces then at least a blood vessel or two. He picked up the lamp where it stood next to the phone and hurled it across the room. The plug popped out of the socket like a cork from a bottle, and the lamp thudded into a wall with a satisfying crash, and fell to pieces.

'Temper, temper,' Youngblood said, but there was admiration in his voice as he viewed the lamp's total destruction. 'Didn't want to play, huh?'

Naumann crashed a fist into his open hand; he was white around the lips. 'He will,' he rasped. 'I promise you he will.'

The six men had all arrived by midnight and were posted around the house. Youngblood left with a cheery, 'See you in the morning.'

Naumann paced for a while longer, then went to bed, but he didn't sleep very well.

Chapter Twenty-two

Bradshaw lay awake a long while after the phone call, his anger cooling in stages. Finally, he dropped off to sleep, but was up early and had Glen Stingley, the president of the Imperial Petroleum Corporation, on the phone at 7.30 a.m. He outlined the call he had had from Naumann in terse sentences. Stingley agreed that they should meet at once.

Glen Stingley came out from behind a massive rosewood desk to shake hands with Bradshaw as he was ushered into the office. He was taller than Bradshaw's six-foot-one by three inches, and the strong face generated vibrancy and power. The handshake was a bone-crusher.

'We've got a problem, huh?' he said in a deep baritone.

'Maybe, maybe not. I think the Kraut is coming apart at the seams. He is real spooked.'

'What's the story?'

Bradshaw sat down in the indicated chair and Stingley returned to his seat behind the desk.

'There's a guy running around named Sebastian who has got it in for Newman. He has already knocked off another guy from the company, over in London, named Swift. I don't know why for sure, but I can make a damn good guess.'

'Tell me.'

'Well, I doubt that Newman is his real name, or that other little fink they call Spicer, and that probably goes for Swift, although I never met him. They are supposed to be Swiss also. Crap. They are about as Swiss as Mercedes-Benz. I figure they are ex-Nazis and something happened during the war which pissed this Sebastian off.'

'What makes you think so?'

'Shit, I saw enough of them. I was with Patton, G2 Intelligence. I bet my last buck that they are SS.'

Stingley mulled it over. 'Okay, so what?'

'So nothing, so Sebastian probably has a legitimate beef. And I don't much care for Newman, I hope he gets him.'

'It's OK with me, but let's get our priorities right. This Sebastian can get him after Newman completes the deal. Do you know how much it's worth?'

Bradshaw was disgruntled. 'Yeah, yeah, yeah, I know – millions. So what do you want me to do?'

'What does Newman want from us?'

'Help.'

'What kind?'

Bradshaw laughed. It was a raucous sound. 'What he would really like us to do is to get this Sebastian for him. The last time he suggested it I told him to go chase himself. I told him we were in the oil business, not Murder Incorporated.'

'Is that what he still wants from us?'

Bradshaw shook his head. 'No, this time it's a little simpler. He tells me that he knows what kind of a car Sebastian is driving and he can't go to the cops with it. So he wants us to find him.'

'That doesn't sound too unreasonable.'

'And how are we supposed to do that? You would have to have a couple of hundred guys out looking.'

Stingley flicked a speck of dust from his desk. 'I don't know, there might be a way. Do you remember a guy named Ted Sherman?'

'Ted Sherman – hmm, it rings a bell, but I can't place him.'

'Went to college with me at ANM. Then changed his mind and took a law degree and joined the FBI.'

'Oh, yeah, I remember. He used to be down here.'

'Right. Well, he has been head of the LA office for the last two years. I think I could get him to make a request through LAPD about this car.'

'Shit, he's the FBI. Why should he?'

'Well, let's just say that he owes me a whole mess of favours. And it's no skin off his nose. I will tell him that we just want to have a quiet talk with this guy 'cos he ripped us off a touch. Nothin' serious, and we really don't want to bring in the law.'

Bradshaw shrugged. 'Well, hell, if you think it'll work. He's your buddy.'

'I might as well have a try. It'll keep Newman happy and out of our hair, and I really want him to stay alive for a while yet.'

'He wants us to send him some protection also.'

'So, we'll send him some protection. We have a couple of good old boys from down here who'll jump at having a little vacation in Hollywood. They don't have to do anything. We've got to show the flag, Darrell, my boy.'

Chapter Twenty-three

Naumann was on the phone very early in the morning after the explosion. The first call was to his doctor, who agreed to transfer Spitzweg again, this time from the hospital in Santa Monica to a private sanitorium with which he dealt. It was an extra precaution to prevent the police from interrogating Spitzweg before he had a chance to brief the man, and to make sure he would stand up under the questioning. The next call was to Kessler in Hamburg. Naumann filled the lawyer in on the latest events. Kessler expressed shock and commiserations. Naumann brushed the sentiments aside and told Kessler to send over four or five men – Germans.

'I want them to be professional, you know what I mean, Kessler. Get me men who have done jobs for you in the past. I want to get rid of the men I have here. They are Americans and don't know what loyalty is, what a commitment is. You understand?'

Kessler waffled. Of course he understood, but men like that were difficult to find. It is not like the old days.

'I don't care how difficult it is – find them and send them immediately.' Naumann slammed down the phone. He was breathing hard.

To Kessler's credit, he chose to ignore the imperative, attributing it to the stress of the situation, and with several phone calls, found four good men. They would all arrive in Los Angeles within four days.

Darrell Bradshaw called. He was brusque, but managed to sound agreeable. He told Naumann that he had met with Stingley and that he thought he could help him with finding the car, and IMPETCO would send two of their security men out to LA. Naumann was less gracious.

'I don't know if I need them now, but send them anyway.' When he put the phone down he felt much happier.

Nothing much happened in the next few days. The Germans arrived to replace the Americans, and were Naumann's constant companions. The two IMPETCO men were posted to guard the outside of the house, which was beginning to resemble an entrenched battlement.

Naumann went to the sanitorium to visit Spitzweg. The little man was pallid and jumpy, a vein throbbed in his temple, he twitched. Naumann explained to him, as he would to a child, that he would be questioned by the police, and was to tell them that he knew nothing. That would be the extent of his story and he was to stick to it . . . or else.

Lieutenant Helder was angry and getting angrier by the minute. When he arrived at the office the next morning, he was told that the man at Mt Sinai had been transferred to a private sanitorium, location unknown. He called Naumann to ask about it, and was told coolly that Mr Spicer's doctor had insisted on him having complete rest, and that he was not to be bothered by anyone until he recovered fully.

Helder put down the phone in frustration and vowed he would get to the bottom of what was going on. His subordinates tiptoed past his door for the rest of the day.

Two days later, the information from the inquiries he had initiated began coming in. He sifted the reports. The Immigration Department reported that Carl Newman, a Swiss national, had entered the States some fifteen years previously, that he was a resident and a corporation officer of a Swiss-based pharmaceutical corporation that did business in America, with offices in New York, Chicago and Los Angeles. The information was about what Helder had expected. He pencilled a note in the margin to make inquiries in Switzerland about Carl Newman and William Spicer. He put the report in his 'out' tray.

The next set of reports concerned the driver and two other passengers whom he had correctly identified as bodyguards. All three had records. They ranged from 'drunk and disorderly' to 'grievous bodily harm'. One of the men had been charged with armed robbery, but the case had been dismissed for lack of evidence. Helder's mouth twisted into a grim smile. He made some notes and tossed the reports into the 'out' tray. The last report was from Interpol. Helder read it quickly and sat back in his chair.

Interpol had received Helder's circular requesting information on Carl Newman. They had nothing on him, but when they ran the name and the company, Forsche-Brandt, through the computer, a match was made. An official of the very same pharmaceutical company, Swift by name, had been murdered just outside London about six weeks earlier. Interpol gave the name of a Chief-Inspector Digby Warren, who was dealing with the case. Helder asked the switchboard to try to reach him at Scotland Yard.

It was the following morning when Warren returned the call. He apologized for being unavailable, explaining that he had been out of town on an investigation, and how could he be of service? Helder told him about the explosion of the car, of a man called Carl Newman and how the Interpol computer had connected the man's company to a murder in London.

Warren was silent for a long moment, and Helder wondered if the connection had been broken.

'I knew it,' Warren said. 'I knew the bastard was hiding something, but of course, I couldn't prove it.'

'What's it all about?' Helder asked.

Warren told him about the triple killing and about the note that had been found with the body. 'And I just found out something very significant. There was a murder of a man in Bremen a few weeks before ours, where the exact same note was left. The only difference was that our note had two names crossed out on it instead of one. One assumes that the names correspond to the individuals who were killed, although those were not the names they went by.'

Helder could hardly contain his excitement. 'You say there are two more? What are they?'

'Naumann and Spitzweg.'

'V-e-e-e-r-y interesting.'

'Yes, isn't it? You have, of course, noticed that Naumann is not a million miles away from Newman, and Spitzweg and Spicer are similar.'

'Now this thing is beginning to make sense. Can you get a line on any of these guys? I mean, what is the connection and who's the guy who's wasting them one at a time?'

'No news yet,' Warren said. 'I have only just received the information and am instituting inquiries. I thought the Federal Government of West Germany might be the place to start,' he added drily. 'Also, in the light of what you have told me, I think I would like to interview this Newman once again. It might aid my inquiries here which have stagnated.'

'Well, you come right ahead,' Helder enthused. 'We'll give you all the cooperation we can. I'd like to nail that smug son-of-a-bitch!'

Helder curbed his impatience until Warren arrived two days later. He itched to get his hands on Newman, but knew that rushing his fences wouldn't accomplish anything. Warren filled him in on all the details that he had, and Helder 'requested' that Newman come in the following day.

Naumann arrived promptly for his 10.00 appointment with his lawyer in tow – just in case. The two men were ushered into Helder's office, and Naumann's reaction on seeing Warren sitting next to Helder's desk was a brief flicker of the eyelids. They sat down.

'I think you know Chief-Inspector Warren,' Helder said.

'We have met,' Naumann replied.

'And this,' Helder indicated the lawyer, 'is Ben Marzy. How are you doing, Counsellor? I haven't seen you for quite a while. Ran out of ambulances to chase?'

Marzy, an overweight, balding man with a bulbous nose and loose-lipped mouth, grinned sourly. 'Just as funny as always, Lieutenant. You are a real riot.'

'Yeah, that's what they tell me.' He turned to Naumann. 'But I didn't call you in here to swap jokes. Chief-Inspector Warren has come all the way over from London – again, because of what happened to your car.'

Naumann was belligerent. 'What does it have to do with my car?'

'That's what we thought you could tell us. Seems to me that the people in your company are a little accident-prone. The only difference is that, in your case, it wasn't fatal.'

'That is stupid and illogical. They are separate incidents. I don't know why my colleague was killed, but it is obvious that it has nothing to do with the bomb placed in my car.'

'Is it?' Warren asked quietly. 'Obvious, I mean. It seems to me, sir, that violence has been perpetrated on both you and your former associate. That seems to be more than a coincidence.'

Naumann raised his voice, and his face flushed. 'I tell you, one had nothing to do with the other!'

Marzy put a hand on Naumann's arm. He directed his statement to Helder. 'You're badgering my client, Lieutenant. How many more times does he have to tell you that he knows nothing about what happened in England?'

Helder slapped the desk with the flat of his hand .A ballpoint pen jumped an inch. 'Until I'm convinced it's the truth.'

There was a silence in the room. Helder sat back, regretting his outburst. The chair creaked under the strain. Warren had a serene smile as he took out a cigarette and lit it. Naumann averted his eyes and shifted his chair. He also lit a cigarette – it gained him some time. Marzy folded his arms across his chest, stuck out his lower lip and glared at Helder. Into the silence, Warren dropped his well-timed little bombshell.

'I know that two men died and had notes left by their bodies. What does the twelfth of December 1940 mean to you . . . Herr Naumann?'

Naumann was totally unprepared for hearing his real name. He flinched and went deathly pale. His voice came out in a croak. 'My name is Newman.'

'Oh, didn't I say that?' Warren asked blandly. 'Silly of me. Newman, of course. I must have been thinking of one of the names on the note, one that hasn't been crossed off yet. Easy mistake to make. Newman, Naumann, very much alike, aren't they?'

Naumann was treated to an ingenuous smile. Marzy's head moved back and forth between the two men in a way that was reminiscent of watching a tennis match. He looked puzzled. His shrewd little eyes had missed nothing. There was certainly something going on, but something to which he was not privy. He thought he'd better jump in, his client was looking distressed.

'What's this date in 1940 got to do with anything?' he challenged in a loud voice.

'That's what we would like to know,' Helder said. 'We think Mr Newman might be able to help us.'

'Now c'mon, Lieutenant,' Marzy shook his finger at him, 'I don't know what the hell kinda game you're playing. None of that shit has anything to do with my client's car. It looks like I have to remind you that he's the innocent victim, the man who, but for the grace of God, would have died tragically at the hands of a vicious felon – who you should be out trying to catch, instead of coming down on my client like a ton of bricks. I know you are a hard-nosed cop, but you are out of line.'

Helder clapped his hands in a slow rhythm. 'Bravo, Counsellor, that was a real stirring speech. Save it for a jury; I'm not impressed.'

Marzy's pudgy face went red. 'My client and I don't have to sit here and listen to this abuse. We came down here in good faith, thinking you had some new information on the people who blew up the car, and, obviously, all you want to do is insult us both. You can be sure that the Commissioner will get a full report on this fiasco. C'mon, Carl.'

The two of them stood up and trooped out of the room. Marzy slammed the door behind him. Helder and Warren stayed where they were, exchanged glances.

'I think I blew it,' Helder said. He got up from behind his desk and walked to the window. It had begun to rain.

Warren shrugged. 'Don't worry about it, Sam. I think we got more than I reasonably expected. He was bound to fight shy of a connection to my little lot in London, but his reaction to the name "Naumann" was far better than I had hoped for.'

'Yeah, maybe we dug ourselves up a skeleton.'

'I gather you know his lawyer?'

Helder turned back from the window. 'That's what got me pissed,' he said, reddening again. 'I've had several run-ins with that shyster. He'll represent anything that will make him a lot of bucks – rapists, child molesters, oddball religious cults and dope dealers. I knew that Newman was involved up to the roots of his hair as soon as I saw Marzy walk in. You don't get that kind of mouthpiece unless you got something to hide.'

'Hmm, we have solicitors like that in Britain also, but more to the point, where do we go from here. There seems to be little point in pursuing the line we took with Newman. All we can expect is more of the same.'

'I agree. We have to hit him with something more concrete next time. How long can you stay?'

'Oh, at a pinch, I might be able to stretch it out for another four or five days,' Warren smiled, 'in pursuance of my inquiries, of course.'

'Good, we need some hard facts. When do you think you will hear from Germany?'

'Oh, any time now. In the best of all possible worlds, I will receive information which will connect Newman with Naumann. Then perhaps I can solve my own murders.'

Outside, Marzy waited until he was seated comfortably in

the back seat of Naumann's new Mercedes. He leaned forward and shut the glass panel that separated them from the driver and bodyguard. 'Now, what the hell was that all about?'

Naumann had his head turned. He watched the passing scenery. 'Nothing to concern you. I am employing you to stop the police from asking awkward questions,' Naumann leaned back in his seat, crossed one immaculate trousered leg over the other, 'which you did admirably.'

'Hey, c'mon, Carl, I'm the only one in the dark here. There is nothing wrong with my eyesight. You know who it is who booby-trapped your car, and those damn cops know you know. How am I supposed to defend you if you don't let me in on it?'

'Very shortly, I won't need defending. The source of my . . . discomfort will be removed; so you see, you don't really need to know any more.'

'Didn't you ever hear of privileged communication?' Marzy said in agitation. 'I'm on your side, I'm not going to talk to anyone else.'

'No, you're not,' Naumann agreed, and that was all he said until he reached home and grunted a good-bye.

Chapter Twenty-four

Sebastian stayed close to Malibu for the next ten days and brooded. The only trip he made was to go to the supermarket once and lay in a supply of groceries, so that he was unaware that a request had been made to all the police departments in LA and Orange Counties to be on the look-out for a brown Camaro, licence number FRT 142. The request was to identify and locate, but not to apprehend. All information on the car was to be forwarded to Ted Sherman, FBI, Los Angeles office. Apart from the one brief trip, the car remained parked outside the Malibu house, invisible from the road. Sebastian was able to brood in peace and what he thought was security, a combination of factors which made him careless.

He sat for hours watching the ocean, listening to the surf

pound the beach. Sometimes he would take long walks on the sand, deserted in January. His isolation was nearly complete. Only occasionally would a figure emerge from one of the houses, usually with a dog in tow. Sebastian never exchanged greetings, avoided all contact.

Sometimes he would jog along the beach two miles to the south, then back again past his house to where the wealthy Malibu Colony began, and back to the starting point. Then he would work out for another solid hour, straining muscles with an excess of pushups, situps, karate exercises, until, at the end of it, he could collapse in a heap without having to think about any more than getting his breathing back to normal.

Sometimes he would reflect on the lengths he had gone to to acquire some particular skill. His expertise with the knife had taken time, hour after patient hour of practice. His first knife came from a sports equipment shop where Grandfather Sebastian had taken him to buy him his own deep-water rod and reel. While the old man enthused about the equipment, young Mark's attention was elsewhere on the display of hunting knives pinned to a cork board to the left of the gun counter. His grandfather found it difficult to refuse him anything, and he came away with a gleaming knife of his own.

There were woods on the property of the Gustavus Adolphus Academy. They extended for a quarter of a mile beyond the buildings proper. Mark found a small clearing and put a crude target up on a tree. Then he would practise.

The knife was heavy and hard to handle in flight. The eight-inch blade and sturdy hilt were not meant for throwing, the balance was wrong. Mark hitch-hiked into Monterey and bought two proper throwing knives with his allowance; then he practised whenever he could get away. In the end, he could put both knives into the bull's eye of his target from forty feet away, with only a hair's breadth between them.

Then there were the hours of flying he had put in when that was high on his list. He had concentrated on learning to fly figure eights, outside loops, split esses and, like everything else, once he had mastered it, he went on to something else. He had done the same with parachuting where he showed great promise as a sky-diver before he quit; and archery, where he was good enough for competitions; and stunt driving where he had been offered a contract by a film studio who wanted him to jump the car seventy feet in the air – he turned it down, just because he knew it was easy.

Then there were the courses he took in electronics; and the job he held for three months at a small factory in Downey which made bugging devices on government contract; and his expertise with locks – that was a funny one, an accident, or destiny.

It was while he was taking his acting lessons in New York. He had a small apartment, a third floor walk-up in the Village. He could have afforded better, but all the other students lived in the area and he wanted to be looked on as just another one.

There wasn't much of value in the apartment, other than a good stereo and tape deck, so that he was surprised, when he reached the second landing of his building, to hear somebody fiddling with the lock on his door. He went up the last flight of stairs without making a sound, lunged and grabbed the figure bending over the lock by his collar. He swung the intruder round, fist poised for a punch. He stopped. The man was old, fifty-five Sebastian guessed; the bald head gleamed with sweat, the eyes were mournful. The man had only one arm.

'What the hell are you doing?' Sebastian hissed.

The man tried to shrug in the grasp, failed. 'I guess,' the man said, 'I was trying to break into your place.'

Sebastian looked down at the man's one arm. He held a set of lock picks. Sebastian reached into his pocket, took out his key, unlocked the door. He dragged the man in and threw him into a chair. He slammed the door and sat down across from him. 'And what did you expect to find in this dump?'

The man had a sheepish grin. He shrugged again with his one good arm and this time succeeded. 'Didn't expect to find nothing. It was just for practice.'

'Practice? You look kinda old to start learning how to be a cat burglar.'

The man drew himself up and sat stiffly erect. The expression hardened, the eyes snapped. Pride emanated in waves. 'I was the best damn second-storey man this town has ever seen . . . before this' – he indicated the missing arm where the empty sleeve was pinned to the jacket – 'so don't make fun of me, kid, because you don't know nothing.'

Sebastian softened. He sat back and smiled. 'OK, I'm listening.'

The man looked at Sebastian with suspicion. 'You gonna turn me in?'

'Don't know, it depends on how good a story you tell.'

The man was belligerent. 'Well, I don't give a damn if you do turn me in, there's nothing on the outside for me anyway. I'd just as soon get three squares on the State . . . you really want to know?'

Sebastian nodded. So the man started and seemed pleased to find a willing audience. He introduced himself. He was very formal.

'I am William Henry Seaton . . . the Third, but everyone calls me Angel.' That was, he told Sebastian, because at times it seemed as if he could fly up the side of a building. He related how, when he was a boy, he had run away from his comfortable home in upstate New York to come to the Big Apple, and how he had fallen in with 'bad company'. Seaton was given to using old-fashioned turns of phrase that made Sebastian smile. Seaton told him how he had been apprenticed to the best lock man of the twenties and thirties and how, as he learned his craft, he was called in by the various criminal factions to pull off some spectacular jobs. He told Sebastian about the safe he had cracked in the millionaire's apartment on Fifth Avenue, where he found a fortune in jewels, and papers and ledgers that proved the millionaire was an embezzler on a grand scale. The robbery was never reported.

There were many other jobs all over Manhattan and Long Island and wealthy resorts like Newport and Miami Beach, and he said with pride that he had never been caught, arrested on more than one occasion, but never convicted. 'The cops knew who I was, but couldn't do a damn thing.' And then eight years earlier when one top banana crook had taken exception to him doing a job for a rival, his right arm had been run over by a Caddy limousine, deliberately. After he recovered, with the arm missing, he had scratched out an existence ever since, training himself to do what he knew best, left-handed.

It was exactly what Sebastian was looking for. He became a pupil of William Henry Seaton the Third, gave him money to live comfortably, learned everything there was to learn about locks and safes, became good friends with the man.

Seaton died a year later of a coronary. Sebastian found him in his apartment with a note that said thanks for everything and a legacy to Sebastian, Seaton's own set of lock picks, master keys and tools. Sebastian paid for the funeral and was the only mourner.

Sometimes he thought about his early life that, for most kids, would be the formative years, from which he felt excluded. He had formed his own conclusions in solitary. Although there were always people around him, he remained in seclusion as no one was allowed to penetrate the barriers he erected.

It came from a hard core of obstinacy, a trait from both sides of the family. He had found a purpose for living, for being, and would run roughshod over anyone who would try to deter him.

He had no parents to rely on, but two sets of very rich, very influential, very demanding grandparents. They vied for his attention, haggled over the time he spent with either set. The division was calculated to the last day. So there were times when he spent whole summers in Chicago with his mother's parents, the Goldmans. They had a huge house in the north Chicago suburb of Skokie. They had servants and a patio and a barbecue and a backyard the size of a football field. They built and installed items they thought would amuse young Mark – a pool, a tennis court a cabin-sized playhouse. He would use the pool when no one else was in it; shunned the playhouse, except very late at night when everyone else was asleep when he could sneak out to it, sit in the dark and think. The pro they brought in to teach him tennis finally gave up in exasperation when Mark refused to learn the more delicate touches of the game. He tried to kill every ball that came his way.

Morris Goldman tried to amuse him. He took Mark to Cub games at Wrigley Field and introduced him to the players. Mark barely responded. He took him to the science museum and the art institute and to Marshall Fields and told him he could buy anything he wanted in the department store. Mark chose a deck of cards with which he could play solitaire, and nothing else.

The Goldmans tried to make him go to the synagogue they supported. He was adamant in his refusal. But then the Sebastians had tried to get him to go to church and he had been just as adamant with them. Both of them tried to persuade him to leave the Gustavus Adolphus Academy, which was for misfits, and to go to a more conventional school. He refused that too. It suited him.

Sebastian reflected that he was not a loving child. He knew that there were times when both the Goldmans and the Sebastians would have loved to have put an arm round him when introducing him to their friends and say proudly, 'This is my grandson. He is a great kid and a fine example of what having children is all about.' But they refrained because they could never be quite sure what his reaction might be. He was always polite and courteous, and just as often stand-offish. His mouth would smile, his eyes wouldn't. It was disconcerting. There were times when he really tried to be different. He would castigate himself for being a 'problem'. He would resolve to turn over a new leaf, to be what they wanted him to be, but was never able to sustain it. The energy required just seemed to drain away, leaving him as flat as a dead battery.

Finally, his grandparents squelched their exasperation. They established a wary *détente* with their grandson. They were grateful for the progress he had made, which he insisted on doing at his own speed. They respected his wishes when he said no. They still didn't, couldn't, begin to understand him. He was not a 'normal' boy, but they were at last satisfied that Mark – in his own way – would be a credit to them, a quality that ranked high in their respective spheres of influence.

Sometimes he would sit and read snatches of *Paradise Lost* and Dante's *Inferno.* They suited his mood, but he found them vaguely unsettling, especially the part in the *Inferno* that dealt with the Seventh Circle of Hell in the City of Dis, the level that included those who did violence to others, the murderers.

This was the most time he had ever spent at trying to understand himself. The concentration was excruciating, the dull ache in his head constant, conclusions still beyond his reach.

Sebastian drove into town. He'd finally had enough of his self-imposed exile. On the last day he thought that, by speaking to Pamela, he might reach a conclusion. He picked up the phone a dozen times, and an equal number of times set it down before dialling.

He realized that he didn't even know what the date was until he passed a newsstand and saw it displayed: 5 February.

He found a film theatre on Wilshire Boulevard, and a parking space just outside, left the car and went in.

Fifteen minutes later, a police car on its regular patrol passed the Camaro and stopped to check the licence plate because it was brown. The licence matched the car on the list. The patrolman called in for instructions. Ted Sherman was contacted at the FBI, wrote down the present location of the car, told the caller he would handle it from there. He rang Stingley in Dallas. Stingley phoned one of his security men back in Los Angeles and, in forty-five minutes, that man and one other were parked a few cars behind the Camaro. They didn't have long to wait. Sebastian came out of the theatre, got into the car and drove west on Wilshire, with the other car following fifty feet behind.

Sebastian was so preoccupied that he never even glanced in his rear view mirror. He was, perhaps, the most vulnerable he had been in years.

When Sebastian turned north on Pacific Coast Highway, the other car was right with him; and when Sebastian slowed to turn into his house, the other car slowed and went past, making a note of the address.

The two men rode back into town and informed Naumann that they had found his man. Naumann sat motionless for a long time, savouring it. At last, he had a chance to do things his way. He reached for the phone to call Youngblood, got as far as lifting the receiver, then replaced it. The idea had been for Youngblood to wait until Sebastian had been located when he would then do the job for which he was employed. An idea burst on Naumann that was like a brilliant flash of light. Youngblood, indeed, would get a chance to do the job, but not in the way he expected. Naumann went to see Spitzweg, who was installed in one of the spare rooms.

'We have him now, Max,' Naumann gloated. 'I know where Sebastian is.'

Spitzweg's eyes widened. 'Really, Carl?' he whispered. 'It will all be over soon?'

'Very soon.'

Spitzweg sighed and fell back on the bed. He looked ghastly.

Naumann took the four Germans, and all of them piled into the Mercedes and drove out to Malibu. It was just after seven when they arrived, and quite dark. It was raining again.

They parked the car across the highway from the house and fifty yards further down the road. Naumann dispatched one of the Germans to reconnoitre. He was back in a few minutes to say that the Camero was parked in front of the house and that there were lights on inside.

'Then we wait,' Naumann said, and lit a cigarette.

Naumann couldn't have known, but he was lucky that Sebastian had decided to come out of his shell, or he might have been sitting there for the next week. But the brief trip to the film had whetted his appetite for the great outdoors. What really drew Sebastian out was that he was bored to death with his own cooking. He drove out around 8.00 p.m. and went north further into Malibu to find one of the many steak and seafood places that dotted the coast. Naumann waited until the tail lights were out of sight, then he and three of the Germans (he left one with the car) crossed the highway and went over to Sebastian's house. They were cautious, but there was no need. There wasn't a car in sight and it looked like all the houses were unoccupied. They opened the gates, went down the steps and along the path that led to the entrance door. Naumann gestured to the German, who was reputed to be the most adept at picking locks. The man went to work.

Strangely enough, Sebastian, ever security conscious, had been lax about his own house. There were reasons for it. He kept nothing visible that was worth stealing and he felt safe in the house about which nobody knew. The man took only a minute to open the door, and the four of them went inside.

Sebastian had a good meal at a table next to the window where the ocean slapped at the glass at high tide. He took his time so that it was already 10.00 when he retrieved his car from the parking lot attendant.

The rain was coming down in a steady drizzle as he drove back down the highway and parked in front of his home.

The entrance door opened into a long narrow hallway with a door to a spare bedroom on the right, the second bathroom on the left. At the end of the hallway was a lounge, rectangular in shape, twenty feet from the doorway to the picture windows that fronted the ocean, and twenty-five feet long that extended to the left and right of the doorway in equal proportions. The kitchen was tucked in behind the door with a serving bar acting as the dividing line between the lounge and kitchen. Access to the master bedroom was through a doorway to the left.

Sebastian's shoes clattered on the woodblock flooring of the hallway. His mind was dulled with his problems, his sixth sense inoperative – until it was too late.

He stepped into the lounge reaching for the wall switch. He was half-turned, a sense of something being not quite right trying to penetrate his hazy brain.

The light that flooded the room and the door that smashed into his unprotected back, knocking him forward, happened simultaneously. Sebastian had lightning reactions, but he still wasn't quick enough to block the fist that thudded into his stomach, taking his breath away, and he never saw the black-jack that clipped him from behind.

He crawled his way up from the blackness and into a shower of coloured light that separated into individual sparks and pin-wheeled crazily, exploded, and coalesced into fingerpaint blobs. He reached full consciousness but kept his eyes shut. His head ached. The noise around him separated into speech. German registered on his fogged brain. He felt that the pit of his stomach had dropped to the floor. He suppressed a groan. A pointed toe-cap kicked him in the ribs. Sebastian hoisted his eyelids to half mast. The room swam for a moment, and then the face that bent over him steadied.

The sheen of sweat on the man's forehead glistened in the overhead light, the blue eyes were arctic, the scar on the cheek twitched. 'So we meet at last,' Naumann said.

Sebastian licked his lips; they felt dry. 'Somehow, I guessed that you would say some melodramatic crap like that,' he said. 'That's straight out of a Sydney Greenstreet movie.'

Naumann laughed softly. It was not a sound calculated to amuse. 'Nowhere in your dossier does it say you were a comedian. I must remonstrate with my investigator . . . to have slipped so badly.' He lifted his eyes and nodded to the two men standing behind Sebastian's prostrate form. They each grabbed one of his biceps and roughly manhandled him to his feet. He felt weak from the blow, but was recovering quickly. He tried to take stock of the situation. He had only just realized that his hands were tied behind him. He tested the knots. They were solid, and his wrists had already begun to ache.

Naumann stood in front of him, hands on hips, twisted smile on his face. To his right, a solidly built man in his early thirties with fair hair and an expressionless face held a revolver that was pointed in the approximate region of his belly-button. The man was dressed in a black suit and tie, a white shirt suitable for a funeral. Sebastian twisted around. The other two men, also expressionless, were dressed the same. Except for the fact that one had black hair, the other white-blond, all three of the men carried with them the same deadly air of menace. Sebastian dubbed them Fritz 1, 2 and 3, and turned back to Naumann.

'You have caused me much trouble,' Naumann said. The smile broadened. 'But I think for not much longer.'

Sebastian was diffident. 'Oh, I don't know. As Yogi Berra once said, "The game's not over until it's over." But then you wouldn't know who Yogi Berra is. He's one of our great philosophers.'

Naumann's hand shot out and slapped him hard across the face. Sebastian had expected that something like that would happen and rolled with it as best he could. It still made his head ring and he tasted blood.

Naumann was breathing hard. He started to pace the room, twisting his head so that he always kept Sebastian in sight, and he began ranting. He turned to Sebastian, his face flushed a deep crimson. He stamped his foot, pounded an open hand with his fist.

'You piece of Jewish shit! You dare to come after me, dare to think you are better. I will eliminate you as I did that filth that spawned you. Yes, I killed your father, shot him in the head, and I fucked that bitch whore of a mother of yours before I killed her also.'

Sebastian stiffened, his jaw clenched, his lips whitened to a narrow line, but he kept his expression the same, his eyes riveted on Naumann.

'You have the audacity to think that you, one inferior man, could beat me?'

The man with the gun glanced at Naumann and shifted uneasily. The shouted words bounced around the hard surfaces of the room. Naumann's stream of curses echoed back from all sides. He lunged forward, still screaming and attacked Sebastian with both fists. Sebastian tried to keep out of the way, but it was impossible. Fritz 1 and 2 held him rigid for the onslaught. Finally he blacked out.

*

When Sebastian came back to consciousness for the second time, he crawled back, step by painful step. Sections of his body checked in with his brain one at a time. The first that intruded was a right hip. It seemed to be in contact with something hard and irregular. It sent out pain signals. His wrists came next. They were still tied and he had very little feeling in his hands. His head seemed to be resting on the same irregular surface that his hip tried to tell him about. Now he had additional information: It was also cold and clammily wet . . .

He opened his eyes. The darkness remained velvety and impenetrable. He panicked, thinking he had gone blind. He moved his head, and his cheek scraped on what he now recognized as a rough stone floor. His shifting body made a slight echo. He seemed to be in a spacious room, empty and pitch black. The pain in his hip eased when he rolled off the pebble he'd been lying on. He struggled to sit up, using his shoulder for impetus.

He sat cross-legged in the dark and shook his head to clear it. Nausea swept over him and he almost threw up, but gulped in a large lungful of air and managed to keep it down.

He struggled to his feet, rolling over on his knees, first planting one foot on the ground and then the other. He stood, swayed, felt dizzy and completely disoriented. There was no reference point, just total blackness.

He took a tentative step, then another. Five steps later, his shoulder brushed the wall. He leaned his back against it, panting from the effort. He straightened up and, keeping his right shoulder in contact with the wall, shuffled forward. His heels made a hollow ring in the room.

He found the next wall when he banged painfully into it with his forehead. He turned his back to the wall again and tried another approach. He trailed his fingers along the wall as he shuffled crab-wise to the next corner; still solid stone. He turned the corner and continued his progress. His fingers registered a difference. The surface was wood, smooth in places, roughened in others. He slid along it for what he estimated to be three feet. Unquestionably a door. He turned around and kicked it with the heel of his shoe. It sounded thick and solid.

He went on and made a complete circuit of the room. There was just the one entrance, all the other wall unbroken rough stone.

He decided he was in a storage room of some kind, and couldn't even begin to guess where. It could be California or Romania, although, judging from how the bruises on his face and body still ached, he supposed that he had not been unconscious for that long – California, and most probably within a reasonable distance from his Malibu house. He made another guess that he was in a basement; no other logical reason other than it felt like one. So if that were the case, it was probably part of a house, and he could extend his guesses to its being unoccupied and probably away from built-up areas. He couldn't see immediately how that was going to help him out of his predicament. So first things first.

His hands were getting more numb with each passing minute, and that became his first priority. He moved down the wall until he found a particularly rough spot where a chunk of the stone seemed to overlap and might provide a cutting edge. He started to rub his bonds on the stone. They were thin, probably nylon, and a good portion of his skin rubbed along with the rope. He gritted his teeth.

The black Mercedes slid noiselessly on the narrow roads that ran up and down the hills on Topanga Canyon. Naumann looked at the luminous hand of his watch. It was almost 1.00 in the morning and the few houses that they passed were dark and shuttered for the night. A lone dog, wakened from its sleep, barked furiously after them.

Naumann paid no attention. It would take distraction of earthquake proportions to penetrate his sense of euphoria. He sat and gloated, and the other four men in the car watched him covertly, but remained silent.

Everything was crystal clear. There was nothing to thwart him any more. Soon there would be no one left to hinder him in any way. Mexico and all that it promised lay open in front of him. He had known for two days that Luis Montez would receive his appointment to the Ministry officially in one week's time. The news hadn't gladdened him as it should have, but then Sebastian was still loose and the future unresolved.

Now it was different. Sebastian was his prisoner. He languished in the basement of the deserted house in Topanga Canyon, where he would remain until he put the next phase of his plan into operation. Sebastian could shout his head off if he wanted to. Nobody would hear him. The house was isolated from his nearest neighbour by a good half-mile, and Naumann owned all the surrounding acreage – a parcel of land he had picked up cheaply, speculating that its value would increase with the passing years. He had never dreamed that he would put his purchase to such swift and excellent use.

The car turned into Beverly Glen and then left on Mulholland Drive that bisected the Hollywood Hills. Naumann's eyes glowed in the faint light from the dashboard instruments. He felt a quick burst of admiration for the driver, a good German, who was unfamiliar with Los Angeles, but who could apparently read a map and commit it to memory with the best of them. They proceeded by stages to his house in Beverly Hills.

Ben Marzy sounded wide awake when he answered the phone. Naumann could hear music in the background and the low hum of female voices. He identified himself.

'Hi, Carl. I'm having a little party. Do you wanna come over?'

Naumann ignored the question and asked one of his own. 'You know the boat I asked you about? When can I get it?'

'Boat? Oh, yeah. Well . . . hell, I don't know for sure, It's down somewhere south of Ensenada. Couple of days maybe.'

Naumann hesitated a moment before answering. 'All right, a couple of days. It's as you told me, this boat? Not traceable to you, I mean.'

'C'mon, Carl, this is an open line. It's a good boat. Nobody I know has anything to do with it. You know what it's used for.'

Naumann knew exactly the use to which the boat was put. It made the run regularly from Mexico, carrying good grass or coke or brown Mexican heroin or all three to Los Angeles, where it was picked up and distributed by one of Marzy's 'clients'. Marzy had told him that it was a fifty-foot cruiser with twin high-speed diesels that could out-run almost anything, and so far had. Naumann was far more interested in its anonymity than in its speed.

'You will take care of changing the name . . . ?'

'Like I said. It'll all be done. You haven't told me what you want to use it for.'

'That's correct,' Naumann said, and put the phone down.

Naumann made one more call. It was hard for him to tell if Youngblood was awake, even when he was awake, when he affected that maddening drawl. Instead of music, Naumann could hear a noise in the background that sounded like a pot of boiling water.

'What's that,' Naumann asked, 'that noise?'

'Noise? Oh, you mean the bubbling. I'm in my jacuzzi.' A female giggle told Naumann that Youngblood was not along in his jacuzzi. 'What can I do for you?' Youngblood asked.

'What I am paying you for,' Naumann said grimly. 'I have Sebastian.'

There was a silence on the line. 'No kidding?'

Naumann had always wondered why Americans uttered those inane words every time a statement of truth was made that seemed to stretch their incredulity. He had never figured it out.

'No,' he answered, 'that was not a joke. I am not in the habit of calling people in the middle of the night to tell funny stories.'

There was a long silence on the line. 'What do you want me to do?'

'I want you to come to my office the day after tomorrow at precisely nine-thirty a.m., and I will tell you then.' Naumann broke the connection without saying good-bye.

At the other end of the line, Youngblood held the phone to his ear for long seconds listening to the dial tone before he replaced the receiver. He was thoughtful, so deep into it that he was oblivious of the girl next to him, whose soft hand had slid across his thigh and was gently massaging his penis.

Naumann went to see Spitzweg. When he flipped on the light, he saw that the little German was huddled in his bedclothes, eyes wide and staring wildly.

'What's the matter, Carl, what's the matter?'

Naumann didn't bother to conceal the contempt in his voice. 'There is nothing the matter. You must pull yourself together; you are becoming a vegetable. I have come to tell you that Sebastian is my prisoner. I have him locked in the cellar at the house in Topanga Canyon. He will not bother us any more.'

Naumann turned on his heel and left the room.

Spitzweg lay on the bed, quaking with fear. Slowly, Naumann's words sank in and he began to relax, but he didn't sleep much and kept the light on.

Sebastian had lost track of time. The sawing motion that his hands made on the sharp stone had become mechanical. He concentrated his mind away from the pain. The rope had become slick and wet, Sebastian judged, from a combination of the sweat that flowed freely and his own blood.

He continued sawing away at the rope for an additional minute before he realized that the strands had parted. He staggered away from the wall. The rope unwound and he was finally able to get his hands free. They felt like two lumps of raw meat. He kneaded them together. Circulation returned at a snail's pace. It was heralded by the pins and needles that started in his palms and worked their way to his fingertips. The pain was even worse than rubbing off layers of flesh.

When sensitivity returned, he touched his face with careful fingers. One eye was almost shut, although in the complete dark of the cellar, there was nothing to see anyway. His left cheek was swollen, a dull ache in the cheek-bone along its entire length. His lip was cut in two or three places, his front teeth felt loose. There was a sharp pain in the area of his ribs where he had been kicked before he blacked out, and aches in other parts of his body that must have happened after he lost consciousness. He took a deep breath while holding his ribs. It hurt, but he didn't think anything was broken.

He looked at his watch. The luminous dial read just after 4.30. Morning or evening? If it was morning, as he surmised, then he had been in this place for four or five hours. He set out to explore it.

This time he held one hand on the wall and the other in front of him so that he wouldn't bang himself again. He counted his steps. Fifteen paces on the two long sides of the room, twelve paces to accomplish the two shorter sides. He calculated, using a thirty-inch step. Approximately thirty-seven and a half feet by twenty-eight feet. A good-sized room. It reinforced his original idea that he was in a basement.

He made several forays across the room, striking out from one wall and holding both hands out in front of him to tell him when he reached the other side. He zig-zagged back and forth, found nothing else in the room but himself. He jumped as high as he could, holding his hand above him. His fingertips just grazed the ceiling. It was also stone. He went to examine the door. He kicked at it with his foot and thrust his shoulder hard against it. It was solid and gave no more than a quarter of an inch. He tried to find the keyhole. There wasn't any. So, that meant the door was secured from the outside, either by a bolt or a heavy block of wood that slotted into iron holders. The hinges, too, were on the other side. He crashed into the door repeatedly until his shoulder was sore. The door barely quivered. He sat down on the floor with his back to the door trying to think what to do next.

Recriminations flooded in that revolved around how he could have been so careless, how he could have been caught with such childish ease. He thrust the thoughts away viciously. They wouldn't help him to get out.

Chapter Twenty-five

Chief-Inspector Warren arrived at Police Headquarters early. He looked dapper as ever in a charcoal grey suit that looked like Savile Row, but which had cost him less than half the price in Fulham Road. He wore over it a fawn-coloured Burberry and carried a soft felt hat in one hand. The drizzle had abated to a fine mist. Warren carried a rolled umbrella in case it should start again. He was used to London.

He was surprised when the desk sergeant told him that Helder was already in. He went directly to the office, knocked and entered. 'Bit early, Sam, isn't it? A quarter-past seven?'

Helder grinned sourly from behind a paper cup of coffee. 'This damn thing's bugging me. I couldn't sleep. What's your excuse?'

'Oh, I'm still on London time,' Warren grinned. 'It's a quarter-past three this afternoon. No, really, I was on the phone. They called me about this Swift case . . . or should we call him Rascher? They've picked up a suspect called Jimmy O'Brien. He's a hard nut who hires his muscle out to the highest bidder. We have reason to believe that he was at the stable when the three men were killed.'

'Hey, that's great. What did they tell you?'

'Not a lot yet,' Warren admitted, 'but we can make several surmises.'

'How did you get on to him?'

'Through one of the dead men, Jack Poggin. He was another one who hired himself out as a heavy, and the two of them usually worked together. O'Brien, of course, claims to be an innocent victim. It was only after the stable owner identified him from the line-up that he admitted to being there at all.'

Warren sat down on the chair and lit a cigarette. 'He says he knows nothing, only that this Swift – or Rascher – hired him as a bodyguard. He says that there was supposed to be some sort of meeting and that Rascher was scared. The only name he knows is Sebastian, but whether it is Sebastian-somebody, or something-Sebastian is anyone's guess. I wish I had been able to interrogate him myself, but never mind. From what I can gather, he appears to be telling the truth . . . or most of it. There is something I have not mentioned to you. When we took samples of blood on the ground, there were four blood types and only three people accounted for. O'Brien was not injured, so that leaves this Sebastian or some other unknown party. O'Brien is not saying. His story is that he was on guard, waiting for this character to arrive, when he was coshed from behind, and he doesn't know anything until after he woke up, found his friend and former employee dead and left the scene rather quickly. And that is all he will say. I am sure there is more, but we haven't been able to shake him into telling us.'

Helder sat bolt upright hanging on every word. 'Well, by God, that's enough to go on with. I would like to ask this Newman character about someone named Sebastian, and see what his reaction is.'

'Are you going to call him in?'

'No, I don't think so. He will just bring that shyster with him and we won't find out anything. I think we'll drop in to see him at his office . . . unannounced.'

So just after 10.00 that morning, Naumann's secretary informed him that a Lieutenant Helder and Chief-Inspector Warren were in the outer office requesting an audience.

Naumann frowned and then smiled. 'Tell the gentlemen to come in,' he said.

Helder and Warren came in and sat down. They both noticed

how relaxed Naumann looked. Helder decided to plunge straight in. 'What does the name Sebastian mean to you, Mr Newman?'

Naumann was surprised but not completely. He had decided at the previous interview that it was likely that Scotland Yard would unearth the name. 'Sebastian who?' he asked blandly.

Helder and Warren looked at each other. 'We thought you could tell us that,' Warren said.

Naumann shook his head. 'I'm sorry, gentlemen, I don't know the name. Am I supposed to?'

Warren leaned forward in his chair. 'Your associate, Mr Swift, he never mentioned him?'

'Sorry, I've never heard the name. Does it have something to do with my colleague's death?'

The rest of the interview went about the same way, so that in ten minutes the front entrance of the office building disgorged two very disgruntled policemen.

'Something has happened since the last time,' Helder said. 'That smug son-of-a-bitch is completely different.'

'I had the same impression. What can we infer from that?'

'That they got this Sebastian? – If he's the one that's been knocking them off.'

They walked round the building and towards the underground garage. Helder was deep in thought. 'Damn it,' he said, 'you know what I'm going to do? I'm going to stake out Newman's house. It's going to play hell with my budget, and I might even get some flak from above about why I'm wasting the Department's money on a supposedly innocent victim – not to mention what I'm doing to his civil rights – but I think it's worth it. Maybe we'll find out something we can use, because Newman is sure not going to tell us.'

The hours dragged on with excruciating slowness for Sebastian. The only thing he could see was the luminous dial of his watch. He started to play games with himself to pass the time, tried to estimate the time in half-hour units before he looked at his watch again. He was getting good at it.

Twice each hour he would get up, pace back and forth. He got to know the dimensions of the room so well that he stopped short of banging into the wall, without the benefit of a groping hand in front of him. He tried to get a little closer each time and was satisfied when he could pull up in front of the wall, his nose a mere two inches away.

He finally resorted to meditation. It was a throwback to his days in the foothills around Kyoto, when he was training with the Master, intent on achieving the various plateaus of karate expertise. But it had been much more than just karate. It was a way of life. It provided him with inner peace when he needed it most.

The Master had advocated Zen for the initial part of his training, and taught him to increase his knowledge throughout the three years.

Now he sat in the dark, in the lotus position, and the Master's words came back to him as tangible as the stone floor.

'When you first look at Zen, a bowl is a bowl and tea is tea. While you are studying Zen, the bowl is no longer a bowl and tea is no longer tea. When you are enlightened, a bowl is again a bowl and tea is again tea.' And, 'What is the greatest single thing a man can do in his life? To know himself.' And the story of the archer: 'The archery master says that Zen is easy. The target is myself, I reach the point of no effort, the arrow leaves the bow, the arrow and the target are one.'

Sebastian was so deep into his meditation that the real world meshed with the dream world. He no longer felt the stone floor on which he was sitting, but seemed to be floating just above it. At one point he thought he felt a slight rumble, bass overtones below the level of his hearing, transmitting themselves through his body. He thought he heard the room shake, but it was momentary. A mere fragment of time, and he dismissed it as one of the manifestations of his deep meditation.

Sebastian felt comforted in his solitude.

Would he be left there to die of thirst and starvation? Or would Naumann come back and take a personal part in his demise? Sebastian decided that that would be the case. From what he knew of the German, he wouldn't be allowed to just languish. Naumann would have something much more positive planned for him.

He had ample time to reflect on the circumstances that brought him there. His thoughts ran along different channels from the previous period he spent at Malibu. He realized now that he had been in a mental fog looking for justifications for his so-called mission. By the end, he had almost decided to leave it, to pack up, to go away, back to England, make an attempt at some sort of a life with Pamela.

Meeting the girl had been the most disconcerting of events in his life. It had forced him to think of something that he had consciously avoided – the future. Beyond his revenge, there had been only limbo, now there was substance. And now it might be too late. The hours dragged on, thirty of them now.

Naumann was all business when Youngblood arrived. He was crisp and authoritative, a changed man from the one Youngblood had known for the past few weeks.

'You will be able to complete your part of the agreement by eliminating Sebastian, and I want you to do it tomorrow night.'

'Where is he?'

'I have him stored away, where no one will find him.'

'Is that where you want me to do it?'

'No, we'll pick Sebastian up from there. I don't want any dead bodies found in the vicinity of that property. I have arranged for a boat. I want you to take him out to sea and dump him, so that he will never be found. You can run a boat, can't you?'

Youngblood nodded. 'OK, where and when?'

'Midnight at my house. Take a taxi,' Naumann said, congratulating himself on his forethought. He would not have to get rid of Youngblood's car. 'We'll get Sebastian in my car.'

Spitzweg was in torment. He writhed on his bed until he couldn't stand it any more. He forced himself to get up, and stumbled to the bathroom. He drew a steaming hot tub and settled himself in it. It was supposed to relax him. It didn't.

He agonized over what was going on, what had gone before, what the future would bring. He held himself responsible – or at least one quarter responsible – for launching the weapon that was Sebastian.

If only he had not gone along with the other three that night in 1940, Sebastian would never have come after him. If only he had been strong enough to persuade his comrades that what they were doing was wrong, Sebastian would not have come after anybody. If only . . .

Spitzweg was confused. Naumann said he had been captured and no longer presented any problem. Could that be right? Could removing Sebastian remove the problem? The man had done what he thought he had to. He had been driven to it. Could that be right? Sebastian was not responsible for the things that he did. He, Spitzweg, must be held to account for this. Could that be right?

He felt an overpowering urge to throw himself at Sebastian's feet, to confess his sins, to beg forgiveness. Could that be right? It wasn't his fault. Sebastian must be made to understand that. Could that be right? Yes, that was the solution. That must be right. He must save Sebastian from himself. Naumann would understand. It was the only way that the debt could be paid.

Chapter Twenty-six

Naumann turned his head to the direction of the hallway from where the sound of footsteps was making steady progress towards the lounge. At first he thought it was the butler, but no, he had been dismissed for the evening. He glanced at his watch. 10.00 p.m. Two hours more and Youngblood would arrive, then get Sebastian and dispose of him; and there'd be a surprise for Youngblood also.

Naumann's tongue flicked over his lips in satisfaction when he thought of his afternoon's work. He and one of the German imports, the one called Fredrich, had gone to visit the boat which had arrived that morning. It was docked at a little cove north of Malibu.

Marzy and a scurrilous-looking man, whom he introduced as the Captain, had been there to receive him. The Captain showed him how to run the boat, then he and Marzy left. Then Fredrich got to work.

Fredrich was an explosives expert. Several terrorist groups had made use of his talents, both as an assembler and an instructor. He wired the thirty pounds of plastic explosive into the starboard engine, in the floorspace between the engine and the hull, made sure the timer was off, and set it for thirty minutes. The last thing he would do before the boat left was to start the timer. The blast should disintegrate the entire aft section in the first half-second, and the forward section should sink like a stone.

Naumann was surprised to see Spitzweg come into the lounge, surprised because it looked like he had rejoined the human race. He was clean-shaven, his hair was combed and he was nattily dressed in a brown suit and matching tie.

'Carl,' Spitzweg said, a little too loudly, 'how are things?'

Naumann looked hard at the face before answering. The eyes were very bright, feverish-looking, the smile was brittle. 'Are you all right, Max?'

'All right? Of course I'm all right. Don't I look all right?'

'You look fine, like you're dressed for a party.'

'And I feel fine. This is a party, isn't it? Tonight everything will be over, won't it? All our problems solved? Back to business, heh? More of that beautiful money and nothing to stop us.' A high-pitched giggle that sounded like a horse's whinny escaped his lips. 'How about a drink, Carl? We must have a drink to celebrate.'

Naumann frowned. Spitzweg was acting a little abnormally, but on balance it was better than the quivering hulk he had last presented. 'All right, a cognac.'

'A cognac, wonderful. I will get it for you.'

Spitzweg almost ran to the bar and fussed with the glasses and a bottle of cognac, keeping his back to Naumann. He poured the sleeping pills he had crushed to powder into the snifter of cognac, swirled it until it dissolved, then turned; and, with his arm outstretched, he walked over with a big smile on his face and held the glass out to Naumann.

'Here, Carl, to success! *Prosit*!'

The brandy snifters emitted a bell-like 'ting". Spitzweg downed half his drink. Naumann sipped his, sipped again, made a face. He put the glass down.

'Drink up, Carl, drink up! One should never leave a drink when the toast is to success. It brings bad luck.'

Naumann picked up the glass with reluctance and took another sip. 'I don't like drinking cognac this late – it gives me indigestion. I think I must already have it, the drink sours my stomach.'

'For me, Carl,' Spitzweg pleaded. 'After so much bad luck, one must not tempt fate.'

Nauman had another swallow, set the glass down with finality. Spitzweg sat down in a chair facing him and started talking. It was a rambling monologue, full of reminiscences, all accomplished in the full glow of the brittle smile and the too-bright eyes.

Naumann began to nod, his eyes felt heavy. He focused in on his watch with difficulty. Just after eleven. Not long now. He settled himself deeper in his chair. Might as well be comfortable while he waited. In ten minutes, he was asleep, mouth half open, a light snore the only sound in the room.

Spitzweg put his glass down and watched the sleeping man with an intensity that would have frightened him had he been awake. Spitzweg sat unmoving and almost unblinking for a half-hour, until he was sure. He tiptoed from the room, gave an anxious and furtive glance down the hallway, advanced into it for a few steps, stopped, and listened. The murmur of voices was just audible. They came from the den at the end of the hall, where all four Germans waited for further orders.

Spitzweg retraced his steps, went past the lounge with a last glance at Naumann, who was sound asleep, and out to the front door. He pressed the button to open the electric gate and went down the four steps without making a sound, crossed the circular driveway and over to where his Cadillac was parked. He opened the door, slid in behind the wheel and brought the door to, until a soft click told him that it was closed. He fumbled with the key, inserted it into the ignition, but didn't turn it on. He shifted the car to neutral and released the emergency brake.

The car was on a slight incline that led down to the entrance way to the property. The car started to roll, slowly at first, then picking up speed. Spitzweg guided it down the middle of the driveway, where it bounced on its shocks where the driveway met the street, and the momentum carried it into the road which was going uphill.

The car stopped its backward motion, started to roll downhill. Spitzweg turned the wheel and let the car run downhill and around the first curve before switching on the ignition. He slowed the car with the brake, shifted it into drive, switched on his lights, and zoomed down the road.

He hoped he would remember the way to the house in Topanga Canyon. He had been there with Naumann on four previous occasions, but that had always been in the daytime.

He drove recklessly up the narrow roads that took him into the Santa Monica Mountains.

The front doorbell jerked Naumann out of his sleep. He sat up, rubbed his eyes, looked around him in some confusion. The last thing he remembered was talking to Spitzweg or, to be more accurate, listening to Spitzweg. Where had he gone? Naumann's head felt muzzy and his mouth dry. He tried to puzzle out the reason for it, but his thoughts seemed to be encased in mire. The doorbell jarred him out of his lethargy. He stood up, a little shaky, and went to answer it. Youngblood walked in with a curt nod, stopped and looked at Naumann.

'What's the matter with you?'

Naumann was shaking his head. 'I don't know, I feel as if I've been drugged.'

That thought woke him in a hurry. His eyes widened, and he made a dash for the lounge. He picked up the half-finished glass of cognac, sniffed at it suspiciously. Youngblood, who had followed at a more sedate pace, watched from the doorway.

'Someone slip you a mickey?'

Naumann thrust the glass in Youngblood's direction. 'Here, you smell it.'

Youngblood walked over, took the glass, sniffed it, tilted it to his mouth and touched the brandy with the tip of his tongue. 'There's something in here that ain't cognac.'

'That bastard! Spitzweg did it. But why? I don't know.' Then it occurred to him to look for Spitzweg. He ran down the hallway and flung open the door to his room. Empty. Now in a frenzy, he sprinted to the den shouting to the Germans as he ran. They appeared at the door in an instant. Naumann told them that Spitzweg was missing and to look for him. They fanned out through the house to conduct the search. Naumann's wife peeked out of her bedroom to see what the commotion was. She clucked in disapproval and shut the door again. Youngblood leaned against the wall, arms folded, the sardonic expression more evident than usual.

Five minutes was enough to ascertain that Spitzweg was nowhere in the house and that the Cadillac he used while in LA was missing.

'Where could he have gone,' Naumann ranted, 'and why did he drug me?'

'Does he know where Sebastian is being kept?' Youngblood's question was bland but the import deadly. 'Maybe he's going to let him out?'

The scar on Naumann's cheek stood out in bold relief as his face flushed. 'He wouldn't dare. Why would he? He is scared to death of the man.'

Youngblood shrugged. 'Just a suggestion.'

Naumann growled, it was an animal-like sound. 'Let's go,' he shouted. They all trooped out to the Mercedes and were out of the driveway and heading downhill in seconds.

Up the hill, the two detectives in an unmarked car on stake-out looked at each other. 'What do you make of that?' the driver said to his partner.

'Dunno, but something sure as hell's up. Let's roll.'

But the driver had already started the car and jerked after them. The other man was on the car radio and asked communications to patch him through to Helder.

Spitzweg made two wrong turns before he discovered his mistake. He was in a sweat of anxiety. He slammed the car into reverse for the three-point turn on the narrow road and doubled back. He mumbled to himself, 'Yes, this is the way.'

The driveway leading up to the deserted house in Topanga Canyon was overgrown with weeds that had cracked the cement. Spitzweg kept his speed up and the car bounced over the ruts, sliding to a halt at a cock-eyed angle, when Spitzweg jumped on the power brakes just before the entrance to the house.

Sebastian paced the cellar like a caged lion. He was so familiar with the place that he could do it in complete confidence without the luxury of sight. He was hungry, but he could live with that. Thirst was getting to be a big problem. He licked dry lips, barely wet them. He felt dehydrated. And the chill . . . he wrapped his arms about himself trying to keep warm, but it was a losing battle. Forty-eight hours now. How much longer?

When he first heard the noise, he thought he was hearing things. He ignored it, preoccupied with his thoughts, but it persisted. He snapped alert, the cold forgotten. He moved to the door on cat feet. This would be his one and only chance and he wasn't going to blow it. When the door opened, for better or worse, he would rush whoever it was.

The sound of feet on stone steps came closer. They stopped the other side of the door. Then came the sound of a block of wood being lifted. He had been right about that. Sebastian also thought he heard the low mumble of a voice, but that was curious because he had heard only one person descending.

The block of wood lifted free and crashed to the ground. Sebastian tensed himself for the rush. The door swung open and a flashlight beam hit him in the eyes.

The pain was almost physical. After living two complete days with a total absence of light, the sudden brightness blinded him.

Sebastian held up his arms protectively, his eyes screwed up in pain. He was experiencing after-images, the bright glow dulling to a sullen red, fading to orange and pink.

'Mr Sebastian,' the voice said. It was a tentative voice. It was an eerie voice, as the words were spoken at a level just above a whisper.

Sebastian took his arms down with caution. He raised his eyelids a fraction. The flashlight beam wavered, playing on the floor and walls with spasmodic jerks. Sebastian could see just beyond it to the outline of the small man who held the flashlight. He was in shadows, the passage beyond, grey with moonlight. He could just make out the steps.

'Mr Sebastian,' the voice said again, a bit stronger this time, with an added note of hysteria. 'You have to listen to me. It wasn't my fault. I wanted to stop it but I couldn't. I have lived with it all these years. Oh my God, I have suffered it . . . as much as you have.'

Sebastian straightened up. His vision had returned. He could now make out the man's haggard face behind the light. Spitzweg. Sebastian was uncomprehending. Matters had taken too unexpected a turn. He expected to have to fight for his life, and instead, Spitzweg was standing before him, making apologies. Sebastian shook his head to clear it.

'Please say you forgive me, Mr Sebastian. I want to live in peace. I just want to be left alone.' He started to blubber. The rage that Sebastian had primed for years never materialized. He felt nothing but a curious flatness as if he had experienced a catharsis without the use of an emetic. The creature in front of him was pathetic.

'Where's Naumann?' he snapped.

The blubbering stopped as if shut off with a switch. It was replaced by a cackle of laughter. The hairs rose on the back of Sebastian's neck.

'Oh, he was coming, he was coming, but I stopped him. I gave him sleeping pills. He is sleeping like a baby.' Another cackle. 'And when he wakes up, I won't be there and you'll be gone.' The cackle twisted, changed to sobs.

Sebastian sprang to the door and pushed past Spitzweg, ran up the steps. At the top, the door stood wide open and beyond, an empty hallway with bare boards coated with dust. The light came from an uncurtained window in front of him. He looked left. The hallway disappeared into darkness. To the right lay freedom. The front door was ajar. He could hear Spitzweg behind him, plodding one step at a time, each step punctuated by a renewed burst of crying. Sebastian made a dash for the door. He flung it open and stepped outside. A car, its headlights piercing the gloom, was just turning into the driveway. He skirted the Cadillac and set out at an angle away from the approaching car at a dead run. He didn't believe in Christmas coming twice in one year. That had to be Naumann with help, Fritzes 1, 2 and 3 for sure, maybe more, and they would have guns.

'There he is,' Naumann shouted. He pounded the seat in front of him. 'Get him.'

One of the Germans fumbled his revolver out and snapped off a shot. It missed by a mile. He shot twice more with the same success. The driver screeched to a halt and another German on the passenger side thrust open the door and, using the top of the car as a handrest, shot at the retreating figure.

'I'll get him,' Youngblood said. He jumped out and started after Sebastian.

Two miles away, one of the cops from the stakeout was saying to Helder over the radio, 'They were going like a bat out of hell through these back roads and we lost them.'

'Goddam it,' Helder growled, 'which way were they heading?'

'Towards Topanga . . . hey, hang on a second.' The man leaned his head out of the window. He could hear what sounded like fire crackers going off in the far distance. He turned to his partner. 'Did you hear that?' The officer nodded. 'Shots maybe?' He craned his neck out of the window to see if he could spot anything.

'Hey, Lieutenant,' the other officer said into the microphone, 'we think we hear gunfire.'

'Where?'

'Can't tell. Sounds like a long way off but you get all kinds of freak echoes in these canyons.'

'Can you determine the direction?'

'Maybe,' the officer said dubiously.

'Then roll. I will alert other units in your area and contact the valley stations and Malibu. Keep in close contact. Out.'

Sebastian crashed through some brush and didn't see the dip in the land just beyond it. He stumbled and went flying head first, but tucked automatically into a judo roll and hit the ground in a good position to wind up on his feet. Ordinarily he would have, but there were dead branches at the bottom of a small ravine, and he slid on his back when he hit them. He lay winded for a few seconds, then eased himself up on to his haunches. The branches trembled under his weight and threatened to slide out from under him. He scrambled on all fours until he hit solid ground, then was away again up the slight incline that was loose dirt and into a section of calf-high grass. He risked a look behind him. He was being pursued, but it looked like only one man. The high grass disguised the lay of the land, the moon had gone in behind the cloud. Both factors conspired to make him stumble on the ground that undulated in no discernible pattern. And it was rock hard, as he found out to his cost, when a fall brought his knee in contact with a sharp projection. He cursed, got up and limped away. The terrain was going steadily upwards. The grass gave way to low brush and that to a belt of trees. Sebastian plunged in among them for twenty feet, then stopped and looked back again. The cloud lifted at that moment and the figure of a running man was clearly outlined. He was less than a hundred yards away and was heading directly for Sebastian, as if he could see him. It was uncanny and he felt the chill. He started off again through the trees, but changed his original line of flight forty-five degrees. From the position of the moon, he figured he was taking a northerly direction, a few degrees west of north.

Naumann barked out orders to Fritzes 1, 2 and 3 to follow Youngblood and help him to corner Sebastian.

'And,' he shouted after them, 'make sure you bring him back alive.' Then he nodded to the driver and they walked to the front of the house. Naumann took the automatic from his pocket. It was a .45 calibre Colt, black against the white of his hand, and deadly in any colour. Naumann's mouth twisted into a feral grimace that he thought of as a smile.

The two men walked around the back of the Cadillac, kicking up showers of gravel. They reached the one step up to the door when Spitzweg emerged. He blinked in the glare of the Mercedes' headlights, put his hands to his eyes. The flashlight dropped with a clatter.

'Why, Spitzweg? Why did you do it?'

Spitzweg's hands came away from his face in slow motion. When he spoke, his voice had a tone of wonder in it like a child. 'I had to, Carl, don't you see that, I had to. You understand that. It wasn't right, what we did. Now he has forgiven me.'

There was a long moment when an expectant hush seemed to settle around them. The wind stopped blowing, the insects halted their night noises.

'But I haven't forgiven you, Max.' The Colt jerked in Naumann's hand as the first shot came out in a spurt of flame. The bullet caught Spitzweg just under the breast bone and smashed him backwards into the door. His head hit with a sickening crunch, his arms were thrown out to the side by a reflex action, a cry strangled in his throat. Four more shots followed in rapid succession as Spitzweg slid down the door. Two went through the heart, one the stomach and the last one through the throat. But Spitzweg didn't seem to mind, he was already dead.

Wisps of smoke curled up from the gun. Naumann stood frozen. He gulped in great drafts of air. His heart hammered. Slowly, the adrenalin stopped its flow, the arm holding the gun dropped to his side. He turned away and walked back to the Mercedes. The driver, with a glance behind him, followed.

Chapter Twenty-seven

Sebastian came out of the trees. He paused a moment to listen. His pursuer was still coming. He could hear the cracking of twigs as he came. Sebastian looked around him. To his right, the trees continued up the side of a steep hill. In front of him, a narrow space strewn with branches and twigs led up to the same hill that looked like it was covered with loose scree. To his left, the path ran at a sharp right angle to the way he was going, then curved around to the south and out of sight. If he went that way, his pursuer could change direction, bisecting the angle, and cut him off. He would have to take the chance. It was the only logical way to go. Sebastian ran down the path, trying to keep as quiet as he could and put some distance between himself and the other man at the same time. His breath was coming hard. The forty-eight hours in the damp without food and water were taking their toll.

Sebastian followed the path as it curved round. He could see in the moonlight that it branched – the path to the left continuing south and the other fork through a cleft going westward again in the hills. He chose that path.

He ran on, gaining the relative safety of the steep sides of rock. The path widened as he went round the bend. He followed it.

As soon as he turned the corner, he realized his mistake. The path disgorged into an open space that was like a miniature amphitheatre, steep-sided cliffs on all sides and only one way in . . . or out.

He calculated his chances for going back the way he had come. He didn't like the odds. He started to look for a way to get up and over. He examined the rock, ran his fingers over it . . . worn smooth, very few handholds.

He was working his way down the rock with controlled haste when the other man stepped into the clearing. Sebastian tensed. If there was an opportunity . . .

'Hello, old buddy,' Youngblood said. He was breathing hard but the sardonic smile was still in place.

Sebastian had thought himself beyond total surprise, but he miscalculated. He stared with his mouth open. 'Bobby Youngblood?'

Youngblood made a slight bow. 'At your service.'

'You're working for them?' Sebastian was still incredulous.

'Well, shucks, li'l ol' me has to make a living somehow.'

'What happened to the shrink bit?'

'Oh, I gave that up. All I used to see was crazy people . . . and this pays better.'

Sebastian clapped a hand to his temple. 'Wow, this is really hard to believe. You are the hypothetical pro we talked about in New York.'

'Yeah, pretty smart of old Naumann, wasn't it? To hire somebody who knew you.'

'How come you didn't try to take me out in New York. You are the last person I would have suspected. You could have got right up close. You did get up close.'

Youngblood shook his head. 'That wouldn't have been cricket, old boy. I'm not a back shooter . . . at least not most of the time.'

'Terrific! I suppose it would have made you feel better if I was looking at you when you opened the cellar door and shot me full of holes.'

'I wasn't going to do that.'

'Oh, yeah? What then? More to the point, what now?' The two men had been circling warily during the conversation. 'Where's your gun, pal? I sure did expect to see that nasty old gun pointing at me.'

Youngblood's reply was bland. 'It's in my holster . . . and it will stay there.'

Sebastian stopped moving. He straightened from his crouch, put his hands on his hips, smiled.

'Well, well, well, that's very interesting. It's going to take more than just you to stop me, you know. You had better use that weapon while you can. I wonder if you can get to it before I get to you.'

'It's not going to be like that, Mark.' Youngblood started to take his coat off. He did it slowly, made no sudden moves. He threw the coat to one side, moved a careful hand up and took off the shoulder holster by the strap. He tossed it on top of the coat.

'Did you know that I always envied you, Mark?' It was said in a conversational tone and the smile was friendly, all trace of the cynic gone for the moment. 'You always seemed to do everything so goddam easily. I always had to work my butt off to get anywhere near . . . this is going to sound dumb, but you were my hero.' Youngblood laughed a little in embarrassment. 'So I said to myself, I can be as good as Mark Sebastian. I may have to work at it a little harder, but I'll get there in the end and some day I'll prove it. You know what? This is that day.'

'Jesus Christ, you amaze me.' The words tumbled out in a rush, said without thinking. 'I'm in the middle of what I thought was a life and death situation and you're playing games. I think I must be delirious.'

'Hey, buddy, you get past me, you're home free. Look at it that way.'

Sebastian stopped and looked at it that way. He shrugged. 'Okay, so we'll do it your way. Swords or pistols?'

Youngblood held out his hands. 'Just these. You're a fourth Dan, aren't you? Let's see how good that means you are.'

Sebastian cocked an eyebrow. 'You've been reading up on me,' he said. 'And you?'

'Green Berets.'

'I'm impressed.'

Youngblood's smile vanished, and he started forward in a slight crouch, his hands extended.

Sebastian identified it as the classic forward leading stance (*zenkutsu-dachi*), the knee for the forward leg bent, back leg straight. Sebastian could hear the words of the Master in Kyoto echo through his head. 'It has often been said that a good attack is the best defence. In karate a good defence may also be the best attack.' Sebastian crouched into his beginning stance, the straddle (*kiba-dachi*), his arms low at his sides, his fists clenched. He waited.

Youngblood came close and started the attack with the fist of his right hand angled in towards the middle of Sebastian's body. Sebastian countered with a middle wrist block with his right hand (*koken chudan uchi-uke*), then followed through with a strike with the heel of his palm to Youngblood's solar plexus. There was only a minimum of contact as Youngblood danced away. They went back to beginning stances.

Sebastian knew that they were still shadow-boxing, testing each other to gauge proficiency. He decided that Youngblood was very good, his reflexes greased lightning. He would have to be careful.

Youngblood attacked with his left fist with a strike to the head. Sebastian blocked it with his left hand and counter-attacked. He pivoted first on his right foot, grabbed Youngblood's wrist with his right hand, then changed direction and punched Youngblood in the ribs with his left fist. The move was called *seiken-mawashi-uchi.* Youngblood grunted and broke away. He approached again. Sebastian waited.

Youngblood feinted with a right-hand thrust. Sebastian reacted with a right-hand punch of his own aimed at the heart. Youngblood blocked it with his left hand, grabbed the outside of Sebastian's wrist, applied a wrist lock and aimed a kick at Sebastian's groin with his left foot. Sebastian just managed to avoid it by twisting away. Youngblood still held the wrist lock. He pivoted behind Sebastian and stamped the hollow behind his left knee with his foot. Sebastian's leg was still a little weak from the gunshot wound and collapsed under him. He went with it and rolled away from Youngblood and up into a crouch in an instant.

The three Fritzes were on the other side of the cleft of rock deciding where to look next, when they heard the noises of the two combatants. They entered the passage.

They faced each other again in the fighting stances. Youngblood tried to catch Sebastian off guard with a jumping front kick (*tobi-mae-geri*). He jumped high in the air and, at the apex of his jump, kicked out at Sebastian's head with the ball of his foot. Sebastian had been expecting something like it, and moved his head to avoid the kick. Youngblood had a little difficulty in maintaining his balance when he landed, and Sebastian lashed out with the instep of his foot aimed at Youngblood's groin (*kin-geri*). Youngblood shifted at the last moment and caught the kick on his thigh. He staggered backwards but recovered at once.

For the next few minutes the silent battle carried on, each of the men looking for openings, making offensive strikes and counter-attacking in turn.

Youngblood tried another attack to Sebastian's stomach with the hand open in the cutting position. Sebastian blocked it with his right hand (*seiken chudan soto-uke*), then whirled behind Youngblood, putting his right leg behind Youngblood's right leg; at the same time he wrapped his arm round Youngblood's right arm from underneath. He tripped Youngblood, pushing him over at the same time.

Sebastian landed on Youngblood, a knee in his chest, the flat of his hand poised to strike.

Fritz 1 stepped out of the shadows. 'That's enough,' he said. His gun was levelled at the middle of Sebastian's forehead.

Sebastian let his hand drop slowly. He stood up, held out a hand for Youngblood. They were both breathing hard.

'You are good, Mark,' Youngblood said. It was a grudging admission. 'I guess the cavalry arrived in the nick of time or li'l ol' Bobby Youngblood would be chopped liver.'

Sebastian said nothing. He brushed himself off, saw Fritz 2 and 3 come into the clearing and spread out, levelling their own weapons on him.

The little procession back to the house was accomplished in silence, Sebastian in the van, the three Fritzes and Youngblood behind.

'So nice to see you again,' Naumann's greeting was a taunt. 'I would so hate for you to miss the festivities – when you're the star attraction.'

Sebastian glanced over to where Spitzweg was huddled on the ground like a bundle of dirty clothes. He turned back to Naumann. 'That's kind of drastic, isn't it?'

Naumann split the night with a harsh laugh. 'That's very funny, coming from you, Sebastian. You were going to kill him, remember? I saved you the trouble.' He turned to the driver. 'Get the rope and make sure you tie him tight.' Then to Youngblood, 'You did that well, I thought he'd get away.'

Youngblood didn't reply. He put his hands in his pockets and walked away.

Sebastian's hands were tied behind him and he was pushed roughly into the back of the Mercedes. Naumann detailed two of the Fritzes to pick up Spitzweg's body and stow it in the trunk. The third man was ordered to drive the Cadillac and follow behind them. They all got into the Mercedes and took the road that went towards the beach. It was twenty-five past one in the morning.

Less than a mile away, the police cruisers pulled off at the side of the road, the officer radioed to Helder.

'We've been up and down every goddam road in the area. Nothing. Can't see a thing.'

'Are you sure it was gunfire you heard?' Helder asked.

'Hell, no. You want us to keep looking?'

Helder thought about it. 'No, come on in. If you haven't found anything by now, we might as well forget it. I haven't received any reports about gunfire from anyone else. Maybe you were mistaken. Go back to Newman's house for the rest of your shift and log the time he gets back. I'll think about what to do in the morning.'

Chapter Twenty-eight

Sebastian identified the cove at which the Mercedes arrived as one about five miles north of his house in Malibu. The Mercedes stopped in a small empty parking lot. The Cadillac drew up behind it. The half-dozen or so buildings that faced the ocean were closed and dark. There were a couple of shake bars, shops that dealt with bait and tackle, a novelty shop selling items for the tourists, the usual cluster of small businesses about an area where boats were docked. The odour of stale fish came through the clean smell of the rain. Off to the left of the concrete pier, a strip of beach was deserted. Sebastian counted twenty-one boats rocking gently at their moorings. They, too, were dark and difficult to see in any detail. It had begun to rain again, a steady drizzle that made for poor visibility. Pools of water that collected in the hollows of the parking lot reflected the light from the lamps out on the highway.

Sebastian was prodded from the Mercedes and, with one of the Fritzes holding on to one arm, led down to the pier.

The others followed. They stopped in front of an old boat a quarter of the way down the line. The name on the stern was so badly faded that Sebastian couldn't read it. A narrow gangplank led on to the boat. They skirted the bollards and stopped. No one had yet said a word.

Sebastian twisted round to look at Naumann. He could just make out a smile in the gloom. The man gave a low chuckle.

'Well, Sebastian, this is good-bye, adieu. I will not say *auf wiedersehen* as I never expect to see you again. This is a very good moment for me, Sebastian. You almost spoiled things for me, and I don't even mind telling you now that you caused me some slight anxiety. But all is now well again. How could you expect to win? You have, after all, Jewish blood in your veins.' To Fritz 1, 'Take him below.'

The German tugged at Sebastian's sleeve, pulled him on to the gangplank and boarded the boat. Fritz 2 followed to make sure he wouldn't cause trouble.

'Go ahead, Youngblood, I will come with you to the bridge to make sure you know where everything is.'

Naumann turned to Fritz 3, who was Fredrich, and the driver. 'Get Spitzweg from the car and put him on board.'

He followed Youngblood up the gangplank and down the narrow aisle to the bridge.

'It looks pretty easy,' Youngblood said. They were the first words he'd spoken since Topanga. 'How old is this tub?'

'Perhaps ten or fifteen years old.'

'Then it's had a pretty hard life.'

'It looks like many other fishing boats, I am told. It isn't. They have converted to high speed engines and, as you can see, there's a new radar. The boat, of course, is used for smuggling.'

'I kinda guessed that. One of your buddies, no doubt.'

Naumann shrugged. 'It was lent to me. It is exactly what we need to dispose of evidence on a permanent basis. Start the engines; let's make certain they are working properly.'

Youngblood turned the ignition key and pressed the switches. The engines roared in turn, caught and settled down to a deep-throated burble.

'Good,' Naumann said. 'Now come, I will show you where we have stored the heavy chain to wrap around the bodies.'

He pointed forward and Youngblood went ahead of him. Naumann turned to look back. The two Germans had just come on board carrying Spitzweg. They dumped him on the deck with an audible thump. Fredrich looked around him, then opened the hatch to the engines. Naumann smiled, looked at his watch. 2.15 a.m. He followed Youngblood. He was kicking a pile of chain that reposed in the well, just to the side of the bows.

'Make sure you wrap them well. It would be very embarrassing to have them bob to the surface and be picked up by some passing fisherman.'

Youngblood gave Naumann a look, turned away and went back to the bridge. Naumann followed. 'We'll go now. I suggest you go out about four miles before you dispose of them. Sebastian is locked in the storeroom below. Ah, here's the key.'

Naumann took the proffered key from Fritz 1 and handed it to Youngblood. 'Come back here when you are finished. We will be waiting for you. You can come back to my house to collect the rest of your money.'

Youngblood nodded.

'Good luck,' Naumann said. He held out his hand and smiled.

Youngblood gave it a perfunctory shake. 'I shouldn't need any. It's kinda like shooting fish in a barrel.'

'True, but what else does one say at such a momentous time.' Naumann turned away and left the boat, the four Germans following.

Youngblood hauled in the ropes as they were untied, then went to the bridge, put the engines in gear and pushed the throttles forward. The boat eased out of its slip and headed for open water.

Naumann stood on the pier looking after it. He looked at his watch again. Ten minutes had passed since the time clock had been activated, twenty more to go. The five men stood in silence until the boat was out of sight, then – on a signal from Naumann – went back to the cars and drove away.

Youngblood kept the boat on a westerly heading, two hundred and eighty degrees. He opened the throttles and felt the boat speed under him. The vibration increased. The sea was fairly calm, small waves rolled by, flattened by the rain.

When Youngblood reached what he estimated was a mile and a half from shore, he swung the boat around in a wide arc and put it back on a reciprocal course. He pulled the throttle back so that the craft was just making steerage way and locked in the auto pilot. He rummaged in a drawer and found a waterproof flashlight, then went aft.

Youngblood had been wrestling with his conscience for some days now, a more than usually interesting phenomenon, because he hadn't realized that he possessed one. And he did at last make a decision. It was at the precise moment that

Sebastian had a knee in his chest and was about to chop his head off. It flashed into his mind that if he survived, he would have nothing to do with eliminating Sebastian. The man had a strength of will that Youngblood had never encountered, and besides that, he approved of what he was doing, when the targets were men like Naumann. His active dislike of Naumann had become passionate, and he felt sure his mistrust of the man was accurately judged. He knew far too much about Naumann for Naumann's liking, and was pretty sure that the man had plans to kiss him good-bye also. That would be in character. He was certainly a threat to the German and what Naumann didn't realize was that he intended to remain a threat.

Had Naumann already made the first move? 'Maybe,' he thought. 'Why was that sneaky Kraut fooling around with the engines? I wasn't supposed to see that.' Youngblood lifted the hatch to the engines, turned on the flashlight and shone it into the engine well. The engines were running smoothly and there was nothing immediately discernible. He played the flashlight around the space, a glint of metal in the beam caught his eye. He bent down to take a closer look. 'Shit,' he muttered. He fingered the time clock gingerly. It had seven minutes remaining before it would go off. He traced the wires with the beam where they ran into the crawl space. He sat down on the edge of the open hatch and bent to take a closer look, careful not to touch anything. He recognized the plastic explosive.

He scrambled back up and headed for the companionway that would take him below. The flashlight shone on the door to the storeroom; he picked out the padlock. He took out the key and unlocked it, swung the door back.

Sebastian was jammed into the narrow locker, sitting with his back to the wall, his knees drawn up in front of him. He blinked in the light. 'Time for you to do your thing, Bobby?' The words belied the fierce determination in the eyes.

'Uh, uh, pal, you got it wrong.' Youngblood took out his pocket knife and opened it.

Sebastian glared at him. 'What the hell is that for then? To clean your nails?'

'Now don't get pissed off, buddy,' Youngblood said reasonably. 'This is just to cut your ropes.'

'Why?'

'Because I decided I don't like your Nazi pals very much, and because I'm going to help you get rid of them.'

'I don't need your help.'

'I wish you weren't so goddam ornery. With just a little effort, you could get to love me. I grow on people.'

Sebastian snorted. 'Why the sudden change? I thought you were being paid to kill me.'

'Changed my mind. Decided I couldn't be bought.'

Youngblood bent over and cut the ropes and helped him up. 'And beside that, I have decided I like you. You are the closest thing to a friend I've got.'

Sebastian looked at him in disbelief. 'You're crazy!'

'So I've been told, but it's not catching. Now, I don't want to be rude with all this nice little chat we're having, but I got to change the subject. It's getting just a mite pressing. How are you on explosives . . . like a bomb?'

Sebastian rubbed his hands together to get the circulation back. 'Why?'

' 'Cos there's one ticking away on this boat and I guess there's less than five minutes to go before it goes off.'

'Naumann?'

'Who else? I don't have a death wish.'

'Show me.'

Youngblood led the way in a dash up the companionway ladder and to the open hatch. He pointed into the engine well, held the flashlight for Sebastian to see.

Sebastian grabbed the flashlight from his hand, stepped down into the well and made a quick examination. The clock showed four minutes to go.

'What do you think?' Youngblood asked, sounding a little anxious.

'I think that I don't have enough time to defuse it.' He reached down and felt along the crawl space. 'There is a hell of a lot of C4 here. Thirty or forty pounds worth. It looks straightforward enough, but if the guy who put this together stuck in anything that's even a little devious, like a trip wire or a dummy contact, there won't be enough of us left to scrape into an ashtray. Where are we anyhow?'

'Over a mile from shore, maybe a mile and half.'

'Skiff?'

'None.'

'How's your breast stroke?'

'Looks like I'm about to find out.'

'Right, let's get the fuck out of here.'

Sebastian stepped back up on to the deck, peered through the drizzle. 'Which way we heading?'

'Back towards shore.'

'Okay, we don't have much time to lose. We'll turn the boat around and head it out to sea and hit the throttle on full. We want to put as much distance between the boat and us as we can. I don't want to go into detail about what the concussion from an explosion can do to a swimmer near by. And get rid of those clothes. They'll drag you down.' Sebastian started undressing.

'It's cold out there.'

'Well, I'd rather be a little cold than a little dead.'

'Yeah, yeah,' Youngblood muttered. He shed his clothes down to his shorts. Sebastian had already reached the bridge and was swinging the boat around one hundred and eighty degrees. He leaned out of the cabin. 'Okay?' he yelled.

'Okay.'

'Here we go.'

Sebastian jammed the throttles forward and the boat leaped ahead again. He ran back aft to join Youngblood.

'Let's go, and stay together.' Sebastian jumped on the transom and dived off with Youngblood right behind.

Sebastian had prepared himself for the shock of hitting the water and he cleaved it cleanly, but it was even colder than he expected. He fought his way to the surface, gulped in a lungful of air and looked for Youngblood. He spotted the fuzzy outlines of a bobbing head through the rain.

'Bobby, are you all right?'

'Yeah, perfect.'

Sebastian almost laughed at the depth of misery expressed. He swam over to Youngblood with an easy crawl and trod water. 'Look, I don't want to do much talking. We have got to save our breath. It's going to be a long haul. The main problem we have besides staying afloat is a point of reference.'

'What about it?'

'We don't have any. It is going to be real easy to get off-course. So stay close. I'll try to keep us heading in the right direction. How's your distance swimming?'

'I'm better on water skis.'

'If you get tired, yell and we'll stop.'

'Okay,' Youngblood said in resignation, 'let's go.'

Sebastian took one last look at the boat that was roaring away from them, and started swimming.

They had been going for only a short time when the sound of the explosion rushed at them. They stopped and looked back. An orange glow diffused by the rain lit up the dreary horizon. It collapsed in on itself and in a few seconds was gone. They were silent throughout the brief spectacle. Wavelets in neat rows set off by the blast washed over them. Sebastian kept his head high out of the water, drinking in the pure rain water he had been denied for so long.

'I'll bet Spitzweg never thought he was going to get such a grand send-off,' Youngblood said. 'Just like a Viking funeral.'

Sebastian was distracted, deep in thought. 'No, I guess he didn't.'

'And neither does that mother-fucker, Naumann, know what he's going to get.' Youngblood's tone was venomous. 'But he will soon.'

Sebastian was weary in mind and body. All the events of the last few days seemed to crowd into a small space in his brain, like the boat – ready to explode . . . 'Let's swim,' he said.

They swam on through the rain until they had lost all track of time. Sebastian disengaged the mechanical action of swimming from his mind. He would stroke on and on, one arm after the other, while the grey haze seemed to settle on his brain so that thinking was impossible. He had almost forgotten about Youngblood swimming on his right. He adjusted his pace to fit the other man, slower than he liked, but it would conserve energy if they were in the water for any length of time.

He had minimized the task ahead of him. They were literally swimming blind. He would try to swim on the exact reciprocal compass bearing on that which the boat was heading, but that didn't allow for drift. It was fortunate that the usual crests and troughs experienced in the Pacific were smoothed out that night, a direct result of the steady rain, but what they gained from that was off-set by a sacrifice in visibility. No moon, no stars to guide him. It would be easy to get off-course. They might wind up swimming towards Hawaii.

The first half-hour, Sebastian glanced over every few strokes to make sure Youngblood was still with him, but then he was lulled by the steady tattoo of the rain beating down on the water, the slap-slap of his hands as they stroked in a continuous rhythm, his own breathing, intake of air, stroke-2-exhale-3, 4-intake of air. He tried to hold on to thoughts, but they kept slipping away like eels through his fingers. But weren't his fingers webbed?

Something deep inside his head urged him to break out of his lethargy. He glanced over to where Youngblood should have been, panicked. The man was nowhere in sight.

He stopped swimming to tread water, eyes darting around him. Nothing. He made a complete circle. No sign of Youngblood. 'Bobby,' he yelled. 'Bobby, where are you?' His voice seemed enclosed in a velvet box, deadened almost before he uttered the words. Only the hiss of the rain came through, loud and clear.

He shouted several more times with the same response. He stopped when his throat began to go raw with the effort. He tried to calculate on what tangent Youngblood might have gone off. Chances were, not to the left, as he would have had to cross in front of him. Sebastian struck off to the right at about a thirty-degree angle. He decided to swim in that direction for five minutes then turn back on his original bearing. He hoped that would be sufficient, in geometric terms, to form a new triangle so that he might catch Youngblood at the apex.

He swam on with quick determined strokes, ignoring the fatigue that began to weigh him down. He made brief pauses every few strokes to yell out Youngblood's name, then swam on when there was no reply.

It seemed that he had been doing it for hours, although in truth it could only have been minutes. Despair settled in. Youngblood was lost and he would have to face the fact. He could only hope that wherever Youngblood was, he was still on a course for the shore, and could hold on long enough to reach it. Then he heard a faint yell to his left. He stopped to listen and it came again. He felt a renewed burst of energy and set off with powerful strokes.

He caught sight of Youngblood in less than a minute. He was flailing his arms and half out of the water.

'Jesus Christ! What's the matter?'

Youngblood was thrashing around wildly.

'Something bit me.'

'Where?'

'On the ass, goddam it.'

Sebastian swam closer to Youngblood and dived underwater. He circled around the man. At the extreme edge of his vision, which was not more than six feet away, he could just make out a long narrow shape. He surfaced. He gulped in air and laughed. It was a nervous laugh. He peered at Youngblood. He fancied that the man's face had turned chalky white, but of course that wasn't possible to tell in the gloom.

'What is it?' Youngblood croaked. 'If it's a shark, don't tell me.'

'No, not a shark. I would be surprised if it was. Barracuda. They are curious little bastards and they will sample anything.'

'Barracuda!' Youngblood moaned. 'All those sharp teeth.'

'Don't worry about it. You are too big for them to eat much of you.'

'Boy, you're a real comfort.'

'No, really, it'll be okay. You probably scared the shit out of him with all your thrashing around. They won't bother you again. I don't think you realize what a good turn that fish did you.'

'What do you mean? You call it a good turn to get a chunk taken out of your backside?'

'I hate to tell you this, Bobby, but you were lost.'

'What do you mean, lost?' Youngblood spluttered. 'I knew exactly where I was – swimming right next to you.'

Sebastian kept his tone matter of fact. 'I've been searching for you for about twenty minutes, I figure. If you hadn't yelled . . .'

'Son-of-a-bitch,' Youngblood said. He sounded scared. 'I thought I was swimming next to you, I mean that was the last thing I remember, until that damn barracuda bit me.'

'Like I said, it did you a good turn. We'll get moving again but this time we take breaks every five minutes or so, so that we don't get separated any more. Now let's . . .' Sebastian broke off with a loud gasp. He grabbed for his recently wounded leg.

'What's the matter?' Youngblood yelled. He reached out a hand. 'Did that fish get you?'

'Cramp,' Sebastian said through gritted teeth. He knew about cramp, the pain could be excruciating and a swimmer could drown because of it.

'Bad?'

'Only enough to drown with. Just give me a minute, I'm trying to massage it away.'

A couple of minutes elapsed before the cramp began to ease. Youngblood stayed close by and kept silent. Sebastian took a deep breath and let out a sigh of relief. 'Okay, let's go.'

They stopped several times after that, every time that Sebastian felt his mind going numb, the zombie-like state returning, he would call a halt.

The chill of the water cut deep into them. The rain was warm by comparison. Youngblood took to floating on his back during the rest periods, and would have gone to sleep if Sebastian had not slapped him on the shoulder and urged him on again.

They swam on, fell into the same routine.

His arms felt like lead, his mind in fresh fog. How long had they been in the water? Hours? It felt like days. Sebastian could feel the corners of his mouth crack as the salt from the water embedded itself – and the briny taste in his mouth. It seemed that he had reached the limit of how bad it could be, but it got worse. And his eyes were sore . . . and his nasal passages. When he rubbed his fingers together he could feel the wrinkles from too much immersion. They felt old as cracked parchment. And his body heat, flowing out, floated away at an alarming rate. He began to hallucinate. It took the form of a memory. Seventeen he was, and aggressive, and too damned smart for his own good. He was back at the Newport Beach house with his grandparents for the spring vacation and informed Grandpa Sebastian as soon as he set foot in the door that he wanted to learn scuba diving. It was phrased more like a demand, but Grandpa had learned to tread warily where young Sebastian was concerned. He was aware of the damaged psyche and would do anything to prevent a relapse.

Grandpa Sebastian never did anything by halves. The very next day, he presented Mark with a brand new set of scuba gear-tanks, professional mask, regulator, wet suit, flippers, weight belt, heavy duty diving watch. He told Mark he had made arrangements for him to be taught by the best scuba diver on the coast. He was a man called Chris Bonaventure, ex-navy underwater demolitions expert and current salvage diver, who had dived on wrecks looking for treasure all over the world, who the oil companies called in to survey the rigs. Mark met Bonaventure the following morning when they took off in his forty-foot Chris Craft heading for deep water. The day was brilliant and sunny – in the high eighties – the sky an almost unbroken blanket of blue. Only a few fleecy clouds, way up high, marred its perfection. The water was rolling gentle swells and narrow trough white-capped foam as the bow split the waves. Bonaventure stopped the boat and anchored it a couple of miles from shore. 'About sixty feet of water,' he told Mark, 'and near a wreck I know about. Once we get you going right, we'll go down and take a look.'

'What kind of wreck?' Mark wanted to know.

'It's an old Russian freighter that sank around 1890. They used to do a lot of trading up and down this coast.'

'Great,' enthused Mark. 'When do we get to see it?'

'Just as soon as I am satisfied that you can use the equipment without drowning. Now the first rule before we start is never dive on your own in deep water. In fact, if you can help it, never dive alone, even if you're only in six feet of water. You don't know what can happen down there. Believe me, you might think you've thought of everything, and then something'll sneak up on you that never crossed your mind.'

Mark promised to take heed, and Bonaventure spent the morning teaching him the basics of the diving techniques, and then went on to the advanced course, as the boy caught on to everything at once. They broke for lunch and when they had finished the sandwiches and a beer each, Bonaventure said he was going to take a nap for an hour after which they would continue.

Mark sat in the bows, legs dangling over the side, staring at the placid water. He was itchy to get back in, looked over to where Bonaventure was still asleep. 'To hell with it,' he thought, 'I'll be careful.' So, disregarding Bonaventure's first rule, with flagrant ease, he donned the scuba gear with a fresh tank and let himself down the chain into the water so that he didn't make any noise.

The sun slanted into the water, the rays distorted. Visibility was excellent. A host of small silver fish passed by in the water, eyed him with curiosity. Mark dived deeper, confidence oozing from every pore. Bonaventure had taught him how to clear his ears, and Mark tried, pressing the mask against his nose, mouth shut, blowing. There was only partial relief. There was a sharp stab of pain in his ear drum. He chose to ignore it. The wreck was in sight. He passed the 33 foot level, 29.4 pounds per square inch, two atmospheres of pressure. The ear hurt but not so bad now. The deeper he went, the darker it became as the sun's rays failed to penetrate. The reds in the lower end of the spectrum were filtered out first, as he approached the wreck. The colours around him were deep blue and purple by the time he reached the old freighter.

It was hard to tell how big the ship had been. Mark thought well over two hundred feet, but he couldn't be sure. The hull was pitted and rusty, barnacles had grown over most of it. The ship lay canted on its side, a huge gaping hole near the bow, twisted girders sticking out at odd angles. With more courage than brains, Mark entered the hole head first. He used his flippers to turn himself round without seeing the girders in the blackness. His tank wedged and he was stuck fast. He panicked, tried to wriggle out. He was still caught. He tried for purchase on the section of the hull where it had been bent back; the tank still held. His breathing became more ragged as his panic increased and put more pressure on the apparatus than the demand valve could handle. He tried to calm himself, tried to think of a way out. His mind was blank, all instructions forgotten. He should have remembered the quick release harness but he never thought of it.

When he had just begun to give up hope and submit to the idea that he was going to die, a bright light flashed into the hold and pinpointed him. Bonaventure had him freed in a moment and escorted him to the surface.

Mark Sebastian received the longest, loudest, the most articulate tongue-lashing he had ever received before or since for his crass stupidity. And he paid the penalty – he had a burst eardrum. On the plus side, it would keep him out of the service, but he would never do any deep diving again.

Sebastian stopped to clear his head, looked around him.

'Bobby!' he said sharply.

Youngblood kept swimming.

'Bobby!'

Youngblood faltered, then stopped. 'Huh? Did you say something?'

'Look over there to your left. Is that a light or am I seeing things?'

Youngblood looked in the indicated direction.

'That's a light,' he yelled. 'Son-of-a-bitch, that's a light! Let's go.'

It took them another twenty minutes to come in close enough to shore so that they could finally stand, and then the waves buffeted them. The light had resolved itself into a street lamp where Highway 101 dipped in close to the water. They stumbled out of the water, holding on to each other for support, and fell on to the beach. They both lay there for minutes without saying anything.

'I didn't think we were going to make it,' Youngblood croaked.

Sebastian turned over on his back, took deep breaths one after the other. 'I did. After everything that's gone down, I wasn't going to be lost at sea.' He rolled over and got up on his knees, stood up, staggered, maintained his balance. The drizzle had almost stopped, a fine mist in its place. Sebastian shivered as his body temperature, already chilled from the water, received another shock from the February wind. He wrapped his arms around himself, started to jump up and down to force some heat back into his body. He looked around him trying to determine where they had landed. Straight ahead of him, the light revealed the deserted highway and the hills beyond. To his left, he could make out a cluster of buildings in the far distance, pinpoints of light. The layout seemed vaguely familiar.

To his right, the beach widened from its narrow V, the point at which they were standing, and a line of houses began perhaps 300 yards from where they stood. Sebastian looked at them hard, turned back and looked at the buildings in the other direction again.

'I'll be a son-of-a-bitch,' he said.

Youngblood was sitting up rubbing himself with vigour. He looked up. 'What's the matter now?'

'I think . . . maybe nothing, and that our luck is changing.'

'What, from bad to worse?'

'Just the opposite. Unless I am badly mistaken and that sea

water has blurred my vision more than I thought, my house is about a quarter of a mile from here.' He pointed down the beach.

Youngblood jumped up and looked. 'You're not putting me on, are you?'

'I sure think so, no, I'm positive.'

'Fan-fucking-tastic. Let's go.'

Sebastian caught up with the trotting Youngblood. 'You want to guess how far we had to swim?'

'I don't think so, I'd rather forget all about it.'

'I'll tell you anyway. The boat was moored about five miles north of here – I recognized the cove – plus a mile/mile and a half out? And the distance we had to cover from there – nine or ten miles.'

Youngblood stopped and gave Sebastian a searching look. 'Are you kidding? Did we really swim that far? The furthest I've ever been is about a dozen lengths of my pool.'

'Amazing what you can do – if you want to live.'

Youngblood grunted a yes. His mind was racing with all the juicy things he could do to Naumann. They started off along the beach.

There were only two passages in the wall-to-wall houses. Sebastian led the way through one of them to the strip of pavement used by the house owners as a car park.

'How far?' Youngblood asked.

'A few houses down, we're almost there.'

'This may sound funny,' Youngblood said, 'but one of the things that kept me going when we were out there with nothing in sight was that I was worried about what we were going to do after we landed. Dig the optimism? How we were going to get taken in somewhere when we were running around practically bare-assed naked. Can you imagine some poor slob opening his door to us? And seeing these two guys looming up in front of him like creatures from the black lagoon. Incidentally, you don't look that great.'

'I've seen you look better, too.'

'Probably, but can you imagine it?'

'I didn't know you have such a bashful streak running through you.'

'Well, I don't usually make house calls this way. Come to

think of it, I don't feel too undressed, I've still got my watch on.'

'You've been swimming all that way with a watch on?'

'Hell, I wasn't going to throw it away, it cost me a couple of grand.' Youngblood put his wrist to his ear. 'Shit, the damn thing has stopped working!'

Sebastian laughed heartily. It was the first time in weeks he had felt like it.

'Hey, my car is still here,' Sebastian said, 'which is how I figured they got on to me, but I haven't worked that out yet.'

'My fault,' said Youngblood sheepishly. 'I traced you to Burbank Airport and let Naumann know the car you rented. I guess he took it from there.'

'Hmm, that means cops. I wonder how he worked that. I'll have to unload it and get something else.'

'Well, while you're thinking about it, do you think we can go in? My teeth are chattering so hard they might jump out and do a fandango right down the road. How we goin' to get in? Break a window?'

'I've stuck a key away for emergencies.' Sebastian stooped next to the door, lifted a cement tile and took out a key. He fitted it in the lock and they went inside.

He turned on all the lights and put the thermostat up to eighty degrees. 'It'll be warm in here soon.' He went to a closet, reached in and tossed a bathrobe to Youngblood. 'The other bathroom is over there to the right. I'll take a quick shower. The booze is on that shelf above the bar.'

Sebastian steamed himself for ten minutes. He couldn't remember anything feeling so good. He came out, dried himself, rummaged through the closet, found underwear and socks in a drawer, jeans and a sweat shirt, put them on along with an old pair of sneakers, and pulled out another set for Youngblood. When he returned to the lounge, he found Youngblood sitting Buddha-fashion on the couch, cradling a large glass of brandy. He tossed him the spare set of clothes.

Youngblood let out a deep sigh of contentment. He picked up the clothes and was back in a couple of minutes, dressed, and with the level in the glass appreciably lower. He found Sebastian chewing on a large mouthful of bread and cheese.

'A little loose, but not a bad fit.'

Sebastian nodded and took another long swallow from his

brandy. He was sprawled in one of the cane chairs that looked out on the ocean. Youngblood saw which way he was looking.

'Haven't you had enough of that for one night?'

'It'll be light soon,' Sebastian said.

Youngblood didn't seem to notice the *non sequitur*. He flopped down on the couch. 'I'm really beat,' he said.

Sebastian just stared ahead of him. The next few minutes passed in silence, while he wolfed down the rest of his food.

Youngblood broke it. 'Mark?'

'Huh?'

'Let me ask you a couple of questions.'

Sebastian returned from the far horizon. His eyes came back into focus. He turned to Youngblood. 'What do you want to know?'

'Why? No, I don't mean that exactly, I know they bumped off your parents. Why now? Hell, we are both thirty-four years old. You could have done this ten years ago. Why did you wait so long?'

Long moments passed before Sebastian answered. 'I've been asked that before. The answer I've always given is that I wasn't ready. I convinced myself that there was always one more thing to learn, one more skill to acquire, before I began.' Sebastian took a swallow of his drink, turned back to the ocean and stared at it moodily. More time passed before he continued. 'I was lying to myself. I think I only just realized it. It had nothing to do with being ready. I'll tell you something I never told anyone else, and one of the reasons I'm going to tell you is because you were hired to kill me. In a way, that makes us kind of close – almost Siamese twins, maybe more like Yin and Yang. I was scared.' Sebastian let that sink in.

Youngblood kept his expression non-committal and didn't seem inclined to utter a comment.

'When I say scared, I don't mean in the conventional way. I wasn't afraid for myself and I wasn't afraid to take these guys on. Hell, I've killed people before. Sure, that was a wartime situation and I didn't know them, but the principle is the same.' Slight pause. 'In fact, I used to dream at night about tracking each one down and what I would do when I had them . . . they were very bad dreams. I was scared because my whole life was taken up with catching these guys and all the training I put myself through was exclusively for that purpose. I never considered what would happen afterwards. It was a blank.' Another pause. 'When you've finished something that you have devoted all your energies to, what's left? That scared the hell out of me.' More silence. Youngblood waited, but Sebastian had stopped talking and was brooding over his drink.

'And now?' Youngblood asked.

'I don't know, I just don't know. Have you ever been in love?'

The question caught Youngblood by surprise. 'Who me?' He gave a short laugh. 'Sorry, Mark, but it seemed like a funny question . . . and the answer is uh, uh. Never even been close. We psychologists call that ultimate gratification of self. No room for a chick when I got me. My ego wouldn't allow it.' He paused. 'I take it you asked the question because it is relevant to our conversation. You found somebody maybe you are in love with?'

'Maybe.'

'Wouldn't happen to be a tasty blonde with a broken arm, would it?'

Sebastian jerked around. He stared at Youngblood with hard eyes. 'How the hell did you know that?'

Youngblood laughed again. 'Take it easy, man, I was going to tell you some time. I saw her in Chelsea one day. I tailed that little chubby guy who works for your company back to the building you were holed up in. I saw the doctor go in and that blonde come out, with a bunch of bruises and broken wings, and I put two and two together.'

'You knew where I was? Why didn't you complete your contract then?'

Youngblood shrugged and smiled. 'Didn't seem fair, figured you were wounded and flat on your ass and that would have given me too big an edge.'

'I don't believe it – a true romantic. You're in the wrong century, pal, the hit man with a heart. What did you tell Naumann?'

'Exactly what he wanted to hear. He didn't figure you were dumb enough to hang around, so I just confirmed that.'

Youngblood told Sebastian about his skiing trip while Naumann had sweated it out in Mexico. Sebastian shook his head throughout, mainly in disbelief, and then guffawed with laughter. The laughter died down and they got serious again.

'Let me ask you one,' Sebastian said. 'How did you get into your line of work?'

'Do you want the flip answer or the long version?'

'I'm a good listener.'

'Okay . . . I guess it was expected of me.'

Youngblood went into his wry smile routine. 'I don't mean I was born to be an assassin, but I come from a long line of individualists. My grandfather disappeared into the Yukon for five years and never found a damn thing. All he ever wound up with was a severe case of frostbite and four less toes than he started out with. My father went on three expeditions to climb Everest, all unsuccessful, and one trip down the Amazon where he contracted a fever which almost killed him, and he spent the rest of his life alternating between malaria and hives before he died. My mother's family were pioneers in Oklahoma and Texas before they came here. They did the whole bit, fighting Indians, or Mexicans, or Indians and Mexicans together. I've got a relative who died at the Alamo. My mother is a tough old broad who had some kind of religious experience when she turned fifty, and is now off on a reservation somewhere in Washington teaching Indians about Christ and Christ knows what else. I got a sister who rides the rodeo circuit and walks funny because she has broken her legs about a dozen times riding bulls, and I have an older brother who is a Buddhist monk in Kashmir. Now we come to me. After I got my degree, I enlisted because I wanted some action. With my background, I guess you would have to call it staying in character. It seemed like the thing to do. And I learned . . . how to kill people.'

'Ever have any doubts about it? Moral questions?'

Youngblood took a long time to think about it. 'Well, maybe. Although I always considered myself amoral. No, that's not completely accurate, it's not as strong as that . . . more . . . a neutral.'

'That sounds like a cop out. I'm sure all your victims would be a lot happier if they knew you were neutral instead of amoral.'

'Well, I'll tell you something, since we are exchanging confidences. When I was in 'Nam, I told you I was a Green Beret, but it was a lot more than that. They wanted to use my shrink training, so they made me an interrogator, inquisitor, whatever you call it. None of the thumb screw bit. We were after accurate information, troop dispositions, times of attack, that sort of stuff. We didn't want to wind up with a vegetable that would tell us anything just so we would stop. So we developed some very sophisticated techniques – a combination of drugs, psychedelics, sounds, sensory deprivation, and a lot of mental gymnastics. I was very good at it. In fact *numero uno.* I looked on it as a challenge – how to extract the maximum amount of information with the minimum amount of damage to the subject.' Youngblood laughed. 'Another ego trip. And you know what? Through it all, I didn't like what I was doing. I started to have doubts. Nothing to do with morals or ethics, just that the whole damn thing smelled.'

'You started hitting guys instead. Was that better?'

'Jesus Christ, you're starting to sound like a sixty-year-old virgin with a Bible in both hands.' He dismissed it with a wave of his hand. 'I'm not trying to justify anything. The only thing I can tell you, and you'll have to take my word for it, is that all those creeps I hit deserved it. They were either rip-off merchants or pirates, tyrants, murderers, you name it – boils on the backside of society. I never felt I was doing anything wrong. If I hadn't taken them out, somebody else would have. They were no loss to anyone, and it paid well.'

'What about me?'

'That's where the credible parted with the ridiculous. I was a lot more into x-ing out my employers than my target . . . well, hell, if I'm going to be completely honest . . . not at first. At first, it was an intellectual exercise, and my ever-present ego. I wanted to know how good I really was, coming up against you.'

'Well, what changed your mind?'

'Don't know for sure.' Youngblood laughed again. 'But I assure you it wasn't a religious experience. Anyway, here we are . . . on the same side.'

Sebastian sighed. 'Okay, maybe it's a good thing not to probe motives too deeply. Neither one of us is innocent. For sure you have as much reason to get Naumann as I do, so we'll do it together.'

Youngblood made a vicious swipe for the bottle of brandy and poured himself a large slug. 'Now what do we do about Naumann?'

Sebastian nodded towards the window where the grey light

of morning had caused the darkness to retreat into featureless shadows. 'It's day, my friend. Let's sleep first, then we'll work it out.'

Youngblood yawned. Sebastian's reminder had caused the weariness to enfold him like a cloak. 'Okay. Where do I sack out?'

Sebastian showed him the spare bedroom and went to his own bed. He just managed to get out of his clothes and under the covers before he passed out.

Chapter Twenty-nine

Chief-Inspector Warren looked haggard when he turned up at Police Headquarters that morning. He turned bleary eyes on Helder when he entered the office and greeted him.

'You look like you were up all night.'

'I feel like it,' Warren said with fervour. My damned sergeant thinks that because it's the middle of the day for him, it applies to everyone. He woke me three times between four and six this morning. I finally threatened him with a transfer to Glasgow.'

'Is that bad?'

'It's obvious you have never been to Glasgow. Suffice it to say that he promised not to bother me again.'

'What was so important?'

'It's actually because of the information that he gave me that I didn't send him packing the first two times. I think we have Sebastian identified.'

'No kiddin'?'

Warren held up a hand. 'Wait, there is more . . . and I'm fairly certain that we know who Carl Newman really is.'

Helder pounded the desk. 'Sit down and tell me. Wait, we'll get coffee and Danish.'

Helder was tense until everything arrived. 'Okay, shoot.'

'We have very good cooperation with the West German police. One of our men was sent over to Berlin to coordinate the inquiries, and with some effort, I think we have really hit the jackpot. Let me go over it for you as I understand it. You know that the note left at the murder site in Bremen and our note were identical. A list of four names and a date. Schmidt and Naumann are fairly common names; the other two – Spitzweg and Rascher – not so. So that when we went through the SS and Gestapo files, we had several possibilities. No way of telling which were our men. We then went through the newspaper file for the twelfth of December 1940, and the days afterwards, going on the theory that if this event, whatever it was, had occurred on the twelfth, it would have been in the newspapers for the following day or some time thereafter. And . . .' Warren paused dramatically, 'there it was, in the Berlin newspapers for the thirteenth of December. A Mr and Mrs Robert Sebastian, brutally murdered in their apartment by a person or persons unknown. Mr Sebastian was a Second Secretary at the American Embassy. They had one child, a son Mark, aged four at the time of the murder.'

'Mark Sebastian,' Helder said. 'He would be in his thirties now. You figure he's the guy who's knocking these Krauts off?'

'I'd say there was more than a reasonable possibility to presume so. But there is more. The article went on to say that the assailant may have been wounded, as there was blood leading away from the apartment. So, one bright spark had the idea of going through the hospital records for the twelfth of December. And what do you think we found?' Warren didn't wait for an answer. 'Schmidt, Rascher and Naumann treated for injuries, and another SS officer called Spitzweg who brought them in.'

Helder bounded up from his chair, came around the desk and clapped Warren on the back. 'Great work,' he enthused. 'Newman has got to be Naumann, right? That little guy, Spicer is probably Spitzweg.'

'That's the way I see it, Sam. And additionally, this Naumann and one other, Rascher, who we reckon is Swift, now deceased, are still on records as war criminals with an open warrant for their arrest.'

'Let's get the son-of-a-bitch,' Helder said. He was on his way to the door.

'Hold it, Sam. Don't go off at half-cock. We don't have definite evidence that they are one and the same man. If we arrest him prematurely, he is liable to slip away before we can receive hard evidence, which I am expecting by tomorrow.

There are pictures, fingerprints and records on file which are being forwarded here at this moment.'

Helder paced the room, then went back behind his desk and sat down. 'Goddamn it, I hate to wait. What's to stop him from going now?'

'He doesn't have any idea that we are on to him. That is, with the total knowledge to arrest him.'

Helder put his head in his hands. 'I guess you're right.'

'What did your stakeout produce?' Warren asked.

Helder's face reddened. 'Not a lot,' he admitted. 'They lost my two detectives around midnight. They didn't get back till after three this morning . . . okay, we'll wait. Did you get anything more on this Mark Sebastian character?'

'Not on file with us or Germany. Inquiries pending with Interpol. But he is American. Can you see what you can find out about him?'

Helder picked up the phone and gave orders for a search of the records for one Mark Sebastian. Coffee and Danish lay forgotten.

Naumann awoke early, in spite of the late hour at which he had returned. He skipped the usual transition between sleeping and waking. He was aware in an instant and he felt wonderful, marvellously refreshed from his short sleep, full of self-righteous satisfaction and with a feeling of boundless benevolence towards his fellow men.

He hopped out of bed, whistled throughout his bath and shave and tripped gaily down to the breakfast room where he greeted his wife with a cheery 'Good morning,' thereby frightening the good woman out of five years' growth. He thanked the four Germans for an excellent job and said he would make reservations for them to leave the next day and, with an extra burst of generosity, said that they would all receive a bonus.

The feeling of euphoria persisted until 7.00 in the evening, when he received the phone call.

Consciousness came back slowly to Sebastian. He turned over and saw, through a slit in the curtain, that it was broad daylight outside, the sun shining in through the crack and making a jagged pattern on the carpet.

He felt as if every bone in his body ached, every muscle protested with the effort of moving. His skin felt rough, dry and hot to the touch. He guessed that was from the long immersion in salt water. He rested for another hour before he dragged himself out of bed, put on a bathrobe and padded into the lounge.

The aroma of the coffee he made started him salivating. His stomach rumbled, deep sounds that protested at the misuse to which it had been put. He was starving. The bread and cheese had only served to fill one corner of what seemed like a bottomless pit. He took the makings out of the refrigerator and went to it with a will – toast, ham, eggs, sausages, juice. He went to wake Youngblood while the ham was grilling, and the two of them finished off everything down to the last crumb.

Sebastian found a packet of cigarettes in a drawer for Youngblood, who was experiencing withdrawal symptoms, then walked over to the windows. The storm had completely blown away and there wasn't a cloud in the sky. The winter sun shone brightly on the landscape that looked newly washed. It dazzled the eyes where it struck the sand and made the white caps sparkle as they broke on the beach in endless succession.

Youngblood, smoking with contentment, watched Sebastian from the couch. 'Make you feel good to be alive, huh?'

Sebastian turned from the window and faced Youngblood. He wore a sad smile. 'Makes me want to stay that way. I've been thinking that maybe I should give it up – forget about Naumann.'

Youngblood's reaction was disbelief. He straightened up and looked at Sebastian as if seeing him for the first time. 'You're kidding! – give it up – now? After all he's done to you? And he's the last one. You can't be serious.'

Sebastian turned back to the window with a sigh. 'No, I guess I'm not, but it was a nice thought – to leave it and maybe start living for the first time.'

Youngblood was angry. 'Suit yourself, pal. I can't let things like that lie. If you're not going after him, I am, for goddam sure. And those other four Krauts also.'

Sebastian went over to a chair and sat down, turning a curious gaze on Youngblood. 'Why them?'

'Why them!' Youngblood was exasperated and agitated enough to wave around the hand holding the cigarette, making swirls of smoke in the air. 'You seem to have a short memory, or some kind of forgiveness quotient, which floors me. In case you've forgotten, those are the guys that helped beat you up. Just take a look in the mirror, pal, you bruises are looking pretty good. And one of those bastards tried to blow us both up! If it offends you, I'll take them out. It will be my pleasure.'

'They were just working on Naumann's orders.'

'And Naumann was working on Hitler's orders.'

Sebastian felt very tired. He slumped in his chair. 'You're right,' he murmured. 'How do you want to do it?'

'That's better. I've been thinking about it. We've got a couple of big things in our favour. Naumann thinks that we're dead and that he is home free – nothing else to worry about. I think we can apply enough pressure to make him a nervous wreck, I mean wild enough so he can't think straight. I want to force him into a mistake before he realizes it – get him out in the open on terrain that we choose. If we rattle him enough, we'll be able to get him out of that house. The place is like a fortress and he could just sit there playing the chief dude surrounded by the Praetorian Guard, and we couldn't get close.'

Some of Youngblood's excitement communicated itself to Sebastian. 'How are you going to do it?'

Youngblood told him, improvising as he went along.

Sebastian considered. 'Okay, why not? It could work.'

Naumann went to the phone with expectation. He thought it would be Luis Francisco Montez confirming their meeting in Acapulco in two days' time, where the newly appointed Minister would receive his final instructions.

'Hello,' said Naumann. He had a large smile on his face and it reflected in his voice.

The voice that answered was muffled, not much more than a whisper, so that it was difficult to determine with any degree of accuracy what sex it might be.

'Mr Newman?' it said.

Naumann felt the chill of premonition. His voice went hoarse. 'Yes?'

'I have something to tell you,' the voice whispered, 'that I know is going to interest you.'

'Wait a minute, there is nothing . . .'

'Don't interrupt me,' the voice said. 'You have a house in Topanga Canyon.'

Naumann tried to cut in.

'Don't bother to deny it. I saw you there . . . last night. There were some very interesting things going on.'

'Who are you?' Naumann croaked.

'It don't matter who I am, just think of me as the guy who's going to keep you out of the slammer.'

'What do you want?'

'Goddamn it,' the voice said, 'if you shut up long enough, I'll tell you. I want ten thousand dollars.'

'For what?' Naumann was now belligerent.

'For a set of pictures I took that show you killing a guy. They're very good pictures. Your scar shows up real good.'

Naumann wanted to say something but he was speechless.

'Then I got more pictures of you dumping that guy in the trunk of your car – a black Mercedes, right? – and some more pictures of a second guy with his hands tied that you took away with you. Got the picture? Newman?' The voice gave a whispered laugh at the joke. 'Ten grand, I want for them . . . or I'll make like a good citizen and send them to the cops.'

'How,' Naumann strangled out the words, 'how did you get the pictures?'

'Don't matter how I got 'em. You didn't think anyone was around, but I was there with my camera and my telephoto lens. Now, do you want a deal or do I get on to the fuzz?'

'Deal, yes, I want a deal.'

'Good, ten grand. You bring it.'

'Where?'

'To Topanga. The road that runs up to your house. There is a hill fifty yards past it. Right there, and no funny stuff. You bring it on your own. I saw all those other guys with you.'

Naumann recovered much of his composure, his brain clicking away like a pinball machine.

'What time?' he said.

'Five o'clock this morning.'

'Five!' Naumann shouted. 'Why such a ridiculous time?'

' 'Cos that's the way I want it, it'll be nice and quiet then. All right, we got a deal? And I ain't no dummy, so noooo funny business.'

'Okay, we got a deal.' Naumann almost smiled.

'Five o'clock,' the voice said, and the line went dead.

*

Youngblood was very satisfied with his phone call. 'Well,' he demanded from Sebastian, 'what do you think?'

Sebastian nodded. He had his ear close to the phone and heard both ends of the conversation. 'I think he's hooked, he can't afford to let it alone.'

'And I tell you something else,' Youngblood said. 'I'm pretty good on stress factors, the kind you can pick up from the voice. Something I picked up from the interrogations. At the end of the conversation, Naumann recovered. I could almost hear the gears going round in his head. I think I got across exactly what I tried to do, that he thinks I'm some local clown with not too many smarts who got lucky with some pictures and who is trying to make a quick score. I think ten grand is just the right touch. It's a piss in the ocean for Naumann, and a fortune for the guy I'm supposed to be. I think we can count on him having the troops up there.'

'I agree. Have you any more thoughts about how we deploy?'

'No, I'm satisfied. Let's work on it like we planned. We have command of the high ground on both sides of the road, and when we commence a sweep-in towards the middle, we ought to catch Naumann in the net. The only thing we got to worry about is that we are not out-flanked. If we secure our positions early enough, that shouldn't happen.'

'So you figure midnight gives us enough time?'

Youngblood ran through all the facts again before committing himself. 'Yeah, I think so. It gives us five hours, right? I don't figure he's going to move his soldiers in until three, at the earliest. He's got to think he's dealing with only one guy.'

'I hope you're right, because it's a lead-pipe synch that we're going to be out-manned and out-gunned.'

'He's only got four guys.'

Sebastian shook his head. 'That's now. Are you willing to bet your life that he's not going to get more in? Naumann is a cautious man, you ought to know that better than me.'

Youngblood lit a cigarette, took a deep drag. 'Yeah, okay, it still doesn't change our strategy.'

'Except that when we start picking them off, it had better damn well be in complete silence. I don't feel like being a target.'

Youngblood shrugged. 'I haven't forgotten how, it's like riding a bicycle. You're the one without the formal training.'

Sebastian's mouth creased into a wry smile. 'I learned all the fine points from a Wehrmacht commander. It'll do.'

'Okay, we got weapons to choose. I have some handy little items at my place.'

'And I've got a few here,' Sebastian said. 'I'll show you.'

Naumann's thinking, indeed, was as predicted. He ran to tell the four Germans of the emergency and that they were to stand by for further instructions, then went to the phone and traced the American bodyguards he had previously employed. He told them to report to his house that evening. Then he called Marzy.

Marzy was very unhappy. A phone call earlier in the day from Naumann had informed him that, due to a set of most regrettable circumstances, the boat had been lost. Naumann, of course, had glibly offered to compensate the owner for the loss. And Marzy had been left to tell the man.

The offer hadn't assuaged the Captain's anger. The man was in a murderous temper and, as Marzy knew, capable of acting on it. The worry that shared equal prominence, was that it endangered the future dope-running operation, from which Marzy derived much of his income. The Captain threatened to break off all future contact, and Marzy's attempt to smooth it over by saying that it was only a boat and that a new one and better one could be found, served only to further the man's anger.

So Marzy felt himself in a precarious situation, betrayed on one hand by a client who displayed no conscience over losing the boat – Marzy privately thought that Naumann had intended to do so from the start – and on the other hand, by a lunatic who held him responsible, and who was in a position to do him injury – both personal and financial. And now Naumann was asking him for another favour, and perhaps throwing him a small bone at the same time.

Naumann needed a couple of thousand dollars in cash. He kept none around and the banks were closed. He explained to Marzy that he was being blackmailed and would probably have to show some cash to the blackmailer before he sprung his trap. He hinted that this was the man who was responsible for the loss of the boat.

Marzy seized on it at once. This was a way out of his difficulties, and he insisted that he and the Captain go along on the appointed rendezvous. As irrational as it sounded, the Captain would be able to vent his anger at a specific person. Marzy would be seen to be doing something, and therefore be able to protect his position. The blackmailer would be the sacrifice that would distress nobody but the man himself. Marzy felt sure that Naumann intended to kill the man anyhow, so he agreed to Naumann's request with the one proviso that the Captain be allowed to administer the *coup de grâce*. Naumann readily agreed.

Naumann put the phone down with extreme satisfaction. This time, and this would be the very last time, he would leave nothing to chance.

He counted up his forces. Eleven men including himself. It was pathetic to have to use so many to catch one, small-time, penny-ante blackmailer. The word for it was certainly 'overkill', but he didn't care what anyone called it.

Too much had happened in the last few weeks, too much nervous energy expended, too many people killed, too much attention drawn to his private business, too much money at stake, to leave even the slightest thing to chance. He had to have those pictures and the negatives, and to find out if anyone else was involved. Only then could that book be closed for ever, and only then could he relax.

Chapter Thirty

Sebastian left the brown Camaro parked down the hill from Youngblood's house. It was the last time he would use it.

They went through a checklist before leaving, ticking off each weapon, and making sure – for the third time – that everything worked. It was a formidable arsenal. Youngblood chose a Smith and Wesson M-28 .357 magnum – the highway patrol model – and a BM-59 assault rifle that had a 20-shot magazine and was the weapon that NATO used. In addition, he had a blackjack that was a solid chunk of lead that slid into a leather handle, a seven-inch blade Marine Corps combat knife, and his pride and joy, a garrotte made of piano wire attached to a pair of handles.

It was one of the most effective methods for ensuring a silent kill, and one that the Green Berets had practised diligently.

Sebastian stayed with the Walther. He had a duplicate in his store. He also took an Armalite AR-18 .223 calibre rifle that had a handy collapsible stock, a 20-round magazine and enough muzzle velocity to shock someone to death if he was hit in the toe. He also strapped two throwing knives on to his belt and accepted a blackjack from Youngblood.

They left in Youngblood's Ferrari, just after 11.00. They were identically dressed in black; both men wore crêpe-soled shoes. They carried burnt cork with them to blacken their faces and hands when they reached their destination. There was always the one long chance that they would be stopped by the cops for a minor traffic violation.

Youngblood drove well within the speed limit, kept to the back roads, and they arrived at their destination without mishap.

They had scouted all the roads that might lead to the house in Topanga, after walking the terrain that afternoon. They found one that was narrow, that would just allow two cars to pass if you were careful about it. It ran uphill in a north-easterly direction and petered out on top of a hill, surrounded by scrub, that was a site for a new house. The foundations had been dug. About a quarter of the way up, the road widened on the east side on to a level patch of scarred earth. Youngblood backed the car in and turned it around, so that the nose was pointed downhill. He left the keys in the ignition, and they took their weapons from the trunk and hiked over to where they were to lay in wait, a distance of perhaps a mile. It was seven minutes past twelve when they reached the hill.

The road they had chosen ran southeast to northwest. It would eventually emerge from the Topanga area and connect with a main boulevard to the beach. The point they chose was at the top of a rise, approximately fifty yards from Naumann's house. On the north side the ground was level for about twenty feet, covered with tough scrub grass that gave way to a patch of broken rock that sat like an island in the middle of the scrub. There were huge boulders jumbled together from some pre-historic upheaval, one of which – at the perimeter point of the rough triangle – stood eight feet tall. During their exploration, Sebastian had found a narrow passageway where he could squeeze behind the rock, and from there on to a ledge that would give him a commanding view of the terrain, and from where he couldn't be seen in return. Going further north behind the rocks, the woods started – the same ones through which he had crashed on his earlier flight.

The other side of the road, south, ran down a slight incline for about fifteen feet, then edged back up into a screen of trees – sycamores, elms, oaks and eucalyptus. Youngblood had found a pair of gnarled old oaks that had sprouted so close together that the bases touched. The trunks leaned out to form a V where the branches had pushed them aside at head height. It provided an unimpaired line of sight to the road and the house beyond. They blacked their faces and hands and held a whispered conversation on the side of the road.

'Are we all set on the procedure?' Youngblood asked.

'I guess so, but I still don't like the idea of being without communications.'

'What's to communicate?' Youngblood was bright-eyed in the moonlight. 'You take care of your side of the road and I'll take care of mine.'

'What if they get behind you?'

Youngblood remained unconcerned. 'So I'll slip back and take'm out.'

'You mean all the way out?'

'Hell, yes, this is war. And I'm not taking any prisoners.'

Sebastian turned away so that Youngblood wouldn't see his face. The fatigue that he had felt was creeping back again. There was going to be a lot more blood spilled before he got to Naumann and he was already finding it difficult to maintain the kernel of hate he had nurtured for so long, without it dissipating. Youngblood was making it a personal vendetta on everyone concerned. Everything was clear and concise, black and white. Sebastian's dilemma was that he didn't know how he would react. He shuddered, made an effort to shut off the thought processes. He would have to play it by ear.

Youngblood showed no sign that he had noticed Sebastian's turmoil. He cocked an eye at the moon and watched as a cloud obscured it, plunging the road into darkness. A few seconds later the moon re-emerged from the wispy tail.

'Damn, I think it's going to start raining again'. Sebastian looked up and stared, more clouds were approaching. 'Yeah, it's gonna rain, I can smell it. The old Schnoz never fails me. I can sniff a storm at fifty miles. Well, what the hell,' Youngblood continued philosophically. 'I suppose that's good news and bad news. We don't have to worry too much about making noise, the rain will cover that, but it sure is going to cut down on our visibility.'

Sebastian's rifle clattered against his belt buckle as he turned to face Youngblood. 'As long as there's enough light to see Naumann when he comes, I guess I can stand getting wet again.'

Youngblood had his wry grin in place. 'Okay,' Sebastian said. 'Let's go over it once more. How do you figure they'll place the men?'

'Well, if I was him, I would send at least three guys up around here and stick them off the side of the road. That means somewhere in the rocks and off in those trees where I am. I would leave one guy down there,' he pointed east down the road, 'to give him an all-clear as he went by. That would be one of two things. Either to say that everything is cool and the men are in place to snatch the little bastard, or that they already have him and are awaiting his pleasure.'

'I agree as long as he is sticking with the four guys.'

'You still think he's going to have more?'

'I would be willing to put money on it.'

'Okay,' Youngblood shrugged, 'so there's more; they're still going to do the same thing. The only difference is that they will have more area covered.'

'It also means that they will be closer together – certainly within earshot – and we are going to have to move quietly, or else get into a firefight.'

Youngblood smiled and raised the rifle. 'That's what we got these for, pal.'

'Just do me one favour,' Sebastian said sourly. 'Angle your fire so that you're not aiming in my direction.'

Youngblood laughed. 'I promise. Scout's honour,' he said.

'All right, one last thing. We can't start taking anyone out too early. They are likely to check in with each other at regular intervals, and if they can't find their buddies and we get into a shoot-out, the only thing that's going to accomplish is that it will spook Naumann, who will go thundering off into the blue, and all we'll be left with is the hired help. That's not the object of this exercise.'

Youngblood patted Sebastian on the arm. 'Don't worry, I won't get over-anxious. There were plenty of times in 'Nam where I had to make like a statue for five or six hours maybe. I'll sit tight before I have to act. The ground rules are, the only time we do anything before four-thirty is if we are in danger of being discovered. Let's see, I got twelve-twenty-six.'

'Check,' Sebastian said.

'Luck,' Youngblood grinned. They touched hands briefly and separated. Sebastian went to the rocks, Youngblood to the trees.

Sebastian squeezed behind the boulder and up on to the ledge. He wedged the rifle into a crack alongside of him, and leaned back against the rock.

The three-quarter moon shone like an eye that had just started to wink at the clouds all around it. It bathed the surrounding landscape with enough light to etch the shadows into clearly defined shapes. An owl hooted, crickets chirped, nothing moved.

Youngblood settled himself behind a tree, but checked the ground around him first. He did some housekeeping, picking up dead branches and moving them away from the paths he might have to take. The wood was dry and brittle and it would snap with a loud crack if stepped on by an unwary foot. He put the rifle in the crook of the tree and sat down beside it. He felt keyed up and alive. The time passed with agonizing slowness for both of them.

They both heard the car at about the same time. It was five minutes to three, and a light rain had started. The car came on past the house, stopped at the top of the hill, mid-way between their two position. Five men got out, leaving the driver to take the car off and park it somewhere. They all carried flashlights, and Sebastian was able to recognize the Germans he had dubbed Fritzes 1, 2 and 3, and the two American bodyguards who had been with Naumann when he had blown up the Mercedes.

One of the Germans was giving orders in a voice which carried clearly to where Sebastian was hiding. He told the two Fritzes and one of the Americans to hide themselves in the area where Youngblood was waiting, and that he and the other American would come over to Sebastian's side.

Sebastian heard the other car just as the German finished giving orders. It rolled up and stopped where the other men stood, and three more men got out that he didn't recognize. The driver moved the car off to park it.

Ed Marzy looked around him nervously. He was completely out of his element and knew it, and had decided with certainty that he had been crazy to come along. 'What are we supposed to do?' He addressed the question to the Captain.

'Just stay out of the way,' the man rasped. 'When we catch the cockroach, I will take care of him.' He took out a large pistol from his jacket pocket and fondled it.

Sebastian cursed under his breath. He had expected more than the original four men, but not this many. His position was now vulnerable. The place was beginning to resemble Times Square at rush hour.

He hoisted the rifle from the crevice in the rock and eased himself back around the boulder. Fortunately, he had taken the precaution of reconnoitering the entire area and had a clear picture in his mind of the whole of the boulder outcrop and the byways that traversed it.

He stepped off the ledge and on to the footpath and melted deeper into the rocks.

All ten men were gathered in the middle of the road. Sebastian had found another vantage point, thirty feet back from his original position. He peered cautiously over a splintered boulder and down at the party of men. He glanced up. The moon was completely hidden by the drizzle. He could make out just enough of his hand to see that most of the burnt cork had washed off, and guessed that his face was just as streaked. 'No way for them to see me, unless I make a sudden move to attract their attention.' He shivered and put the collar up on his windbreaker. He already felt wet clean through.

The German, who had been giving orders before, was gesturing at one of the Americans and pointing down the road. The man took off at a dog-trot.

Sebastian realized that another of their assessments had proved accurate. The man would be the advance guard for Naumann.

The others separated, four coming over to Sebastian's side, the other five to hide themselves in the woods where Youngblood sat poised to act.

There was a good deal of scrambling among the rocks by the four men, along with muttered curses. It was obvious that they had not checked out the hiding-places until that very moment, and barked shins were the result. But after a time they settled down and the quiet returned.

Sebastian had seen the four men spread out in a ragged line from east to west with a distance of about fifty yards between the two extremities. The man closest to him was about ten feet to his right and twenty feet in front of him. When he peered around the rock, he could just see the back of the man's head. Sebastian's watch read 3.22.

On the other side of the road, the five men spread out in the trees, forming a line that ran more or less parallel to their counterparts across from them. They penetrated only about ten feet into the tree line, each finding a trunk to hide behind.

Marzy was so nervous that he was finding it difficult to breathe. His heart hammered away, his palms were clammy. Perspiration dripped off him. It was hard to control his body. When he tried to turn his head and look for the other men, he made it only after three spasmodic jerks. The only rational thought he had was to keep as far away from the action as possible. He waited until the other four men seemed settled, and then started to back away deeper into the wood. When he looked behind him, all he could see were patches of black that were other trees, only millimetrically different from the deep graze of the open spaces. He kept backing up, bumping into trunks, tripping over roots, grabbing wildly at branches that brushed him.

Youngblood heard him coming before he saw him. He crouched behind his double tree until the outline of the man solidified. He was backing straight towards Youngblood's hiding-place, and so Ed Marzy, lawyer, shyster to some, sometime dope-dealer, was the first casualty of the skirmish at Topanga Canyon.

The garrotte snaked around his neck, and was already being tightened for the inevitable finale before Marzy had his first conscious thought about what was happening to him.

It was, coincidentally, his last conscious thought.

Youngblood dragged the dead man ten feet further into the trees and left him, then resumed his position. The minute hand seemed to crawl around the watch until it reached 4.30. A hush had descended on the wood as the wind eased and the tempo of the rain increased. There was the faint odour of rotting vegetation, now sodden. Water dripped from the foliage in a random tattoo. A dead branch fell off a tree and whispered to the ground. Youngblood's nightsight was so adapted by this time that he caught the movement. He took his rifle and edged out from behind the tree.

He moved in a slight crouch, testing each step for dead branches that would give him away before he put any weight on the foot. Despite the rain, they were still dry enough to make a loud snap.

He'd heard, more than seen, how the men had deployed themselves in the wood. The only thing of which he was certain was that the man he had killed was at the end of the line. So he worked his way forward for about fifteen feet, and then latterly to the west, to where he should come up behind the next man in line. He accomplished it with stealth and without haste, and again he heard the quarry before seeing him.

The man was standing behind the tree, one arm against the trunk for support. One foot was crossed over the other. Youngblood could almost imagine what the man was thinking. 'Here I am playing kid games in the middle of the night, getting wet, to catch one little bastard who is about as dangerous as a poacher.'

Youngblood crept closer until he was only five feet from the man.

He made a careful search of the area further down the line. None of the others were visible. Youngblood drew his knife and from a crouch advanced another three feet, then sprang.

The man was taken completely unawares. The arm that went around his neck cut off his windpipe, so that he was unable to utter a sound. The knife slit the jugular to ensure it. The blood pulsed out in a torrent, and Youngblood held on until there was no danger of the man making the tiniest noise.

He eased the man to the ground and remained in his crouch for several seconds. All his senses were alert, his hand on the pistol ready for instant use. After half a minute, he relaxed, straightened up and started to drag the man out of the way. He made very little noise. He retrieved his rifle and began to work his way further down the line.

Sebastian made sure that his rifle was wedged in securely, then edged his way out from his hiding-place. He had to go down three uneven steps to ground level and put a hand flat against the rock for support. The last step dislodged a trickle of gravel. To his highly attuned senses, it sounded as loud as a waterfall. He froze. Time passed and nothing happened. He set his feet on the narrow track and took one cautious step after the other. The path started to wind to the west, and he thought it would lead him to the place where the first man in line was hiding. But as he swung round the bend he was brought up short by a boulder that blocked his way. He looked over the top of it.

The man was about fifteen feet away with his back to Sebastian, left shoulder leaning on a rock. He could see the glow of a cigarette held in cupped hands. That at least was good; the man seemed unconcerned. Sebastian backed up with careful steps. He would have to find another route.

He got back to his starting point, and followed the channel. It was going in the right direction, westerly, but also angled to the north. He kept low as he followed it, and came to the point where it virtually doubled back on itself, heading in what he estimated was due south. It narrowed even further, coming together at one point so that he had to scramble over where the rocks joined at a height of about four feet. He made it with no noise.

On the other side, the channel widened and branched into three directions. Sebastian was unable to see more than a few feet down any of the three routes, as they all twisted away behind the rocks. He chose the middle seam as the one he thought would bring him closest to the man.

The channel brought him closer than he anticipated. When he turned the corner, the man was not much more than an arm's length away. It took only a fraction of a second for him to duck back behind the covering rock, but it seemed like an age. He stood and waited until his pulse rate slowed. Luck had been on his side. The man was still in the same position as he had last seen him, leaning on a rock, his back to him, smoking a cigarette, both hands occupied, protecting the butt from the rain.

Sebastian touched the knives at his belt, left them, took out the blackjack. The thick rod of lead pivoted away from the leather case, which was then used as a handle. He grasped it and tested the lead on his palm. He took a cautious peek around the rock. Everything was the same, the man still unsuspecting.

Sebastian weighed the possibilities. The man was just round

the corner to his right. He could take one step out and clobber him left-handed, which might be awkward, or he could take a couple of steps out, swing his body around and do it right-handed where he would be more confident. He balanced one against the other, left hand and less time, or right hand and the risk of being exposed. He took a grip on the blackjack with his left hand.

He took a long step out, arm already raised, and almost froze. The squelch of his wet shoes as he stepped into the gurgling water that ran down the channel sounded loud enough in his ears to wake the dead. Only a bare fraction of time elapsed and he was going on again. His arm came down and caught the man behind the ear. He followed through quickly to catch the falling body. Even then he was a little too late. The cigarette went spinning into the dark, raising a shower of sparks before it hissed out, and the man's arm brushed the narrow ledge, dislodging a score of pebbles. They clattered and bounced on the rocks.

Sebastian let the man drop and had the Walther in his hand at once.

A few feet away, although the speaker was invisible, a testy whisper in German asked what the matter was.

Sebastian replied in German, also in a whisper, that he was sorry but he had slipped.

The other man said to be more careful in the future and relapsed into silence.

Sebastian was just beginning to realize the difficulty of the task ahead of him. It had taken a quarter of an hour to manoeuvre himself behind the first man, and he still had three more to go; impossible to accomplish in the time remaining before Naumann showed up. He checked on the huddled form on the ground. The man was still alive, the breathing shallow. Sebastian reached in and removed the pistol from the shoulder holster. He might not be able to get to all the others, but at least this one shouldn't present any further problems. He doubted that the man would regain consciousness in anything under an hour, well beyond the time when it would make any difference, but it was still prudent to remove the gun.

He went back to reclaim his rifle and then to work his way through the rocks that would take him behind the other three. He had a fuzzy idea in mind that when the time came, he would be able to order those three men to put down their guns, as he had the drop on them. All he really wanted was Naumann.

Youngblood worked his way through the trees, taking it slow. He, like Sebastian, realized that it was going to take more than the half-hour before Naumann arrived to eliminate the three men left on his side. Unlike Sebastian, he was unconcerned. He had the assault rifle and a couple of extra magazines, and all that the opposition had were pistols. Youngblood had few doubts of the outcome if it came to a firefight. There was only one difficulty – that was not to alert Naumann. Everything would have to look normal until Naumann was in the bag. He would have to drive up the hill, stop the car and step out. After that, it wouldn't matter. Youngblood stared through the trees at the road that was black and shiny from the rain pelting down on it. Naumann would probably stop just in front of where he was at the crest of the hill. And, he had just realized that, because of the direction from which Naumann was expected to come, the driver's side of the car would be towards him. He would have a clear shot at the Nazi, Sebastian wouldn't. It was only right that Sebastian should finish him off. Maybe *if* he just shot him in the legs . . .

Youngblood's watch read twelve minutes to five, just about enough time to get one more before Naumann was due. He flitted from tree to tree, then stopped. If they were keeping roughly the same distance apart, then the next man wasn't where he was supposed to be. Youngblood was even more careful now, as he went from one point of cover to another. Then he heard the voices.

He cursed articulately, mouthing the words, although no sound came out. Inexplicably, all three men were together, speaking in low tones. They were clustered behind a tree only a few feet from where the wood began, engaged in conversation. They didn't seem disposed to separate, and Naumann was due any time.

Youngblood settled down, positioning himself in such a way so that he had an unobstructed view of the road. There was nothing else he could do. He would have to disable Naumann, then take care of the other three.

Five o'clock came and went. No car appeared. Sebastian almost held his breath, he was so tense, but the minutes dragged by and still nothing happened. Five past five. Ten past five. The rain came down harder. Sebastian heard noises in front of him as the three men moved about, restless as he was with the waiting. Five-twenty and still nothing. Sebastian began to doubt that Naumann was going to show up at all. After all their elaborate planning, maybe this was going to be a double bluff. Maybe Naumann never had any intention of coming. Maybe he was going to leave the supposed blackmailer to his men, or even worse, perhaps he had seen through the ruse and had guessed that the two of them had survived and were lying in wait.

Sebastian had almost convinced himself that that was the case, but then, he thought, why had the one man been sent down the road if not to signal the all-clear to Naumann.

Youngblood was having similar thoughts. He ran over in his mind the whispered conversation he'd had with Naumann, line by line. He could find no fault with it. It was logical and possible, even probable. Five-thirty and everything remained the same. At 5.35 an approaching car was heard. The three men on Youngblood's side shuffled expectantly, and spread out to adjacent trees. Sebastian could hear feet scraping on rocks as his three men prepared for the arrival.

Sebastian could see down the road from his position. The headlights came closer, piercing the curtain of rain. The car paused for some moments, then carried on, the twin beams cutting a path through the darkness. The Mercedes passed the house at an unhurried pace, rolled up the hill, and stopped on the crest. A minute crawled by, then Naumann stepped out. Youngblood was just about to put a bullet into Naumann's leg when his plans were changed radically for him.

Sebastian had completely forgotten about the man he had laid out, so intent was he on the scene before him. The Mercedes had stopped, Naumann had at last stepped out. Two of the men, hiding in the rocks that he could see, were inching their way closer to the road.

When the shout came, it was so unexpected that Sebastian's keyed-up body made a convulsive jerk.

'He's here,' the man shouted, 'he knocked me out. He's hiding somewhere.'

Naumann dived to get back to the car and shut the door. The shout had caught Youngblood off guard and spoiled his aim. The bullet whanged into the rear door and ricocheted off with a whine. Out of the corner of his eye, Youngblood picked up the three men turning his way, and levelling their pistols at the point from where the shot had come. Youngblood had no time to think, just act.

He switched to automatic fire, swung the rifle in a ninety-degree arc and depressed the trigger at the same time. Most of the bullets from the bursts smacked into trees, but two of them found their mark – in the neck of the Captain. He let out a gurgled scream, grabbed for his throat and fell on his face. The other two men fired back, getting close, but their aim was high. Youngblood was in motion. He stayed low and darted for the next tree.

The Mercedes was already picking up speed as Sebastian reacted. His priorities were clear. He levelled the Armalite and the burst of automatic fire shredded the right front tyre. The car veered wildly, ran straight off the road, bumped over the scrub grass, and came to rest with a bang on a boulder that crumpled the fender and grillework. A bullet from the man closest to Sebastian slammed into the rock two feet in front of his face, throwing dust in his eyes, showering him with splinters. He tried to blink it away, aimed and fired where he thought the man was. A piercing scream told him that he had been accurate.

Sebastian ducked as three more shots hit the rocks around him. He found a channel that paralleled the road and ran along it.

Youngblood threw himself flat, rifle ready for the next target. Shots followed his progress. He could hear shooting from across the way and he caught a glimpse of the car through the trees as it veered off the road and smashed into the rocks. Youngblood felt in complete control, cold and deliberate. When the man fifteen yards away revealed himself for an instant, in an attempt to find a target, he made himself the target. Youngblood thought of the navel as a bullseye and put a burst of fire into it. A convulsive pull on the trigger of the pistol was a last wild shot, as the man was flung backwards to land in a contorted heap. His agonized groans weakened and stopped.

The last man left in the woods had had enough. He broke from cover and made a dash for the road and over to the other side, where he could hide himself in the rocks. Youngblood jumped up, looking for a line of fire, found a slot, went down on one knee and aimed. The man's frantic dash had just taken him to the other side of the road, when the bullets caught him in the small of the back, flung him sideways, and left him lying face down, arms and legs spread.

Youngblood let out a grunt, as a bullet from one of Naumann's men in the rocks got him in the calf. He ducked behind a tree and checked the wound. It wasn't too serious. The bullet had hit nothing but flesh and had gone straight through. Youngblood was more concerned with his weapon. The last burst had emptied the magazine. He took it out, chucked it away, and put in a fresh one.

Naumann was dazed. He had tried to control the careening car but it had been no use. In fact, he had compounded it when he stepped hard on the accelerator, when he thought he was reaching for the brake. The sudden jolt, as the car fetched up against the rocks, threw him forward, and his head banged hard on to the windshield, starring it into thousands of spiderlike cracks. When he reached up to his head, his hand came away wet. He looked at it, uncomprehending – blood. He wiped his hand on his sleeve, tried to wipe the blood away from his face as it ran into his eyes, blinding him, but it kept flowing. He remembered the handkerchief in his pocket, took it out, and dabbed at the wound. Firing was going on all around him. He knew he had to get away from there. The engine on the Mercedes had died with the crash. He tried to start it. The motor kicked and whined as the starter made contact, but it didn't catch. Naumann was frantic. He cursed the car and its makers. The Mercedes, impervious to the above, remained obstinately dead. He fumbled for the door handle, his hands slippery with blood, grasped it firmly, pushed. The door opened and he tumbled out on to the wiry grass and sank into the yielding ground. He started to crawl on hands and knees, keeping the car and a line of rocks as cover. Only a few feet away, the rocks ended, and open land that dipped into a gulley began. He made for it.

The channel Sebastian was following came to an abrupt stop at the base of a boulder. He looked around him. There was nowhere else to go. He wedged himself in the space that was like a chimney and, putting pressure on both sides, hoisted himself on top of the rock. He kept flat as he looked over to where the other men were firing. He saw the flash of a gun ahead and to the left. It wasn't firing at him but across the road. He brought up the rifle and snapped off a single shot. It missed the target and ricocheted. A hail of bullets came in his direction from two sides and he lunged forward and rolled off the rock, landing heavily on the other side. He winced as his ankle twisted on a stone that rolled out from under him. He hobbled down the new channel that weaved in an erratic fashion, first to the left, then to the right, and then back again. There was open space twenty yards ahead where the rocks ended.

Somebody hurtled across a path that bisected it, and was out of sight before he could bring up the rifle. Now he felt exposed and looked for some cover. He reviewed the positions of the other men in his mind's eye. There should be two left on his side of the road with guns, and they both had been to his left, but one had crossed over now, leaving him in the middle with two directions to cover. Sebastian found footholds up the boulders to his left and climbed up. He could hear somebody creeping along in front of him out of sight.

'*Achtung*,' Sebastian said. The man jerked into sight looking for the 'friend' and received a bullet in the exact middle of his forehead. He disappeared again.

Sebastian climbed down from the rocks and back into the channel, edged along it until he came to the path that had bisected it. He switched to automatic fire, stepped into the passage, firing, and across to the other side. The brief glimpse he had in the light of the gun flashes told him he had been firing at nothing. The man who had gone down that channel had found a way out somewhere else. Sebastian did a quick count. One opponent left with a gun, and the man he had knocked unconscious with the blackjack, whom he had disarmed.

Sebastian knew that there was a chance that the man would pick up a gun from one of his dead friends. He would have to watch his back, but in the meantime . . . he plunged into the channel down which the armed man had gone.

Youngblood ran awkwardly on his injured leg. He kept just inside the trees as he made his way west to a place just opposite where the Mercedes had crunched into the rocks. He dashed out into the open space and crossed the road, reached the back of the Mercedes, crouched down using it as cover.

He was getting reckless and didn't check behind him. He had forgotten about the sentry who had been left down the road to signal Naumann, but then again, everyone else had forgotten him also.

That man had run up the hill when the firing started, keeping to the line of rocks. He saw Youngblood dash across to the car, but the indentation in which he stood made it a bad angle for a shot, and now the car's trunk was in the way. He stepped away from the rocks and crept into the roadway, holding his revolver with both hands to steady it for a shot.

He stopped when he had Youngblood in his sights, crouched, ready to shoot. Sebastian emerged at that precise moment – saw the man, emptied his rifle into him. Youngblood jumped up ready to shoot, took everything at a glance, and waved at Sebastian. Neither one of them saw the man that Sebastian had been chasing. He stepped out from concealment and fired at Youngblood three times.

Sebastian had caught the movement in his periphery, and had swung the Armalite immediately and pressed the trigger. Nothing – the magazine was empty.

Between the first and the second shot he had dropped the rifle and torn the knife from his belt. Between the second and third shots the knife was winging its way towards its target. It caught the man behind the shoulder blades, just as he was about to turn and shoot at Sebastian. He sank to his knees with a gasp, then fell forward on his face.

Sebastian sprinted to where Youngblood lay.

The first bullet had missed, the second had hit Youngblood in the right shoulder, the third, just below the heart.

Sebastian bent over, calling Youngblood's name. The eyes flickered and opened.

'Bobby,' Sebastian said urgently. 'Bobby! Hang on, buddy and I'll get you outa here.'

Youngblood managed a weak smile. 'Don't bother,' he croaked, 'it's bad.'

'C'mon, it's not that bad, we'll fix you up.'

Youngblood shook his head. 'No,' he whispered. 'Just listen, I'm not big on deathbed scenes . . . they're so corny.' The voice trailed off. Sebastian moved to shield Youngblood from the rain, that was slanting down. Youngblood reached out a hand and grasped Sebastian's wrist. He licked his lips. 'Listen . . . you know where I keep guns . . . in my house . . . go back there. There is a leather case.'

'What the hell are you talking about?' Sebastian said angrily. 'Tell me later.'

'Now,' the voice was fainter. 'I found Rascher's money, gems . . . all in Switzerland . . . my account . . . all numbers in the case . . . use it.'

'Goddamn it, Bobby, I don't want it.'

'Use it.' The voice got stronger. 'Give Naumann hell. I'll be seeing him there soon.' Then he died.

Sebastian stood up slowly. He looked down at Youngblood and the tears started, and mingled with rain streaming down his face. He didn't bother to wipe them away. His mind was a jumble of thoughts. The man who might have been an enemy, who wasn't an enemy. The man who had turned into the friend he had never had . . . and now the dead friend. He felt cheated; and Naumann was still out there somewhere, alive.

Sebastian wiped his face with his sleeve, took a last look at Youngblood and walked away. He picked up the Armalite and reloaded it. He was going hunting.

The man that Sebastian had knocked out, looked at the carnage from where he was hiding behind a rock. He'd had enough. He turned and ran the other way.

Sebastian gave the car and the body a wide berth. He went past it to where the rocks ended and angled in to where the gulley started.

'Naumann,' he shouted. 'I'm coming, you son-of-a-bitch, do you hear me?' The sound of the rain beating down was the only response to his challenge. 'I know you're shaking, Naumann. And I'm coming to get you. Yeah, it's me, Naumann, Mark Sebastian. Still alive. The boat blew up without me on board. Now it's your turn, you're the last one.'

Sebastian plunged into the gulley, and sank to his ankles in mud.

Naumann was quaking like a leaf in a cyclone. He was so petrified that his teeth chattered and his limbs shook uncontrollably. He had followed the gulley until it had deepened to eight feet and it ended in steep overhanging banks, and he had been too afraid to return and get in the way of the gun fire. Why hadn't he brought a gun? He'd asked himself that question dozens of times. He just hadn't thought he would need one. All those men, all those guns, one lone blackmailer – or so he thought. And now Sebastian was coming.

Naumann turned and tried to haul himself out of the gulley, but the strength in his arms had gone and he slipped back each time. Large clumps of mud rained down around him from the effort; the bank was soaked. He heard Sebastian splashing through puddles and clumping over the dead branches, turned in his panic and tried to dig himself a hole in the bank.

Sebastian saw the white face reflected in the faint streaks of dawn from the east, saw the man hunched and cowering against the steep-sided bank. He came on at a steady pace, as inexorable as a moving glacier, and stopped two feet in front of Naumann, the barrel of his rifle poking the man's belly. He stood like that for long moments, wordless, while the German gibbered and moaned, and pleaded for his life in a mixture of German, Spanish and English.

Sebastian moved his arm with deliberate slowness so that Naumann could see what he was doing. He reached for the second of the two knives, took it from its sheath, moved it to Naumann's face in slow motion, and slashed open the unscarred cheek.

Naumann screamed. It was a high girlish shriek, and he covered his cheek with his hands as the blood gushed out.

'I wanted you to have a matching set,' Sebastian said, but the words didn't penetrate Naumann's numbed brain.

Sebastian stepped back, put the knife away, levelled the rifle on Naumann's chest.

A torrent of rain poured down as the storm reached its zenith. It was as if the whole of the skies had emptied at once. Sebastian tried to blink away the screen of water from his eyes. He rubbed an arm across them, and had the distinct impression that he was looking out from the inside of a waterfall. The heavy drops of water pounded into him, battered his head and body. He could barely see Naumann, who had pressed himself as far back as he could go into the shallow depression.

The mud overhang had the last of its vegetation stripped away by the torrents of water. The last root from some long-dead tree was torn away and washed down into the gulley. For years it had provided a tenuous link between the overhang and the more solid ground. When the anchor disappeared, the overhang collapsed.

A ton of mud slid into the gulley, dragging chunks of earth and scrub grass with it.

Naumann disappeared from view, as his former shelter became his tomb.

Sebastian was flung back by the advancing mud avalanche that buried him up to his waist. In his heightened state of awareness, he thought he heard a final piercing scream from Naumann. Then there was just a continuing noise from the torrent. A flash of lightning split the skies open and a crack of thunder shook the ground, then rumbled away in a series of diminishing cannonades.

Sebastian lay on his back, pinned by the mud slide, and watched the pyrotechnics unfold. 'Götterdämmerung,' he thought, 'the doom of the gods.' He started laughing hysterically. Was this the final cosmic joke? He could hear the swell of Wagnerian music in his head, and certainly God had arranged for the thunder and lightning as an accompaniment to 'the end of the world'. It was the end of the world. It was all over, retribution complete, Naumann dead, not by his hands, but by those of a higher power.

'Now, I can rest,' Sebastian thought in his hysteria. 'I can just lie here and sink deeper in the mud. Soon it will close over me and I will have peace. Everyone's dead except me.'

'I'm not,' Pamela said. 'I'm still alive. I'm waiting for you. You have to come back to me. Don't you remember our last talk. You told me you had to go. You said you had to finish what you started, because that was your only reason for living. And after it was all over, then you could truly start living for the first time. Don't you remember how I finally understood. I love you, Mark and now you're free, you can let go.'

The vision of Pamela was so real that Mark reached out to touch her. 'I love you,' he said. 'I really do love you.'

'I know you do,' said the smiling vision of Pamela. Her voice seemed deep in echo. 'Hurry back,' she said, 'and don't forget Bobby,' she scolded him gently. 'He's lying there in the rain. He should be in a dry place, where he can rest. You have to move now . . . move now,' said the fading vision, 'move now . . .'

Gradually, Sebastian became aware of the cold drops of rain splattering in his face, filling his mouth, and nose, stinging his eyes. Gradually, his sanity returned. He started digging himself out.

Chapter Thirty-one

It was five days, 14 February, St Valentine's Day in fact, before Lieutenant Helder gave the Sebastian case another thought. Like every other policeman for miles around, he had been fully occupied in coping with the aftermath of the rainstorm and resulting floods and mud slides. 'The heaviest rain in fifty years,' the papers were saying.

Fifteen people had died as a direct result of the storm. Most of the deaths occurred when cars aquaplaned off the mud-smeared roads. Three people died when their house slid off its foundations and tumbled down the hill on which it was built. Two others were electrocuted by cut power lines. One was struck by lightning.

Beverly Hills had not suffered as much as some other areas. Most of the homes in the wealthy section were solid and well built, and suffered a minimal amount of flooding. A half-dozen of the streets in Beverly Hills were awash, but only for a short period of time. Still, there was enough damage to occupy the time of every man on the force. Gas and water mains had been fractured.

Chief-Inspector Warren had gone back to London, commenting, 'If this is the way it's going to be here, I might as well go home, where at least I know how to find a good pub, and where I will drown my sorrows. 'There was a tiny twitch of a smile for the joke there. Because of the emergency, it was impossible to pursue the inquiries any further for a time, and he was glad to get back to the normality of England.

In truth, Helder had almost completely forgotten about Sebastian and Naumann, until he started working his way through the routine reports that had piled up. The paper that brought it back to mind was the missing persons report filed by a Mrs Carl Newman from an address in Beverly Hills that Helder knew to be the German's residence. According to the report, her husband had gone out on the night before the storm and had never returned.

Helder also found a report that was the reply to his inquiries about Mark Sebastian. According to it, he was indeed the surviving son of the Mr and Mrs Sebastian murdered in Berlin in 1940, and he was the heir to the Sebastian Arms Corporation, but not employed by the company. The president of the company had stated that Mark Sebastian lived in Europe, had done so for many years, and, to his knowledge, had not been back to America for a very long time.

Appended to the report was a statement from Immigration that Mark Sebastian had not entered the States for over five years. Helder put the reports in his out-tray and shrugged. That line of inquiry was a dead end. He would have to tell Warren. He wondered what had happened to Naumann. Could he have been caught in the storm? Could his car have run off the road, and could he perhaps, be lying dead somewhere in a ditch? In some of the hilly areas surrounding Los Angeles, a crashed car, lying at the bottom of a ravine, might go undetected for years.

In Hamburg, Reinhart Kessler had received a full report from the one German who escaped from the Topanga Canyon battle. In a way, he was relieved. Everything had changed since the old days and Naumann had been like a dinosaur – unable to adjust to the new order of things; and like the dinosaur, he, too, had disappeared.

In Mexico City, Luis Francisco Montez, the new Minister responsible for oil exploration, had waited with apprehension for Naumann to arrive. When he didn't come at the appointed time, Montez wondered what had happened to the man. No word had been sent. He relaxed only after several weeks more had passed.

From Dallas, Glen Stingley, president of the Imperial Petroleum Corporation, had started calling Naumann the day of the storm to see how he had fared. He became progressively more worried when Naumann's wife told him that he had gone missing, and had not been seen again. Stingley gave up the calls after two weeks. He and Bradshaw, both glum, held a post mortem on the Mexican oil deal. They agreed that they had no recourse, that Naumann had been the key to the deal. They didn't even know for sure who the contact was, as Naumann had never disclosed it. Even if they had known, there would have been no leverage to exert on the man. All the incriminating documents had been cached by Naumann in a secret place. They wrote off the deal and turned to other matters.

*

During the month of June, the temperature in Greece had already climbed into the eighties. The couple, he tall and handsome, she blonde and beautiful, drifted lazily from island to island on a forty-foot boat they operated themselves. They stayed in one place as long as they felt like it, and moved on when the mood hit them.

In the brightly decorated saloon hung miniatures of Napoleon, much admired. On many of the sultry evenings, the man would stare at them, toast absent friends and start to reminisce. The girl was an attentive listener.

Everyone with whom they came in contact remarked on how nice they were, how well they looked together, how much in love they seemed to be. Honeymooners, perhaps?